DON'T SCREAM

BLAIR DANIELS

STORIES

THE HITCHHIKER

I was driving through rural New Jersey when I saw him.

A hitchhiker, standing by the side of the road. Surprisingly well-dressed – black suit, slicked-back hair, narrow briefcase.

Now, I know I shouldn't pick up hitchhikers. But I'm 6'4", 230 pounds, with all kinds of hunting equipment in the back of my truck. It's not like this prissy-assed businessman is going to beat me to death and leave me on the side of the road.

Besides, I need gas money.

"Hey, man," I said, pulling over to the side of the road. "I'll give you a lift, if you pay me for gas."

"Of course," he said in a polite, almost British, accent. He reached for his wallet, and pulled out three crisp, $20 bills. "This enough?"

I grinned. *That's way more than enough.* I greedily snatched the money from him and clicked the locks. "Get in, bud."

He climbed in. His blue eyes shifted from the crumpled Wendy's wrapper on the dashboard, to the mysterious, sticky goo on the middle console.

"Sorry, the car's not clean. I'm going hunting," I said, turning back onto the highway.

"Hunting. Interesting," he said, in a strangely enthusiastic tone. "Have you always liked to hunt?"

"No, it's the funniest thing. Never thought I'd ever hunt. Love animals, got three dogs at home. But there are so many deer around these parts, when the winter comes… a lot of 'em starve to death. Not to mention all the car accidents they cause." I trailed off, and we fell into uncomfortable silence.

"Just hunting for the day, then?"

"No, my buddy Matt and I will be out there the whole weekend."

He let out a laugh. "The *whole* weekend? Your wife's a saint for letting you go."

My wife? How did he – But then my eyes fell on the steering wheel, and the silver ring on my finger. "Ah, yeah. Mary's a doll. She's actually pregnant, you know. 5 months with a little girl."

He gave me a crooked smile. "A girl, huh?"

"Yeah."

I could feel him staring at me long after we had fallen into silence. It made me feel uncomfortable; I clicked on the radio.

"How did you meet Matt?" he asked, fiddling with the dial. All that came through was static.

That's a weird question, I thought. "Um. He and Mary were close friends. So when we got married, I got to know him well."

"Mmm-hmm," the man said. He stroked his chin thoughtfully, and I was suddenly reminded of a psychiatrist.

"Are you a psychiatrist?" I blurted out.

He laughed. "Definitely not. I work in finance."

"What type of finance?" It was *my* turn to ask the questions, now.

"Futures," he replied, noncommittally.

I glanced over at him. A small smile was on his lips, and I noticed his fingers had gravitated from his lap to the briefcase at his feet.

My heart began to pound.

Click, click. He undid the clasps; the case creaked open.

"What's in your briefcase?" I asked.

"Work."

"What kind of –"

His long fingers disappeared into the darkness of the case. He was pulling something out! My body began to seize up; the steering wheel felt like ice under my fingers. "I have a lot of hunting equipment back there," I said, "so you better not be –"

I stopped.

He was only pulling out a sheet of paper.

For a few minutes, he was quiet. Reading the paper, intently and silently, as if his life depended on it. *Scrtch, scrtch* – his fingers slid over it, as they traced the text.

. Then he slipped it back into the case, and snapped it shut.

What was he reading? I thought. But before I could get the question out, he turned towards me. I could barely see his face in my peripheral vision; but I knew he was staring at me, for minutes on end.

Then he broke the silence.

"Don't go hunting," he said, his ice-blue eyes boring into me.

"What?"

"Turn the car around. Go home to Mary."

"What?!"

"She needs you." He paused. "*Madeline* needs you."

I paled.

I never told him we were going to name our baby Madeline.

"How did you –"

"He's going to make it look like an accident," he said, his voice gravelly and halting. "Just a simple hunting accident. The most punishment he'll endure is thirty-five minutes in the police station, writing out his statement."

"But –"

"Let me off at that diner, up ahead. I like their Cobb salad very much."

"Matt's going to kill me? What are you talking about?"

He turned to me, eyes wide. "What are *you* talking about?"

"About what you just said!"

"All I said is I'd like you to let me off at the diner, please." He pointed to the exit, curving off the highway. "You're going to miss it if you don't slow down."

With a shaking hand, I clicked on my blinker. Pulled off the exit, into the parking lot. My heart pounded in time with the *click-click-clicks* of the cooling engine.

"Thank you for the ride," he said, pulling his briefcase out with him. "Have a good drive, will you?"

I couldn't squeak out a reply before the door slammed shut.

***

I didn't believe him. But my nerves were too shot to continue the trip, either. I texted Matt that I was sick, turned around, and went home to Mary. Mary was thrilled; Matt was disappointed. A little *too* disappointed, if you ask me.

A month later, after ignoring most of Matt's calls and texts (which became increasingly frequent and desperate), I heard a faint thumping noise at the door. When I flicked on the porch light – there was Matt, hunched over our doorknob.

Holding a lockpick.

We called the police. Since then, life has been great. Just a few months later, our wonderful little Madeline was born. And as soon as we got back from the hospital, on our doorstep was a little teddy bear, a pink bow sewn on its head. There wasn't a return address, or a card of any kind.

But I think I know who it's from.

RECAPTCHA

Have you ever seen a photo reCAPTCHA?

Instead of a checkbox, it's a low-quality photo split into 16 square sections. It'll say something like: "SELECT ALL SQUARES WITH STREET SIGNS," and you have to click every square that contains a street sign.

At 11 PM on Sunday night, I got one while downloading free stock images. It was a photo of a path through the forest.

SELECT ALL SQUARES WITH PEOPLE.

Okay. That was easy enough. In the center, there was a jogging woman in pink shorts. She took up a few of the middle squares, and I clicked them all.

I pressed VERIFY.

It didn't work.

SELECT ALL SQUARES WITH PEOPLE, the message said again. I took off my glasses, placed them on the table, and squinted at the image.

No. She wasn't the only person.

Several feet off the trail, at the very edge of the image, I could see it. The edge of an arm clad in a black sweatshirt, with a pink thumb poking out.

I triumphantly clicked the two squares containing it. VERIFY.

The image blinked as it refreshed. Then the same text popped up, as if to taunt me: SELECT ALL SQUARES WITH PEOPLE.

I rubbed my eyes and stared at the image.

The trees cast low-resolution, blocky shadows across the path. The woman's ponytail swung to the left, mid-motion. Patches of yellow sunlight dappled the surrounding forest. I studied some of the darker shadows, far from the path; but none of them matched the silhouette of a person.

I glanced to the edge of the image.

No.

The image had changed. The arm at the edge of the photo was now further in the frame, taking up three squares instead of two. Bulky shoulders and dark jeans followed it.

And the jogger was just slightly further down the path – as if she'd just taken a step.

The touchpad was slick under my fingers. My heart pounded in my chest. Slowly, I dragged the cursor over the three squares and clicked them all.

VERIFY.

The image blinked.

SELECT ALL SQUARES WITH PEOPLE.

I leapt back from the computer.

The image was different again. The man was further in the frame, taking up five squares. His hand was stretched out towards the jogger, just inches from her shoulder.

And the jogger...

She was turned towards him, eyes wide. Mouth open in a silent scream.

Click, click, click. I furiously clicked all the squares. VERIFY.

Loading...

SELECT ALL SQUARES WITH PEOPLE.

The man's face was finally in frame.

The hood of his sweatshirt was pulled tightly over his head. A translucent Halloween mask poked out from underneath, pressed against his features.

His hand was latched onto her arm.

She was screaming.

Click, click, click.

VERIFY.

The image disappeared.

I'd passed the reCAPTCHA.

***

I reported what I'd seen to the police. At first they thought I was crazy, but as I gave a detailed description of the images, they frantically took notes and asked me questions.

The woman matched the description of a local woman, Kaylee Johnson. She went missing a week ago, during an afternoon jog on the wooded Lakewood Trail.

She was never found.

MY AIRPODS MAKE
TERRIFYING SOUNDS

I first wore the AirPods to the Stop and Shop.

It was an incredible, other-worldly experience. I listened to the soothing voice of Neil deGrasse Tyson while picking through the broccoli. I learned about quasars while waiting in line for the deli.

Things got weird, though, when I got to the checkout line.

The cashier was one of the annoying ones. I'd talked to him before—he was the type that makes cute little comments about the items you're buying, while you stand there in embarrassment.

"Oh, these are good," he said, as he slid my pack of lemonade iced tea across the scanner. *Blip.*

I turned the volume up on *StarTalk*.

"These are *so* useful. Own a few of them myself," he said, as he scanned the car phone stand. *Blip.*

He reached for the truffles. He looked me straight in the eye and said, "More chocolate for your fat ass, huh?"

I stopped dead.

"Excuse me?" I asked, slipping out my AirPods.

"More chocolate for your art class, huh?"

"That's not what you said."

"What?"

"You said..." I trailed off, looking at his pimply, juvenile face. He looked so innocent. "Nevermind."

I walked out in a huff.

Maybe I did mishear him, I thought, as I charged across the parking lot. After all, I was listening to *StarTalk* at the same time. Maybe the phonemes got all tangled up in each other.

Or maybe he was just a jerk.

I got home in a bad mood. Opened the box of truffles and inhaled three of them. Just to spite him.

Then my roommate got home.

"Tara! Want to join me?" I said, patting the cushion next to me.

"Nah," she said, over the low thrum of *Kansas* coming through the AirPods. "I got to take off my shoes and just smell my feet for a while."

I stared at her blankly.

"When are you taking your shower?" she asked.

"Not sure, why?"

"I'm going to sneak into your room and stalk your search history, like I do every night."

"What?!"

"I can't believe you still stalk Adam on Face —"

I ripped out my AirPods.

"— bok choy with chicken. Do you want some? I can make extra."

I stared at her. "Are you going to go through my computer when I'm in the shower?"

She paled.

Then she ran into her bedroom and slammed the door shut.

Did I mishear that too? No. There's no way.

I packed a few things and left for a friend's house. When I got there, she was sipping whiskey while watching the evening news.

"The search is still on for MacKenzie Johnson," the newscaster said. "If you have any information, please call the hotline."

"What's this?"

"Some local woman is missing," Amanda said.

The film cut to an older man — MacKenzie's husband. "Please, if you have any information on my wife's whereabouts, go to the police," he said, his lip trembling. "I need her back. Please."

Something stirred inside me. A whim. A realization. I grabbed my bag and reached inside. Pulled out my AirPods.

"Please, if you know anything about my —"

His voice changed as soon as I stuck them in.

"Little bitch."

My heart stopped.

"It was easy. She's so weak, so fragile. Just got the rope from the garage and —"

I yanked the AirPods out.

18

His voice returned to halting sobs. "Please, if you know anything, call the police."

Oh, I will.

I picked up the phone.

***

"The husband did it."

"And how exactly do you know that?" Detective Babanuk asked, with an exasperated sigh.

"Uh… just trust me on this."

He raised a scraggly white eyebrow. "*Trust* you? Look, Ms. Hofstetler, we get thousands of bogus tips a day. You know how the system works —"

I grabbed the AirPods out of my bag and shoved them in my ears.

"— when you're married? You do the dishes like 20 times just for *the chance* to have sex with your wife. Oh, God, it's awful. I'm so tired. My back hurts. When I get home I'm going to take a nice, long bath. With one of those lavender bath bombs. Yeah."

I stared at him. He stared at me.

"You like taking lavender baths?"

His face flushed red. "What?"

"Do you like taking —"

"I think it's time for you to leave," he growled, standing up.

"But —"

"Get the hell out of here!"

I took the AirPods out.

19

"Get the hell out of here!"

Oh. He's actually saying that.

I walked out of the station, put my AirPods back in. This time, for their intended purpose — to listen to music as I walked back to my car. The soaring vocals of *Bohemian Rhapsody* filled my ears. *Mama, just killed a man...* My heart sunk. *I may not have killed a man, but I'm guilty all the same. I know David Johnson killed his wife, and there isn't a damn thing I can do.*

I stopped.

There was a voice. Soft and low, barely audible above the music.

"That's her."

I whipped around.

What? The street was empty. No cars, no passersby — except for the rows of parked cars that flanked the road.

"But it's broad daylight."

I stared at the cars. They were utterly still. Statues of metal, silently watching me with their blank, dead headlights.

"Really? Now?"

I broke into a run. My feet slapped on the pavement; my breath came in short bursts. I finally got to my car and dove in. Panting, high on adrenaline, my fingers raced across the screen. After several tries, the address came up.

His address.

I swept out of the parking lot.

Knock, knock, knock.

My heart thundered in my chest as I waited in front of the red door. Within a minute, I heard his heavy footsteps on the other side.

Click.

"Can I help you?"

"D-david," I stuttered. "You're here."

So it wasn't him, parked on the street. I laughed, internally. *Why did I think it would be? He had no idea I even existed until this moment. God, I'm an idiot.*

Well, at least I'm doing the right thing.

I sucked in a deep breath of air and forced the words out. "I'm a friend of your wife's. An acquaintance. And I need to talk to you."

His face lit up with fake hope. "You know where she might be?"

I nodded.

"Come on in."

"Actually, can we talk out here?"

"Uh, sure."

I took a seat on an old, rickety bench on his porch and pulled out the AirPods as discreetly as possible. My hands shook; they nearly slipped from my hands. *Try to get as much information as possible. Like where her body is. Or where he killed her. Then submit it anonymously to the police...*

I popped them in.

"So what do you know? Come on, tell me. I'm freaking out over here."

For a second, I thought maybe the AirPods weren't working. But then, he continued:

"You sneaky little whore." He shook his head and clicked his tongue. "Who are you? Undercover police or some shit?"

This close, I could tell his lips didn't match up with the words I was hearing. It was a strange, jarring feeling — like hearing a song played on an out-of-tune piano.

I ignored his words and said: "I saw her the evening she disappeared. A woman was coaxing her into the car. A blonde woman."

He can't know that I know he killed her.

"You know that I killed her."

What?

He reached up to his ear, grinning. With a small tug, he pulled out a tiny, spherical piece of silver metal.

"How do you think I found out about MacKenzie's affair in the first place?" he asked, his blue eyes gleaming in the light. "These little things are neat. Worth the price, for sure."

I shot up and scrambled towards the yard. I grabbed my phone, dialed 911 — just as he pulled me back.

"Get away from me!"

"No. I'm going to make sure you don't tell a single fucking soul." He grabbed me by the hair and yanked me towards the door. I screamed.

I'm going to die.

"Yeah. You are."

But he didn't notice my phone. By a stroke of luck, it'd fallen underneath the bench. Out of sight.

Within minutes, sirens pierced the silence.

After a brief struggle, the police wrestled him to the floor. Even though he might get away with MacKenzie's murder, he wasn't getting away with this.

As soon as I got home, I opened my laptop.

I went to eBay — where I'd bought the AirPods in the first place. They had been "gently used" for $89.99, from a seller named listen_tech5.

I shot them a message.

Hi. I was wondering if you could supply more information about the AirPods you sent me.

Then I collapsed on the couch and turned on the TV. An infomercial for some cleaning solution came up.

"I'M JUST GOING TO SHOUT, SO YOU THINK I'M REALLY EXCITED ABOUT THIS STUFF!" the man shouted. "I HAVE NO IDEA IF IT ACTUALLY WORKS OR NOT!"

Click. I changed the channel.

"I really don't want to be on this herpes commercial," a blonde woman was saying. "But I'm behind on rent and my *Game of Thrones* audition didn't really work out..."

Click. "Oh, yes! Gone with the wind!"

"Darling, move your arm," Scarlett O'Hara asked, throwing herself at Ashley and fluttering her lashes. "I want them to get my good side."

"This script is the most abhorrent thing I've ever read," Ashley replied. "I feel like a fool."

Ding.

I looked down at my phone.

listen_tech95 sent a message about Apple AirPods

I immediately opened it.

Hello

It appears we have sent you the wrong item. Please RETURN YOUR AIRPODS IMMEDIATELY

Do NOT use your AirPods. Using them could be VERY DANGEROUS as they have an electrical malfunction. Simply put them back in their case and send them to ███, *Broadland, SD 57350 AS SOON AS POSSIBLE.*

Appended to the bottom of the message was a single, foreboding sentence:

If we do not receive them in three days, we will find you.

***

Of course I didn't send the AirPods back. Those things had the power to uncover every lie in the world. Condemn the guilty. Exonerate the innocent. I wouldn't part with them for the world.

Maybe that was a mistake. At 2:45 AM, I jolted awake to a clicking sound.

Click, click, click. Reverberating through the little house like metallic, off-beat ticks of a clock.

I extricated myself from the tangle of blankets. I crept over to the window, parted the blinds, and peered outside.

Two figures stood on the doorstep. One stood in the shadows, immensely tall, his eyes hidden in the shadows of a baseball cap. The other hunched in front of the door. Hands deftly working to pick the lock.

"No, no, no," I whispered. *What do I do?* Slowly, silently, I grabbed the AirPods.

As soon as I popped them in, I heard the man's voice. Four words.

"Shit. She heard us."

I jumped out of bed. Backed away. Grabbed a coat hanger from the closet with a grunt. *I can poke them in the eye —*

"She thinks she can bring us down with a coat hanger, George!"

They're wearing AirPods too.

They can hear what I'm thinking.

I threw the coat hanger to the floor and grabbed my phone. My fingers raced across the screen. *9-1-1 —* "Come on, come on —"

"Don't do it. Look... we're just coming to take the AirPods back. You give 'em back and there's no trouble. If you call 911 — *then* we'll have trouble."

I stood in the darkness, frozen with fear, for several minutes. I didn't make a sound; neither did they.

Finally, I lifted a trembling hand up to my ears. Popped the AirPods out. Slipped them in my pocket.

And grabbed the second pair I'd bought at the Apple Store earlier that afternoon.

As long as I don't say anything, they won't know what I'm thinking. Stay. Absolutely. Silent.

My fingers tightened around the doorknob.

I pulled.

Two men stood on the doorstep. The short one held a lockpicking set. The other loomed over him, holding an axe.

I swallowed.

Do not make a sound.

I handed over the dummy pair.

"You're a smart girl," the lockpicker said. The other didn't say anything — he just inclined his head in a half-nod.

***

Twenty minutes later I was coasting down the highway. Journey's *Only the Young* beat through my AirPods, low and soft. Other than that – silence. Either the other cars were too far away from me, or their drivers weren't speaking.

Those were the two laws the AirPods operated by, I'd figured out. They only worked in a certain range — I couldn't hear someone's thoughts more than 10-20 feet away (unless it was a TV or radio broadcast.) And, second, the person had to actually be speaking at the time.

I wasn't a mind reader.

And that was a good thing.

As I drove, deciduous trees and shrubs transformed into spiky black pines. The moon rose above the pines, terracotta red.

My parents had a little cottage up in Michigan. A tiny, one-room house with warped windows and no hot water.

But it was miles from the nearest neighbor and virtually impossible to find. I would be safe.

At 4:30 AM, I pulled off the interstate and into a tiny diner. "Coffee and a cheeseburger, please," I said to the waitress, as I collapsed into the booth.

"Fuck you," she replied.

I couldn't help but laugh.

As she hustled away, I noticed someone staring at me. A man, just a few booths away. Greasy hair. Blue eyes. A torn leather jacket.

As soon as my eyes reached his, he broke into a grin.

I immediately gestured to my AirPods — to signal I wasn't interested in conversation.

He didn't care. He came over, slid into the booth across from me. Took a big gulp of coffee, smiled, and opened his mouth to speak.

I expected to hear a disgusting proposition. *I just want to bend you over this countertop right now.* Or, maybe, a confession. *I always drink a cup o' joe after dumping the bodies. Really picks me up.*

But I heard something far worse.

Static.

Fuzzy and high-pitched, like a mesh of white noise and tinnitus. Throbbing in my ears like a warning siren. It grew louder and louder, reaching a fever pitch that vibrated every cell, every molecule in my body.

I ripped the AirPods out.

His voice faded in. "— and you should try some of their pie. Chocolate chess pie. It's heaven."

I popped the AirPods back in. Static.

27

He talks. But his thoughts... are static? What does that even mean?

Oh, no. Maybe they're broken.

Maybe Listen Tech found out I gave them the wrong pair – and remotely deactivated mine.

Only one way to find out. I leaned out of the booth and flagged down the waitress. "Excuse me! When will the cheeseburger be done?"

She pursed her lips.

"Go fuck yourself."

Nope. Still working. I looked back at the man. He opened his mouth, with a large grin; the static filled my ears again.

But this time, I wasn't listening.

I was staring at the sharp gleam of silver, sticking out his jacket pocket.

A knife.

I shot up – but I was too late. He grabbed my wrist and pulled me towards the door. The static screeched in my ears. My hand tingled underneath his grip, as if a thousand needles pricked at my skin.

I screamed.

But all I heard was static.

He dragged me out of the diner. Out of the halo of golden light, into the inky darkness that lay beyond. The gravel bit into my feet. The cold burned at my fingers.

"What are you going to do to me?"

I couldn't even hear my own voice over the static.

He just grinned, his yellow teeth glinting in the light. One hand latched to my wrist. The other holding the knife. With a jerk, he pulled me against him.

He said something to me. I couldn't read his lips. I didn't want to.

The steel pressed against my throat.

Maybe if I...

With my free hand, I reached up. Ripped out the left earbud – and smashed it into his ear. His eyes widened.

Then he crumpled to the ground.

I raced across the gravel, leapt into the car. The engine rumbled under my feet. As I swung towards the main road, I glanced in the rearview mirror.

The man glowed red in the taillights, as if lit by hellfire. Thrashing, writhing, rolling. Blood pouring out of his ear.

Listening to static echoing static.

As I raced down the highway, I called the police. I learned that they caught him; the waitress called the police on him, and no one else had been hurt. "By the way, you might want to keep the AirPod you find in his ear," I told the officer, with a grin. "I think you'll find it *very* useful."

Then I hung up.

I spent the rest of my trip listening to *Journey*, feeling the cold breeze whip through my hair, and trying to unravel the mystery of the static.

After several hours in the car, the best theory I came up with was his thoughts were so corrupt, so perverse, they couldn't be perceived by anyone else. Either that – or a failsafe was built right into the earbud, to block out such evil.

I'll never know for sure.

A little after 2 PM, I arrived at my parents' cottage. It was miles from the nearest neighbor. Well out of range of the voices. The thoughts. The static.

Everything.

I collapsed in the dusty, rotting armchair. I turned on the lights, cranked up the heat, and popped the single AirPod out of my ear.

Then – for the first time in days – I listened to the silence.

HOMEOWNERS' ASSOCIATION

"This – this house has an HOA?" I stuttered.

The real estate agent nodded.

No. I'd heard the horror stories. Fines for walking your dog. Fines for the wrong color curtains. Fines for obscenely-shaped stains in your driveway. A homeowners' association was just about the worst thing a house could have.

"Do you have a copy of the HOA agreement?"

The real estate agent avoided eye contact. "How do you like the house?" she asked, trying to change the subject.

"I'd like to read the HOA agreement, please."

After rooting through some drawers, she pulled out a thick stack of papers. "Here you go."

With a heavy heart, I began to read.

PELICAN PEAK: HOMEOWNERS' ASSOCIATION RULES

1. Your garage must be kept closed at all times, unless you are currently entering or exiting the house.

2. The community has a strict curfew of 10 PM. You may not make any noise between 10 PM and 6 AM, and you must also keep all the curtains closed during this time.

3. Food scraps cannot be mixed with regular trash; we have a compost bin. Discard food scraps in the red plastic bin provided to you, and leave it on the curb on evenings shortly before curfew. We will pick it up and bring it to the compost bin. Do NOT attempt to bring it to the compost bin yourself.

4. You must always wear neutral-colored clothing when exiting or entering your home, and when walking around the development.

That's where I raised an eyebrow. *What? Neutral-colored clothing?* I looked down at my own outfit – aqua-blue jeans and a hot pink, fluttery top. *What is this? Some kind of dystopian nightmare? Making us conform, to all look the same in these cookie-cutter townhouses?*

"So I wouldn't be allowed to wear this outfit?" I asked the real estate agent.

She hemmed and hawed. "Uh, well… probably not. But, you know, you can just get one of those long duster cardigans, or a jacket, in a neutral color and wear it when you go out. It's not a super-strict rule – you can have *some* color showing –"

"Not a super-strict rule," I repeated, pointedly nodding in her direction. "I see."

I continued to read.

> **5. Never knock on a neighbors' door unannounced. Similarly, never answer the door if you aren't expecting anyone. As a community, Pelican Peak values privacy and safety above all else.**
>
> **6. When walking your dog, keep him or her away from the cul-de-sac on Petunia Lane. The compost bin is back there, and sometimes animals are triggered by the smell.**
>
> **7. Never leave children that weigh under 50 pounds playing unattended outside.**
>
> **8. The homeowner dues are $150/month, due on the first weekday of every month.**

I stared at the sheet. "This is pretty restrictive."

"But look at what you're getting for the price," she said. "Granite countertops and mahogany cabinets. Stainless steel appliances. A rain shower in the master bathroom. All for under two-hundred thousand!"

I *did* love rain showers...

***

I made an offer the next week. Several weeks later, I was moving in – along with several new black cardigans and jackets. My corgi, Buff, seemed to like the place well enough. She liked watching the squirrels run by –

something she couldn't do from the window of my 11th-floor apartment.

That first night, I followed the rules to a T. At 9:47 PM, I put my food scraps out – chicken bones, kale stems, and an apple core. At 9:58 PM, I locked all the doors, drew the curtains, turned down the radio, and settled into bed.

(I wasn't going to *sleep*, of course. It was time for my three-hour Seinfeld marathon before bed.)

Around 10:15 PM, Buff started growling.

Rrrrr!

I groaned, paused the episode, and walked into the second bedroom. "Buff! Shhh!" I hissed, remembering the association rule.

She didn't even turn around. She just sat at the front window, her head poking around the curtain. Hackles raised, staring out into the darkness, growling like mad.

"Buff?"

My fingers fell on the curtain's edge – but then I stopped. *Keep curtains closed after 10 PM.* That was the rule. *But does that mean I'm not even allowed to take a peek?*

And what if it's some crazy guy sitting on my porch or something? Or a rabid squirrel?

I pulled back the curtain.

At first, I just saw darkness. Amorphous blobs of townhouses stuck to each other, speckled with blocks of hazy golden light. Everyone had their curtains drawn. The street was empty. No cars, no people, no squirrels.

Wait.

The street wasn't empty.

A tall figure stood on the sidewalk, right in front of my house. The light from my window barely illuminated his form, but I could still make it out.

He picked up my red, plastic bin.

But there was no garbage truck, or wheelbarrow, or anything else around to dump it in. *Where's he going to dump it?* I thought. *Is he just going to carry the bins one-by-one to the compost? That's really ineffic —*

He hoisted the bin up.

His mouth stretched open – far wider than I've seen any mouth open.

Then he poured the contents in his mouth.

A light cracking sound emerged from the darkness as he chewed up the bones. I stared, horrified, and Buff did too.

Then she began to bark.

Ruff! Ruff!

The thing froze.

"Sssshh!" I said, patting Buff's head. "Please, be quiet –"

Ruff!

He snapped around and ran towards the window at full speed. A flash of a gray, wrinkled face. Hollow, black pits for eyes. A gaping mouth with, somehow, no teeth or tongue.

I let the curtain fall. I backed away, hugging Buff, my heart pounding in my chest.

That's when the knocking started. And I remembered, perhaps, the most important rule of them all:

Never answer the door if you aren't expecting anyone.

LASIK

I'd been saving up for Lasik surgery for years. I'm blind as a bat without my contacts, and after that one got stuck in my eye... *eeuuuugh*. Fortunately, the surgery went great (thanks Dr. Widow!), and soon I was stepping into my Uber home.

"I think there was an error," the driver said. "Are you sure your address is '72 East Mill Rd.'?"

"Uh. Of *course* I'm sure. My wife and I have only lived there for the past ten years."

"Okay," he said, in an uncertain voice. "Just, uh, wanted to double check."

I spent most of the ride looking out the window. The houses, the trees, the cars... they already looked clearer to me. I smiled to myself, as the driver turned onto our street.

And then, suddenly, he rolled to a stop.

"What are you doing?" I said.

"72 East Mill Rd. This is it."

"But that's not my house."

I looked up at the thing. It was a small colonial, like our house, but it was in complete disrepair. It looked like nobody had lived there for years. The white paint was shedding off the wood; the shrubs were tangled and overgrown, some crawling up the sides of the house. A few windows downstairs were shattered, and the flowerboxes underneath – that Maggie so fastidiously tended to, in our *real* house – were empty.

"This is not my house."

He pointed to the mailbox. And there, in chipped white paint, was a number.

72.

This is ridiculous. This is not my house. But the Uber guy already thought I was crazy. "Okay, thanks," I said, stepping out of the car. I was halfway through calling another Uber, to take me to my *real* home, when my gaze caught on the porch.

There, in front of the door, was one of those novelty welcome mats. *GO AWAY. NO ONE'S HOME.*

I *remember* buying that mat. Maggie and I went to the mall, saw it, and had a good laugh about how antisocial we were. I remember the chip reader malfunctioning on my card, and the cashier giving us a really weird look. I remember it all.

Hands shaking, I walked up to the front door. I pulled the key out of my pocket, and put it into the lock.

It fit.

The door creaked open. Inside, the house was in an even worse state. The floorboards were splintered and stained; some of the walls had large, rotting holes in them. On the kitchen table sat a pile of mail, all addressed to me.

On the table sat a half-eaten cinnamon bagel – the one I ate this morning.

There was no doubt about it – this *was* my house.

Then where's Maggie?

"Maggie?" I called. My voice echoed in the empty, rotting house. "Maggie, are you home?"

Silence.

I walked up the stairs. Each step creaked under my weight, threatening to completely disintegrate. When I got to the top level, all the doors were shut.

"Maggie!"

Once again, silence.

My hand fell on the doorknob to our bedroom. With a shuddering breath, I pushed it open.

The curtains were open. Golden sunlight filtered in through the windows, bathing the room in a cheery glow. And there, on the top of the made bed –

Was a mannequin.

Her face was painted on plastic, shiny skin. Fake, brown hair spilled out onto the pillow in elegant waves. Her sightless eyes gazed towards the ceiling, as if she was perfectly at peace.

Like some kind of madman, I began to shake her. "Maggie! Maggie!"

Of course, I was only met with silence.

I collapsed in the corner and cried. The tears stung my freshly-cut eyes – but I couldn't stop. That doctor didn't just fix my nearsightedness.

He'd opened my eyes.

SUBWAY

"Hey, Sleeping Beauty!"

My eyes fluttered open.

I was crumpled in a subway bench, my head resting against the window. By now it was empty – save for the girl who had just spoken.

"What time is it?" I glanced at my phone – 9:32pm. Dammit, I had missed my stop. "What's the next stop?"

"Franklin. We'll be there in an hour."

Franklin? I hadn't heard of that one before. I plopped back down in the seat, and stared at the map on the wall. Thompson, Greenville... but I didn't see a Franklin.

She smiled at me, one finger twirling a lock of her black hair. "I'm Angela."

My heart fluttered. "David."

"So, David –"

The subway lurched.

The lights flickered, sputtered –

And then went out.

"Angela?" I said.

Silence.

A few lights zipped past the window, flashing the car in an eerie green. I could see the faint outlines of the benches, the poles, the windows, and –

A large, black shadow where Angela was sitting.

"Angela?" I said, my voice shaking.

And beside it, something metal, gleaming in the low light...

Thump.

I felt the air shift, as if something walked right by me.

And then –

A cold, bony hand on my shoulder.

"Get off me!" I screamed.

Click.

The lights flicked back on.

Angela stood next to me, her hand on my shoulder. "Did I scare you?!" she said, breaking into laughter.

"Uh – no, of course not. You just startled me, that's all."

"Right, right. I *startled* you," she said, snickering. "Of course."

I crossed my arms – but I couldn't stay mad at her. That pretty black hair, that infectious laugh...

The subway lurched upwards. The black outside faded into the purple of night. Pines lined the track, their branches swaying in our wake. A small sign read: ENTERING AMBLETON COUNTY.

"I've never taken the subway this far," I said.

"Of course not. You city slickers never go out into the suburbs."

"Aren't you from the city, too?"

"No, just visiting."

My heart sank. "Visiting? For how long?"

She laughed – a warm, tinkling laugh that filled the entire car. "Don't worry. We'll see enough of each other."

"Uh – what?"

"We've still got almost an hour, stuck here."

"Oh, right." I laughed uneasily. "How much longer do we have?" I slipped the phone out of my pocket, and turned it on.

9:32pm.

Huh. Weird.

"So, David, tell me about yourself," she said, as the subway dipped back underground.

"Uh, I'm 27 years old, an accountant for Bauer & Hofstetler –"

"No, no, no. I don't want the standard name, age, job. That's what resumés and obituaries are for." She leaned against me, ever so slightly, and I blushed. "Really tell me about yourself. Your likes, your hopes, your dreams."

"Okay. On weekends, I play Magic the Gathering –" no, no, that makes me sound so *boring* – "I mean, I go kayaking with my cousin, upstate." I mean, I did do that, once.

"What else?"

"To be honest, I always wanted to..." I paused, glancing over at her; she smiled back, her brown eyes staring into mine. "I always wanted to find that special someone."

"Did you?" she said, her eyes sparkling.

41

"Maybe," I said, softly.

Even in the terrible, fluorescent lighting, she was beautiful. Her warm smile, her brown eyes... and her talkativeness, which I at first found annoying, was actually quite fun. I extended my hand out to hers...

The subway lurched.

Reflexively, I turned back to the window. The black faded, again, as we resurfaced from underground. The pines swayed in the wind, and a sign approached –

ENTERING AMBLETON COUNTY.

"Wait, we've already seen that sign," I said, yanking my hand away.

"Are you sure?"

My heart began to pound. "I'm positive." I stood up, my knees shaking. "Are we – are we just going in circles?!"

But I had not felt the subway turn – not once.

"David –" Angela said, rushing over to me.

I swatted her away, and ran to the windows. "And that fallen pine – I remember it, too!" The windows rattled under my fists.

"Calm down!" she yelled.

I backed away. "You're in on this," I yelled, so loud that the car shook. "Making small talk, keeping me distracted. To think! I was falling for you!"

Her eyes clouded with tears. "David, please..." she said, in a voice barely above a whisper.

"Where are you taking me?" I yelled. I stared out the window, cupping my hands against the glass. "Where in the hell –"

I stopped.

The scenery of the trees, the moon, the sky –

There was something terribly wrong.

I squinted –

And my blood ran cold.

They had no detail. The moon was just a white circle – all the craters were gone. The pine trees were just rough silhouettes.

"Angela – where are we going?!" I cried. My voice was softer now – stripped of its anger, replaced with gnawing fear.

But her hands were already on my shoulders. I could feel her warmth, her calm permeating my body. She snuggled her head against me, and whispered: "I'm taking you home."

"What are you talking about?"

But then I remembered.

9:32 pm.

Bang!

A crushing pain in my chest.

"There was a terrible accident," she said, looking into my eyes. Such warm, beautiful, brown eyes.

I blinked, and – for a second – I saw the black shadow in her place, holding a scythe.

"No!" I yelled, tearing myself away from her.

"David, please, it's not your decision!"

I turned to the door.

I took a deep breath. Shaking, I ran forward, ramming myself into it as hard as I could.

Crack.

I was flying, falling, out in the cold air –

Thump.

My eyes flew open.

The air stung my lungs.

"He's alive!" A flurry of sound – sirens, yells, screams. A rush of motion, as paramedics hoisted me on to a stretcher, asked me my name.

As I was wheeled into the ambulance, I saw, out the corner of my eye –

A dark-haired girl, standing in the crowd.

Watching me.

I WAS EMAILED A VIDEO OF MYSELF

Samsung's AI program can make a video of you from a single photo.

When it came out, the internet erupted with fake videos of famous people, deceased people, or even artwork. George Washington laughing at a joke. Mona Lisa talking and smiling.

It was cool, but I didn't think much of it. Just another brick in the ever-growing edifice of technology. A reason to laud human intelligence. Or just something cool to laugh at.

That's what I thought.

Until I was emailed a video of myself.

***

The email came from <u>me@blackwidowinc.com</u> at 2:14 AM.

I figured it was just spam. An email for "Hot Singles in Your Area," "Enlargement Pills," or "Supplements." But when I saw the subject line was just "Video," my heart began to pound.

"What's wrong?" my roommate Alex asked, from across the room.

"Nothing!"

I opened the email. There was no body – just a video attachment.

Do I really want to click that? It's probably porn. The thumbnail was just a black square, offering no preview.

I glanced at Alex. She was back to texting.

I turned the volume down on my phone and then clicked.

A black image filled the screen. Slowly, it began to fade away, into a photograph.

It was a photograph of me.

My Facebook profile picture. A selfie I'd taken a few days ago in my room. I'd just braided my hair and thought it looked cute. I'd been hoping Christopher would comment – but, of course, he didn't.

He didn't even have the decency to like it.

I sat there, spiraling into anger towards Christopher, as I watched the video. The progress bar inched forward. 0:04. 0:09. 0:13.

Then she blinked.

I screamed.

"River! Are you okay?"

I showed her the phone with trembling hands. "I didn't take this video, Alex. That's not me."

I – or *it* — straightened its shoulders. Shifted in the seat.

And broke into a grin.

Except, when it grinned... it didn't look *exactly* like me. The teeth were too straight, too white. The lips stretched thinner than mine do. The eyes didn't crinkle up at the corners.

That somehow made it worse.

It was my face – there was no doubt about that. But it was mapped to someone else's expressions, someone else's movements.

"What do you mean, you didn't take it? That's clearly you."

"I think someone generated it. From my profile picture. With one of those AI programs."

"Holy shit," she whispered. "Who do you –"

She didn't get the chance to finish that sentence.

The *thing* began to speak. It was not my voice.

"Hello," she said, her grin fading. "I want to thank you for watching this."

The voice had a strange, halting quality to it. Like it didn't know exactly where it should pause, how it should intonate. I couldn't tell whether it was a text-to-speech app – or a person.

"You all have brightened my world so much. I want you to know that," she said. The smile returned. Her arms jerkily rose to her chest, as if she were hugging herself. "Thank you."

"That's actually kind of… sweet?" Alex said. Then she let out a nervous laugh. "That's a lot sweeter than you usually are, actually."

I glared at her.

"I want you to know what happened is *not* your fault," the fake-me continued, her tone growing quieter.

What?

"I just felt empty. Emotionless. Like there was no purpose for me here, anymore."

No.

"So I had to leave and say goodbye."

It was a suicide note.

It ended there. At 3 minutes, 12 seconds in. I turned off my phone. Then I stared straight ahead, my eyes sliding out of focus, turning the world before me into a melted mess of color.

"I don't get it. Why would somebody send you this?"

"Isn't it obvious?"

She shook her head.

"Someone's going to kill me. Then they'll give this video to the police, say I killed myself."

"Well, I'll tell them it's fake. We should go to the police right now, and –"

Ding.

Alex's phone chimed.

She slowly pulled the phone out of her pocket. As she opened the email, her eyes went wide.

It was a video of Alex.

"I just couldn't live without her," the fake-Alex sobbed in the video. "I'm sorry. River was my best friend, my roommate… she was like a sister to me. Now that she's gone…"

I grabbed the phone from her hands and turned it off. "Don't watch it."

I grabbed my phone and called the police.

They arrived only four minutes later. But when we brought out our phones and looked for the videos… they weren't there.

The emails had been deleted.

The police took our statements and left, but there was nothing they could do. We hugged each other and cried for a while. Then we cracked open a pint of Ben and Jerry's and ate, until we passed out on the couch.

The next day went by without event.

And the next, and the next. I eventually forgot about the whole thing, figuring it was some dumb prank.

Until exactly 3 weeks later.

Alex was in the kitchen, smoking up the place with her cooking. I lay on the couch, reading a trashy magazine.

Ding.

Both of our phones went off at the same time.

Our eyes locked for a second. Then I grabbed mine and opened the email.

It was a video. A video of both of us, sitting on the couch in the living room.

Each of us holding a knife.

Pointed at the other.

THE BOY IN THE DEVIL COSTUME

I hate Halloween for many reasons.

I have to answer the door every ten minutes. I have to pretend like I'm excited to give bratty kids free candy. I have to stay inside, because driving on a road filled with crazy, running children gives me panic attacks.

I plopped down in the chair by the window. Hordes of children in garish costumes ran down the sidewalks, shepherded by tired mothers.

I sighed as a group of children crossed the street and started towards my house.

Ding.

The doorbell chimed, echoing inside the house. I heaved myself up, grabbed the bag of Milky Ways, and walked towards the door.

"Trick or treat!"

Five kids stood on the doorstep. A few princesses, a batman, and a devil. I unceremoniously grabbed handfuls of candy and plopped them in each kid's bag. One murmured 'thank you'; the rest were ungrateful little brats.

"Can I have more?"

I looked up.

The Devil kid was staring at me, holding out his bag. His blonde hair shone in the porchlight; his eyes were a piercing, ice blue.

There was something oddly familiar about him, but I couldn't place it.

"Uh, sure," I replied. I dropped a few more Milky Ways in the bag.

He didn't thank me. He just silently turned around and walked off my porch, following the other children.

I shut the door and returned to my perch by the window.

I watched as the four children walked off my lawn, joining a mother at the end of the driveway. Then the group disappeared into the shadows of dusk.

Scarcely two minutes later, the doorbell rang again.

Ding.

I grabbed the bag of Milky Ways and tromped to the door. I straightened my blouse, plastered a smile on my face, and swung the door open.

"Trick or treat!"

A similar mix of kids. Two Elsas, Marshall from Paw Patrol, and a ninja. "How scary you all look!" I said. They giggled and swarmed around for the candy – all except for the ninja.

He stood back from the rest, silently watching. His entire face was covered with black cloth... save for his chilling, blue eyes.

"Thank you!" the kids cheered, stepping off the porch. As they did, the Ninja kid stepped forward. His eyes glinted under the porchlight, and even though his mouth was covered, I could tell he wasn't smiling.

"Can I have more?" he said.

My blood ran cold.

It was the same voice.

I stood there, in the doorway, frozen. The Milky Way bag hung limply from my hands. *There's no way he could've changed costumes that fast. How... how can it be him? This must be some kind of joke.*

"Can I have more?" he asked again.

I snapped out of my thoughts. "Sure, of course," I said. I threw a large handful of Milky Ways in his plastic jack-o-lantern candy bowl.

That's when I noticed it was empty.

If he'd been trick-or-treating all evening, how could it be empty?

"Hey!" I said. "Are you okay?"

But he had already turned away, running back across my lawn. In seconds, he was gone – camouflaged in the dusky shadows, among the fellow trick-or-treaters.

I sat back down on the chair and stared at the floor. I didn't want to look out at the swarms of kids anymore.

I just wanted to be alone.

Those blue eyes... I know I've seen them before.

And not under good circumstances.

Whenever I'd seen them before, something bad or embarrassing must've happened at the same time. Seeing them again filled me with an inexplicable dread.

I ran my fingers through my hair. *Maybe he came to my house last year.* But that didn't make sense, either. Last year, I'd been over at my ex-boyfriend Drew's house. We'd gotten into a terrible fight that lasted for hours, and I'd left late.

I hadn't handed out a single piece of candy.

Tap.

My head jolted up.

Tap-tap.

Through my own reflection in the glass, in the dark shadows of dusk, I could make out something.

A pair of blue eyes.

I jumped back with a terrified shriek. Then I grabbed the cord and pulled. The blinds dropped with a clatter. His footsteps raced over the damp grass, fading into the night.

Who the hell is he?

I didn't have time to think about it.

Ding.

I didn't move. I didn't want to answer the door and see that kid again.

Ding. Ding.

But I also couldn't listen to the doorbell ring for ten minutes. I heaved myself out of the chair, forced a smile, and swung it open.

"Trick or treat!"

My eyes glanced over the trick-or-treaters nervously. A fairy with curly hair, an Incredibles boy with brown eyes, a little girl in a tutu. None of them were *him.*

I breathed a sigh of relief.

"Here you go!" I said with a grin. I was so relieved, I gave each of them about ten Milky Ways. They squealed in delight and scampered back towards their parents. I slowly pushed the door closed. It squeaked against the hinges, and then slammed shut.

I returned to my chair. I glanced at my phone: 8:19 PM. The din of children outside was finally fading. When I peeled back the blinds, the flow of little costumed figures was heading towards the main road.

Within twenty minutes, the noises faded to silence. I flipped through a book, checked my texts, and got comfortable.

Ding.

I picked up the candy bag, which was now nearly empty. Only four fun-size bars floated in the bottom. *I hope it's not more than four kids.*

It wasn't.

It was just one child.

He was wearing some sort of werewolf costume. The outfit was black, tufts of fur haphazardly taped to his body. On his head was a hideous mask. The plastic snout was contorted into a snarl, revealing yellow teeth. Fake blood dripped from its mouth, caking the fur on his shoulders.

"Do you want some candy?" I asked, my voice starting to waver. I glanced at the road; it was empty. All the kids were gone.

A terrible dread sunk in my heart. My hand quivered on the doorknob.

"Can I have more?"

I slammed the door shut in his face. I clicked the locks. I ran to the back door and locked it. I closed the windows.

Then I threw myself into the chair and sobbed.

The costume was familiar. Horribly familiar. The yellow, sightless eyes... the pointed, plastic teeth... familiar and alien, all at once. I wrapped my arms around my knees and sat there, motionless on the couch, listening to the silence.

Thump.

I jolted up.

My heart throbbed in my chest. I whipped around, looking for the source of the noise. "Hello?" I called.

Thump.

It was coming from the living room. I squinted in the shadows, trying to make sense of the shapes. I could see the silhouette of the floor lamp, near the window. The bulky outline of the couch.

Something stood between them.

Something short with a horrible, contorted face.

"Can I have more?" the voice quietly called out of the darkness.

"How – how did you get in here?" I scrambled back into the family room. The golden light enveloped me, and I felt slightly better. *He's probably just some lost kid,* I told

56

myself. *I'll call the police. They'll find his parents. It's all just some misunderstanding...*

"We'll find your parents, okay?" I said, choking back the fear. "Let me just make a call. We'll get you home safely, okay, buddy?"

He didn't reply.

Instead, he took a slow step forward. As he came towards the light, I saw there was something terribly off about him. His head tilted strangely to one side. His left arm was twisted and mangled. With each step, his body lurched forward unnaturally.

"Are you okay?" I asked.

Silence.

The fake blood that dripped from the werewolf's snout now soaked him. His pale little hands were covered in the red, shiny liquid. The black outfit glistened in the light. The fur was caked and matted.

"Can I have more?"

I backed into the family room. I fumbled for my phone; it was gone. I grabbed at anything I could find, and my hands latched onto the nearly-empty candy bag. "This?" I asked. "Is this what you want?"

The child didn't reply. He took a step forward.

"Here, you can have it!" In my terrified state, I threw it at him. The bag bounced off his chest and landed at his feet.

He didn't pick it up.

"Can I have more?"

"I gave you more!"

He looked at me with those horribly familiar yellow eyes.

Then he stopped. He stood just a few feet from me, bloody hands hanging stiffly at his sides. I took a step back and hit the wall.

I was cornered.

"Who are you?" I yelled. My plan to stay calm and call the police was long gone; I descended into panic. "Why won't you leave me alone?!"

The tiny black pupils fixed on me, and he spoke. For the first time, he didn't ask for more.

"Do you remember me?"

"What are you talking about?"

"Do you remember what you did to me?" His high-pitched, lisping voice was muffled through the mask. "Do you remember what you did, one year ago?"

One year ago...

One year ago, on Halloween night.

The memories flooded back to me.

I was storming out of my Drew's house, fuming. Swearing I'd never see him again. *Slam* – the sound of my car door cut sharply through the night. The engine revved underneath me. The headlights blinked on in the darkness.

I wasn't paying attention. I was thinking about the fight.

I didn't even glance behind me before I backed out of the driveway. And even if I had... I never would have seen him. The black werewolf costume rendered him nearly invisible in the darkness.

When I ran out of the car and saw the broken, mangled body of a little boy in a werewolf costume... and ripped the mask off, to see his lifeless blue eyes staring back up at me... I didn't call the police. I didn't call for help.

I panicked. I got back into the car, drove over the grass, and peeled out of the neighborhood before anyone could see what I'd done.

"Do you remember, Eliza?" The child cocked his head at an even greater angle, as he stared at me through the mask. "Do you remember now?"

"I do," I choked through sobs. "I'm so sorry. I didn't mean to... I was upset, I wasn't paying attention –"

"Can I have more?"

I looked up.

He'd taken off his mask.

The left side of his head was crushed. Blood dripped down his face, staining his pale skin, caking his blonde hair. One ice-blue eye was squashed deep into its socket; the other was perfectly intact. His neck was bent at a horribly unnatural angle.

"Can I have more?" he asked. His lips parted to reveal shattered teeth, a scarred tongue.

"Can you have more *what?*" I asked.

"Can I have more time?"

"More time?"

"More time alive."

"I wish... I wish I could give that to you." My breath shuddered in my throat. "I *wish* I could give you life."

"You can," he replied. His voice suddenly became raspier, darker. "Just give me yours."

I stared at him. Numb. Weak. My heart ached for the poor, pathetic, mangled child in front of me. It was all my fault. I ran him over. I did this to him.

"I can't give you mine," I said. I backed away, further into the room. He advanced quickly, walking towards me in swift, lithe strides.

"You don't have a choice," he said.

"What are you talking about?"

His mouth widened into a crooked grin.

"Trick-or-treat!"

I bolted for the door. I yanked the door open, ran out across the yard, screamed out into the night. I didn't stop until one of the neighbors found me, standing in the middle of the road, absolutely incoherent.

That was one year ago.

In 2 days, it will be Halloween again.

I've already seen him. A small figure across the street, dressed in all black. Watching me. Waiting.

Wearing a hideous werewolf mask.

SECURITY QUESTIONS

"What's your name?"

"Adam Lu. I want to close my American Express Gold Card," I said hurriedly into the phone. The train left in twenty minutes. But I needed to get the account closed, before they charged me that damn annual fee.

"Okay, we just need to verify your identity," the woman said. "I'm going to ask you a few security questions, okay?"

"Okay."

"What's your current address?"

"XX Hyacinth Court."

"And what's your mother's maiden name?"

"Greenberg."

"Thank you for that, Mr. Lu. We just need to ask you a few more questions to verify you. First, which of the following addresses have you lived at? [redacted] Maple Avenue, [redacted] Emory Circle, [redacted] 5th Street, or none of the above?"

"None of the above." Oh, *these* security questions. The weird multiple-choice ones, that you didn't actually ever

pick. I sighed into the phone and checked the clock. 8:12...
sixteen minutes to go.

"Okay. What security system do you use, or have you
used in the past? ADT, Ring Alarm, Adobe, or none of the
above?"

"None of the above."

A pause. I heard what sounded like papers shuffling
on the other end. Then: "How tall are you? Five-nine, six
feet, or –"

"Five seven. Listen, how many questions are you
going to ask me? I just want to close my account. I have to
catch a train."

"Okay. One last question," the woman said. Her voice
took on a smooth, soft quality. As if she were smiling on
the other end. "Are you a gun owner?"

"Uh, no."

"Thank you! We've verified your identity." Her voice
grew suddenly chipper. Excited.

"Okay. So I'd like to close my account," I said. 8:21.
Dammit, I'm going to miss it.

"That's not possible, Mr. Lu."

"You can't cancel my card? Why not?"

A pause. "I can't cancel your account, Mr. Lu, because
I don't work for American Express."

"...What?"

"It's a common mistake, Mr. Lu. American Express is
528-4800; you dialed 529-4800."

"I don't... I don't understand."

"Do you know how many people misdial American
Express's phone number? Hundreds. Per day. And those

people tend to be just what we're looking for — wealthy, dumb."

"I don't —"

"They'll be there in a minute. You can make it easy on yourself, and leave the house... or you can stay and fight. But I don't think the odds are good, Mr. Lu. They have guns... and you don't."

A pause. Then her peppy voice continued: "Anything else I can help you with, Mr. Lu?"

"I —"

"Thank you for calling! We *do* hope you have a wonderful day."

Click.

I pulled the phone away from my ear.

Just in time to see a shadow flit across the curtains.

"Hello?" I called. I took a step back, heart beginning to pound. "Hello?"

Thump, thump.

And then a man.

Just a glimpse of him, running by. Wearing all black, complete with a cap over his head. Dashing madly past my window.

I backed away.

Click, click.

The locks turned and clicked. Heavy footsteps at the back door.

I turned on my heel and ran. Threw open the front door, ran as fast as I could through the front yard. Until the cold stung my lungs and my legs were weak.

Then I pulled out my phone and called the police.

***

They came too late.

The house was ransacked. I was missing my TV, almost a thousand dollars in cash, and my iPad. I reported it all to the officers, and told them about the phone number. But when we called it, we only heard:

Beep, beep, beep! The number you have dialed is no longer in service.

They left. Then I sat in silence, my mind reeling.

Then I got on my computer — an old, half-broken thing, no wonder it wasn't stolen — and wrote this post.

To warn you.

There are hundreds of different ways you could misdial 528-4800. Whoever these people are jump from number to number, pretending to be American Express. They ask "security questions" to get information out of you. To rob you blind… or worse.

Don't fall for it.

Next time you pick up the phone…

Don't answer any strange security questions.

MATERNITY CLOTHES

Packing was going well.

Until I found the maternity clothes.

They were folded neatly, sitting in the back of my closet. Two pairs of pants, three shirts. At first I thought they were my sister Amanda's – but when I checked the tags, they were Large. *My* size, not hers.

I brought them out and examined them. They looked like my style – short-sleeved, hues of purple and blue. Maybe a gift I bought for someone, and forgot to give? Or maybe I just thought they looked cute, and bought them even though I wasn't pregnant... But maternity styles aren't exactly flattering on someone who isn't pregnant.

I shrugged, threw them into one of the boxes, and continued packing.

But then I found something else. Shoved in the corner of the closet, under some blankets and old dresses, was a toy fire truck.

I picked it up, turned it over in my hands. It looked vaguely familiar, with the little yellow ladder and painted blue windows. *Maybe it's Brayden's?* Amanda, her husband, and their one-year-old son often came over to visit. Maybe they'd left it behind.

Shrugging, I slowly lowered it into the box.

Riiiing.

"Hey, Mom," I said, layering clothes on top of the box.

"Hi, Rosie. We'll be there in about twenty minutes. How's packing going?"

"Pretty good," I said, folding another shirt on my lap. "Actually, do you remember if Brayden has a toy fire truck? I just found it in the closet, and I think it's his."

A strange silence came from the other end.

"Mom? You still there?"

"Yeah. We'll see you soon. Bye!"

Click.

When they finally made it to the apartment, they were eerily silent. Amanda was scratching at her neck, like she always does when she's nervous. Eliot held Brayden, refusing to make eye contact with me.

"I need to tell you something," Mom said, sitting at the table. The grim look on her face made my heart start to pound.

"Is that why you were so weird on the phone?"

She nodded. Then she sat down, and with a shuddering sigh, said: "That little fire truck... belonged to your son."

"What?" I burst into laughter. "Mom, what are you talking about? I don't have a kid."

"No, but you did. You gave birth to a little boy, last year." Mom pulled out a crumpled tissue and brought it to her eyes. I glanced at Amanda and Eliot. Neither met

66

my gaze; both stared at Brayden, pretending he needed attention.

"When he was about three months old, you took him to the grocery store. On the way back, you got into an accident. You were badly injured, and he..."

He died?

Mom fell into quiet sobs. After several seconds of silence, Amanda spoke. "Dr. Albright said you have retrograde amnesia. When we realized you didn't remember him, and saw that you were happy... we decided to leave it that way."

"You've been lying to me this whole time?"

They nodded.

"I had a little boy... that I can't even remember?"

"We were just trying to protect you," Amanda said. Mom nodded.

I didn't reply. I just sat there, in shock, staring into space.

And then I felt something on my leg.

I looked down. Brayden was standing there, holding the truck. With a pointed finger, he lifted the little ladder up, then smacked it down again.

Smack, smack.

I jolted up.

Images shot through my head. Cloudy and vague, in disjointed pieces, but that was it – I remembered something. *I was lifting the ladder, snapping it down, showing him how it worked...*

Smack, smack.

And then Mom walked in, carrying a bowl of oatmeal.

"Oh, Mom, thanks – but I'm not hungry."

"Come on, it's good for your milk supply."

I took a few bites. And then I felt sleepy – so sleepy. "Why don't you take a nap?" Mom said. "I'll watch him. You get your rest."

And when I woke up…

I was in the hospital, and he was gone.

My head snapped up. I stared at the three of them, my heart pounding.

And that's when I realized it. Mom's eyes were dry. Her sobbing sounds were the same rehearsed *gasp* of air, the same weak whimper of grief.

"You're not crying," I said.

Mom looked up at me. "What?"

"You're faking it."

Her eyes faded to anger. "Ridiculous! What kind of a daughter –"

Smack!

"What kind of a daughter does that to her mother? Ridiculous!" She was talking to Amanda in the kitchen, unaware I was standing right outside the door. "It's an embarrassment! What am I supposed to tell Grandma?"

A loud clink, as Amanda set down her cup. "And it's not fair. Eliot and I have been trying for six months. Nothing. Then Rose goes to a party, fucks some random guy she doesn't even know, and – bam! – gets pregnant. I'm the one that deserves a baby. Not her."

"I agree," Mom replied, her voice taking on a strange, light tone. "That should be your baby. Not hers."

I stared at the three of them. Acting, pretending like they cared.

Then I grabbed Brayden. Hoisted him onto my hip, held him tight against my chest.

And then I ran out of the apartment. I heard their yells echoing behind me – of confusion, of realization; but I kept running.

Brayden squealed with delight in my arms, still holding the little fire truck.

THE LOVE SIMULATOR

"You are so *fucking* self-righteous!"

"I'm just doing what I think is best —"

"For you, or for *us?*" I asked. "You know what? I wish — I wish I'd married Dan instead!"

Of course I didn't mean it. Exes are always better in retrospect, eroded to perfection by the sands of time.

But it was too late. Tommy slammed the door in my face.

I plopped down on the couch, my heart pounding. After staring at the wall forever, I pulled out my computer and typed into the search bar: "what to do if you married wrong man." Hoping for a self-help article, or maybe even some sort of wikiHow on divorce.

I got something else instead.

Marriage Troubles? Try the Love Simulator™! Only $19.99!

Curious, I clicked. I half-expected a porn site — which, honestly, would be fine by me.

But it wasn't. A page loaded up. Hot-pink Times New Roman on a black background, like some sort of '90s Geocities monstrosity.

Welcome to the Love Simulator™ by Black Widow, Inc.

Worried you'll marry the wrong person? Or that you already did? Find out below!

Below were rows. *Your name. Your love's name. Your Facebook page. Your love's Facebook page. Click here to upload photos, videos, and sound clips. Remember — the more information you give us, the more accurate the simulation!*

It's probably nonsense. But I needed a distraction, anyway. Maybe I'd get a good laugh.

My cursor hovered over the Submit button.

Click.

The scene that loaded reminded me of the Sims, with crappier graphics. A 3D living room. Blocky armchairs with ugly brocade textures. A vase with some bubbly things that only mildly resembled flowers.

A man sat on the sofa. His face was Dan's — but it was weirdly stretched and warped. His Facebook profile picture was a texture, mapped haphazardly to the cylindrical face.

"Hi. Kasey," an automated, stilted voice said from the speakers. "I. Love you."

Despite myself, I laughed. "Uh. Hi. I love you, too." The words felt weird on my lips, spoken to someone other than Tommy. Even if it was just a computer program.

"How. Are. You. Doing?"

"Uh, not so good, Dan, to be honest."

"I'm. Sorry," the voice said. *Oh, this is kind of neat. Must have some sort of speaking recognition... and an AI... like those old AOL chat bots.* "Is it. About. The fight?"

"Uh, the fight?" I said into the microphone.

"I'm. Sorry. I fought. With you." The pixelated, still eyes from Dan's profile picture stared out at me. "I. Love you. Kasey."

"I love you too."

"Also. Also," it started, tilting its head. "I am. Not. Self, righteous like Tommy."

My blood ran cold. "Wh-what?"

"I would. Never. Slam the door. In your face."

My cursor hovered over the x. *Click, click.* The window didn't close.

"Don't. Try to. Leave." He leaned in closer with his deformed head. "You're with me. Now. Kasey."

I slammed the laptop shut.

For a second, I thought I'd been successful. But then his voice came through the speakers, muffled through the plastic: "Do you. Remember. How we met?"

I nodded, scrunched into the corner of the couch. "You, uh... you stopped me on campus. I dropped my phone. You gave it back."

"Did you ever. Realize. You didn't actually. Drop your phone?"

"Uh... what do you mean?"

"I. Stole. It."

A buzzing silence filled the room. My ears rang.

"And did you. Ever realize? I wasn't. Even a student." A rustling sound from the speakers. "I worked. At the auto body shop. Next to campus."

I grabbed the laptop and threw it to the floor. Bits of glass and plastic exploded, covering the rug.

His voice continued, distorted and low:

"I wasn't. Even a student. Watched you for days. A pretty little co-ed —"

Rap, rap, rap.

Three knocks on the front door.

I bolted up. Stepped into the foyer. "Tommy — is that you?"

No reply.

"I'm so sorry for what I said. I'm so, so sorry."

A pretty. Then five words came through the heavy oak door:

"Get out of the simulation."

Click. The sound of a key fitting into the lock.

Creeeeeaaaak.

I shut my eyes and screamed. A hand grabbed my wrist, yanked me onto the porch.

"Kasey! Kasey!"

I opened my eyes.

I wasn't standing on the porch.

I was sitting in a bed, in a dim room. The damp smell of must flooded over me; a dim beeping sound came from somewhere in the shadows.

"Kasey."

I turned to see a figure in the shadows, sitting at the computer.

"I'm... back? What are you talking about?" I pulled myself up further. My forehead suddenly itched. I reached my hand up to scratch; my fingers brushed wires instead of skin.

"Yeah. I just pulled you out of the simulation."

The voice was gravelly. Low. Familiar.

No.

The man stood up and walked towards me. His large nose, short dark hair illuminated in the light.

"Dan."

He smiled. "See, I knew it wouldn't take long. You're a grass-is-greener kind of girl. You said you wished you'd married Tommy. So I gave you that... and then, only two days into the simulation, you told *him* you wish you'd married me." He broke into laughter. "Tommy *is* a self-righteous asshole, isn't he?"

My blood ran cold.

The memories flooded back in pieces. The wedding to Dan. The fight, only a few weeks after. *You're a liar and a creep. I wish I'd married Tommy!*

"What happened after that? I don't... I don't remember."

"I dragged you down here and started the simulation." He frowned. "I'm surprised you don't remember that. You were thrashing and yelling quite a bit."

My heart dropped.

Then I leapt out of the bed. Tore the wires from my forehead, ran up the stairs. I heard his yells behind me, his thundering footsteps.

I yanked the door open.

Then I disappeared into the snowy night.

STEREOGRAPHS

"Cross your eyes to see the hidden image."

Becky sat on the floor, the book laying flat across her lap. It was one of those Magic Eye stereogram books. Where you stare at a weird pattern, cross-eyed, until you see the 3-dimensional, hidden image.

She'd picked it up at the library. Because Becky apparently thought that was a cool thing to do.

"I don't see it," she whined.

"Let me try."

I snatched it off her lap.

The first page depicted a pattern of wild flowers in a field. I crossed my eyes; the image split into two translucent, overlapping pieces.

Then they snapped together, forming the 3-D image of a frog.

"It's a frog," I said, tossing the book back at her.

She winced. Then she took off her glasses, brought the page up to her face. Her brown eyes went crooked, her eyebrows furled.

"I don't see it."

"Let's do the next one."

That page was just as boring as the first. A pattern of hearts and polka dots. When I screwed up my eyes, I could see a 3-D cat playing with a ball of yarn.

I can't believe I'm spending Saturday doing this. With Becky. She'd asked to come over in front of my mom — who was, of course, thrilled. *Becky's one of the smartest kids in class! She's a good influence.*

Psh. Good influence.

I picked at my nails. Staring at my signed Ariana Grande poster, my pink wallpaper, my trophy from horseback riding.

I bet Becky just has stupid books in her room.

"Oh! I see it! I see the cat!" she squealed.

We went on like this for nearly an hour. Finally, we got to the second-to-last page. Even I was having trouble with this one; every time I crossed my eyes, the yellow floral pattern just snapped back in focus.

"I can't see it," I finally admitted to Becky.

"That's okay!" she piped back.

I stared down at the pattern and crossed my eyes again. For a split second, I glimpsed something 3-dimensional; that fuzzy, flickering depth in the page.

Then it flattened.

"Don't focus on it," Becky said.

"I know."

I closed my eyes and took a deep breath. Then I looked down at the page and crossed my eyes. The image grew fuzzy — then it locked into place.

My heart stopped.

It wasn't some cute little dog or cat, like the previous ones. It was a woman.

She stood still and straight, hair falling raggedly down her shoulders. No details or clothing. Not even a face. Just that endless, yellow floral pattern.

But I could tell — she was looking straight at me.

"You see it?" Becky asked.

"Yeah, uh, it's a woman." I closed the book. "Hey, let's go watch —"

"I want to do the last page."

"But —"

"I want to finish the book.'

"Okay," I said.

I slowly pulled the book back open. The last page was a pattern of blue flowers, bending in the wind. Heart pounding, I crossed my eyes.

It was the same woman.

Closer. One arm outstretched.

Reaching for me.

I shrieked and jumped back. The image collapsed; the book fell off my lap, onto the floor.

"You saw her."

I looked up.

Becky was staring at me. Hands neatly folded in her lap. Glasses pushed up her nose.

Smiling.

"I — yes, but —"

"Then my work here is done."

She lifted herself up off the floor, still smiling. Picked up the book. Walked over to the door.

Click.

I sat in my room, silent. My heart thundered in my ears. *It's just a book. Just a book.* My heart began to slow.

Just a book.

I stared at the wall, my eyes falling out of focus.

Just a book.

The pink floral wallpaper stared back at me.

Just a —

The image snapped into focus.

A woman. She leaned out of the wall, the pink wallpaper wrapping around her body. Molding to her face.

One arm stretched towards me.

"No, no! Please!" I closed my eyes tight.

When I opened them a minute later, she was gone. Or, at least... I couldn't see her without my eyes crossed.

That night I told myself it was all a joke. A stupid prank that Becky planned to get back at me. For the time I ditched her at the mall with Sam and Marin. For the time I laughed at her in class.

But as I lie in bed, trying to fall asleep, I hear something.

A rippling, crinkling sound.

As if something is moving underneath the wallpaper.

THE HANGING TREE

by *Blair Daniels & Craig Groshek*

"They say the tree bleeds when you peel off the bark."

Liz's eyes flickered in the orange light. Her lips curled into a small smile, as if she enjoyed that particular detail.

"That's ridiculous. There's no way a tree could bleed," Tucker said, yanking his burning marshmallow from the fire.

"There are photos, though. I've seen them all over Instagram. Bright red blood, oozing from the bark."

"It's supposed to be the blood of Monstruo's victims," I added. "The legend goes, the tree absorbed all the blood spilled at its roots. Now instead of sap, human blood pumps through its veins."

Tucker let out a peal of laughter. "Absolutely not! That's ridiculous. Come on, you guys were in my Biology class. You know there's no way *human blood* is pumping through the xylem and phloem —"

"It's true," Liz said, shooting him a glare.

"You know what? I bet the whole thing is a myth. I bet Monstruo himself didn't even exist."

I glanced at the tree. It stood in the shadows, several yards behind us. Blackened bark. Leafless branches. A sore thumb in the forest.

The Hanging Tree. Or *el árbol del ahorcado,* as some of the locals called it.

"It's nothing more than a tourist trap," Tucker continued.

"A tourist trap only the locals know about? Doesn't make much sense to me," I said.

Tucker sighed. "You know what I mean." His marshmallow fell into the fire with an unceremonious *plop.* "It's an urban legend to tell around campfires like this one. A spooky haunted tree. The legend of a perverted, cannibalistic killer. It sounds like the plot to a Stephen King novel. I guarantee you — Monstruo wasn't real."

"He *was* real. Every single person in this town who's old enough to have seen it, says it happened." I glanced over at him. "And this tree is where he hung his victims' bodies."

Tucker laughed. The sound echoed off the trees, making it sound like a chorus was laughing with him. "Yeah, and those same locals just call him 'Monstruo.' The Spanish word for 'monster.' If he's real, why don't they call him by name?"

"Because they don't want to give him the dignity."

It was Liz speaking, now. The smile had faded from her face. She scooted closer to the fire; the black shadows faded from her face. "He did such terrible things. Referring to him by name would only glorify that."

"That's a clever lie. But it doesn't fool me."

I shifted closer to Tucker, who was plucking another marshmallow from the bag. "Come on, Tucker. Ever notice how this part of town is basically abandoned? And no one ever builds on the empty lot a few feet over, even though it's dirt cheap?" I laughed. "The things Monstruo did are so terrible, even money won't get anyone near it."

"So terrible. So, so terrible. That's what I keep hearing. Yet, funny how I've never heard any details or facts."

"You want facts? I'll give you facts. He killed 17 men, women, and children. And you do a hell of a lot of disrespect to those people, when you claim he didn't exist."

Liz nodded, her dark eyes glancing at Tucker.

"Look, I'm not trying to disrespect anybody. I just —
"

"I'm not done." My voice cut through the cold air like a knife. Tucker jumped. "He didn't *just* abduct and kill those people. It was a lot worse than that."

Tucker's marshmallow burned and crackled. Liz shuffled her feet across the dry leaves.

"He led each victim, blindfolded, to the tree." I glanced down from their faces, and into the blinding flames. "Then he killed them, and strung their bodies up in the tree as if they were trophies to show off."

Liz's eyes shone brightly in the orange glow. She wiped her sleeve across them.

"And then he eviscerated them."

82

"Oh," Tucker said, softly.

"Then he took them back to his house. But not before he removed their right shoes — and added them to his creepy-ass memento box. And then... do I have to say it?" I asked. The pillar of smoke billowed up between us, shrouding Liz and Tucker in a gray veil.

"He ate them," Liz whispered to him.

"Oh, come on! What a load of nonsense." Tucker stood up and rolled his eyes. "I can *guarantee* you, there is not a shred of truth in that story. No Monstruo, no cursed tree. Someone probably just made it up on the internet."

"You just think you're so smart, don't you?"

He laughed, blowing on the blackened marshmallow. "Yeah, you bet I do."

"Then how about this? The day after Monstruo died, the tree died. Then all the foliage, within a few feet of it. Nothing grows there to this day." I gestured to the tree, barely visible from our spot near the campfire. "You can't deny that, Tucker. You can get your lazy ass up and see it for yourself."

Tucker didn't reply.

"Go on. Look at it," Liz said. Her smile was back. "Or are you too *scared?*"

Tucker grumbled and turned around. "I can see it from here. And you're right — but, obviously, the tree died because everyone peeled off its bark."

"Okay, so that's why the *tree's* dead, maybe. But what about the fact that nothing grows around it?"

"The tree's roots probably choke everything out. Or the soil's too compacted, from all the teenagers visiting and stomping it down."

"Right. Let's talk about those teenagers." I smiled, leaning closer to the fire. My face grew uncomfortably warm. "They climb it, decorate it, have sex under it —"

"Hang effigies from it," Liz added. Even now, a stray piece of rope hung from the lowest branch, swaying in the wind. I tried not to look at it.

"Yeah. And do you know what happened to those teenagers?"

"No."

"Adrian Keller climbed it to take a selfie. A month later, he was committed to a mental hospital because he violently attacked his mother."

"Okay, so? He was probably crazy before he even saw the tree."

"I'm not done yet," I snapped. "On a fine Wednesday afternoon, Greg Patel skipped school to have sex with Aria Stewart underneath the tree. She got pregnant — and, months later, miscarried something so terribly deformed, the doctors didn't even call it a fetus."

Tucker didn't have a snarky reply for that one.

"And Sidney Taylor. Let's talk about her. After hanging an effigy from the tree, she started sleepwalking. At first, she'd wake up under the tree. Then she'd wake up in neighbors' lawns. Finally she woke up in one of their houses — surrounded by a pool of blood and two corpses."

"That's enough," Liz muttered. "He gets the point, you don't need to repeat it —"

"She'd taken off the right shoe of each corpse and stripped them naked. And each one… each one was missing large chunks of flesh. When doctors pumped her stomach, they found —"

"John, okay! You've made your point!" Liz snapped.

A thick silence fell over the three of us.

Finally, Tucker said: "I still don't believe it."

"So touch the tree, then," Liz shot back. "We'll write you at the sanitarium, we promise. Right, John?"

I raised my eyebrow at her.

"Fine. I will." Tucker heaved himself up off the ground. With heavy footsteps, he started into the darkness.

"Shoot. I didn't think he'd actually do it. Wait! Tucker!"

I followed them through the trees. Soon enough, the three of us were standing before the Hanging Tree.

Swaths of bark were peeled off, and a thick sap — almost blood-like — oozed from the wounds. The bits of rope swayed in the wind. Initials and hearts were carved all over the bark that was still intact. I noticed a faint marking that read *Greg+Aria*, near the roots, and my heart dropped.

"Tucker, please, don't do it."

Tucker stood on the border of the dead circle — where the weeds and shrubs dwindled into sticks, leaves, and rotten mud. His arm was stretched out, fingers inches from the trunk.

"Tucker. I was just joking. Don't do it." Liz tugged at his sleeve.

"Relax, Liz. It's just a tree."

Of course, Tucker was going to do it, now. He'd always had a crush on her. No way he'd pass up this chance to impress her and be some sort of macho man.

"Tucker, please, don't." Liz looked at me expectantly — as if she expected me to dissuade him. I was silent. "Come on, let's just go to sleep. This whole idea was dumb."

"I want to touch the tree, Liz." Tucker took a step forward. "I want to prove to you I'm right. That this whole thing is an elaborate hoax."

He took a step forward, arm outstretched.

"No!"

Liz grabbed his shoulders.

But it was too late.

His fingers pressed into the bark. When he pulled them back, rusty-red sap covered them.

Liz stepped forward, eyes brimming with tears. "No. This is all my fault. Now you're going to go crazy and kill people and —"

"Get a hold of yourself, Liz," Tucker said. "It's just a tree. And a dead one at that."

The three of us walked back to the tent in silence. Tucker handled the fire; I cleaned up a bit around the campsite. By the time I got inside, Liz was already asleep — only her messy hair poked out from the sleeping bag.

I opened my own sleeping bag, snuggled in, and closed my eyes.

I jolted awake.

For a second, I couldn't place where I was. It was cold; colder than I'd remembered it being that evening. I fumbled through the darkness for my cell phone.

2:06 AM

The light from my phone lit the inside of the tent. I saw Liz, sleeping peacefully in her bag. Her mouth hung slightly open, a wet spot of drool on her pillow.

The other sleeping bag was empty.

"Tucker?" I said. Softly, at first.

No reply.

"Hey! Tucker!" I called. Liz stirred next to me.

I slowly stood up, careful not to rustle the sleeping bag too loudly. With one hand, I peeled back the entrance of the tent.

Everything was pitch black.

I pressed the flashlight button on my phone. It lit the clearing in bright, white glow. The charred remains of our campfire; depressions in the dirt, where we'd placed our folding chairs.

And in the distance — a silhouette. Standing right under the tree, facing away from me.

"Tucker?" I shouted, running towards him. I stopped a few feet away; he didn't turn around. "Tucker, are you okay?"

Silence — save for a *schlick, schlick* sound.

I grabbed him by the shoulders. "Tucker, what —"

I stopped.

The entire tree was covered in carvings. *Hundreds* of them. All in Tucker's handwriting, all of the same word:

LIZ.

"Tucker! Hey! Are you okay?"

As if waking from a deep sleep, Tucker jolted and glanced around. "Uh, yeah, I'm fine." He glanced at the trees. "Why am I out here?"

"Doesn't matter. Come on, let's get you back to the tent."

I didn't sleep a wink the rest of the night.

***

Liz and I were incredibly worried about Tucker. But days, and then weeks, passed without event. We began to believe that the Hanging Tree really *was* just a tree, and he was right all along.

Until that fateful Saturday night.

I was sitting in my house, eating a late dinner alone, when someone knocked on the door.

I jolted upright. "Who's there?" I yelled, glancing at the deadbolt. Locked.

"It's me! Liz! Open up!" Her voice warbled with emotion.

My heart sank. Something was terribly wrong. "Liz, are you okay?" I called, as I hurried to the door.

"I'm okay. Just open the door, John. I need to tell you something."

I yanked the door open.

"Don't move."

Tucker stood next to Liz on my porch, smiling. The barrel of a gun poked against her skull; he slowly turned it, so that it pointed at me.

"I'm so sorry," Liz said to me, starting to sob. "I didn't want to. But he said he'd shoot me if I didn't. I panicked... I'm so, so sorry."

Tucker motioned for me to step forward. "Come on, John. Or are you *scared?*"

"Okay. Okay. Calm down, I'm coming." I held up my hands and stepped into the cold. Tucker grinned.

"In the car," he said. "Backseat. Both of you."

I climbed into the backseat. Liz cried against my shoulder. "I'm so sorry," she kept repeating, over and over.

I felt numb. Like I was watching a terrible movie. Watching the scene unfolding in front of me, utterly powerless to stop it.

The car tore through the night. My shoulder hit the door, hard, as we made turn after turn. "Where are you taking us?" I asked, trying to keep my voice as calm as possible.

He didn't reply.

But I didn't have to wonder long. Soon enough, I saw the empty lot approaching. The forest rose up behind it, shrouded in shadow.

"You're taking us to the Hanging Tree, aren't you?"

Silence, save for Liz's soft sobs.

He drove right across the empty lot, through the weeds and shrubs. We skidded to a halt at the forest's edge. "Out," Tucker grunted, as he swung the door open.

We trudged through the forest in silence. My feet rhythmically crunched the dry leaves and sticks with each step. Like a clock, ticking down to the moment of our death.

We stopped in front of the blackened tree. Its branches twisted and crossed the indigo sky. A cold wind blew; the shreds of rope swayed.

"Stand over there," he commanded Liz.

"Why are you doing this?" she cried.

"He doesn't know what he's doing, Liz. He's sleepwalking."

"I'm *not* sleepwalking." Tucker snapped towards me, his blue eyes wild and dark. "I'm not doing this because some cursed tree infected me. I'm doing it because two friends who *betrayed* me."

"What are you talking about?" Liz shouted.

"Oh, come on. Who do you think I am? Some kind of an idiot?" He reached into his bag and pulled out a length of thick rope.

"I don't know what you're talking about."

"Oh, don't act so innocent. You and Liz have been fucking behind my back, for weeks. When you knew I was in love with her," he spat.

"That's not true," Liz said, softly.

"Oh, don't deny it. And then you call me as some kind of idiot just because I don't believe in a cursed tree! What kind of friend is that?"

He grabbed me roughly by the waist. In one swift, strong motion, he looped the rope around my shoulders. "A fit punishment for a fit crime, don't you think?"

I tried to wriggle free. I thrashed and kicked and shouted. But Tucker had at least six inches on me. I didn't have a chance.

After fumbling with a knot, he looped the rope over the lowest branch and tugged. My feet left the ground. Slowly, inch-by-inch, I was pulled up the tree. The blackened, leafless branches came closer into view.

And then I noticed the scratch marks.

Hundreds of them. White like scars, covering the bark. Desperate. Anguished. *Human.*

"Monstruo didn't hang dead bodies from this tree," I muttered. Liz looked up at me, eyes wide.

"He hung them alive."

I tore my eyes away from the bark. Below me, Tucker was looping the rope around Liz. She wasn't crying anymore; instead, she was thrashing. Kicking. Fighting.

But she wasn't strong enough. In minutes, she was hanging next to me.

Tucker dragged his bag over the ground. *Zip* — he pulled it open and reached inside. A steel knife glinted in the moonlight. Then he walked over to us.

First he gently pulled off my right sneaker.

Then he pulled off Liz's boot.

"Please. Don't do this," Liz pleaded, one last time.

I remained silent. Instead, I wriggled against the rope. Jumped. Thrashed. Tried everything in my strength to get free.

The rope began to loosen.

Liz met my eyes. I tried my best to make a face at her, to signal what I was doing. Catching my drift, she started: "Tucker, listen. I've only ever liked you. Not him." She forced a smile. "Look at me, Tucker. I'm telling you the truth."

He took a step towards her. Finally tilted his head up to look at her.

I fell to the ground.

I ran at him and tackled him. After getting in a few good punches, I leapt up and pulled down Liz's rope.

"We need to call the police," Liz said, latched onto my arm. "We need to —"

THUMP!

Tucker collided with her.

The scene played before my eyes as if in slow motion. Tucker grabbed her by the wrists. He dragged her across the mud. In one frenzied motion, he pressed her hands against the tree trunk.

She screamed.

I leapt at them. But it was too late. Liz was shrieking, looking at her hands. They were covered in sticky red sap.

"I touched it. I touched it," she said.

"Come on, let's go." I grabbed Liz's wrist and yanked her towards the lot. "We need to go." Tucker was already reaching for the knife, his face twisted in an expression of anger.

"Liz! Come on!"

We ran through the forest, through the empty lot, and into the night.

***

That night, Tucker was arrested for assault. The next morning, they found his cellmate dead, on the floor, in a pool of blood. Missing chunks of flesh.

Liz started sleepwalking a week after the events. She committed herself to a mental institution the next day. We exchange letters sometimes, but I don't think she's ever going to leave that place.

So that's my experience with the Hanging Tree. And, listen — I'm not telling you this tale to scare you. I'm telling you because I need your help

A week ago, builders broke ground on the empty lot. As we speak, they're cutting down bits of the forest — including the Hanging Tree.

To build a daycare center.

Toddlers and caregivers will be on that cursed ground. Learning, playing, growing. Utterly unaware of the darkness that once stood.

Maybe it won't have any effect.

But if Tucker and Liz are any indication, it will.

I've tried calling my local representatives. I've tried calling the daycare company. I've tried protesting on the street.

Nothing helped.

So now I'm telling you.

If you live near El Bosque, Texas, do everything in your power to stop it. If enough people complain, maybe they'll get discouraged and give up.

And if not…

Leave town — and never look back.

THE BABY MONITOR

"I got you something." John reached into the Buy Buy Baby bag and pulled out a sleek, white box. "A baby monitor! One of the fancy video ones!"

"My 3 AM visits to the nursery starting to bother you, huh?" I asked, with a smirk.

"Maybe a *little*. I think this'll help us both sleep better."

I glanced down at the mug in my hands – my fourth cup of coffee. "Let's do it."

We set it up in the nursery that night. I pointed the camera right at the crib and placed the monitor on my nightstand. I fell asleep watching the black-and-white video feed of our son. Gracefully sleeping, with his face in a puddle of drool and his butt in the air.

Thump.

I jolted awake.

I grabbed the monitor. The feed showed James sleeping peacefully – butt still in the air, now in an even bigger puddle of drool.

I smiled, rolled over, and fell back into a deep sleep.

The next night, as John and I were getting ready for bed, I asked him about it. "Last night I heard a weird sound from James's room."

"Oh, no. You think we have mice again?"

"Oh, I didn't even think about that." I turned to him. "Maybe I should sleep in there tonight. Just in case. I wouldn't want mice getting into the crib, or –"

"You have the monitor."

"But maybe if I was *right there* –"

He frowned. "Come on, Carrie. He's over a year old — he needs his own room. The monitor is to help you work through this."

I glared at him. "Work through *what?*"

"The anxiety."

"Anxiety? Is that what you call *concern for our child's well-being?*"

"I didn't mean it like –"

"Goodnight," I said sharply, and pulled the covers over me.

I woke up again at 3:21 AM.

Instinctively, I reached for the baby monitor. The blue light blinded me in the darkness. I waited for my eyes to adjust.

There was my little man. Facing away from the camera, little tufts of hair sticking every which way. Sleeping peacefully.

I set the monitor back down on the nightstand and closed my eyes.

Click.

My eyes flew open. James was facing towards me, now. Eyes closed peacefully. Puffy little cheeks smushed against the mattress.

Just go to sleep. He's fine. Stop checking him.

Maybe John has a point.

I forced my eyes closed. *He's fine.* The fog of sleep filled my mind, melting my thoughts into dreamy nonsense. *He's fine. Fine, fine, fine –*

Thump.

He's fine. Don't check on him. Just go to sleep. Go to –

Waaaaah!

A loud cry came through the wall. Then through the monitor, a second later. My eyes flew open. James lay in the same position.

But despite the cries coming from the nursery —

His mouth was closed.

What the hell? I leapt out of bed. Stumbled across the hall. I grabbed the doorknob and yanked it open, running blindly into the room.

James was lying in the crib. Crying his lungs out.

And dark figure was leaning over him.

"Get away from him!"

I ran to the crib. The figure darted across the room and – in an instant – slipped out the window. I grabbed James out of the crib. Held him tight against my chest. "James! James, are you okay?"

"Carrie?" John came stumbling in.

"Call the police!" I shouted. "Someone was in here!"

As I held James tight against me, something caught my eye. The baby monitor camera, its red light blinking in the darkness.

There was something propped up in front of it. A piece of paper.

I reached out and turned it over.

No.

It was a photo.

Of James, sleeping peacefully in his crib.

GRAFFITI IN A GAS STATION BATHROOM

The car swung into the parking lot. The neon sign cut through the darkness, through the mist of drizzling rain.

"Try to be quick," Derek said, as the car rolled to a stop. "We're running late."

"I told you, I'll just be a minute!"

I ran towards the convenience store, hands thrust in my pockets, rain dampening my hair. I hurried through the aisles of chips, chocolate, and twinkies until I reached the bathrooms.

Creeeaaak.

"Wow." I expected the bathroom to be bad – but not *this* bad. The walls were pocked with holes. The floor was covered in a sticky wet film. The place reeked of air freshener.

There were only two stalls: one closed, the other open. I walked into the open one and plopped down on the cold toilet seat.

As I went, I read the graffiti on the back of the stall door.

It was full of the standard stuff. Declarations of love: *Marisa <3s Jay!!!* That stupid, stylized S thing all over the place. *S S S.*

But the weirdest thing was a drawing that took up half the bathroom door. It was a drawing of a man in a suit – though clearly done by an amateur. The limbs were way out of proportion with the body; they were far too long. And, for some reason, the face had been scribbled out with marker.

I sighed and pulled on the toilet paper. The roll thumped underneath my fingers, as clumps of white fell into my hands.

Then I saw it.

There was writing down there, too – a few inches under the roll of toilet paper. Six words, written in tidy, small handwriting.

don't look in the other stall

Huh. What does that mean? But I shrugged, pulled up my pants, and flushed the toilet.

Fluuuusssshh!

The noise echoed in the small room, bouncing off the metal and brick. I walked over to the sink, washed my hands, and glanced in the mirror.

Writing in black, bold Sharpie caught my eye.

A single sentence, just above the mirror, in the same tidy handwriting.

don't turn around

That's when I noticed the shadow in the second stall.

It spilled out from underneath the metal door, stretching across the wet tiles. *Okay, so someone's in the other stall,* I told myself. Yet the bathroom was – and had been – perfectly silent. No footsteps. No humming. No awkward splashes.

If someone was in there... they were *deliberately* staying silent. They didn't want me to notice them.

"Hello?" I called, my voice sounding more fearful than I meant.

No reply.

There was only one way to find out if someone was there. I crouched down, inhaling breaths of stale piss, peering underneath the door. The edge of the toilet came into view, grime crusted on where it met the floor. Then the curve of the toilet bowl, white and glistening in the fluorescent lights. Then the edge of the toilet seat. Then –

"Shit!" I jumped back, nearly toppling onto the sticky ground.

Way at the back of the stall, up against the wall... were two feet. Clad in men's black dress shoes.

I whipped around. I ran over to the door and yanked the handle.

It didn't move.

"What the *fuck?*" I hissed under my breath. I gave it a few more tugs; it didn't budge. I grabbed my phone out of my pocket and dialed Derek's number, my nails racing against the screen. "Derek? Derek, I'm locked in the bathroom!"

Footsteps sounded from the closed stall. The shadow shifted.

"What are you talking about, Amber?!"

"I can't get out of the bathroom! Someone's locked me in here!"

The slam of a car door came over the line. Derek's ragged breathing filled the earpiece, with the *thumps* of his hurried footsteps. "Okay, I'm coming to get you. Don't freak out, the door probably just got stuck –"

He stopped.

"Derek?"

"The store… it's locked."

"Bang on the door until someone opens it!"

His fist pounded through the door first; then through the earpiece a second later. "No one's coming. I'm not sure anyone's in there…" he panted.

Shhhhhhhhwwwwp.

Click.

I whipped around.

The sound of a lock disengaging. Coming from the stall. The two black shoes stuck out from under the door, shining in the fluorescent light.

"There's someone in the bathroom with me!" I shouted into the phone.

Pause. "Amber, are you serious?" His knocking grew louder, more frenzied. I yanked on the handle with all my strength.

That's when I noticed another bit of graffiti.

A short paragraph, in different handwriting, etched right above the handle. The first letter of each sentence was drawn over with marker, to make it bold.

Right now, he's behind you

Under the door, you see his shadow
No – never let this door close!
Creeeeeaaaak.

I heard the stall door swing open behind me. *Thump. Tck. Thump. Tck.* The clicking sound followed each step – the sound of his shoes unsticking from the tacky, grimy floor.

The air shifted. The flowery smell of air freshener faded into the acrid smell of dust and decay. The room suddenly became hot and dry. Sweat beaded on my forehead.

Don't turn around don't turn around don't turn around –

The footsteps came to a stop a few feet behind me.

Silence.

Then –

Sph, sph. The loud rustling of clothing. I felt the air shift over my neck. I closed my eyes tight, utterly paralyzed. *Don't turn around, don't turn –*

Click.

The bathroom door swung open. *Derek.* He grabbed my arm and pulled me into the blinding light of the store. He didn't let go of me until we were in the car, driving as fast as we could away from that place.

After twenty minutes of stunned silence, as the dark scenery whipped by on the highway, I finally spoke.

"When you opened the door… what did you see?"

"What do you mean?"

"Did you see… anyone in there with me?"

"No. The bathroom was empty."

"But I mean –"

"I didn't see him, Amber," he snapped back. "And the door wasn't locked. It was just stuck."

We fell into awkward silence. I stared out at the hills and pine trees whipping by in the dark. And as I watched, I realized something.

I never told Derek it was a *man* in there with me.

In the days since then, Derek has been acting stranger and stranger. Two days ago, I found him slumped against the toilet, muttering to himself. The day before that, he was knocking on the bathroom door for ten minutes, claiming the door was locked.

And yesterday…

I thought I glimpsed two black men's shoes, sticking out from behind the shower curtain.

PEANUTS

I'm deathly allergic to peanuts.

When I eat one… it's awful. My throat seizes up. My blood pressure drops. My mouth feels like it's on fire. I can't even sit near someone else eating peanuts. The dust hangs in the air like some sort of lethal, invisible tear gas.

But there was a silver lining: I wasn't allergic to anything else. *Just* peanuts.

That all changed in 2011. My dad, stepmom, and I moved into an old house on the edge of town. That's when my allergies started getting worse.

I vividly remember our first dinner there. Seconds after taking a bite of chicken, I felt it. The familiar itching tingle in my lips. The swelling. The pain. The lightheadedness.

"Dad! I think I'm allergic!"

"What? You're not allergic to this!" he said, through a mouth full of chicken.

"Dad!" I shouted. My voice already sounded different. Deep. Hoarse. "Get the Epi-Pen! Now!"

He dashed off to the bathroom. My stepmom stared at me, terrified and awkward. "Do you want to help you, um, throw it up?"

My poor stepmom had already witnessed one of my reactions a few years ago. She had the privilege of accompanying me to restaurant's ladies' room while I forced myself to vomit.

"No, I'm okay," I said, my voice sounding like a monster from the depths of Hell.

Dad ran to my side, uncapping the Epi-Pen. Without warning, he thrust it into my thigh. "Ow! Dad!" I screamed.

I spent the night drifting in and out of sleep.

The next day, we started a list. **Samantha's Allergies.** Taped right to the fridge. We added chicken and paprika underneath PEANUTS.

I thought that would be the end of it. But the next week, I got another reaction.

After just one bite of burger, that horrible, tingling pain spread through my mouth and throat. "Dad, I don't feel so good." I said.

He ran to fetch the Epi-Pen.

The next day, I talked to my Dad. "I don't get it. I *just had* cheeseburgers three days ago at Maddy's house. I was fine then."

"Maybe something different in the buns?"

"I guess."

"Also, allergies can change really quickly."

"Where did you read that?"

"WebMD."

I laughed. But inside, I was miserable. All I could imagine was that list on the refrigerator, growing and growing, until it hit the floor. And me, sitting down to a dinner of mushy rice and tofu every night.

Or worse.

And it wasn't just my food allergies that were getting bad. I found that just *standing* in that dusty old house made my throat get that awful, itchy feeling. I tried to spend a lot of time outside. Sometimes I just sat in the backyard, under the oak tree, hungry. Wondering if it was even worth it to go inside and eat dinner.

Over the weeks, the list continued to grow. Ground beef. Broccoli. Rice. Things that were supposedly "hypoallergenic."

Hypoallergenic. Psh. What a joke.

Finally, after weeks of this, Dad sat me down. "I got you an appointment with an allergist. We're going to do a bunch of blood tests to find out exactly what you're allergic to. Okay?"

"But we... we don't have insurance, Dad."

"I don't care," Dad replied. "We need to get you better."

***

"Okay, good news," the doctor said, shuffling the papers in his hands. "We got your test results back."

I looked up at him and for the first time in a long time, I smiled. "Yeah?"

"You're only allergic to one food!"

"What?"

"Peanuts. That's it!"

I glanced at Dad. "No. That can't be right. I've been getting allergic to *everything*. Beef, broccoli…"

"Nope! All those foods came up negative!" he said in a chipper tone, waddling over to the desk.

"Look, Dr. Avery, we paid a lot of money for those tests. They're supposed to be accurate," Dad said, annoyed.

"They *are* accurate. I mean, nothing's perfect, but —"

"My daughter has been getting allergic reactions *daily*. To tons of different foods. We don't even know what to feed her anymore!" he said, practically shouting.

"Dad," I whispered. His eyes met mine and he softened his tone.

"Sorry, just, uh… I'm at wit's end, here."

The doctor turned around, nonplussed. "Well. Is there any chance of cross-contamination?"

"What?"

"Cross-contamination. Like, if you use a knife to spread peanut butter on your sandwich, and then use that knife to cut Samantha's chicken. She'd get a reaction, then, since her peanut allergy is so severe."

"You think we'd do that? We don't even keep peanuts in the house!"

"Well, then I don't know what to tell you," Dr. Avery said.

We left the allergist in confusion – with Dad bemoaning the $350 he'd just paid out of pocket.

***

Several weeks later, I found out the truth.

I'd gotten out of school early. It was a half day, because a bad snowstorm was forecast that evening. When I walked in the side door, though, my ears were assaulted with the whine of the food processor.

Whiiirrrr! Whiiiirrrrrrrrrrrrr!

My stepmom was standing over the kitchen island. A large pan of uncooked lasagna stood in the middle. She pulsed the food processor; a light brown powder spun inside.

Whiiiiiirrrrrrr! Whiiiiiiirrrrrrrrrrrrr!

She grabbed the skillet on the stove and gave it a good shake. Something rattled inside. I leaned over to get a better look.

No.

They were peanuts.

She dropped a handful into the food processor. *Whiiiirrr!* Then she twisted the lid off and reached a hand inside. With the finesse of a chef, she carefully sprinkled the powder over the lasagna.

All while humming to herself.

I ran outside. My throat already felt like it was closing up. Like I couldn't breathe. I heard the muffled shouts of my stepmother behind me.

But she didn't have a chance to stop me.

I pulled out my phone and called Dad.

LIME-GREEN PAINT

My boyfriend and I are in a long-distance relationship. To make up for it, we Skype all the time. We were on one of these late-night video calls when it happened. Steve stopped mid-sentence and said: "Rae, what's that behind you?"

I turned around. There was nothing behind my chair but a blank wall.

"What are your talking about?"

"The crack in the wall. Harry's going to have a fit."

"There's nothing wrong with the wall."

"Oh, really? You don't see the huge crack spanning your entire wall?"

I turned around again. All I saw was that ugly lime-green wall. Harry, the landlord, painted all the apartments in the building like that. All the walls white, except for one blinding lime-green "accent" wall in the main room.

"No. I don't see it." I sighed, and said in my most seductive voice: "Can't we get back to what we were doing?"

"Maybe it's a glitch? Or some dirt on your camera?"

I sighed.

"Check your webcam."

"Fine."

I clicked on the tiny image of myself in the corner. It filled the screen.

I froze.

Whether it was dirt or a glitch, I couldn't tell. But there *did* appear to be a jagged, thick, black line running through the lime-green paint. "That's so weird."

I rubbed my camera, but it didn't go away. I hung up and re-entered the call, and it didn't go away.

"It looks bigger now," he said.

"What?"

"At the beginning it was just a thin crack. Now it looks a like, two inches wide."

"Okay. Can we talk about something else now?"

"But it's so weird."

We continued talking. Steve's eyes stayed fixed just over my shoulder the entire time. I tried to ignore it. "So Mary said, *what are you doing here at the salon, in the middle of the night?* And I said —"

"Rae! Behind you!"

"What?"

But I didn't have to ask. As my eyes glanced to the small camera feed in the corner, I saw the crack behind me was wide. Much wider than before.

And four fingers were poking out.

I got up and ran. Out of the apartment, down the stairs. I swung the door open and leapt out into the cold night. As I tried to collect myself, I looked up at the apartment building.

And saw a dark shadow flitted by, from behind the sheer curtains, on a third floor room.

I pulled out my phone and called the police.

***

I found out a few days later that someone on the third floor went missing that night. A young guy named Charlie Hayworth. After a few days of searching, they found his body.

Inside the wall.

Yet — there was no damage to the wall at all. And the body they found — though it matched Charlie's body by DNA — was in a severe state of decomposition. He was little more than a skeleton... even though he only disappeared a few days ago.

And there's one other thing.

As the police continued their investigation, they found out the ugly lime-green paint Harry used wasn't just paint. It was laced with some sort of weird chemical that even the scientists had trouble identifying.

And Harry?

He disappeared the night the body was found.

MY COLLEGE ROOMMATE

Last fall, I started college.

I hated it. The classes were hard. The people were cold. I had a hard time making friends.

And then there was Addison.

Addison was my roommate. We were randomly assigned by computer – and it couldn't have been more obvious. We had *nothing* in common. I was a nerdy, self-conscious, tall girl that frequented the computer labs. She was a blonde, petite softball player, that spent her Saturday nights partying and her Sunday mornings in church.

She was friendly enough – when we both happened to be in the room at the same time, she'd say hello. Sometimes she'd 'borrow' my shampoo (without asking, of course.) Sometimes I'd 'borrow' one of her fancy-schmancy granola bars in retaliation. Generally, things were okay, even though they weren't great.

Until the night of October 19th.

I got back late from an engineering class. As I felt the chill leave my cheeks in the warm hallway of our dorm, I heard a scream from our room.

Addison.

Then, she yelled: "No! Get out!"

I ran to the door, shoved my key into the lock. I thought I was about to stumble on an attempted rape. Addison didn't exactly hang with the best crowd – and she had a posse of frat guys that followed her like bees after honey.

"Addison, are you okay?"

She was alone.

Just lying there, crumpled on the bed, all by herself. When she heard me, she whipped around in surprise. "Oh, sorry, I must've fallen asleep," she said. She sat up and stretched. "Sorry, what were you saying?"

"No, just... I heard you yelling. Are you okay?"

"Yeah. I'm fine. Must've been talking in my sleep... haven't done that since middle school." She let out a little giggle.

Sleeping...

My eyes fell on the bed, where her phone lay.

It was mid-call with someone. I could see the little phone icon on the screen, see the numbers timing the length of the call.

"You were on the phone with someone?"

"No, I was asleep."

I stared at her. "Um, okay."

I decided not to press it. *Maybe it's just a fight with a hometown boyfriend or something. Or her parents.* But then why did she say *get out?* No one was in the room with her.

The next week went by without anything too exciting. My classes got a bit harder, and I spent more and more time over at the engineering school. Every night, by the time I got back to the dorm, Addison was already asleep. I could hear her light snores coming from across the room, see her cross necklace dangling from the jewelry hook on her dresser.

On Friday night, I got home a little earlier than usual. I didn't have a problem set due until Tuesday, so I figured I'd relax a bit.

As I walked down the hallway, it was dead silent. The light flickered overhead, and I felt a chill course through my body.

I've never seen the building this empty.

I immediately shook my head, trying to extinguish the thought. *There's nothing wrong with a dorm being empty on a Friday evening. People go into town, hang out with their friends. Some even take trains into the city for the weekend.*

The light flickered again.

And besides, there probably are *people here. They're just sleeping, or on the computer, or something.*

My footsteps softly thumped across the carpet. The gold 21 screwed to our door came into view. I pulled out my keys with a jingle and put them into the lock.

I twisted the doorknob.

The room was dark. *Addison out partying, as usual,* I thought to myself with an eye-roll. I set my backpack
114

down against my dresser, unhooked my bra, and climbed into bed. I pulled out my phone, scrolled through reddit, sent off a text to my mom.

The silence remained. The minutes ticked by, and I realized I hadn't heard a single sound in almost twenty minutes.

My heart began to pound. A prickly, uncomfortable sensation crept up my arms, up my neck. *Something is wrong. Something is very, very wrong.*

I looked up from the phone.

The dim glow of the screen lit up the room in a soft glow. The shadows were black and blurred; but as my eyes adjusted to the dark, they came into view.

There was something on Addison's bed. Something long, stretching up to the ceiling...

I squinted in the darkness.

It was Addison.

Standing on the bed, her head almost touching the ceiling.

Staring down at me.

I yelped and jumped back. "Addison, what are you doing up there?" I shrieked. "You nearly gave me a heart attack!"

She opened her mouth. It seemed to stretch wider than ever before, in a sunken O-shape that was blacker than the shadows around her.

"I already got the others."

I ran out of the room, down the hallway. Footsteps pounded behind me. I raced down the stairs; the lights flickered.

I swung open the door.

Then I collapsed, gasping in the cold, crisp air.

**

They found the bodies the next day.

17 people total. All of them found dead in their rooms. Cause of death? Asphyxiation, even though none of them were hanging from ropes or showed any signs of being strangled.

Addison, herself, was found dead in our dorm room. Splayed out across her bed.

The cross hanging from her neck, upside-down.

COSTCO'S SECRET BASEMENT

My husband is dying.

Despite his good prognosis after the accident, he gets weaker every day. After he couldn't even say my name, I got desperate.

I posted details of his condition on every forum I could find. Medical, accident survivors... I even posted it on a sketchy "deep web" forum called *Help Yourself.*

That's where I got the PM from "Crimson87".

I can help you. I'll send instructions tomorrow morning. -C

The next morning, I didn't get a PM.

I got a letter. A real, paper envelope, tucked into my empty mailbox. After I got over the initial terror – *he somehow knows where I live* – I greedily opened it and read the note inside.

Dear Blair,

Here are the instructions. Be sure to follow them exactly, or they might find you. Then we'll have a real problem on our hands. -C

1. Drive to the Costco in ███████. Bring a photograph of your husband and something that is likely to have his DNA on it (like a toothbrush.)

2. Go to the refrigerated produce room in the back. You will see a red-haired woman standing there, pretending to sort through the lettuce. She will be wearing a red vest and a Costco badge – but don't be fooled. She is *not* an employee.

3. Go up to her and ask: "Do you have organic blueberries? My son's allergic to the other kind."

4. As long as the produce section is empty, she will smile and lead you over to the blueberries. As she picks up a box and hands it to you, she will purposefully drop it. "Oh no!" She'll pretend it's an accident. Play along.

5. Such a mess. Blueberries all over the floor. She'll say: "I'll stand out there and make sure no one comes in while we wait for the janitor."

5. No janitor is coming, of course.

6. She will stand guard outside the produce room. Go to the right wall, where the crate of mushrooms is. Push it back towards the wall – it will roll into a small alcove. Beneath it, you will see a rectangular hole cut into the floor, and a ladder leading down.

7. Climb down it.

My eyes flicked to the bottom, where he had scrawled in red marker: *WARNING! READ BEFORE PROCEEDING!*

1. Don't just make a beeline for the produce section. They'll know what you're doing. Get a cart, fill it with some junk. You should blend in with the other shoppers as much as possible. For that same reason, don't wear bright colors or heavy makeup.

2. If a short woman with an infant strapped to her chest asks you for help, kindly refuse. She is one of them. If you look closely, you will notice that the infant pressed face-first into her chest is a doll.

3. Don't talk to the man at the front of the store advertising flooring. (He's not one of them; he's just rude.)

4. Don't buy any food from the café.

I folded up the paper and jammed it into my pocket. Then I rushed into the house, grabbed the items he requested, and jumped in the car.

With a squeal of tires, I was on my way.

***

It had been a decade since I last set foot in a Costco. Everything looked different. Bigger. Emptier. The shelves stretched up to the ceiling far above; a seasonal section of glittering Christmas trees and dancing Santas sat far below.

I rolled the cart into one of the first aisles. Napkins and disposable dining ware stared back at me. I grabbed a huge stack of paper plates and dropped it into my cart. *Thraaang* – the metal rattled.

When I got to the end of the aisle, I turned left.

"Excuse me?"

I turned around.

A pretty blonde woman stood behind me.

"Yeah?"

She flashed me a sweet smile. "I don't want to bother you, but can you help me get that?" She pointed to a jug of maple syrup on a high shelf. "I can't reach it... and you're so tall."

I stared at her, my heart beginning to pound. My eyes flicked down.

A motionless infant was strapped to her chest.

"No, I'm sorry, I'm in a hurry."

"But –"

I quickened my pace. The cart rolled across the floor with newfound speed. I didn't slow until I'd rounded the corner. Then I grabbed a few more decoy items – some corn muffins from the bakery, a bag of clementines – and arrived at the produce room.

When I entered, there she was. The red-haired woman, sorting through the lettuce. I cleared my throat. "Uh... do you have organic blueberries? My son's... uh... he can't eat them. I mean – he's allergic to the other kind."

Fuck.

She gave me a smile and walked over to the blueberries. "They're right over here." She picked up one of the boxes.

Splat.

I watched her walk out. When she was firmly stationed at the entrance, I ran over to the crate of mushrooms.

I gave it a push. It rolled easily under my hands.

With a final glance at the red-haired woman, I descended into the pit.

The metal rungs were cold under my hands. They felt rough, as if covered in rust. The square of light above me shrunk, until it was little more than a twinkling star in a black sky.

Smack. My feet hit the hard floor.

Drip, drip, drip. The sound of water came from somewhere in the darkness, along with a soft rustling sound. I pulled my phone out and turned on the flashlight. Before me was a tunnel, roughly hewn out of stone – like some strange hybrid between a basement and a cave.

I walked forward. The floor was uneven, and I had to concentrate to keep my footing. The damp walls glistened in the white light. After a few minutes, I found a wooden door set into the stone.

I pulled it open.

Inside was a dark, cavernous room. The smooth walls and rectangular shape looked like a traditional basement – but it had a rotten, swamp-like stench to it. In the center was a table. One leg was bent and broken.

There was a sheet of paper in the middle.

Leave the items here. We'll take care of the rest. -C

I pulled the toothbrush and photo out of my pocket. I placed them on the table. I looked around the room – but as far as I could tell, it was empty. The closest thing to a person was a heap of clothes in the back corner.

My heart filled with doubt, but I tried to focus on Dan and the happy life we deserved as I exited the basement.

***

Dan came home from the hospital two days later.

That first night home, we sat on the couch in front of the TV, eating ice cream. Like nothing had happened. "Guess I'm living on borrowed time," Dan said, though a mouthful of cookies and cream. "Better make it count."

"By eating tons of ice cream?"

"By leading a good life."

"Oh."

He smiled at me. I reached out for his hand, squeezed it, and smiled back.

But our smiles faded when the news came on.

The newscaster was standing outside of the Costco. Dozens of police cars were parked around it, their red and blue lights cutting through the night. "Tonight, police found evidence of violent cult activity at the ▮▮▮▮▮ Costco," she began.

I jabbed nervously at my ice cream.

"Human remains, belonging to dozens of individuals, were found in the basement. They ranged from a few days to a few years old. Police believe some match the missing locals, but we're waiting on forensics to answer. The most recent one, however, has already been identified – it belongs to 24-year-old Carlie Bessinger."

A photograph flashed up on the screen. Blonde hair, blue eyes, a warm smile.

It was her.

The blonde woman who asked me to reach something on the shelf.

"Security footage shows her walking around the store two days ago, alive and well. Until she entered the produce section…"

The reporter's voice faded. I wasn't listening anymore.

Crimson lied. There was no *them*. No woman with a doll strapped to her chest, waiting to pounce on me. No evil entity watching, thinking, plotting.

He just didn't want me talking to a witness. A victim. A sacrifice.

I looked over at Dan. He watched, oblivious, a generic look of concern spread over his features. I looked down at the floor, unable to watch anymore.

Dan's not on borrowed time –

He's on *stolen* time.

THE FORGOTTEN ROOM

Three weeks ago, I bought my grandma's house.

She was selling it to move into a nursing home. While other buyers turned their noses up at the shag carpets and green wallpaper, they filled me with happiness. Every nook and cranny of that house held a memory for me. The parque floor – riding a tricycle across it, while my grandpa chased after me, cursing under his breath. The wood-paneled walls – taping my drawings of monsters and unicorns up there, like it was my own private art gallery.

When we moved in a week ago, though, I noticed something different. Something I'd never seen before.

Off the kitchen, between the bathroom and the pantry, there was a door. Danny got to it first. "Hey, Brie! Look at this!" he said, pushing it open.

It didn't open to a closet or a pantry — it opened to a room. It was small, maybe 6 feet by 10 feet, and had a little window at the end, framed by tattered yellow curtains. The walls were painted sky blue, and the floor was hardwood, like the rest of the house.

Other than the curtains, the room seemed to be in good condition. Better condition than the rest of the house, even.

"Weird. I've never seen this room before." In all the days I'd spent at my grandma's house, I'd never seen it. And I was one of those curious kids who opened every cabinet, closet, and drawer.

"Oh, your grandma got it added on after?"

"I don't think so. She's too cheap for that." I scoffed and motioned to the surroundings. "I mean, if she didn't take down this peeling, floral wallpaper, do you really think she added a whole room?"

"Oh! Wait." Danny's hand snaked around the door. "It's got a lock. She probably locked it because she didn't want you messing it up." He grinned. "Or maybe she kept her liquor in there."

"Yeah, I guess that's it."

But I still felt uneasy. First, my grandma wasn't the type to hide stuff from us. She let my brother and I play with everything — even her authentic Matryoshka doll from Russia. *Our time together is the most important thing,* she always said. *Nothing else matters.*

Second, it was an old '70s house. Except for a few of the bathrooms, none of the doors had locks.

"Maybe we shouldn't be in here," I said, suddenly.

Danny laughed. "Brie, this is our house now. We can go wherever we want."

"That's the point. I don't want to be here."

"Fine, fine."

We walked back into the kitchen. He shut the door behind us.

That night, though, I had trouble falling asleep. I played through my memories, trying to remember that little wooden door. *I must've seen it before. I know every inch of this house like the back of my hand.*

I imagined it there in the kitchen, across from the table, as Grandma and I made mushroom soup for Christmas Eve dinner. I imagined it when she held my hand, telling me it was all okay, I'd find a different date for prom. I forced it into my memories, like I was hammering a rusty nail into a board of wood.

But every time I forced it into a memory, my heart sank. My mind swam. I felt no moment of reckoning, no epiphany, no déjà vu.

I'd never seen that door in my life.

***

When I got home from work the next day, I found Danny moving our loveseat into the room.

"What are you doing?!" I screeched, leaping at him.

"I thought we could hang out in the room."

"Why?"

"It's cozy, isn't it?"

"No."

"Look, if you don't like it, fine," he grunted, as he slid the loveseat a few feet. "But I like the room, okay? I'll just sit there, alone, and play Skyrim or something."

I laughed. "You still haven't beaten Skyrim? Didn't that come out like, five years ago?"

"Yeah," he said, looking at the ground in embarrassment.

I walked over and helped him slide the loveseat the last few feet. When it was finally in the room, even I had to admit it looked nice. Cozy. The loveseat was almost the same width as the room, and when it faced the window, it gave a sort of 'reading nook' vibe.

Danny flopped down on the couch and pulled out his laptop.

"No, I'll sit with you," I said. "As long as you don't make me watch you play."

He smiled.

The two of us sat there on the loveseat, arms around each other. While he fixed his eyes on the computer, I stared out the window. Beyond the tattered curtains, I could make out the Ralston's backyard. Even after all these years, their swingset was still up.

Two little kids were playing on it. The girl was on the swings, while the boy sat in the little fort atop the slide.

"Those must be their grandkids," I said. "I remember playing with the Ralston kids, when I was younger. Jenny and James Ralston. Did I tell you about them?"

"Yeah. Jenny's the one that smashed all your Play-Doh sculptures, right?"

"Yeah. And she lied about it too. Said the wind did it. Like really, did she think I was going to believe that?" I laughed and got off the couch. "It's cold in here. I'm going to get my sweater."

"Oh, good idea. Can you get my jacket, too?"

"Sure."

I slipped around the loveseat and out the door. I walked through the kitchen and into the dining room.

I froze.

Out the dining room window stood the Ralston's swingset. It was old. Splintered, sagging, decaying. The yellow plastic of the slide was stained with brown. One chain of the swing was broken, swaying limply in the wind.

The children were gone.

"Brie?"

I heard Danny's muffled voice, through the dining room wall.

That's when I realized. The room didn't face the outside... it faced the dining room.

There was no way it could have a window.

"Danny!"

I ran into the kitchen. The door hung open. Light rippled and flashed against it, like sunlight reflecting off a lake.

"Danny!"

He didn't turn around. He sat, utterly still, on the loveseat. He wasn't looking at the computer, which was making random dragon noises. He was staring at the window.

I looked up.

Through the window, the children were coming closer. The girl had abandoned the swings and was several feet from the glass. The boy had hopped down from the fort and jogged towards us.

Neither had a face.

Just skin, stretched and smooth, where their faces should have been.

Slam!

Before I had time to react, the door shut in my face.

"No!" I screamed. I grabbed the doorknob and pulled. It was locked.

"Danny! Danny, can you hear me?" I screamed. I pounded on the door; it shook underneath me. "Danny, unlock the door! Let me in!"

Silence.

I screamed. I cried. I pounded on that door with all that I had. Breathless, weak, gasping for air. But when I finally stepped back, it wasn't a door anymore.

It was a bare wall.

I stared at the floral wallpaper for several minutes, the strength draining away from my legs.

Then I ran into the garage. Rifled through the boxes of our stuff. Found the hammer. I ran back inside, and with a primal yell, flung the hammer into the wall.

Crrrack!

I pulled it out and swung again.

Crrrack!

After twenty or so swings, the wall began to crack and crumble. I stuck my fingers inside the cracks, tearing at the drywall. "Danny!" I screamed. I dug faster, harder, until my hands hit something hard.

I yanked away.

Wood.

The door, the room... it was all gone.

I ran through the kitchen, the foyer, to the front door. The Ralstons could help me. Maybe they even knew about the room, knew what was going on. They'd lived there, right next to my grandma, for years. I yanked on the front door, half-expecting it be locked in this cursed house.

It opened.

I leaped out of the house. Ran down the front steps, across the lawn. The cold air burned my lungs. "Mrs. Ralston! Jenny! Help!" I shouted, as I ran towards the house.

I stopped dead in my tracks.

The swing set in the backyard was new.

The wood was no longer splintered. The slide was bright yellow, no longer stained with mud and dust. One of the swings swayed, its chain making a horrendous *creeeeaak*.

I ran faster. When I got to the Ralston's door, I nearly pounded it down. "Open up!" I shouted. "Please! I need help! Mrs. Ralston?" My throat went dry. "Danny?"

I suddenly felt a prickly feeling on the back of my neck. A horrible tingling sensation that rolled down my spine, drained the strength from my legs.

I turned around.

The street was empty. Silent. The breeze sent a few dry leaves skittering across the pavement. No cars on the street, or in the driveways. No lights on in any of the houses.

I looked up at the house across the street.

My blood ran cold.

There, in the window, was a woman. Watching me. She looked like the neighbor, Mrs. Patel. Red dress. Black hair in a braid. Tan skin.

Except, like the children… she didn't have a face.

I glanced at the next house. The Johnsons lived there — an elderly couple, who'd always given me caramel candies whenever I walked over. Trembling, I looked up at the windows.

They were in the window.

They stood there, in the shadows, huddled next to each other. Their wrinkled, pale skin stretched smooth over their faces.

I glanced from house to house. In every single one, I could make out a faceless figure in the darkness. Turned towards me. Watching me without eyes.

I took a step back. The Ralston's front door hit my back. "No, no," I whispered. "Where am I?"

The door suddenly gave way underneath me.

I fell through the darkness. Pain shot through me as I hit the floor. I watched, in horror, as the door slammed shut in front of me.

"Brie?"

I looked up to see Mrs. Ralston standing over me. Relief flooded through me – she had a face.

"Brie, sweetheart, are you okay?"

She was older than the last time I saw her. Much older. Gray hair tied back in a bun, wrinkled skin. She helped me up, giving me a smile in the dim light.

I walked over to the door and looked through the window. The windows across the street were empty. The driveways were filled with cars. Two kids kicked a ball in the street.

Everything was back to normal.

Mrs. Ralston lay a comforting hand on my shoulder. "What happened?"

I lost it.

The tears came hot and fast. I shook with every breath, every sob. "Danny's gone. There's this secret room in her house, and now it's gone. And I saw these people — these people without faces —"

At that, her face paled.

"Do not go back there," she said, her soft touch turning into a vice grip. "Do you hear me, Brie? Do not go back there."

"You've seen them?"

"Once." She turned towards the window, her wrinkled face cast in white sunlight.

"What... what are they?"

"You do not want to know, sweetheart. Trust me."

"Please."

She finally turned towards me, folding her legs neatly underneath her. "Do you ever wish you were a child again? Playing at your childhood home, with not a care in the world?"

I nodded.

"Or, if you were older, like me... you would be reminiscing about the early years of marriage. When Don and I were young, raising Jenny and James. We spent quite

132

a lot of time longing to be back in the good old days. Back in this neighborhood, when we were younger, happier. It's a normal part of the human experience – nostalgia."

"What's that got to do with anything?"

"Nostalgia takes on many forms, sweetheart. And it can be awfully dangerous." She sighed and stared at the floor. "These creatures – the Faceless – made the secret rooms. This whole second dimension, overlaid underneath ours. But they need the nostalgia to live. It's their sustenance, sweetheart. Like a good burger. Or one of those pumpkin spice lattes."

She laughed. I didn't.

"Why are they faceless?" I asked, finally.

"Memories are imperfect. Especially remembering exactly what someone's face looked like twenty years ago. So they don't wear a face."

"But –" I started.

I was cut off.

By a resounding, sharp thump at the front door.

"Don't move," Mrs. Ralston said.

She slowly got up and paced to the door. She pushed the curtains aside and peered out through the window.

Then she breathed a sigh of relief.

"Don't worry, sweetheart. It's just the mailman."

She opened the door and accepted the package. I sat still in the kitchen seat, the hard wood clawing into my back. All I could think about was Danny in that place. Wondering if he was okay.

Or if he was gone forever.

She walked back to the table, limping slightly, and lowered herself back onto the floor. I glanced around in the awkward silence and noticed a photo of Mr. Ralston hanging over the fireplace.

"Where's Mr. Ralston?"

Her expression darkened. "Passed away three years ago. Prostate cancer."

"I'm so sorry."

"I miss him every day," she said, wistfully glancing at the photo. "The life of a widow... I'd never wish that on anyone."

I stood up, the heat rising to my face. "Then help me get Danny back."

Her face paled. "We cannot go there."

"I need to try. And I'm going to. With or without you."

She stared at me, her blue eyes fearful.

"You don't have to come with me. Just help me get back to that place. Tell me everything I need to know about the Faceless."

She stood up and motioned me to follow. She walked up the old steps of her house, covered in brown shag carpeting and yellow floral wallpaper.

"Why didn't Grandma tell me all of this?" I asked, as we made it to the second floor. "You would think —"

She cut me off.

"I don't believe your grandma ever saw them," she said. "The less nostalgic you are, the less likely you are to slip into their world. Your grandma... I don't think she dwelled much on the past."

We stopped. Five doors lined the hallway, cut into the green wallpaper. All closed tight. She pointed to the middle one.

"I'm afraid I wasn't quite honest with you. I've seen the other world... far more times than just once."

She looked at me, her lip trembling.

"That middle door leads to a room that is not in the floorplans. Sometimes I go in there, just to look out the window..." Her voice cracked, and a flush of red flooded her face. "I see Don out there. Mowing the lawn, in his cargo shorts and red T-shirt. I know it isn't him, but sometimes I just need to see him again." She took in a deep, shuddering breath.

I awkwardly touched her shoulder. "I'll see you when I get back. Okay?"

She nodded.

I swung the door open and stepped inside.

It was a small room, like the one in Grandma's house. Even though we were on the second floor, the window opened to ground level. The swingset was new again, the lawn freshly mowed.

I pulled the window open and climbed out it.

The air was warm and breezy, fluttering my hair. The sun seemed to glow supernaturally bright, veiled by a thin layer of clouds. The grass was too green, too soft.

And everything was too quiet.

I walked down the sloping hill, towards the swingset. *Where would they have taken Danny? Probably inside the house, right?* But last time, the front door just led me back to reality.

So not the front door, then.

I walked over to one of the windows. Cupping my hands and looking inside, it seemed to be the kitchen window. I cracked it open and climbed inside.

Thump. Thump. A faint sound came from above. I crept over to the stairs and climbed up them quietly. It grew louder — like the dull throb of a heartbeat.

Thump. Thump.

My hand tightened around the first doorknob. I pulled it open.

"Danny!"

He was bound to a chair in the center, a piece of duct tape stuck to his mouth. He stomped on the floor rhythmically, trying to struggle free. A deep slash ran across one side of his face.

As if they tried to slice his face off.

I ran over to the cords, yanked at them. His muffled cries sounded over the duct tape. "I know, I know, I'm working as fast as I can!" I hissed back.

The ropes fell to the floor. More frantic murmurs from him. I bent over and ripped the duct tape off.

As soon as it came off, he spoke.

"They're behind you."

I whipped around.

Jenny and James Ralston stood in the doorway, their blank faces pointed right at me. The skin was smooth and pale, stretching over the contours of their face. It rippled and roiled, as if something moved beneath.

They took a step forward.

"Jenny! James!"

136

The two Faceless stopped in their tracks.

"Jenny! James!" the voice called again, from downstairs.

It was Mrs. Ralston's voice. The Faceless mother of the family.

Jenny and James immediately retreated, eagerly running down the stairs.

"Okay. We'll go down, go out the front door, and then come back in. The front door goes back to our... dimension, or whatever. I don't know."

"You shouldn't have come back for me," he whispered. "You might get —"

"Of course I'd come back for you. Now, come on!"

I grabbed his wrist and yanked. We crept out into the hallway; I peered down the stairs.

The foyer looked empty.

We slowly, quietly, walked down the stairs. The wood creaked underneath us. As we made it into the foyer, a low murmuring sound came from the kitchen.

Danny's hand fell on the front doorknob.

"Wait," I said.

I tiptoed into the hall and peered into the kitchen.

A faceless Mr. Ralston sat at the kitchen table, in front of steaming plate of chicken. Jenny and James sat on either side of him, making soft, murmuring sounds. Mrs. Ralston stood in front of them, smiling.

She had a face.

"Mrs. Ralston!" I shouted.

She looked up.

So did the Faceless.

137

"Run!" I screamed.

She slowly shook her head.

"It's not really them! You know that!"

"Brie!" Danny shouted, from the foyer.

"Mrs. Ralston, please —"

Sccchhhhrrrip.

A ripping sound echoed through the house. The three, smooth faces split down the middle. Then their heads snapped open — to reveal rows of needle-like fangs.

"Mrs. Ralston!" I screamed.

She ran.

She zipped out of that kitchen faster than I've ever seen an old woman run. She grabbed my hand, and the two of us ran. Danny yanked the door open. *Slam* — it rattled shut behind us.

We fell out into the damp, bright green grass.

"Quick! Back inside!" I yelled.

I wrenched the door open.

The foyer was empty.

The three of us collapsed onto the floor, panting, hearts racing. I grabbed Danny and hugged him as tight as I could.

***

Over the next few weeks, we helped Mrs. Ralston board up the middle door in her upstairs hallway. We tried to get her to move away, but she refused to. "At least let me relive my memories in this old house," she said. "Even if I can't be with him."

138

Danny and I moved out soon after. We visited my Grandma at the nursing home about once a week. I never planned to tell her about the secret room, but one day, it came up naturally while we were playing checkers. Taking in a deep breath, I started: "Grandma, did you ever see an extra door in the kitchen? Between the pantry and the bathroom?"

I expected her to give me her classic *What the hell are you talking about?* look. But instead, she just smiled.

"Beautiful little room, isn't it?" she said.

"You... you went in that room?"

"Of course! And I would have stayed there, too," she said. "But this nursing home is so wonderful. The nurses go the extra mile to make sure you're comfortable. The food is great, too."

"Really?" I asked, thinking about the mushy chicken and green Jello I'd shared with her last week.

"Oh, yes," she said, with a smile. "Everyone's so deliciously nostalgic here."

That's when I noticed the scar. Hidden among her wrinkles, cutting from her forehead to her chin.

She just smiled.

HANGING FROM A TREE

I left her alone for 30 seconds to grab some water.

When I came back, she was gone.

"Kasey?" I yelled. "Kasey, where are you?"

As if she could reply. She's only 16 months old. She knows, like, 5 words.

"Kasey!" The panic set in. I ran over to the pile of toys in the living room, the stairs she liked to climb, the bookshelf with the new *Goodnight Precious* laying on top. She wasn't there.

"What's wrong?" Mark asked, poking his head out of the den.

"I can't find Kasey."

"Wasn't she just in the family room? Weren't you watching her?"

"I was, but I went to get some water... now she's gone."

A look of panic set into his face. He ran out of the room and followed me around the downstairs, shouting for her. I walked across the foyer.

The front door was slightly open.

No. There's no way she could have opened that all by herself. She was barely even tall enough to reach the handle. "Mark! Over here!"

I swung the door open. Cars whizzed by on the road. Puddles collected in the damp grass. *No, no, did she go out in the road?* The dread settled heavy in my heart. *This can't be happening. Oh God, oh God, no, please no.*

Mark took off running towards the road. "She's not here," he called back, peering into the bushes along the side of the road.

I whipped around, scanning the front yard. "Kasey!" I screamed, as loud as I could muster.

I listened. For her soft little babbling, for pattering footsteps through the mud.

But only silence reached my ears.

Right now she could be dying. Running into the woods, tripping in the brambles. Falling face-down into a puddle. I glanced around the yard; it became a blur of green grass, white sky. The gravity of the thought – that what I chose to do in the next few minutes could decide life or death for my daughter – fell upon me. I was paralyzed.

And what if someone took her?

No. There was no way. We would have heard them come in.

"Amanda?"

Mark was calling from the backyard.

"Amanda!"

I took off across the grass, my feet slipping in the mud. As I rounded the corner of the house, a terrible sight came into view.

A tiny pink dot, at the far end of the yard.

Hanging from the gray, twisting branches of a *tree.*

"Kasey?" I screamed, my voice now hoarse. "Kasey!" Mark stood at the base of the tree, paralyzed, staring up at her.

I got to the tree.

There. I recognized everything. Her little mouse-print, pink shirt. Her brown curls. Her light blue, stretchy pants pulled over motionless legs. She hung there, in one of the lower branches, as still as a corpse.

"Oh God, no, no..." I kicked off my shoes and pulled myself up. I grabbed her by the arm and carefully pulled her through the branches.

She was too cold. Too light.

"Kasey?"

I was staring at a doll.

A doll *made* to look like my daughter. Brown curls, blue eyes, an outfit I often dressed her in.

I began to sob. Aching, scratched by branches, I slowly lowered myself into the grass. The doll fell to the ground. Mark let out a strangled cry. We stood there, frozen, trying to process what was going on.

Crack.

We both looked up.

In the shadows of the forest, beyond the backyard, something was moving. *A deer?* I took a few seconds to process the shifting, brown shape among the trees.

I froze.

It was a man, wearing hunter's camouflage, running back into the woods.

A heavy, brown bag swung over his shoulder.

***

We chased after him. Called the police. Shouted and screamed and made all the noise we could.

About a quarter of a mile into the forest, he dropped the bag and continued by foot. When we ripped it open, there was Kasey – terrified, red-faced, mouth taped shut. I cannot even begin to describe how I felt when I saw my daughter alive.

The police caught him half an hour later, hiding in the brambles by the old creek.

I bought some guns. I added shiny new locks to the front door. I installed a ton of security cameras, overlooking our backyard and the woods.

If it ever happens again... we'll be ready.

THE TERRORIST

I was *not* enjoying my flight.

I was in a middle seat, crammed between a purple-haired teenager and a woman with a screaming baby. I'd tried to nap about twenty times. And when I finally *did* doze off, a loud noise woke me just a few minutes later.

Snap!

I turned. At first, I wasn't sure where the sound was coming from. But then my eyes fell on a strangely-dressed man across the aisle. In a weird way, he kind of reminded me of Neo from *The Matrix* – black hair, black clothes, and dark sunglasses. He was holding a small leather briefcase in his lap, emblazoned with the words *Black Widow, Inc.* The sound was from undoing its gold clasps.

Snap!

For lack of anything better to do, I watched him. He opened the briefcase just a few inches, peered inside, and smiled. A small smile, as if he didn't want anyone else to see it. I watched him curiously as he began to pry it open, his smile growing wider.

Snacks?

A laptop?

A… bomb?

But no. It was none of those things.

The briefcase was empty.

Weirdo, I thought, snickering to myself a bit. *Guy probably forgot all his stuff at the airport or something.* I smiled to myself, nuzzled my head against the pillow, and closed my eyes.

Thump! Thump! Thump!

My eyes flew open.

The person who'd been sitting next to Neo – a sixty-year-old, rotund man – was suddenly beating on the window with his fist. It shook and rattled dangerously.

"Crazy old dude," Purple-Hair laughed.

But it wasn't funny for long.

Old Man grabbed his laptop, and with as much strength as he could muster, began smashing it into the window.

Crack! Crack! Crack!

"He's going to break the window!" I shouted. I pounded the stewardess button. *Come on, come on…*

The silence of the airplane swelled into a cacophony of panicked voices. The person on the other side of Neo – a 12-year-old girl, wearing a yellow flowered shirt – ran out into the aisle. For a second, I thought she was getting help.

But then she ran a few rows ahead of us –

And began climbing over the passengers in the emergency exit row.

Clawing for the door.

"What's she *doing?!*" Mom cried. Baby, sensing the panic, began to wail too. Purple-Hair was finally afraid, her brown eyes wide.

"Hey! Stop!" The stewardess came running down the aisle, panting and shaking. "Go back to your seat," she reprimanded, yanking the girl by the arm.

"Let me go! Let me go!" she shrieked. "I have to get out of here!"

Then she lurched forward – and bit the stewardess as hard as she could.

She screamed and let go.

The girl ran for the exit again. But the passengers were ready this time. One of the guys leapt out of his seat and grabbed her by the waist.

Crack! Crack!

"Over there!" I yelled to the stewardess. "He's going to break the window!"

Old Man was repeatedly hitting the glass. Surprisingly, Neo wasn't making any move to restrain him; he was just sitting there, in the middle seat, with that tiny smile upon his lips.

And as soon as the stewardess's eyes fell on him, the smile grew.

I leapt out of my seat. A few others did the same, and we descended on Old Man. As soon as we touched him, he whipped around, staring at us with wild eyes. "Don't touch me, filthy whores!" he spat, brushing our hands away.

Crack!

"Sir, you need to calm down –"

146

Crack!

"The window's cracked!"

Crack!

"Fucking stop him!"

Crack!

We finally wrestled him away from the window. Dragged him across Neo, who just watched us with a knowing smile.

As soon as we got Old Man in the aisle, we thought it was over.

But it wasn't.

Because now two more people – the people in the middle seats directly in front of and behind Neo – were standing up, that frenzied look in their eyes. One, a nerdy-looking woman with glasses, ran for the front of the plane. The other, a bearded college guy, went towards the back.

The stewardess paled. "They're going for the emergency hatches," she whispered.

We ran after them.

We didn't get there in time.

But, as it turns out, airplane hatches are wonderfully built. And it would take a few tons of force to open one of them mid-flight. That didn't stop those two from trying, though. Nerdy Woman screamed and pulled until she collapsed into a sobbing mess on the floor. Bearded Guy grunted and pushed until he was vomiting from overexertion.

We made an emergency landing in Raleigh. The four passengers were taken into custody by the FBI upon landing. Somehow, Neo slipped out unnoticed – and, even if he didn't, how could they take him in? He *technically* hadn't done anything wrong.

To this day, I still don't know what happened on Flight 3310. Maybe it *was* just the random insanity of four people. Or maybe they had planned their attack for months, even though it seemed random.

I don't know what happened –

But I'm pretty damn sure that Neo's briefcase was not, in fact, empty.

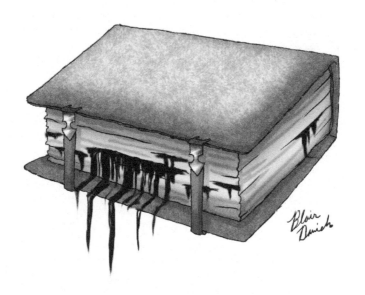

THE BOOK OF SKIN

The bigger the house, the harder it is to clean.

That's what I learned working for Sharon. *She* liked the big houses, sure – she got to cook in the gorgeous kitchens and chit-chat with the wealthy residents. Me? I got the scut work, scrubbing bathtubs as big as jacuzzis and mopping floors three times the size of my apartment.

We pulled into the Thompson's driveway on a Wednesday afternoon, just as the sun began to set. This house wasn't like the others. The faded, rust-red brick façade reminded me of all the other crumbling institutions in town – not old-time elegance. The driveway buckled and cracked, tufts of green grass creeping through the gaps.

"Nice, isn't it?" Sharon asked, sticking her key in the lock.

"Sure. Beautiful."

We stepped into the foyer. The house was dark; heavy shadows stretched across the carpet. The high ceiling stretched above her, dark and cavernous.

Sharon led me through a dark hallway, into the living room. "I'm here, Mildred," she said to the lump of blankets on the couch. "Brought a friend to help me. She'll clean the library while I cook your stew, okay?"

The red blanket slipped, revealing the other half of the woman's face. She looked as most old women do: sunken skin, brittle white hair. The only thing that set her apart were her brown – nearly black – eyes.

"The library?" she said – a feeble murmur.

"Yes. You said you wanted everything dusted and polished, didn't you?"

"Oh. Yes." She nodded. Her old bones crackled with the movement. "What's your name?"

"Mary."

"Mary. Come closer."

I took a hesitant step forward. The smell of must and bad breath washed over me. "Yes, Mrs. Thompson?"

Snap.

Mildred's hand shot out from the mess of blankets. It latched onto mine in a painful, vice grip. "Don't touch the books," she rasped.

"Uh, what?"

"Whatever you do, don't touch any of the books."

"But I'm supposed to clean–"

"Don't touch the books!" she hissed. "They're my David's! His research, his journals. Don't touch the books, or –"

"Okay, Mildred!" Sharon stepped forward, laying a hand on her. "She won't touch the books. She heard you."

The grip released. Mildred sank back into the blankets and closed her eyes, her breaths ragged and loud.

"Are you okay?" Sharon asked, tenderly stroking the old woman's hair.

"Fine," she whispered.

"Okay. Come on, Mary. I'll show you where the library is."

I followed her through the corridor, nervously fidgeting with my necklace. Deer heads hung on the walls – black eyes, fur matted with dust. An old, dented suit of armor leaned against the corner, missing a few panels.

At the end of the room stood ornate French doors.

"Here it is," Sharon said, swinging the doors open. She forced a mop into my hands. "Mop the floor. Polish the globe. I'll meet up with you in about an hour, after I've got dinner on."

"But not the books?" I asked, my voice quavering.

"Ah, don't worry about her. She's just a little nervous around new people." Sharon spun to leave. "But sure, don't clean the books. Less work for you, right?"

She pulled the doors shut.

I plopped the bucket on the floor; the soapy water sloshed inside. I dipped the mop in, ran it across the oak floor. The wet swipes glistened under the light of the chandelier.

The library *was* beautiful – even under the layers of dust. Oak-paneled walls, covered in bookshelves. A bay window, facing the woods. Above the stairs, a painting of an olive-skinned man with gleaming black eyes. *DAVID THOMPSON,* according to the nameplate.

I swiped the mop across the floor. *Swish. Swish.* In less than twenty minutes, I was done. The library wasn't that large, and nearly empty, save for the books.

I turned my gaze upwards. *Do I really have to mop the upstairs?* I thought, eyeing the curved staircase snaking up the wall. *Mildred probably can't even climb the steps, right?*

Ah, but Sharon can. Knowing her, she'll check my work.

I sighed and climbed the stairs. Each step groaned beneath me.

"Woah," I muttered.

The books up here were different. Not battered textbooks and encyclopedias, or trashy paperbacks, like on the shelves below. These were dark, leather-bound tomes, bearing no markings on the spine. "Bet these are old… and valuable," I said to myself, skimming a finger along the spines.

Curious, I finally pulled one from the shelf.

On the cover was no writing – just a symbol. A seven-pointed star, embossed in gold. I flipped it open. Snatches of sentences leapt out to me from the yellowed paper: *place a lit candle at each apex … represents darkness, plague, infection … one drop for each year on this earth.* One page in the middle had no text – just a large drawing of a seven-pointed star, and a woman kneeling in the center.

Schliip. I pushed the book back onto the shelf. When I finished mopping, I collapsed into one of the armchairs next to the small coffee table.

That's when I noticed the book on the table.

Unlike the rest of the library, it was clean. Not a spot of dust on it. *That's weird. No one's been up here for months, probably. Mildred can't even climb these stairs. So who pulled it from the shelf?* She grimaced, deep in thought. *Unless Sharon pulled it out? Sharon, snooping... that was difficult to imagine.*

I stood up and leaned over the book.

The cover was a lighter leather than the other books. Golden tan, with darker patches and few brown dots speckling the surface. No title, no symbols, no markings of any kind.

I reached out a hand. Softly, my fingers skimmed the cover.

I froze.

A light touch caressed my back. I whipped around. "Sharon?" I called out. "Hello?"

No reply.

The room was empty. Just the dark oak walls, the endless rows of strange books. The portrait of David Thompson watched me, his dark eyes glittering with mirth.

Even I'm going crazy in this creepy old house. I guess that's how Mildred got to be... how she is. I plopped down on the armchair again, massaging my temples. My legs ached; my back stung. My eyes fell on the book again.

I picked it up.

Hands pressed into my back. *Hard.*

I leapt off the armchair. "Who's there?" I yelled. But the upstairs of the library was completely empty.

I peered over the banister. But everything was as I left it – the wet floor, the shining globe, the untouched books. No one was there.

My heart thrummed in my chest. Goosebumps spread up my arms. *What the hell is going on?*

Shaking, I returned to the seat.

No.

The leather of the book was covered in small, prickly bumps.

"What the hell?" I looked down at my own arms. Then at the book. There was no mistaking it – they were both covered in the same, miniscule bumps.

Heart pounding, I pressed two fingers into the tan leather, depressing it.

At the exact same moment – I felt two fingers press into my spine.

I backed away. Panting. Heart pounding. *What the hell is this thing? What sort of crazy illusion is this –?*

My foot caught on the mop.

I flew backwards. Hot pain shot through my back, as the mop handle jabbed into my shoulder blades. The stairs lay a dizzying few feet away from where I'd fallen.

Missed by an inch, missed by a yard...

I stumbled to get to my feet. I grasped the railing, the wood growing slick with my sweat. As I did, I took one last glance back at the book.

A purple line ran across the cover.

The impression of a mop handle.

***

"Sharon! Sharon!"

I flew towards the kitchen, yelling at the top of my lungs. "Sharon!"

The aroma of beef stew hung heavy in the air. On the stove sat a pot, curls of steam rising towards the ceiling. "What?" Sharon asked, not looking up.

"There's a book in the library," I panted.

"Well. Of *course* there's a book in the library, Mary."

"No. I mean, a terrible book. I touched it and –"

Sharon laughed. "Didn't heed Mildred's warnings, I see."

"Sharon." I grabbed her by the shoulders. "Listen to me!"

"Hey! Get your hands off me!"

"Come with me to the library!"

"Okay! Fine. Fine." Sharon fiddled with the dial on the stove. The flame underneath the pot shrunk. "I'm coming."

I led Sharon into the library, my legs shaking underneath me. Without a word, I yanked Sharon up the stairs. We stepped over the mop and stared at the little coffee table.

"*That* book."

Sharon raised an eyebrow. "Okay. It's a little weird-looking, I'll give you that."

"Touch it."

Sharon shot me a weird, questioning look. Then she approached the table. With a steady hand, she reached out and poked the front cover.

She jumped.

"Hey! Don't go poking me like that!"

"That wasn't me."

"What are you talking about? Of course it was you."

"I'll leave the room. Then touch it again." I decisively turned around and descended the stairs. As soon as I shut the library doors behind me, I heard the scream.

I pulled the doors open to find Sharon clamoring down the stairs. "Don't touch that book," she said shakily, bits of auburn curl falling around her face. "That one is... well – never mind. Just stay away from it."

"Why? What do you know about it?"

"I don't know anything about it. I just think... Mildred asked us not to." Sharon ran a hand across her forehead, pushing the damp curls from her face. "Just finish up cleaning, okay? Come to the kitchen when you're done. I'll drop you off at home."

I waited until Sharon's footsteps faded into silence.

Then I raced back into the library and up the stairs.

The initial shock had worn off. My fear had evaporated, leaving behind an itching, morbid curiosity. I ran over to the table, poked the cover of the book. I felt the familiar warm poke on her back, and a small smile flicked across my lips.

I wonder how it does that.

I flipped the front cover open, felt a warm hand brush against my shoulders. The pages were stiff and warped, as if water-stained, and a deep yellow color. The first page had only two words on it, handwritten in fancy scrawl:

DAVID THOMPSON

I flipped through the next few pages. *NOVEMBER 10, 1958... JANUARY 21, 1959.* Beneath each date were walls of frenzied, almost illegible, script. Words popped off the page: *a cold feeling, like plunging into Cayuga Lake in May... thumping sounds in the attic, above Mildred and my bedroom... the books in the library were all gone, back the next day...*

I flipped through the pages, faster and faster, the script turning into a smudged blur of yellow paper and black ink.

The last entry was dated *APRIL 26, 1968.*

The handwriting was significantly messier, shakier. The words ran into each other, overlapping in illegible scribbles. Smudges of gray covered the page – ghosts of the written words. As if David's palm had touched the wet ink and stamped it all over the page.

I squinted, trying to make it out.

The door's locked [illegible] can't open [illegible] something's in here, I hear it upstairs [illegible]

Oh, Lord, please help me. I am sorry sorry [sic] for my sins. The way I treated them, [illegible], and Mildred. I hear it closer... please help me.

Let me out. LET ME OUT! LET ME OUT LET ME –

"Mary?"

Sharon's voice echoed down the hall.

i glanced at the book, heart pounding.

Then I slipped it into my bag, before Sharon had the chance to see. As I did, I felt the rough burlap of the bag scratch against my entire body.

"I'm ready!" I called.

***

As soon as I walked into my dingy one-bedroom apartment, I pulled the book out of my bag. It hit the round, metal table with a loud *slap*. Almost instantly, pain shot up my chest.

I forgot, I thought, rubbing my collarbone under the thin golden chain of my necklace.

I pulled the flimsy plastic chair across the tile. It made a deafening scraping sound. I snuck a hand inside the cover and flipped it open.

My heart stopped.

Now, there wasn't just one name written across the page.

There were two.

DAVID THOMPSON

MARY GIORDANO

I turned the page. The same writing of David stared up at me. *Thank God. For a second... I thought there might be something about me in this crazy book. Schlip. Schlip.* The old pages crackled and bent under her fingertips.

But when I got to the last page of David's journal, I gasped.

There, on the page opposite his frantic scribbles, was a date. *MARCH 10, 2017.* And below it, were familiar words:

Thank God. For a second... I thought there might be something about me in this crazy book.

"What the hell?" I yelled.

As the words escaped my mouth, black ink bled onto the page.

WHAT THE HELL?

Snap.

I slammed the book shut. Then I pulled out my phone and dialed Sharon's number.

"Hello, you've reached Sharon Tillery. Please leave a message after the beep."

I hung up the phone. Then I glanced out the window. Somewhere, less than five miles away – in the sea of black to the west, that made up the forest surrounding the mansion – was a very special library. A very special set of books.

And some very special answers, that I would get out of Sharon tomorrow.

***

"Tell me everything you know about this book. *Now.*"

I stood in the kitchen at Sunshire. The book sat in front of me on the granite island, still and silent. *I wonder if it's recording this entire conversation,* I thought. Sharon pretended the soup on the stove needed urgent stirring. The steam billowed up towards the ceiling in puffs of cloud.

"Sharon? Tell me."

"I only know rumors," she said finally, fidgeting with her red ponytail. "Only things I've heard… nothing based in fact."

"Then tell me rumors."

"You know, you weren't supposed to touch the books. Really, Mary, I should send you home —"

"If you won't tell me, Mildred will." I grabbed the book, feeling the familiar press of hands across my chest. "Mildred! Hey, Mildred —"

"Don't!" Sharon hissed. She grabbed me by the arm and dragged her back into the kitchen. "What are you trying to do, give the old lady a heart attack? Geez." She ran back to the stove, stirred the soup once more. *Clink* — the spoon smacked against the pot. Then she took a seat across from me and pursed her lips. "The book… it's David Thompson, I think."

"I already know that it's his. His name's right there —"

"No. It's not *his*. It's *him*."

"What?"

"If the rumors are true… that book is bound in his skin."

I instantly recoiled. Nausea flooded my body. I stole a glance at the cover, imagining that tan, speckled skin belonging to the man in the portrait.

Sharon stirred the soup again, nervously. "David was a seedy guy. Liked women – especially those with rings on their fingers, if you know what I mean."

"You know him?"

"No. He died about 12 years ago, long before I started working here. Back when Mildred could afford a full staff. I heard all about David from the old handyman – more than I wanted to know, to be honest."

"How'd he die?"

"I don't know how he died, exactly. Maybe a heart attack, but like, they say that didn't make much sense

162

because he was such a health nut." Sharon rapped her fingers on the granite, blue eyes cast downwards. "I do know *where* he died, though."

"Where?"

"In the library."

The nausea threatened to burst into full-on gagging. I swallowed, hard, and tried to regain my composure. "So how did the book happen? After he died, did they, um –"

"When they found David, he was missing two large patches of skin. One on his chest, one on his back. That was the gossip, anyway — don't know how much of it is true."

For a second, I considered telling Sharon everything. That I took the book home. That it seemed to record my thoughts. Instead, I forced a smile, and said: "Thanks for telling me, Sharon."

"You're welcome. Now, put that book back where it belongs."

For the first time, I obeyed her. I cradled the book in my arms, walked back into the library. David stared down at me from the confines of his portrait.

I climbed the steps and walked over to the table. I set the book down, feeling the familiar stroke of a finger across my back as my hand left the book. "There. Back where you belong," I said, shakily.

I began to descend the stairs.

Snap.

I whipped around. The book was open on the table, its yellowed pages facing towards the heavens.

I took a tentative step forward. My heart began to pound in my chest. "Hello?" I called, though I knew it would go unanswered.

I took another step. And another, and another, until I was standing in front of the table and staring down at the pages.

Words bloomed in black ink on the yellowed paper.

HELLO?

Above it was my entire conversation with Sharon — annotated with my own thoughts next to the dialogue.

My body began to shake. Waves of nausea rolled over me. Numbness crept up my body.

"Stop it!" I yelled.

STOP IT.

My heart pounded faster in my chest. *It's copying everything I say. Everything I think. How? Why?* "Stop it! Stop it!"

This time, different words appeared on the page. Words in a blocky, jagged scrawl.

No. I won't stop.

"Sharon?" I screamed. But the doors to the library were now shut. There was no way my voice could travel through the thick wood, through the cavernous mansion, all the way to Sharon in the kitchen.

I glanced back at the book.

No. I won't stop.

A sound filled my ears. Whispers, hissing and muttering, overlapping each other in frantic tones. Then more words bloomed on the page:

I know what you did.

"What? What did I do?"

One word bloomed on the page, in red instead of black:

THIEF

"No!" I yelled.

You stole this book.

"I was just curious –"

No. This isn't the first thing you stole, is it?

"It is –"

You steal something at every house. Even the chain hanging from your neck. It's from that old, blind woman that Sharon knows – isn't it?

My fingers touched the necklace. "That's – that's not true –"

It is. You know it is.

I picked up the book. Felt the familiar brush of hands across my back. Then I placed it on the floor, raised my foot. "Stop it! Stop it! *Stop it!*"

I brought my foot down on the book as hard as I could.

Smack.

A crushing pain hit my chest. I toppled backwards, gasping for air.

Thump.

I fell to the floor.

The library twisted and spun above me. David Thompson's eyes stared down at me. A burning heat pressed against my chest, my back.

Then the world faded to black.

***

"I don't understand," Sharon choked through sobs. "I just – I just saw her, an hour ago. She was asking me about... well, never mind. We were talking."

The police officer offered her a consoling smile. "I'm so sorry."

"How – how did she die?"

The officer bowed his head, and answered: "We'll have to wait for the official autopsy. But it looks like a heart attack."

As he disappeared into the darkness, Sharon turned back to the mansion. Its hulking shadow rose up against the indigo sky, dotted with stars.

She turned and went back inside. Ran into the library, up the stairs. The book lay on the table, where it was supposed to be. The cover, somehow, looked lighter. Paler. Smoother.

Sharon picked it up, feeling the brush of hands over her back.

"Mildred?" she called, walking through the dark hallways. "Mildred?"

She found Mildred on the usual sofa, wrapped in her blankets. "Sharon," she whispered, her eyes widening. "Don't touch that book."

"This is *him*, isn't it?" Sharon spat, throwing the book on Mildred's lap. "He killed her."

Mildred's frail, old hands poked out of the blankets. As her fingers grazed over the cover, her lips curled into a small smile. "David... oh, David." Then her eyes grew

166

sharp, and her smile faded. "I wouldn't put it past you to kill a poor young girl."

"What happened, Mildred? What *really* happened?"

She ignored Sharon's question. Instead, she pulled the cover open. Only one name was inscribed on the first page: *MARY GIORDANO.*

"You killed that poor girl so you could be free of this place, didn't you?" she said into the book. "I see you haven't changed a bit, David. Still not a shred of respect for women – or for life itself."

Sharon pursed her lips, clasped her hands, looked at poor Mildred with sad eyes.

"You were supposed to be trapped forever," Mildred whispered. Suddenly she shook the book with all her might and let out a shriek of anguish. "You were supposed to be trapped! For what you did to me! For what you did to your family! Do you hear me?"

"Mildred!" Sharon lay her hands on her shoulders. "Easy, it's okay, it's –"

"You were going to be trapped forever," Mildred yelled. "All that effort! Locking the doors shut. Telling the police I never heard your screams. All for nothing!"

Mildred sunk back into the sofa and closed her eyes.

"All… for nothing."

TRAPPED

I didn't *want* to spend a night at the Southfield Inn.

But we didn't exactly have a choice. It was 3 AM. We'd been driving 10 hours. Every hotel we'd passed was booked solid.

So when I saw the small hotel on the side of Route 22, its red sign blaring *VACANCY* – I almost cried.

We ran in. "You have rooms?" I asked, breathless.

"Of course." The tall, thin woman at the counter smiled.

We checked in as fast as we could. "I'll bring James up to the room," Caroline said. "He needs a diaper change, bad. You bring up the luggage, park the car, okay?"

"Sure. What's the room number, again?" I asked, as she disappeared towards the elevator.

"213!"

I trudged out into the cold and loaded our suitcases on the cart – plus the random toys and books strewn around the car. Fifteen minutes later, I was yanking the cart across the ugly brocade carpet, hotel key in hand. Fantasizing about a soft, feathery bed to collapse into.

I slowed down as I got close.

210... 211... 212...

214.

I stopped short. The cart rolled a few inches past me.
Wait. Where's 213?

210 and 212 were on the left. 211 and 214 were on the
right. But no 213. I shook my head and started walking
further down the hall. *Maybe it's one of those weird corner
rooms, that seem to defy numbering conventions.*

But no. The rooms at the end were numbered
correctly. 213 wasn't there.

Weird. I walked back down the hall, dragging the cart
through the silence. *Maybe 214 is really be 213?* After all, 214
was on the wrong side of the hallway. Should've been on
the even side, not the odd. *I bet it's just misnumbered.* I
pulled out my key and touched it to the door.

Brzt. Red light.

In the off-chance it wasn't Caroline's room, I didn't
want to wake up whoever was inside. But desperate times
call for desperate measures, eh? *Knock, knock.* "Hey,
Caroline! Is that you in there?" I called.

The door swung open.

A middle-aged, bald man in a fluffy white bathrobe
stood before me. "Yeah?"

"Uh. Sorry. Wrong room." I walked back towards the
elevator, yanking the cart behind me. *Maybe I missed it
somewhere –*

He-he-he!

A high-pitched giggle. Muffled, faint.

James.

I stopped in my tracks. Ran back over to 214, pressed my ear against the door.

Silence.

Confused, I stepped back, towards 211.

Giggle.

"What the hell?" I ran over and pressed my ear against 211.

Silence.

I stepped forward. *Giggle.* Stepped back. *Silence.* Forward, back, forward... My heart began to pound. I knew exactly where the sound was coming from.

Not from 214. Not from 211.

From the tiny stretch of wall *between* the two doors.

"Caroline?" I yelled into the wall. I felt like an idiot. That guy in the bathrobe probably thought I was nuts.

No reply... except for my son's pattering footsteps. *Thump, thump, thump. Giggle.*

I pulled out my phone and dialed her number. A few seconds later, the muted tones of *I'm Bringing Sexy Back* – her ringtone for me – came through the wall. Through that tiny, foot-wide gap between the two doors. *How?*

"Hello?"

"Caroline!"

"Where are you?"

"I can't find the room."

"What are you talking about?"

"I can't get into the room."

"What, lost your key already? Okay." Her classic annoyed sigh. "I'll open the do–"

She cut off.

"Caroline?"

"Oh my God." Her ragged breaths came through the line. Labored, panicked. "It's a wall. I opened the door, and there's just a *wall* on the other side." Her voice cracked. "Tom, what the hell is going on?"

"I don't know. But I'm going to –"

"Wait, there are people outside the window. I'm going to ask them what the hell is –"

The line cut to silence.

"Caroline?"

"Oh, God. They don't have faces." Her voice was cut with static. "They don't have faces and they're coming –"

"Caroline? Where are you?" I pounded my fist on the wall. Like that would help anything.

"Dani— p-pl— hel—"

Static.

"Caroline? Caroline, can you hear me?"

Static.

I pounded the wall as hard as I could. My wife's voice, my son's footsteps, were impossibly faint. Whispers in the wind.

Then – silence.

I don't know what the hell is going on… but I got to get them out of there. Maybe they got trapped in a crawlspace or something. Somehow. I whipped around, looking at the cart. My eyes fell on Caroline's suitcase.

Yes.

I grabbed her "self-defense" knife from the pocket.

I ran at the wall. *Crack.* The blade punctured it, crumbling bits of drywall everywhere. I yanked the blade out, stuck my fingers in, and began clawing my way through. I didn't stop until I'd created a sizeable hole.

I raised my eye to it and peered inside.

Darkness, wires, wood...

And a sliver of light.

It was a hotel room, on the other side. Only four or five feet in width. The walls looking almost as if they were closing in. As if the very room was winking out of existence.

Caroline stood in the center, holding our son. Silhouettes shifted outside the window, tapping on the glass.

"Caroline!" I screamed.

She whipped around. Ran towards me. Her brown eyes appeared in the crack, wide with fear. "Get me out of here!"

"I'm trying!"

I reached in and grabbed her hand. But there was no way I could pull her out of that tiny hole. No way I could take down the wall with my bare hands.

But I pulled anyway, shutting my eyes.

Crack!

The sound shook the entire floor, echoed around me in waves. My eyes flew open.

I was standing in the hall. But my arm wasn't reaching into the wall – it was reaching into one of the rooms.

Room 213.

But the room was no longer lit with golden light. It was dark. Pitch black.

And the hand latched onto mine... wasn't Caroline's.

I yanked my hand back, jumped out of the way. Then I raced down the hall, my heart pounding in my chest. I didn't stop until my lungs burned and my legs wobbled underneath me.

I collapsed on the carpet. As I caught my breath, I looked around the hallway. To the left, then the right.

There were no windows. No exit signs. No elevators. Just an endless hallway, fading into darkness in either direction.

Only broken by that one door. Room 213.

I've been here for hours. Maybe days. I've tried screaming. I've tried running up and down the halls, but all I've found is more of the hallway. More of the ugly brocade carpet. More of the flickering lights.

I haven't found my family. Or an exit. Or anything else. My phone seems to work, but every time I call someone, it fades to static.

If anyone reads this... I am at the SoutHfiEld. inN aa@AsSs!dDd;!;;-_~ pl-a$e.. hlp. reSC@..uE u!!S23__..

EATING FOR TWO

My husband placed the steak in front of me. "You're eating for two, now. Eat up!"

"Thank you." I grabbed the knife and cut into the steak. A deep, blood-red color that made my mouth water. "This looks perfect."

The first few months were the hardest. I'd projectile vomited more times than I could count. We had to have the rugs professionally steamed, the couch washed. No matter what I ate, no matter how hard I tried, it seemed like the nausea boiled up out of me at the most inopportune times.

And, honestly? I just haven't been feeling like myself.

Sometimes I try to speak, but only unintelligible syllables come out of my mouth. Stefan says that's perfectly normal, and nothing to be worried about. That getting confused and mixed up is part of it. I'm not sure I believe him. Sometimes I say things, and I don't even remember *thinking* them before they come flying out of my mouth. Other times, it's just unintelligible nonsense.

There were a lot of other side effects I didn't expect, too.

Like fainting. A few weeks in, I was walking up the steps to church when I suddenly felt a wave of weakness wash over me. My vision grew dim, spotted with patches of black. *Smack* – I fell onto the cold hard steps.

Then everything went black.

"You fainted," Stefan said, when I finally came to. "Are you okay? I should've been there to catch you. I'm so, so sorry."

My head throbbed and my knees ached, but I was okay. *We* were okay. I spent a week taking it easy — watching my favorite soaps on TV, getting served on hand and foot — and then I was good as new.

But you know what? I somewhat expected the nausea and the fainting. I mean, I've read all the books. They tell you there will be changes. Some will be unpleasant. But it's all worth it in the end, right?

Yet they never warned me about some changes. All the aches and pains! My neck has been hurting something awful these past months. My back feels like it's on fire, and I'm always aching and hurting in one way or another.

And the random allergies and rashes! I've always had a whole host of food allergies... but, suddenly, I was breaking out in a rash from my favorite necklace! It was crazy. Stefan got me some cream right away. But it still made me sad.

And the books never warned me just how bad my anxiety would get. How all those little voices in my head would amp up. Some days I'd just lie in bed, trying to silence them and focus on the positives. But it's hard. Really hard.

Stefan's been so supportive though. I know he's just trying to help. He's been rubbing my back, rubbing my feet, getting me all kinds of gifts. I couldn't ask for a better husband.

He knows that it's hard work. He knows throwing away my cross necklace and listening to the growing voice in my head have been so, so hard.

He knows it's hard being possessed by a demon.

But in the end, it'll all be worth it.

THE METAL DETECTOR

Beep beep beep.

The familiar beeps of the metal detector rang out across the sand. Followed by the furious sounds of digging. When I got there, Elizabeth was already pulling it out.

"Woah. What *is* that?"

"Treasure!" she squealed.

It was a thin, wooden box, faded around the corners. I was a bit jealous — all I'd found so far were a few coins and coke cans. Elizabeth always found the good stuff.

"I can't get it open," she said, prying at it with her fingers. The metal clasp at the front was rusted over badly.

"Maybe your dad can do it."

But her dad couldn't do it. Nor could her older brother, her mom, or me. "Do you have to keep it in the house?" her mom, Mrs. Greenberg, complained. "It smells."

It did smell. Like salty water, hot sand, and rotten fish.

"No way," Elizabeth said. "If I keep it outside, someone will steal it."

We talked about it late into the night, as I was sleeping over. "Maybe it's got real, bonified treasure inside," Elizabeth said, her eyes dancing in the glow of the nightlight.

"Maybe," I yawned. "Or maybe it's just some old dude's stamp collection."

"Hey! We know there's something metal inside."

"No, we don't. The clasp is metal. That could've set off the detector." I pulled my sleeping bag over me and rolled over. "I'm tired, Elizabeth."

"Okay. Goodnight, Jackie." I heard a soft thump and the scrape of wood as she placed the box back in the nightstand drawer.

***

My eyes fluttered open.

My back hurt from the floor. My neck ached. I glanced at the clock — 4:07 AM.

That's when I noticed the smell.

The smell of rotting fish and salty water. Like the box — except amplified by a thousand. I gagged a bit and turned to Elizabeth.

I couldn't see her. It was too dark. *Did she turn off the nightlight?*

I opened my mouth to ask, but stopped short.

Click, click.

Soft sounds, coming from the other side of the bedroom. Where Elizabeth was sleeping on her bed.

"Elizabeth?" I whispered.

178

No reply.

"Elizabeth?" I whispered, a little louder. "Is everything okay?"

I reached for my phone. I pressed the power button, illuminating the room in a dim blue glow.

I froze.

A figure hunched over Elizabeth's bed.

Too tall to be her mom or brother. Too thin to be her father. Its fingers raked over the nightstand, as if looking for something. *Click, click, click.* My fingers fumbled for the power button. *Shut off, shut off —*

Thump.

The phone slipped from my fingers and clattered to the ground.

The figure stopped.

And turned towards me.

Milky white eyes met mine. Stringy hair fell down its shoulders, tangled with seaweed. Its plump, gray, water-logged skin shined in the light.

It took a shaky step towards me.

"The drawer! The box is in the drawer!" I shrieked.

For a moment, it stared at me with its milky eyes.

Then it slowly turned around.

Scrrrrrppp.

The familiar sound of the drawer pulling out. *Clunk.* Then the slap of wet footsteps against the tile. *Creeeaaak.* The door creaked open.

All was still.

***

"You stole my box! How could you?!" Elizabeth screamed. "Give it back! Give it back!"

"Elizabeth, calm down," Mr. Greenberg said. "Now, Jackie, please give Elizabeth her box back. I understand you were jealous, but —"

"Let her take it," Mrs. Greenberg interjected. "That thing *reeked*. Good riddance."

"I didn't take it!" I said.

"Then what happened to it?" Elizabeth spat. "You were the only one who knew where it was! What, did it just disappear?"

"Sort of?"

"Get out!"

"Elizabeth, no," Mrs. Greenberg said. "Stop. Jackie's not going anywhere."

I turned to her and smiled. *Thank you, Mrs. Greenberg. Thank you —*

Mrs. Greenberg turned to me and looked me squarely in the eye. "Jackie can't leave yet. She needs to clean up all this sand she tracked in first."

PORTAPOTTY

I never wanted to use a porta potty.

But that was the risk I took when I drank that 24-ounce cherry coke.

"Be right back," I told my boyfriend, as I slipped away through the crowd.

The pounding bass faded in my ears. The rows of porta potties stood in the darkness, at the edge of the concert crowd, as if watching over the music and chaos before them. *Click* — I latched the plastic door behind me.

Then I was in utter darkness.

Ugh. Aren't these things supposed to have a light?

I fumbled in my pocket and pulled out my phone. In its glow, I could see the toilet paper, the plastic toilet seat. It looked fairly clean – at least in the dim light, I couldn't make out any wayward excrement – and I took a seat.

That's when I heard the moan.

Uuuhhhhh

I immediately felt uncomfortable. *Ugh, no. I don't want to hear some guy in the next stall pooping.*

Uuuuuuhhhhhh

Then I felt bad. *He's probably really constipated. Poor guy.*

I reached for the toilet paper and began pulling at it. As I shifted my legs, the stench wafted over me again. *Ew, ew, ew. Don't they ever clean these things?* It was even worse than the usual bathroom smell. Smelled as if someone had thrown in a few dead squirrels for good measure.

Uuuuuuuuuuuhhhhhhhh

Then a sloshing sound filled my ears. *Sshlssh, sshlssh.* As if something was moving around in the sea of excrement below. My heart began to pound. *What is that? What —*

Something cold brushed against my right butt cheek.

"Ow!" I yelped and jumped off the toilet seat, nearly toppling to the floor. *What the fuck was that?* I pulled out my phone. Hands shaking, I pressed the flashlight button and aimed it at the toilet.

No.

Four fingers clung to the edge of the seat.

I backed away, fumbled with the lock on the door. It wouldn't open. "Hey! Open up!" I yelled. "Somebody, open the door, please!"

Schlick.

I whipped around to see *two* hands clinging to the toilet seat. Wet. Slimy. Covered in bits of... well, you know.

I grabbed the roll of toilet paper and, with all my strength, lobbed it at him. It bounced off his hands. *Uuuuuhhhh!* The same groan I had heard before rung out against the plastic walls.

182

But he never climbed out. Those fingers just clung to the toilet bowl, as he groaned over and over.

And then he slipped.

Uuuuuuuuuuuuhhhhh!

Splash!

That's when it occurred to me that maybe he wasn't some creep. Maybe he wasn't some murderer, waiting to stab any butt that sat on the toilet. Maybe, instead... he was some old concertgoer that had fallen *in* the porta potty.

I cautiously approached. "Hello?" I called. "Are – are you okay, sir?"

Uuuuuuuuuuuuuuuuuuuhhhhhhhhhhhhh

I peered down into the toilet, the white light of the phone shining down.

And screamed.

Below me wasn't just a small pool of sewage. It was an immense room. Dozens of people stood far below, in a pool of black sludge. Some were shackled and collared; others were sitting in the liquid, rocking back and forth, moaning in pain.

One man stood in the center, unlike the others. No shackles, no chains, no red gashes marring his chest. He pulled out a knife and advanced towards the man in front of him.

"No!" I screamed.

He slowly turned his head up towards me.

The image flickered and rippled.

Then I was staring into a plastic basin of poop, pee, and toilet paper. "Hello?" I called. My voice echoed off the plastic.

"Hello? Hello?"

A knocking sound from door. "Are you coming out soon?" a woman's voice said from the other side, annoyed. "I've been waiting out here for 10 minutes!"

I ran to the door. After a few tries, the lock disengaged and I was standing in the fresh air. "Thanks," the woman snapped, rushing past me into the porta potty.

I walked back to my boyfriend in a daze.

See, I'm not a religious woman. I'd always assumed when we die, eternal nothingness awaits us. A void. A lack of existence. I'd assumed Heaven and Hell were just constructs invented by man to cope with the nothingness of death.

I was wrong.

There is a Hell.

And it lies at the bottom of a porta potty.

LATE-NIGHT PIZZA

by Blair Daniels & Michael Crutchfield of The Scarecast

It was ten minutes till close when I heard the door swing open.

Jingle-jingle.

Ugh. A customer this late? It was my first day at Tony's Pizzeria, and I was eager to get home. My manager, Mason, had to leave early – his infant son had a fever – and I was left all alone to close up. Sighing, I put down the broom, and made my way to the front.

"Hi, may I help –"

I stopped.

The store was empty. Everything was as I left it – the chairs lifted onto the tables, the lights dim, the silverware and parmesan shakers sitting on the shelf above the garbage.

"Hello?" I called.

But only silence met my ears.

I shrugged and went back to sweeping.

The store was eerily quiet; the only sound was my broom scratching rhythmically against the floor, as I swept shreds of mozzarella across the floor. *Only five minutes till close,* I thought, glancing up at the clock. *Then I can finish cleaning, lock up, and get out of here.*

But I had scarcely swept another few feet when I heard it again –

Jingle, jingle.

I dropped the broom and ran to the front of the store. "Hello?"

Nobody was there.

But this time –

The front door was open.

"Hello?" I called again, louder this time, hoping my voice would reach the outside.

Beyond the light spilling out into the patio, there was total darkness. I couldn't even make out the parking lot or the trees. *What if there's someone out there? Watching?* If there was, I wouldn't even know.

I rushed over, shut the door, and turned the lock. *Click.* "No pizza left for 'em anyway," I muttered to myself.

I picked up the broom and began sweeping around the tables. But I couldn't silence the voice echoing in my head – *what if someone's out there?* I stared out the glass; the shadows across the patio shifted and swayed with the wind.

What if someone's trying to rob us? I'm all alone... no weapons, no security system, just an old lock on a glass door.

I shook the thoughts from my head and continued sweeping. I was nearly done, when –

Slam!

A loud noise, from the back of the pizzeria.

I jumped. "H-hello?" I called, starting to shake. I gripped the broom tight, as if it were a weapon, and stepped forward.

"Hello?"

Thump, thump.

"Hello –"

I rounded the corner.

The back door was wide open. The stench of the dumpster in the alley filled the room, along with gusts of cold night air.

But no one was there.

I ran over and shut the door. Then I dragged a chair in front of it, and a stack of empty pizza boxes for good measure.

It's a windy night. You're just scaring yourself. I took a deep breath, the mozzarella twirling and sticking under the broom. *Just finish cleaning, lock up, and get out of here.*

I finished sweeping the back, then walked towards the front of the store –

Slam!

I jumped and ran to the back door.

It was wide open.

The chair was kicked over. The pizza boxes were wildly strewn about.

But the room was, still, empty.

"That's it." I closed the door again and grabbed my coat. Then I ran out of the store, through the shadows, until I reached the familiar cold metal of the car. *If he fires me for a dirty floor, so be it. Better than getting murdered over here.* I yanked the door open, dove in, and pulled out of the parking space.

As I turned on to the main road, I heard it.

Tap, tap, tap.

A soft clicking sound, above the rush of the car.

Tap, tap, tap.

I tried to ignore it as I drove. But it got louder.

Tap, tap, tap.

It sounded like it was coming from behind me.

Heart pounding, I slowly lifted my eyes to the rearview mirror.

And there, breaking the darkness of the back seats –

Was a man's face.

I screamed. The car swerved wildly, narrowly missing the gutter. I jolted to a stop, leapt out of the car.

Then I pulled out my phone and called 911.

"911, what's your emergency?"

"There's someone in my car! They were trying to get in the pizza shop as I cleaned up, and then – and then –"

I stopped.

I could see, through the window, that the backseat was completely empty.

***

The next day, I came into work shaken. But Mason only added to that.

"You didn't finish sweeping the floor before closing up," he yelled. "This entire half has bits of food, even a dirty toothpick!" He sat down and sighed. "I'll let it slide this time, but if you do it again, I'm going to fire you."

"Mason, I'm so sorry – I would've cleaned it, but – but –"

He eyed me suspiciously. "I'm not one for excuses. You know that."

"I know, but I swear, this happened. The front door started opening. I thought someone was there, but nope, no one there. Then, after I locked it, the back door opened! I even put a chair against it, and it opened again!" I looked at him with pleading eyes. "I thought someone was trying to rob the place! And then when I drove home – I swear, Mason, there was someone in the back seat!"

Mason stared at me.

And then he broke into jolly guffaws.

"That's just old Paulie," he said.

"Uh – what?"

"The guy who used to run the shop, before he died in '02. He likes to keep an eye on the place." Mason shot me a smile. "*Especially* the new employees."

OLIVES

The grocery store had a new arrival yesterday.

"Dan's All-Natural Olives."

A promotional display was set up by the front door. Dozens of jars were stacked in a neat little pyramid. Next to it was a photo of a woman sensuously eating a plump, glistening black olive. *The perfect snack! Now only $2.99!*

As we passed it, I answered some uncomfortable questions from my son.

"Mom, why is that woman eating poop?"

"It's not poop. It's an *olive.*"

"What's an olive?"

I didn't really know. Are they vegetables? Fruit? Demon eggs? So I just said, "They're gross. Never eat them."

Of course, that only made Brayden want to eat them more.

"Can I try one? *Please?*"

"Okay, fine." I lifted one of the jars and placed it in the cart. Just looking at it made my stomach turn. Sickly-yellow fluid. Black, squishy olives. *Yeeech.*

When we got home, Brayden ran outside to play with the dog, and forgot all about the olives. I put them on a shelf in the pantry, and forgot about them too.

Until yesterday.

"Dana?"

I followed my husband's call into the kitchen. "Yeah, Rob?" He pointed to the floor.

Yellow liquid oozed out from under the pantry door.

I yanked the door open. There, on the shelf – where I had placed the jar of olives less than a week ago – stood a mess of exploded glass, yellow juice, and shards of thin, black, papery material.

But, surprisingly, there was not a single olive in sight.

Rob and I shrugged at each other. He got the broom, and I got the paper towels.

***

I jolted awake at 4 AM to a sound.

Squelch.

"Rob?" No answer. I grabbed my phone off the nightstand and turned it around to illuminate the room. Something glistened oddly in the darkness, just beyond the foot of our bed.

Squelch.

It moved.

I jumped back. "Rob? Rob?" I called, shaking him.

"What?"

"There's something in here! A rat, or something!" I squinted in the darkness, trying to make sense of the shadows. But it was no longer in view; I only saw the crumpled clothes on the floor, the edge of TV stand.

Rustle.

I felt something slick and cold wriggle against my bare thigh.

No. It's in the bed. Oh, God, no, please...

A sharp, stabbing pain cut into my thigh.

I screamed.

Rob flicked on the lights. I jumped out of bed, screaming. "You're bleeding!" he yelled.

I looked down.

A small bite mark lay a few inches above my knee. The flesh was torn away viciously from the wound; it looked almost like a miniature shark bite. Blood dripped down my leg in thin, dark rivers.

Rustle.

My eyes darted back to the bed. The crumpled sheets roiled and churned, as if something was moving underneath them. I clung to Rob and watched in horror.

Plop.

A small animal dropped to the floor. Slick, black, and long like a salamander. A twitching, pink tail like a rat. Long whiskers sprouted from its noseless snout, and its oily, hairless skin gleamed in the light.

It snarled at us, ran across the room, and it squeezed itself underneath the door.

The *squelch* of its feet moved down the hallway.

Oh, no. Brayden.

I wrenched the door open and flew down the hallway. Sticky footprints led across the linoleum, right up to Brayden's door.

Not just one set of footprints.

192

Dozens of them.

I kicked the door open and ran inside. "Brayden? Brayden, are you okay?"

He lay motionless in bed.

One of the creatures was on his shoulder. Several were at his feet. A few clustered on his stomach.

"Brayden!" I screamed.

His eyes flew open.

"Oh, hi Mom," he said. He sat up and smiled. The creatures scampered back from me. Hissing, spitting, squelching. One snuggled under his shirt. Another rubbed against his hand. A third sat on his knee.

"Brayden, what are you –"

"Aren't they cute?" he asked. "Can I keep them, Mom? *Please?*"

THE SHIRT

It was my first time outside the house without baby Taylor.

"Go out and treat yourself to something nice," Dan had told me. "I got her."

When I ran into Kohl's, I nearly cried. Shirts. Jeans. People! There was a life outside Baby.

After some rummaging, I found a really cute shirt on a clearance rack. It was a sort of a blush pink/rose gold color tee, with ruching up the sides. I checked the size: Large. I was about to put it back when I remembered that, since pregnancy and giving birth, I *was* a large.

I grabbed it and made my way to the dressing room.

I pulled my own top off. A weird cluster of stretch marks hung above my belly button. My stomach stuck out a bit over my jeans.

Pregnancy had definitely changed my body for the worse.

I sighed and tugged the shirt off the hanger. Then I pulled it over myself. The cloth felt strangely smooth against my skin. A weird mix between spandex leggings and that weird pleather stuff.

The fit was snug. I had trouble getting my arms through, and had to yank it hard over my midsection for it to fit. *Am I an extra-large now?* I thought, with a pang of sadness. *Or maybe this is a Junior's top...*

I finally glanced in the mirror.

I looked like a sausage.

The top was super tight. My pale stomach jutted out from the bottom, like some sort of upside-down muffin top. My arms felt like they were in tourniquets.

"So much for that," I muttered to myself. I reached around and tugged it off.

It didn't come off.

I tugged hard.

"Ow!"

Sharp pain shot across my back. It was a tingling, prickly pain — like ripping off a band-aid. Or getting waxed.

I tugged again.

Pain flew over my body. Worse this time. I immediately crumpled against the wall of the dressing room. I felt hot. Weak.

I looked in the mirror.

And froze.

The edges of the shirt — the bottom hem, the edges of the sleeves — were gone. As if the shirt, somehow, had melted right into my skin. My reflection, blurred by my tears of pain, looked naked.

Except for the fact that my stomach and arms bulged out strangely where the hem should have been.

"Help!" I screamed. I banged on the walls of the dressing room. I fumbled with the latch on the door, threw it open. "Help! Get it off! I can't... I can't get it off..."

I was out of breath.

The shirt was squeezing my chest too hard. I couldn't take in air. I couldn't breathe.

The dressing rooms shimmered before me. Patches of black swam in my vision. I screamed out the last bit of air in my lungs, making a muffled squeaking sound.

"Hey! Hey!"

Arms grabbed me from behind.

Then, suddenly, the shirt peeled off of me. I sucked in a breathe of air and began to cough.

"Are you okay?"

I looked up.

A woman stood over me. Middle-aged, maybe older. In one hand she held the crumpled, leathery, pink fabric. The other rested on my shoulder.

"I — I couldn't get it off," I sputtered. Sobs shook my body. "It was stuck to me. Stuck to my skin. I — I —"

"It's okay. You're okay," she said in a soft tone. She knelt next to me, dropping the shirt on the ground.

With a shaking hand, I reached out and touched it.

It felt like ordinary cloth.

FORGIVE ME, FATHER [1]

Father Nicholas always weirded me out.

He smelled like stale bread and onions. His gaze seemed to look past you, not *at* you. He had a quiet, sullen demeanor, and he always recited the Nicene Creed in a rasping whisper.

So when he asked me to "join him in his office for a quick chat" after Mass, I freaked out a little.

But I still replied, "Sure, Father."

I glanced around the church. It was nearly empty now; the parishioners were filing out the front door in a thick line, full of chatter and laughter. Behind them, a gloomy darkness had settled in the church–deep shadows behind the pews, behind the altar. The golden tabernacle glinted in the dim light, under the darkened crucifix.

I followed him into the parish office. Father Nicholas closed the door behind us.

---

[1] Originally published in *Shadow on the Stairs*

"I've noticed you haven't been coming to Mass regularly," he said, taking a seat across the desk.

"Uh, yeah, I've been busy," I replied, my heart beginning to race. *What is this? Some kind of interrogation?*

"And you don't wear your cross anymore," he said, pointing to my chest from beneath his robes.

"I forgot to put it on."

Father Nicholas leaned back in his seat, surveying me carefully. I didn't like the glint in his dark eyes, or the fact that his hands were hidden in the robes. *Just tell him you have to go,* the voice inside me urged. Reverence kept me locked in place.

"Is there a reason you didn't get any holy water today?"

My heart began to pound, so loudly that I could hear it in my ears.

The holy water is kept in a tiny basin at the front of the church. How would he know that I didn't get any? Was he watching me that closely? There were dozens–no, *hundreds*–of other parishioners coming into the church at the same time, but he noticed *I* didn't get any holy water?

"Uh–no, no reason in particular."

He sighed. Then he pulled a small vial of clear liquid from the folds of his cloak. He wet his fingers, and– before I could react–flicked them, so that a few drops fell on my face.

"What–what are you doing?" I asked.

Where each drop had landed, it burned, as if he had pricked me there with a poker from the fire.

I shot up, shrieking in pain. "Are you crazy?! What is that?! What did you just put on me?!"

With his face grim, Father Nicholas replied: "holy water."

"What–I don't understand," I replied, clawing at my face like a madman. "Holy water–but –"

"Holy water burns. You don't wear a cross." His tone turned almost humorous. "Need I spell it out for you, Jake?"

I stood there, numb, my cheeks still stinging.

"Oh, what–you thought it'd be like *The Exorcist?*" He laughed–the first time I had ever seen him do so. "No. They're too clever for that. Why, if you all were projectile vomiting everywhere, and speaking Latin with perfect fluency, we'd catch on pretty quick."

I stared at him. My heart was racing; my hands felt numb. I opened my mouth to speak, but nothing came out.

"No, they're subtle." He placed the vial on the desk, halfway between us; I involuntarily backed away. "Ever have an intrusive thought? 'Jump out that window, you know you want to.' 'Stop cutting up those carrots and stab him in the neck.'"

I nodded.

"Most of them are meaningless. Just silly thoughts to cloud your mind. But, sometimes… it's one of them, its voice blending perfectly with yours."

"But –" I faltered.

"Just a suggestion, in the back of your mind," he said. He laughed again–but this time it was a bitter, empty scoff. "That's all it *takes*, for humans to do unspeakable things."

Just a suggestion.

I pulled my arms around me and felt a shiver crawl down my back. "So... what do we do?" I asked, voice quavering, fearing the answer.

"Come back tomorrow. At dawn, we will begin."

That night I tossed and turned. The more the blanket tangled around me, the larger the pool of sweat became, and the crazier Father Nicholas's words sounded. *A possession, really? That's the stuff of movies. He's crazy.*

I flipped the pillow over. Yes, that's what it is. The guy is nuts.

But then... what's his real motive? I stared up at the dark ceiling. *Maybe he wants to do something to me. Something terrible.* I looked at the alarm clock–5:12 AM. The sun would rise within the hour.

You better bring your gun, just in case.

I glanced over at the desk, black in the dusky shadows. At the locked drawer, that held a Smith & Wesson in its bowels.

Bring the gun.

As the horizon lit with the fire of dawn, I made my way to the church, the gun swinging heavily in my pocket.

GOOGLE STREET VIEW

Yesterday, I looked up our house on Google Street View.

I wish I didn't.

The picture showed our little blue A-frame perfectly. The flowerboxes leaning out of the kitchen window, filled with morning glories. The cedar rocking chair. The splotch of brown paint on the steps from when I painted the desk.

But there were two people standing on the porch. Two people I didn't recognize. Even though their faces were blurred out, I knew they couldn't be us – we're Indian, and they were clearly white.

"Who are those people?" my brother, Arjun, asked.

"I have no idea." I leaned in to the computer screen, squinting at the pixels. "Maybe some of my friends from school?" But I knew that couldn't be true. They looked like adults: the man and woman were both wearing gray, tailored suits. I don't know of any 15-year-old that dresses like they work on Wall Street.

"Maybe it's an old picture," I said. "Maybe they're the previous owners."

But that didn't seem right, either. First of all, the text in the corner read "Street View – July 2017." Second, they didn't seem to just be hanging out and relaxing at their own home. The woman was standing at the corner of the porch, weight on one hip, arms crossed over her chest. The man stood unnaturally straight, as if he were posing for the photo, hands deep in his pockets.

"Maybe it's photoshopped."

I turned to him. "Really, Arjun?"

He shrugged. "I dunno. Maybe they photoshopped it purposely. To scare us. To make us move."

"You *really* think Google would let someone mess with their photos?"

He shrugged. "*All* those big companies, and organizations, and celebrities are super corrupt. Like Hillary Clinton. She's been doing Satanic rituals for years, and she's the ringleader of –"

I cut him off. "I see. Another conspiracy theory." Sometimes I think the hospital must've messed with his brain all those years ago. *Don't worry, we'll heal you up, little baby. Let us just upload some crazy theories into your head first.*

"It's not a *theory*. It's true."

"You sound like an idiot."

"Mom says you shouldn't call me that, Diya."

"Whatever. It's not photoshopped."

"Okay, then what do *you* think it is?"

I stared at the photo. Those two people... they looked familiar, almost. Something about them – their gray suits, their matching silver shoes – rung a bell. "I don't know," I said, finally.

202

Arjun eventually returned to his room – probably to tweet some more conspiracy theories to his 51 followers. How they let a 13-year-old own a Twitter account is beyond me. I went back to my homework. At least, I tried to. Every few minutes, my eyes tore away from the algebra textbook and back to the photo.

Where *had* I seen them before?

***

Friday went by at a snail's pace. Between getting a C+ on a quiz and nearly falling asleep in History, I forgot all about the weird Street View image. After school, I grabbed a yogurt and headed straight for my room.

But I froze when my eyes fell on a picture, hanging next to the stairs.

It was a photo of Arjun and me. My mom had taken it when we visited Philadelphia a few years ago. Arjun was holding some sort of toy helicopter; I was wearing weird floral jeans and sparkly hair clips. But there, behind us, were two people.

Two people wearing gray suits and silver shoes.

I grabbed the framed picture off the wall, brought it up to my face. A blonde woman, arms crossed over her chest; a dark-haired man, hands in his pockets. Their faces weren't blurred out in this one, but they were wearing dark sunglasses.

"Mom?" I called, heading back into the kitchen. "Do you remember taking this picture? In Philadelphia?"

"Oh yeah, sure," she replied, through *chops* of broccoli. "Why?"

"Who are those people behind us?"

Mom took the photo and brought it close to her face. Her eyes were calm, searching… and then, suddenly, they widened. "Just random people," she said, brusquely.

"But I saw them –"

"Shouldn't you be doing your homework?" she snapped.

"It's *Friday*, Mom."

"But your grades aren't good." She didn't give the photo back to me; instead, she set it down on the counter. "You should be studying, not inspecting old family photos."

I turned around and ran up the stairs. That stung… a lot. Usually Mom treats me like I'm made of glass – always praising me, hugging me, telling me how wonderful I am. Yelling at Arjun, sure – but *me?* It was out of character, to say the least.

I plopped down in front of the computer, typed in maps.google.com. *I should be planning my 16th birthday party. It's only two weeks away. Or on Facebook, checking if Bria Pierce dumped Chad yet.*

But I wasn't. I was here, on Google Maps, staring at *them*. The gray suits, the silver shoes, the faces that were blurred into blobs of unidentifiable flesh.

Then, on a whim, I typed in a different address. ██ Roxanne Ct. Our old address. The house we'd lived in before moving here.

The image loaded.

There, in the front yard, stood two figures.

Wearing gray suits.

What?! I zoomed in, staring at the screen. Wisps of blonde hair fell on the shoulders of the woman. The man held his hands in his pockets. They both stood there in the front lawn, in plain sight, as if nothing was amiss. The text read "Street View – May 2012."

When we'd lived there.

My hands trembled against the keyboard. My heart pounded in my chest. But I forced myself to type a third address: ▮▮ 6th St. The tiny "starter house" we'd lived in several years ago.

The image loaded. A cute, white ranch with 2 windows in front, a carpet of fluorescent-green grass, and a cracked cobblestone walkway appeared.

The porch was empty.

I breathed a sigh of relief. They weren't there. No one standing on the lawn, in the driveway, or anywhere around the house. *If it those people were following us, they'd be here, too.* I took slow, deep breaths, calming my racing heart.

I was about to click away, when something caught my eye.

Something in the window.

I zoomed in. The window was dark, cut by white lines separating the glass into panes. But in the lower right pane – there was something there. Pale, pressed up against the glass.

I zoomed in again.

It was a face.

Fear coursed through my veins. I slammed the laptop shut, leapt out of my chair. And then I did what any terrified teenager would do.

I ran downstairs to Mom. "Mom!" I called, fear trembling my voice. "Mom –"

I stopped.

The broccoli lay strewn over the kitchen island, half-chopped. The faucet dripped; the napkins lay on the floor. "Mom?"

"We're in here." My mom's voice. Weak. Trembling.

We're? Oh, no, no. The two gray suits – were they here? Holding my mom hostage? I ran into the family room, my heart pounding.

But it wasn't them.

It was Dad.

"Dad? Aren't you... supposed to be at work?" I said. I glanced from the grim expression on his face, to the tears staining Mom's cheeks. "What happened? Oh my God, did Grandma –"

"Grandma's fine," Dad said.

I stared at them.

"We need to talk to you," Mom said, her voice broken with sobs. "About something... something we did a long time ago."

I sat down on the ottoman, a heavy weight settling in my chest.

"Do you remember when Arjun was very sick in the hospital? When you were about six?" Dad asked, folding his hands in his lap.

206

That's random. But I nodded. *The hospital… the red-haired nurse who gave me a lollipop… the vending machine that had the vanilla wafers…* It was all fuzzy, distorted and blurred through the lens of time.

At the time, I was too young to understand exactly what was going on with Arjun. But I was old enough to know my brother was very sick, and that my parents were miserable.

"You remember how suddenly he recovered, right?" Dad said, his tone falling from explanatory to miserable. "The doctors couldn't explain it. Said it was a miracle. Do you remember what we told you?"

"Two angels came down straight from heaven, touched his chest, and healed his lungs." I repeated mechanically. They must've told me that story hundreds of times.

"There was some truth in it. We were approached in the hospital by two people. A man named John Crimson and a woman named Molly. They claimed they could heal Arjun." He averted my eyes. "For a price. We told them we were fine with whatever price they wanted. If we didn't have the money, we'd take out loans. We'd pay them back for the rest of our lives if we had to."

"Two people… wearing gray suits?"

He nodded. "After they healed him, they told us the price. They didn't want money." Dad's voice shuddered, and he looked me in the eye. "They wanted *you.*"

My heart stopped. "Me?"

"They told us they'd come back for you," Mom finally said, her eyes wet with tears. "That they'd take you on your sixteenth birthday."

"But my birthday's in two weeks."

She nodded.

"What do you mean, 'take me'? What are they going to do to me?"

Mom and Dad looked at each other, uncomfortably. "We have no idea," Dad said, finally breaking the silence.

"We never would have done it if we knew," Mom said, her voice muffled through a tissue. "I promise that. We love you, Diya, and never wanted to –"

"We thought we could escape them," Dad broke in, cutting her off. "We'd just move into the middle of nowhere. Change our names, maybe. How could they find us after that? But they always did."

They'd found us at every house we've ever lived in. Street View confirmed that.

Mom got up, and pulled an old photo album off the bookshelf. Wordlessly, she dropped it in my lap. "They follow us, wherever we go."

I flipped it open.

Arjun and I eating ice cream at Cold Stone. At the next table, with their backs to us, two people sharing a milkshake.

Two people in gray suits.

Arjun and I at the lake, hitting each other with pool noodles. In the distance, near the woods, two gray figures. Watching.

Arjun and I at the carnival. In the background, lit by the red-and-white lights of the dragon rollercoaster, they stood. Wearing sunglasses, despite the darkness.

They were always following. Watching. Waiting.

There was nowhere I could hide.

"So that's it? They're just going to... take me... in two weeks?"

My parents looked at each other, tears in their eyes. And then they nodded.

We hugged and cried for a long time. Then I went up to my room, turned on the computer, and opened a new tab.

Not Google Maps.

Google.

I began to type, my fingers flying across the keyboard. Guns. Bombs. Mace. Tasers. Weapons of any and every kind. How to buy. Where to purchase. Expedited shipping? Yes. I've only got two weeks, after all.

They may be coming for me.

But I will not go gently into that good night.

BOTTOMLESS PIT

"Are we there yet?"

My legs burned. The mosquito bites itched. Cory had promised an interesting hike, but so far, the most interesting thing I had seen was a woman wearing sunglasses in the shade. Oh, and a squirrel falling out of a tree. So I was about to abandon them – take my chances with the bears and the moose and whatever the hell else was out here – when Cory replied:

"We're here."

"Finally," I groaned. "This better be good, because –"

My breath caught in my throat.

We were standing on the cusp of a huge pit. A thin fence circled it, covered with signs that read DANGER and NO TRESPASSING. Vegetation crept up to the edge, and spilled over into the darkness, like some kind of grassy waterfall. And an unfortunate tree grew at the edge, its exposed roots stretching towards the bottom.

If there even *was* a bottom.

"What is it? A sinkhole?"

"Beats me," he replied, pacing around the fence. "All I know is, locals call it the Pit of Endless Darkness."

"Oooooh, so spooky," Kat mocked.

"How deep does it go?" I asked.

"Who knows?" Kat shrugged. "And who cares?"

Cory got out his phone. "If we throw something in, I can time how long it takes to reach the bottom. And then, using kinematics, we can calculate –"

"You're such a nerd, Cory," she said, rolling her eyes.

"No, let's do it," I said, reaching into my pocket. I pulled out a water bottle, and chucked it. With a soft rush, it fell down into the pit.

Kat leaned against the fence, peering down into the darkness.

But she leaned a little too far.

Snap!

The fence gave way.

Kate tumbled forward – arms outstretched, face frozen in surprise.

And then she screamed.

And screamed, and screamed, and screamed.

Cory and I lunged forward. But it was too late – her scream was echoing up the pit, fading with every second.

And then silence.

No *smack*, no *clunk*, no *thud*. Just the chittering of the birds above, and the rush of the soft breeze.

"Kat!" I yelled, trembling.

"No," Cory said, his voice cut with sobs. "No, no, no! Kat!"

I stumbled away from the fence, and collapsed in the soft grass. "I can't believe this," I said, my voice quavering. "It happened so fast."

But then there was a noise –

Shrill, high-pitched, reverberating through the trees.

A scream.

Cory and I stared at each other.

And then we ran as fast as we could, the branches snapping beneath our feet. "Kat!" we yelled, as the sound grew louder. "Kat –"

There she was.

Lying in the middle of the ground, caked with dirt and dust, facing away from us.

As we approached, she tilted her head up towards the sky. "I'm okay!" she called up, her hands cupped around her mouth. "Cory, Jen, I'm okay! I'm at the bottom!"

"Kat?" Cory asked, stepping towards her carefully.

"Yes! I'm okay!" she yelled, her face still tilted towards the sky. Then she stretched her arms out, groping at the dirt. "Dammit, I can't see a thing. So dark down here."

"Kat –"

Wobbling, she pulled herself up.

Then she turned in our direction.

Cory stumbled back.

"No," I choked out.

Her eyes –

They were completely gone.

INTRUDER

Someone broke into my house last night.

The police don't believe me. "None of the windows are broken," they said. "All the doors were locked. Nothing is missing. Why do you think someone broke in?"

But I *know* someone was in here.

Because I didn't leave four of my mugs on the kitchen counter. I didn't empty the junk drawer, leaving pens, binder clips, and broken measuring cups scattered across the tile floor. And I certainly didn't paw through the dirt in my miniature herb garden on the windowsill.

But the police were unwilling to help. There was no *evidence*, they said. What more did they need? Muddy footprints on the patio, a burglar's mask on the dinner table?

I did what any reasonable person would do.

I drove to Best Buy and bought a ton of security cameras. The fancy kind – ones that had night vision capabilities. Ones that recorded sound. When all was said and done, I'd spent close to a thousand dollars. That night, I installed the cameras. Two in the kitchen, one in the living room, a few outside the house, even one in my bedroom. It took me a few hours to get everything set up. When I was done, I collapsed into bed and fell asleep.

Rrrriiiing.

My alarm pierced the morning air. I pulled myself out of bed, incredibly tired, even though I'd slept for nine hours. After a long yawn, I finally headed downstairs.

I froze.

More things were out of place. The dining room chairs were pulled away from the table at strange, skewed angles. Entire cabinets were emptied on the kitchen floor, turning it into a minefield of steak knives, serving forks, and cheese graters. I stepped on the citrus reamer – "Fuck!" – and nearly fell headlong into the sink.

As I straightened myself, my eyes fell on the camera in the corner.

The cameras! I'd forgotten all about them.

I ran up the stairs, taking two at a time. I grabbed my laptop from the bed, plugged it in, and pulled up the footage that had been recorded. *Let's try porch first. See how that bastard got in.*

I clicked on the first clip of footage.

I saw the front of my house. White railing, wooden swing, thatched welcome mat. All as they should be. For a while, I didn't see anything. *What tripped the motion sensor, then?* I thought. The cameras only recorded footage when they detected movement.

Then at 02:04:31 AM, I saw something.

A shifting shape in the shadows. I held my breath, my heart raced. *The burglar*, I thought. *I bet it's the teenager next door. With his smug little face and –*

The shape walked into view.

It was a deer.

"Fuck you," I said to its grainy little image.

I clicked on the next clip. A moth of epic proportions, flying around the red light of the camera. The next. An opossum or raccoon, flitting across the front yard.

I clicked out of the Porch camera. My mouse hovered indecisively before I finally clicked on *KITCHEN*.

The kitchen camera had only recorded a single, fifteen-minute clip of footage. I took a deep breath, and pressed *PLAY*.

03:45:21. Some rustling noises off camera. 03:46:52. A gray shadow, slowly creeping into the edge of the frame. 03:47:03 AM. A head of dark hair, facing away from the camera.

I held my breath. *Who is that?*

The person walked further into the kitchen, and I gasped.

It was *me*.

The knotted bun on top of my head. The little images of cacti on my pajamas. Definitely me. Not even a question. *But... how? Was I sleepwalking? I've never sleepwalked in my life!*

As I watched myself crouch over the cabinets, a terrible thought crept into my mind. *What if it's not me? Not really *me*? I've read accounts of doppelgangers, body snatchers. Even a crazy one about clones of people,*

215

growing like vegetables in the dirt. They were all far-fetched, and probably fake... but what if they were real?

What if it's not me... and just something that looks like me?

I paused the video, clicked on BEDROOM. There was a clip marked 3:42:25 AM. I pressed PLAY.

I expected to see myself sleeping peacefully. But no – a few seconds into the video, video-me threw off the covers, got out of bed, and walked towards the door.

So it *was* me.

I clicked back to the KITCHEN video. 03:53:10 AM – I was opening the cabinets. Then I threw pots, knives, and even that damned citrus reamer on the floor.

I suddenly broke into a fit of laughter. *It was me! This whole time, I thought someone was breaking into my house... and it was me, sleepwalking!* I even snorted when I saw my video-self step onto a pot and fall to her knees. Then I looked down at my leg, saw the purple bruise starting to form, and laughed even harder.

But then I stopped laughing.

Video-me was standing next to the window, peering outside.

And then I saw my lips move, as if I were talking to someone.

What the fuck am I doing? I squinted at the screen, trying to make sense of the grainy, black shapes. But I couldn't tell what was going on.

At 04:01:35 AM, video-me pulled away from the window. She carefully stepped over the pots and pans on the floor, then reached into one of the cabinets. Then she stepped back. She was holding the spare key I kept in there, hanging from a tiny hook.

I watched as she opened the window wider.

As she called "I found it!" into the darkness outside.

As a strange hand reached in through the window –

And took the key.

DR. WIDOW'S FACE-TASTIC MASK

I'm not an attractive woman.

I've tried every "beauty" treatment in the book. Waxing. Dyeing my hair. Losing weight. But I'm still ugly.

Every guy I've asked out turns me down. In photos with friends, I'm always pushed to the end of the frame. It's just my face. I've got small eyes, a big nose, and a wide face. Only surgery can change those things… and even if I was willing to go that far, I don't have the money.

I'd almost gotten used to it and given up beauty treatments for good.

Then I got the invitation to Sara Cheung's wedding.

Sara Cheung, the sister of Jeffrey. Aka my childhood crush from the age of 12.

The wedding was in two weeks. I needed to look *good.*

I hopped on the computer, googling every beauty treatment I could find. After an hour of sorting through eye creams, lash extensions, and eyebrow-stimulating lotion, a new item came up: **Dr. Widow's Face-tastic Exfoliating Mask!**

I was about to roll my eyes and click away when I saw the reviews. 2,000 of them. 4.7-star rating.

I clicked.

This mask is amazing! After a week of using it, I look incredible. Thank you Dr. Widow!

WOW!! This stuff is fantastic! My husband barely recognizes me, haha. He thinks I look like 'that one Kardashian girl.' I'm not sure which one but WHO CARES??? I LOOK LIKE A KARDASHIAN!!

I ordered it on the spot.

It came in a small, 8-ounce jar. The label was covered with crazy inspirational sayings like *Feel Brand-New with Dr. Widow's!*

I hurried to the bathroom and twisted the cap off.

My excitement faded.

It smelled *weird*. Like strong cleaning chemicals mixed with a sort of earthy, musty smell. Tan in color, with a strange, gloppy, lumpy consistency. Like cottage cheese mixed with milk.

I shrugged and smeared it all over my face. I'd seen weirder.

The directions said to leave it on for twenty-five minutes. I decided to leave it on for an hour. By the time the bottle arrived, I only had 10 days before Sara's wedding. I needed to do this right.

When I peeled it off, though, I was sorely disappointed. My face was a bit red, but everything else looked the same.

I sighed and went to sleep.

*****

Bzzt. Bzzt.

Sunlight streamed through the windows. I yawned and grabbed my phone off the nightstand.

The clock stared back at me.

10:04 AM

What?! How... how'd I sleep until 2 o'clock?

I grabbed my clothes and threw them on, without so much as a glance in the mirror. I pulled my hair in a ponytail and ran out the door. I drove to the office in record time and arrived at the third floor breathless.

I hurried to my cubicle and threw down my stuff. "Hey, you're late," Daniel said, turning towards me. "Everything oka –"

He stopped.

I looked up at him. "What?"

"You, uh, you just, uh..."

I narrowed my eyes at him.

"What?"

He shook his head and pretended to be suddenly very interested in his spider plant. I turned to my laptop and reached for the power button.

Woah.

I caught my reflection in the screen.

I looked... *amazing.*

My skin practically glowed. But it wasn't just my skin – it was my whole face. My eyes looked wider, brighter.

220

My face looked narrower. Even the mole on my upper lip seemed to have shrunk overnight.

Holy hell. This stuff is amazing!

I ordered 3 more bottles that night. I applied the mask twice a day – once in the morning, once in the evening. Wore each for an hour. And every single day, I got a little bit prettier.

But it also seemed to hurt more with every application. The pleasantly minty, tingly feeling that I felt on my skin had transformed into a prickly sting. And every time, it was a little harder to peel off. Sometimes it felt like I was just ripping a huge swath of duct tape off my face. One time my face even bled afterwards.

But it was worth it. *To be beautiful, one must suffer, right?*

My skin looked like I'd walked out of a Covergirl shoot. Heads turned on the sidewalk. Men flirted with me. Women looked at me with jealous disgust – the same way I used to look at them.

But as fun as it all was, I didn't want it. I wanted Jeffrey.

Every night, I lay down on the bed with the mask on my face, thinking of Jeffrey. Imagining his face when he saw mine. *Wow. You look incredible,* I imagined him saying. *Do you... maybe want to grab dinner after this? Catch up on everything? Make little animals out of clay again?*

I reached into my pocket and pulled it out.

A little cat made of oven-bake clay. He'd made it for me, when I was over his house one night, hanging out with Sara. He was always so artistic. I'd made one for him, but it looked terrible. More like a squashed rabbit. He'd smiled and said, *it's still really cute. I love it.*

I sighed and put the cat back in my pocket.

We'd lost touch over the years. We went to colleges in different states, and then reached that awkward status of 'somebody that I used to know.' We occasionally liked each other's Facebook statuses, or tagged each other in an old memory. I knew he was single from his self-deprecating posts about living alone with his cat.

But we hadn't seen each other since we were 22, at Sara's graduation party.

2 more days.

2 more.

***

I ended up arriving late to the wedding. I'd spent about two hours on my makeup, and also somehow slept in to 11 AM. I missed the ceremony, but showed up at the reception right on time. It was on the terrace, overlooking a garden, and it was beautiful. Dappled sunlight. Verdant leaves and purple morning glories. Delicate violin music floating on the wind.

I scanned the garden. It only took me a few seconds to recognize Jeffrey, standing by the appetizer table. Alone.

I clutched the clay cat in my pocket and walked up to him.

"Jeffrey!" I called, brushing my hand across his arm. "How have you been?"

He slowly turned towards me.

My heart fluttered in my chest. I imagined his eyes lighting up, as he took me in. His smile, a little too wide. His hug, a little too long.

But he didn't do any of that.

He looked at me blankly.

"Uh, do I know you?"

My heart sunk.

"It's me! Grace!"

"Grace... Dunlap?"

"Yeah!" I squealed, nodding enthusiastically.

I waited for the gasp of recognition. *Grace! Wow, you look so different, I didn't recognize you! You look fantastic!* The hug. *How have you been? I missed you so much. So much. How's everything?*

It never came.

Instead, he gave a condescending scoff. "Very funny."

"What?"

"There's no way you can be Grace Dunlap," he said, with a shake of his head. "You look nothing like her."

What?

"But if you see her... tell her to come find me, okay? I was actually just looking for her. I'd love to catch up." He smiled and brushed past me.

As I watched him go, I noticed he was fidgeting with something in his hands.

A misshapen, little clay cat.

I wanted to run after him. Tell him that yes, of course I was Grace. Ask him what the hell was wrong with him.

Tell him that I feel the same way about him. Always have, and always will.

But I felt hot tears brimming in my eyes. Rather than make a scene of myself, in front of him and all these wedding guests, I ran out of the garden.

Past the morning glories. Past the kitchen with all the fancy caterers. Past some old ladies taking a break from the heat inside. I didn't stop until I was in the ladies' room, crying my eyes out.

What does he mean, I'm not Grace?!

I grabbed a tissue and dried my face.

Then I looked in the mirror.

The face that stared back at me was beautiful. A slender face. Big, wideset eyes. A small, button nose. Perfect skin – no freckles, no moles of any kind.

He was right.

I barely recognized myself.

I frantically reached into my bag. Pulled out my phone. Scrolled through photos of me. Not recent ones. Ones from a year, two years, three years ago.

They looked almost nothing like me.

I crumpled against the counter. Hot tears ran down my face, and I sobbed. *Jeffrey… he wanted Grace. The dorky girl who smiled a lot and made crummy clay animals. Not… this. A stranger's face.*

I guess the saying really is true.

To be beautiful, one must suffer.

HOW TO BUILD A
SOULMATE

by Blair Daniels & Craig Groshek

The flyer was stuck in my mailbox. Red paper with big black letters.

ARE YOU UNLUCKY IN LOVE?

ARE YOU READY FOR A NEW, EXPERIMENTAL APPROACH TO LOVE?

FIND YOUR SOULMATE AT XX MAIN STREET...

That's all I needed to hear. I'm 36. I have 14 ex-boyfriends, 5 ex-girlfriends, and 0 current love interests. I'm sick of ramen dinners for one and the judgemental stare of my cat.

But when I got to the address, I was sorely disappointed.

It was a psychic. The large, purple sign read: FORTUNES & READINGS!!!. And the building was in disrepair. Chipped paint. Splintered siding. A few windows covered with large trash bags.

Ah, what the hell. If anything, it'll give me a good laugh.

I parked on the street and made my way to the shop.

As I opened the door, I shuddered. It looked halfway abandoned — paint flaking off the walls, a couch bleeding stuffing. A large painting with a crudely-drawn eye hung askew on the wall. Bookcases lined the back, filled with "spell" books. And the smell — a terrible mix of chemicals and rot, like someone tried to scrub the rotten beef smell out of their refrigerator with Windex.

"Hello?" I called.

Sch-schng.

The hanging tassels at the back parted. Out came a silver-haired woman, peeling latex gloves off her hands. Tattoos of eyes — matching the eye in the painting — covered her arms. "Yes?

"I'm Amy. I, uh, saw your flyer. For the soulmate?"

She looked me up and down. "Sure. You look like you could use my help."

"What's that supposed to mean?"

She gestured over my figure. "You think you're going to get boyfriends wearing stained overalls like that? And *Crocs?*" She waved her hand dismissively. Then she sat down at the crystal ball — which looked suspiciously like a snow globe — and set her hands on it. "Sit."

I did. The chair creaked dangerously underneath me.

"I'm Avelyn. And you and I, together, are going to find your soulmate. Did you bring the items I asked?"

"The items?"

"It says right on the flyer. I need mementos from two of your exes. To connect properly with them, and sense what you're looking for in a soulmate."

226

"No, I didn't... I'm sorry."

She heaved an exasperated sigh.

"What do you mean by *mementos*, exactly?"

"Something of theirs. An old shirt they never took back from you, a keychain, a lock of hair..."

I raised an eyebrow. "I don't keep those kinds of things." *Nor does anybody. A lock of hair? Really?*

"I'm sure you'll find something, hun. Come back and we can start."

"Okay." I started for the door, with no intention of coming back. But she called out to me.

"Look in your bathroom. Your girlfriend left a hairtie there."

And when I got home, and looked in my bathroom, sure enough — there was one of Julie Wysocki's purple elastics. I hadn't even noticed it before. A few of her dark, long hairs still stuck to it. I smiled sadly.

I almost miss you, Julie.

It didn't take me long to find an old T-shirt Matt Goldstein left either, hanging in the back of my closet. It still smelled like his aftershave and BO. I recoiled in horror and dropped it in a plastic bag.

In an hour's time, I was back at Avelyn's run-down psychic shop, handing over the items.

"Very good, very good," she said, her nose trailing the surface of the shirt. *Ew.* "What was his name?"

"Matt Goldstein."

"And hers?" she asked, gesturing to the hairtie.

"Julie Wysocki."

"Let me ask — to better understand you. What were your favorite things about Matt and Julie?" A sly smile crossed her lips. "Your favorite *physical* attributes?"

I pictured Julie and Matt in my head. It was hard for me to admit that I liked anything about them; both had dumped me, one over text. Even just picturing them made me viscerally recoil. "I guess I liked Julie's long, dark hair."

Avelyn scrawled notes in a book. "And Matt?"

"His lips." He *was* an amazing kisser.

"Excellent. I promise you — we will get you that soulmate you're looking for." She sniffed deeply into Matt's shirt, then set the two items inside. "I will do some work tonight, and contact you tomorrow morning. But first... we must discuss payment."

"Payment?"

"All magic comes with a price, hun," she said, her eyes twinkling in the darkness.

A chill ran down my spine. "A price?"

"Yes. And the price for this magic," she said, her eyes glittering in the shadows, "is two-hundred-fifty dollars. Cash or credit?"

"Uh. Credit."

As I drove away from the shop, I instantly regretted my decision. *Two-hundred-fifty dollars? For some psychic nonsense?* I shook my head.

I really am getting desperate.

***

I woke up the next morning to a box on my porch.

It didn't have a return address. Or my address, either — it must have been dropped off in person. Only two words were scribbled in the upper corner: *From Avelyn. Open Immediately!*

I picked up the box and carried it inside. It was light, and something rattled softly inside as I brought it over to the table. Honestly, in this age of anthrax and bombs, I probably shouldn't have opened it. But the curiosity nagged at me, until I was standing over it, butterknife in hand. I slid it under the tape.

I pulled out the flaps and peered inside. Dark hair glistened inside. *A wig?* I reached in and pulled it out.

My heart stopped.

Underneath the hair was an *ear*.

It fell from my hands, onto the floor with a wet splat. "What the fuck?!" I screamed, scrambling back from the counter. *No, it's got to be fake. It's got to be.*

I bent over and, gingerly, picked it back up.

The hair was attached to a thin, soft, tan-colored surface. But there was nothing on the other side — no blood, no stains. *It's fake. See? It's got to be fake.*

I slowly reapproached the box.

There was something else inside.

I reached in and pulled it out. It was tan-colored, squarish. Something hard was underneath it, pulling the material taut. And there — right in the middle — was a set of pink, plump lips.

Lips that looked exactly like Matt's.

I dropped it on the counter, my heart racing.

There was one more item in the box. A sheet of paper, folded neatly and tucked away. I plucked it out and began to read.

INSTRUCTIONS FOR ASSEMBLY

1. *Set the scalp (piece A) and jaw/cheeks (piece B) on a clean workspace. Line up the cheeks with the scalp edge.*

2. *Thread a sewing needle with the included thread.*

3. *Sew A and B together by hand. Do NOT use a sewing machine.*

4. *Store in a cool, dry place.*

A note was scrawled in messy script underneath:

Here you go, hun. - Avelyn

P.S. Don't call the police — or you'll be sorry.

I pulled out my phone and called the police. Sorry be damned. *Riiiiiing. Riiiiiiing.* "911, what's your emergency?"

"Someone sent me a box. A woman named Avelyn Mcallister, XX Main Street. It's got... some awful stuff in it. Please, send someone over. XXX Maple Ave." My voice cracked with panic.

"Okay, stay calm. What are the contents of the box?"

"Body parts. They look real. Like, real, actual body parts —"

"Okay. Here's what I need you to do."

"Yeah?"

"You need to take the parts to the counter. Okay?"

"Uh... that's where they are now," I said, confused.

230

"Now, you need to pull the scalp over — so it's lined up the jaw. Then you need to take the thread included in the box —"

The phone clattered to the floor.

After a few seconds of shock, I re-dialed 911. The man on the other end did the same thing — launched into an explanation of how to sew the pieces together. I dialed my local police station next — again, same thing.

I grabbed my jacket and keys. Then I sped over to her little fortune-teller shop.

I found her in the back — feet resting on the coffee table, cigarette in hand. Plumes of smoke curled towards the ceiling. "Avelyn. What did you do?" Tears burned my eyes. I shakily set the box down on the table.

"I *do* a lot of things. Be more specific."

"You killed Julie and Matt."

"No. Of course not. I'm not a murderer, Amy."

"Then where did you get... *those?* Because those lips look *exactly* like Matt's. And the hair's just like Julie's."

"Relax." Avelyn took her feet off the coffee table and took a long drag. "I took those parts from people who were already dead. The local morgue. I have a deal with the mortician."

Ignoring the disturbing consequences of that alone, I shot back, "Why do they look just like my exes, then?!"

"Because I stalked Facebook. I looked up Matt Goldstein, Julie Wysocki. Chose similar features. Simple as that."

"Okay. Well, whatever you're doing... I don't want any part in it. This is absolutely disgusting and evil. You should be arrested."

"Oh, going to try and call 911 again, are you?"

I paled. "How did you know about that?"

"Simple hex." Avelyn waved her hand around at the bookcases with the bogus spellbooks. "Any police officer, first responder, or family member you talk to about this will give you the same answer. So don't bother trying." She leaned over and patted the seat next to her. "Come, sit. I'll show you how to sew them in person."

"I said I don't want any part of this!"

"Don't you want to find true love? Because, let me tell you, you're not going to find it the way you're going. I can see into the future, too. It's all breakups and lonely nights with your cat, hun."

Those words stung.

But I turned my heel, walked out the door, and drove away. Hoping she wouldn't send any hex upon me.

At least, she didn't follow me out.

***

The next morning, I woke up thinking I was rid of Avelyn and her antics.

How wrong I was.

At about 2 PM, I went to the basement for a load of laundry. Juggling the huge basket of dirty clothes, I awkwardly descended the wooden stairs.

What's that smell?

It was an odd combination of chemicals and stink. Similar to the smell in Avelyn's shop. I'd never noticed that smell in my basement before. *Sniff. Sniff.* I smelled the pile of laundry, just to be sure.

Then I turned around.

No.

A shadow. Laid out on the old ping-pong table in the corner.

What the hell? I walked through the darkness. My heart pounded in my chest, thudded in my ears. *I don't remember leaving anything there...*

I stood over the ping-pong table.

My blood ran cold.

Staring back at me was a jigsaw puzzle of a person. Raw, purple, stitched lines ran across its face and body. I recognized the pieces — the dark brown eyes, the dainty hands with the crescent thumb ring. The legs were still missing.

A piece of paper lay next to it.

If you don't do it — I will. -A

The nausea swelled in my throat.

I ran up the stairs. Two at a time. I slammed the basement door shut, drew the chain over it. Then I collapsed against the door. I halfway expected to hear footsteps. Or it pounding the door down, screaming threats at me. Something — anything — other than the dead silence that followed.

No. It's not alive. It's just an amalgam of dead parts... taken from the morgue. Not from my exes. Calm down.

But I didn't calm down.

***

The next morning, another package arrived.

This one was long, stretching across my entire porch. No addresses. Cardboard that was slightly wet at the bottom. When I bent over to pick it up, a sickly stench rushed over me.

With a grunt, I dragged it into the house. Heart pounding, I slit the tape and pulled it open.

I retched.

Two legs. Sliced cleanly at the upper thigh. Instructions were tucked in on the side, as usual. And handwriting scribbled on top:

If you don't do it, I will.

I'm ashamed to say that I did it. I vomited three times before I finished, but I did it. *They were already dead,* I kept telling myself. *Already dead...*

I washed my hands, made some coffee, and sat down at my computer.

They were already dead. They were already dead. Tingling numbness spread over my body like electricity. Then a different thought pounded in my head, with every heartbeat:

What if she lied?

I'd blocked all my exes on social media. It's a policy of mine — one of the worst feelings in the world is seeing your ex with their new partner. And, believe me, they *always* got a new one before I did.

So, with a shaking hand, I opened up Google. Typed in Julie Wysocki.

The third result made my heart stop.

Springfield resident, Julie Wysocki, severely injured in freak accident

My eyes scanned the article.

On Sunday afternoon, Wysocki decided to go biking around her neighborhood. She couldn't find her own helmet, so she decided to use her daughter's, which was too tight. ... As a car came upon her, she collided with it. In the heat and force of the collision, the tight helmet stuck fast to her scalp and ripped it off.

By the time paramedics were on the scene, the helmet — and the scalp — were nowhere to be found.

I pushed the computer away from me, nausea rising in my throat. Black dots swam in my vision. *Fuck, Julie... you didn't deserve that. I don't care if you dumped me — that's awful.*

Thump.

The sound came muffled through the front door.

Avelyn. Dropping off her package of the morning, I bet. I bolted up and ran to the door. Anger supplanted the terror, the dread, the sadness.

I swung the door open.

Avelyn was gone. But there was a box — a small one. I bent over and picked it up. Instructions were taped to the top of the box.

This is the last piece. The heart.

If you want to find your soulmate, install the heart, and then recite the incantation on the other side of this page. If you want to be done with me and all of this, don't. Bury the body when you've placed the heart inside.

It's up to you.

Either way, you're free of me now.

- A

I took the box down to the basement. The figure lay still and stiff across the ping-pong table, eyes shut tight. I plunged a kitchen knife into the chest, slowly pulled it down to create a slit.

I reached into the box. Wet. Squishy. The nausea rose; I swallowed the urge to vomit. Shutting my eyes, I slipped it into the slit.

Now bury the body.

My life flashed before my eyes — my future life. *Home alone. The cat. The ramen. Aging alone... dying alone. No one caring about me. Ever.*

My hands, stained with blood, grabbed its shoulders and started to shift the body. As I did, I looked down at it. It was beautiful, in a way; Julie's long hair, Matt's plump lips, Madison's dainty hands with the crescent rings and Jack's strong legs.

Could be mine.

My soulmate. Forever.

My eyes flicked over to the incantation sheet.

I began to read.

"Ignite this one with the spark of life. Make them my own, forever, to—"

I stopped at the sound of footsteps overhead.

Someone was in the house.

I froze. "Avelyn?" I called. I left the body and ascended the steps, slowly, my heart pounding in my chest. "Avelyn! Is that you?"

I swung the basement door open, clicked it shut. I walked across the foyer, into the kitchen. "Avelyn, is that —"

Four men in dark suits faced me, expressions grim, guns drawn.

"Freeze! Police!"

***

"We can't detain her. We didn't find anything."

"What do you mean, you didn't find anything?! How stupid are you?"

The voices came through the walls of the interrogation room, loud and clear.

"We searched everywhere."

"Everywhere? Even the basement, the closets?"

"Yes, sir. I think we looked everywhere."

The door burst open.

"Amy Greene? You're free to go."

I stood up, shakily, and walked out of the police station. My mind was abuzz, as if I were drunk or intoxicated. Too many thoughts competing for my attention. Too much shock.

"We can give you a ride home," one of the officers said.

"No, thanks. I'll walk."

It was a two mile walk — but my head still wasn't clear by the end of it. *I can't believe I did all of that. I can't believe... how awful desperation made me become.*

Guilt flooded me, burning like fire in my veins. It was as if I'd spent the past few days in some sort of obsessive trance, and cold reality was finally crashing down on me.

I'm a murderer.

Worse than a murderer. I ruined their lives, forever.

I thought of my poor mother. *What would she think if she knew what I did? My poor, old mother, who always believed in me...*

I stopped in front of my house.

The light in my bedroom was on.

Did I leave the light on?

My heart sank with each step, as the guilt turned to imaginary shackles locked to my ankles. I fit the key in the lock, turned the doorknob.

My footsteps clicked across the linoleum.

An overpowering smell of chemicals and rot. A rustling sound. Something shifting, in the shadows of the kitchen.

And then a soft voice, from the darkness:

"I've been waiting for you."

WINDOWS UPDATE

Updates suck.

I was sitting there, doing important work — ok, no, I was reading Reddit and listening to Kansas — when I got up to get a drink. When I came back, the screen was blue, and it said **Installing. Update. 2%**

Well, fuck, I thought. *There goes my next hour.*

When the screen finally loaded, I entered my password. The startup jingle sounded from my speakers.

Not much was different... except the task bar had disappeared entirely. All my desktop icons were gone, too. Except for one: a folder named **Documents.**

I clicked.

In "Documents" there were three files: "personality," "facemap," and a folder called "assets". None of the files looked familiar. Curious, I clicked on the first one.

Personality took a few seconds to open. It was a huge file, crammed with lines and lines of code I didn't understand. Strange words like "var mood" jumped out at me. Since I've never coded anything in my life, I couldn't really make heads or tails of it.

Facemap was a huge image that took several minutes to load. When it did, it was a strange mosaic of images. Curved swaths of golden tan. Half of what looked like a woman's lips. Cut-out, dark eyes, but then a separate piece of the image next to it that was just a curved line of lashes. It looked like someone had (digitally) stripped off a woman's face, laid it flat, and then cut and jumbled up all the pieces. (And if you were artistically inclined, you could reassemble the images on a 3D face.)

Assets was the only one left. I clicked on it. Inside was a long list of files of every type. Audio files — laughter.mp3, sneeze.mp3, footsteppattern.mp3. Images that looked similar to **facemap** in terms of being cut-out, but they looked like clothing rather than skin. Denim texture, floral patterns, slices of high heels.

Curious, I clicked on laughter.mp3.

I stopped dead.

The sound of my own laughter filled the speakers. Playing on a loop. The same wheezing sound I made when I sucked in air, the same hearty chuckle afterwards.

I closed out of it, my heart pounding. As soon as I did — *blip.* A dialogue window popped up.

Are you enjoying your new Windows experience?
YES
NO

I clicked NO.

Blip. It popped up again, asking the same question.

Are you enjoying your new Windows experience?
No.

Are you enjoying your new Windows experience?

No. No. No!

I smacked the lid down, threw my computer on the couch, and walked out of the room. *This is crazy.* I sat down at the kitchen table and opened a Facebook tab on my phone. *Maybe other people are talking about the update.*

They were.

But not in the way I thought.

As I scrolled through my friends' status updates, my heart started to pound.

Katie G.: the new Windows update is amazing!!! Thank u bill gates haha

Eric C: Did you guys try the new update? It's SO GOOD. Like, how did I even use the computer before this?

Divya P.: If your computer didn't download the new update automatically, you can download it manually. Link & instructions in the comments. Don't miss out!

Strangely enough, none of them went into specifics about what changed, or what was awesome. A heavy dread settled into my stomach.

Blip-do-blop.

I glanced at the phone. DAN. "Hey! When are you going to be home?"

"Oh, soon! Yeah. I just wanted to call you to tell you — make sure you update your Windows system today!"

My heart stopped dead. "Uh... what?" I croaked out.

"The new update is amazing! Anyway, I got to go. See you soon, okay?"

Click. I stared at the phone a long time.

Then I ran up to the front door and locked the deadbolt.

Because I'm not entirely sure that was Dan on the phone.

I don't know what to think. Maybe it's a glitch, a strange string of occurrences. Or maybe, for years, Windows has been gathering data. Taking pictures of us through our webcams. Recording the sounds we make.

Maybe, finally, it has enough data to perfectly mimic us.

So, I'm posting this to warn you. Soon, you're going to see your friends, your family, and even Reddit talking about this "awesome new update." They will do anything to get you to download it.

Don't do it.

Get rid of your computer. Unplug it, take out the battery (or let the battery die.) Stow it in your closet and don't open it again.

If you *need* your computer... the ONLY way to block an update is to go into settings, and set your connection as a metered connection. Windows won't download anything on a "metered connection" to save you money. But I'm sure that, soon, they'll change that. And none of us will be able to escape.

Right now, I'm writing this from my phone. As soon as it's posted... I'm getting rid of it, too. It's not a Windows phone, but I'm not willing to take any risks.

Good luck.

MY REFLECTION

I haven't looked in the mirror in 10 years.

I was diagnosed with a psychological disorder. I can't look at photos – or reflections – of myself. It's not a self-esteem thing; at least, I don't think so. I know that I'm average-looking. Maybe even above average. My fiancé tells me I'm beautiful, and I take his word for it.

It's just something that I have.

For the most part, I don't mind it. There are a few bad things – I can't wear eye makeup, for example, because I'll either look like a clown or poke myself in the eye. I can't drive because there are too many mirrors. I have to avoid social media on Throwback Thursday.

I also have to make sure my pots and pans aren't too shiny.

(Okay, that one's a joke.)

I've accepted that this is just how I am, and how I always will be. But last night, as we were getting ready for bed, my fiancé brought it up.

"Sara, we're getting married. And I totally understand if you don't want a photographer at the wedding, because of… you know." He stumbled over his words, squeezed my hand. "But I want to have photos of our wedding. I want to look at them with you when we're old." He stroked my cheek. "I want you to see how beautiful you are on our wedding day."

"I don't know," I replied, pulling away.

"At least consider it?"

"Okay. I will."

I didn't consider it at all.

Until a week later.

I had just finished showering. I shut off the water, pulled on a bathrobe, and began hurrying for the door. That was always my strategy – run out before the steam on the mirror cleared.

Except this time, I slipped.

Hot pain shot up my tailbone. I cried out in pain, but no one could hear me – Sam was out having lunch with a potential client.

Maybe Sam's right. I hobbled off the wet tile and walked out of the bathroom. I'm trying to pretend like this isn't affecting my life, but it is.

My heart began to pound.

I'm going to do it.

I'm going to look in the mirror.

I swung the bathroom door open. Steam poured out, curling towards the ceiling. I waited ten minutes for it to clear completely.

I haven't seen myself for ten years.

Maybe it'll be fine. Maybe this one time will be so hard, but then it'll be okay. Like getting your wisdom teeth out. Or ripping off a band-aid. Or getting a flu shot. Sure, it sucks – it's painful and terrifying – but once you do it, you don't need to do it again for a long time.

I took a shaky step into the bathroom and turned towards the mirror.

My ear and a bit of my hair reflected in the glass, poking out from the doorway.

I didn't feel anything. No fear, no trauma, no terror. It was a little weird seeing a part of myself – the ear looked bigger than I remembered, since I was only a kid the last time I saw it. But other than that, I was fine. *I have nothing to be afraid of,* I told myself.

I took another tiny step.

My jaw, cheek, and a bit of my chin came into view.

There were a few mild acne scars scattering my cheeks. My wet hair was all rumpled and tangled. And I felt fine. My heart soared. *I'm going to be okay. I'm going to be okay!*

I took another step forward.

My eyes came into view.

I jumped back. A strangled scream came from my throat.

Not my eyes. Large, round, black pits where my eyes should be. As if someone cut away all the flesh from my eyebrow to my cheekbone on each one, leaving only darkness.

I ran down the hallway, into my room. I collapsed into the closet and locked the door. It was pitch black in here.

No light. No reflections.

From outside, I heard a sound. A light chuckle.

Coming from the bathroom.

I sobbed and cried and hung my head in my lap. *No no no.* The memories came flooding back – memories of my reflection, as a child. Or not mine – reflections of *that thing.* The thing in the mirror with the big black pits for eyes, that would talk to me every time I saw it.

Another chuckle. Louder this time.

I flew out of the closet. I ran down the stairs, grabbed my cell phone. *Call Sam. He'll make everything okay.*

I grabbed the phone. But when I glanced down at the dark screen –

I saw *its* reflection, staring back up at me.

THE MISSING POSTER

This afternoon, I found a missing poster of myself.

It was stapled to the telephone pole, several feet away. The edges fluttered in the gusts of wind as cars passed by; the middle was crinkled and stained.

My friend, Ava, got to it first. She was always like that – always helping people. She'd help children cross the street, help little old ladies with their groceries. And she'd always take a good look at photos of missing people.

You never know where they could pop up, she'd say. *We might see them and be able to help.*

But when her voice called out to me, it wasn't her usual cheery tone.

"Carlie, come over here."

"What?"

"Come here. Now!"

I huffed and ran across the sidewalk. "Look," she said, pointing at the photo.

With dread settling in my heart, I looked up at it.

It was *me.*

My star-shaped earrings. My wavy, dark hair. The v-neck shirt with the criss-crossing I liked to wear because it made me look older.

"Maybe... maybe it's someone who just *looks* like me," I said. But my eyes glanced over the text, and I knew it wasn't true. *MISSING – Carlie Rodriguez. Height: 5' 6". Weight: 120 lbs. Age: 13 years old.*

Last seen on: 10/18/18.

Today's date.

"How... how can it say I was last seen *today?*" I said. "That doesn't make any sense. It must be a joke or something."

"Pretty sick joke," Ava replied.

I stared the photo. It was strange – it wasn't like the photos that usually accompanied *MISSING* posters. Usually in those, the person is looking in the camera, and it's a pretty close-up shot. In my photo... I was looking off to the right, and further away.

As if the photo had been taken at a distance.

Without my knowledge.

"Come on, let's go, Ava," I said.

"But –"

I grabbed her by the elbow and gave it a hard yank. We continued down the crumbling, stained sidewalk – getting further away from that awful piece of paper with each step.

But the feeling of dread in the pit of my stomach didn't let up.

It got stronger.

I hurried faster down the sidewalk. Ava broke into a run just to keep up with me. The blue-and-white Walmart sign came into view, twinkling in the distance like a beautiful star.

I didn't feel relief when I saw it.

I felt terror.

That's when I finally turned around.

No.

There was a black van behind us. Just a few car-lengths away. The headlights were off – despite the darkening shadows of impending sunset. It crawled along, driving much slower than it should.

Matching our pace.

"Run!" I screamed to Ava.

She didn't need to be told twice. We ran down the sidewalk, emitting those ear-splitting shrieks preteen girls are so good at. A few people in the distance turned to stare at us; a car going the other way stopped. Someone shouted out the window, "are you okay?"

Vrrrrmmm.

The car roared forward. It passed us up and zoomed into the darkness. In its wake, several sheets of paper fluttered out of the window.

I stooped and grabbed one.

Bold, black letters spelling *MISSING* and my own face stared back at me.

We ran as fast as we could, until we got to the Walmart and called for help. I thought we were safe then. I thought I was safe when Ava got to her house and I got to mine. I thought I was safe later that evening, when Mom and I went for a drive to get our minds of it all.

But I wasn't.

Because as we drove down the road, the flashlights rolled over a MISSING poster stapled to a stop sign.

MISSING

Carlie Rodriguez

Last seen on: 10/19/18

ONE OF MY PASSENGERS ISN'T HUMAN

When we left the dock, five people were in the boat. Now there are six.

I didn't notice it right away. I was focused on driving the boat through the murky darkness of the New Orleans swamp. And pointing out gators.

"Alright, everyone, take a look to your left," I called out, cutting the motor. "Between those two cypress trees, see that pair of eyes? That's a gator."

They ignored me, giggling and whispering to each other. "They're not even *looking!*" I groaned to Eric. "We could lose our jobs for this, keeping the boat out after dark. But no, that one girl just couldn't shut the fuck up about how she wanted to see a gator."

"Eh, that's teenagers for you."

I sighed and looked out at the swamp.

The lights on our boat barely penetrated the murky darkness. The cypress trees stood tall in the shadows, like an endless army of gray, thin, faceless people. Clumps of

Spanish moss hung from their arms; their feet disappeared into the black water.

The swamp was silent, except for the croaks of the frogs.

Then –

Splash.

The boat lurched. I fell forward in my seat, as it rocked back and forth. *Splash.*

"Eric – what *was* that?"

But Eric had his phone out, playing some stupid mobile game. "What was what?" he said, his eyes not leaving the screen.

"The splash, the boat rocking..."

He shrugged. "Probably just a gator, Ellen."

A gator... I shivered. It was one thing to point to a gator's glinting eyes, twenty feet away, from the safety of the boat. It was another to hear a loud *splash* in the darkness, feel the boat rock, and wonder if the gator is slithering up the sides with those tiny little –

Splash!

I whipped around.

Silence.

The kids were oblivious. A geeky guy took sneaky sips from a flask, sidling up to an Asian girl in a purple hoodie. A tall guy put his arm around Blondie, the annoying girl who complained about gators earlier. Two white girls giggled to each other, their ponytails bobbing.

Six teenagers, in total.

Not five.

"Eric? We only... had *five* people board the boat."

253

"Yeah. Why?"

I looked at him, my heart starting to pound.

"There are six people back there."

He turned around, his lips moving as he counted them. "Six. You're right."

Eric and I stared at each other. The boat drifted noiselessly through the water, the light glaring off the surface. Around us stood the cypress trees, stretching up to the sky.

"Okay. Tour's over," Eric announced, turning towards the group. "We're turning back. Should be at the dock in five."

Geeky scrambled to hide his flask. Purple Hoodie rolled her eyes. Ponytails One and Two didn't even look up. Tall Guy pulled Blondie close.

I kicked the motor back on. It thrummed under our feet. I grabbed the steering wheel and jerked it left; the boat slowly turned towards the trees. *Why is a K-turn in a boat so hard?*

"Let me drive. I can go faster." Eric stood over me. His usual laid-back attitude was gone. From the corner of my eye, I could see his arms shake, his eyes dart across the swamp.

"But I'm supposed to do it, to learn –"

"Let me drive!" he yelled.

I got up. He grabbed the wheel, jerked the boat back; it nearly hit one of the cypress trees. Then we were zooming back down the channel, the murky water roiling and churning beneath us.

"We probably just miscounted when they boarded, right?" I said. "I mean, I'm not *totally* sure –"

"I am. Only five people boarded, Ellen."

"So what – what does that mean?"

"Someone got on the boat... *after* we left the dock."

"What?" I forced a laugh, even though I felt nauseous inside. "You're saying someone climbed out of the water and onto the boat?"

He didn't reply.

I looked back at the teenagers again. None of them looked familiar... or out of place. Geeky, Purple Hoodie, Tall Guy, Blondie, the Ponytails... I'd been concentrating so much on driving, I hadn't even given the passengers a second glance.

Then I shook my head. *No way. This is crazy. We must've just miscounted when we left.*

The boat cut through the water. The gray silhouettes of the cypress trees dissolved back into shadows; the churning wake glinted like diamonds in the light.

The boat jolted to a stop.

A felled cypress tree lay across the water, half-submerged.

Blocking the path back to the dock.

"Who the *fuck* put this here?"

"*Put* it there? Maybe it just fell..." I offered, barely convincing myself.

Eric shook his head. "Okay, change of plans. You get back there and try to figure out who's the odd man out."

"You don't really think –"

255

He turned to me, his brown eyes blazing with anger. "Do it, *now*."

"Okay." I climbed out of the passenger seat, made my way to the back of the boat. The kids looked at me with wide eyes. "Hey, guys," I said. "I'm Ellen, your tour guide. We just ran into a little hiccup, but then we'll be –"

"Are we going to die out here?" Ponytail One asked.

"Oh my God, Britney, don't ask that," Ponytail Two said.

"We're going to be okay, though, right?" Blondie asked, her voice quavering.

"Yeah, we're just, uh…" I faltered.

"I have to go to the bathroom," Geeky complained. "Like, real bad. If we don't get back soon, can I go in the water?"

Purple Hoodie shot a disgusted look at him.

"Let's just…" I stopped; I had an idea. "You guys all know each other, right? Did you meet anyone for the first time tonight, on the boat?"

Tall Guy pointed straight at me. "You."

I sighed. "I meant *other* than Eric and me."

Murmured *ohs*.

I stepped closer. "Listen, guys. Only five of you boarded the boat. But there are six of you, sitting here." They stared at me. Silent, as the truth dawned on them. "One of you boarded the boat after it left the dock. So I'm asking you again – did you meet anyone for the first time tonight?"

Ponytail One raised her hand. Ponytail Two elbowed her and whispered "this isn't *school*, Britney."

"What were you going to say?" I asked her.

"Just that our school's, like, really big. I only knew Isabella before tonight," she said, pointing at Ponytail Two.

"Same. I only knew Britney," Ponytail Two said, pointing back at her.

"I met *him* once before," Tall Guy said, motioning to Geeky. "He tried out for the basketball team. Didn't make it, though."

Geeky hid his head in shame.

"I didn't know anyone," Blondie said. "Met them all for the first time tonight."

"Liar," Purple Hoodie muttered.

"What?"

"I said, *liar*." She pulled her hood more tightly over her hair, shrouding her eyes in shadow. "Everyone knows you hooked up with *him* –" she pointed at Geeky – "over summer vacation. You just don't want to tell anyone because it's so embarrassing."

"What? That's not true. And, hey – what about you?" Blondie said, staring at Purple Hoodie. "I've never seen *you* before."

"Oh, come on." Purple Hoodie rolled her eyes.

"I've never seen her, either," Tall Guy said.

I looked at the others. The Ponytails shook their heads in unison. Geeky stared at her, as if looking for a redemptive sparkle in her eyes. Then he, too, shook his head.

"So *none* of you know her?"

Silence. All eyes on her.

257

Purple Hoodie's eyes glinted in the shadows of her hood. "But if I didn't know anyone, how would I know about... you two?" She pointed furiously at Blondie and Geeky.

"Wait," Geeky said. "Do you not know our names? Is that why you keep pointing at us?"

"Of course I do. It's... uh..." She faltered. "Caroline and John, right?"

"*Bzzzt!* Wrong answer!" Geeky stood up, pointing an accusing finger at her. "That proves it!"

"Wait, wait," Tall Guy said, squinting at Purple Hoodie. "I think I remember you. You were the one-eyed cow in the 7th grade Nativity scene, weren't you?"

"Oh, my God..." she muttered, her face flushing.

"Oh, yeah! I remember that!" Blondie said. "Moo! Moooooo!"

I turned to Blondie.

And my blood ran cold.

Her hair...

It was damp.

Suddenly, it all made sense. She didn't know anyone. *She* was the one who insisted on seeing an alligator. *She* was the one who wouldn't shut up until we turned the boat around. *She* was the one who made us drive further into the swamp.

If it weren't for her...

We'd be back at the dock right now.

"Did you know the blonde girl before tonight?" I asked Tall Guy.

He looked at me, wide-eyed.

258

Shook his head.

"Do any of you know her?"

One by one, they each shook their heads. Except for Geeky – he nodded enthusiastically.

I paced forward. The *click* of my footsteps echoed against the bottom of the boat. I crouched to her level, looked up into her face.

Blondie's eyes glittered in the dim light, matching the swamp water below. On her lips was a small smirk, utterly unafraid of our accusations.

And her face glistened with a thin film of damp.

I jumped back. "She's it! Eric, she's it!"

Eric stood up, rushed to my side. He stared intently at her, his expression grim.

"Oh, come on!" Blondie scoffed. "It's not me, I swear!"

"Then how come you're all wet?" Tall Guy asked.

"I… I sweat a lot, okay? It's really humid out here!" she said, face flushing. The rest of the teenagers were silent, watching her closely. "Seriously, come on, guys. I see you around at school all the time –"

"Then how come none of us remember you?" Ponytail Two interjected.

Blondie narrowed her eyes at them. "Maybe because I'm cooler than you."

"You're a monster!" Ponytail One shrieked.

"Oh, shut up –"

Ponytail Two stood up. A fiery anger danced in her eyes. "Stop trying to convince us. We all know it's you."

She stepped forward. *Click, click, click.* Blondie backed away, until she was cornered at the edge of the boat.

"Let me go," Blondie said.

Ponytail Two shook her head.

Blondie tried to dart around her. But Ponytail Two was too quick. She leapt forward, grabbed her arms, and pushed.

Blondie toppled over the side of the boat.

Splash.

"It's not me!" Blondie screamed as she resurfaced. Black rivers of mascara ran down her cheeks; her hair stuck fast to her head. She bobbed up and down as she clung to the side of the boat.

"It *is* you!" Ponytail One yelled.

"Fuck, something just grabbed my foot!" She tried to hoist herself back up onto the boat but slipped back down. *Splash.* "Okay, okay, fine – I'll admit it! Jeremy and I hooked up! On my little brother's bed while the rest of my family was on vacation in Bermuda. Ask him if you don't believe me. That clears my name, doesn't it? Please, just get me out of here!"

"It's true," Geeky said hurriedly. "She's telling the truth, guys."

With a sigh, Eric leaned over the side of the boat and pulled her back up. She sat on the bench, drenched and shivering, her tears mixing with the swamp water.

My eyes fell on her arms.

I gasped.

Exactly where Ponytail Two's hands had grabbed her... were two sets of long, bloody claw marks.

260

Blondie looked at me, then at her arms. "Hey – what the fuck did you do to me?" she screamed at Ponytail Two. "What the *fuck* is this?!"

Eric and I whipped around.

The Ponytails stood close to each other. Separated from the rest of the group. Faces hidden in the shadows.

My heart began to pound.

They said they knew each other...

But no one else knew them.

"It's you," I choked out. "Both of you."

There was still doubt in my mind. Doubt that they were the ones who'd joined us. After all, I'd only counted *one* extra person... not two.

That doubt evaporated as soon as they turned to face me.

Glittering black eyes. Crooked smiles. Hands ending in sharp, black claws.

"Surprised it took you that long," Ponytail One said, taking a step towards me. The words came out with a lisp, from the scaly lips, the pointed teeth.

"But – how could it be *both* of you?" Eric asked, his ragged breaths in my ear. "There was only one extra person..."

"We already threw one of the teenagers overboard," Ponytail Two said.

"Yeah. It was easy. A loner type." She snickered. "When she fell in the water, you all barely looked up."

The *splash.* The rocking boat... I suddenly felt dizzy. Faint. Numb.

Eric dove into the driver's seat. "I'm going to try to get to the dock, the long way around. Keep them safe!"

"How?" I yelled. The two Ponytails were already stepping towards the other four teenagers, hungry smiles on their faces.

"Just do it!"

The motor roared to life. The boat sped through the dark, sending white foam flying. The cypress trees rattled in the wind; the moss swung from the branches.

Splash, splash.

Behind the boat, the water roiled and churned.

"There are more of them! Behind us!" I yelled.

Scaly heads punctured the surface. Wet hair fanned out in the inky water, shading their bodies. Black, empty eyes glinted in the light.

They started towards the boat.

I stood between the Ponytails and the other teenagers, trying to keep my eyes off the water. Blondie cowered behind me; Geeky muttered something incoherently to himself.

The two girls just smiled.

Splash!

The boat rocked back and forth, sloshing water everywhere. I glanced down; scaly hands were grabbing at the sides.

"Go faster!" I screamed to Eric.

"I can't!"

I looked down at the floor. Anchors, ropes, hooks… *what could I use against them?*

I didn't have time to find out.

Something yanked me back.

Hard.

The two girls pinned me to the ground. The rest of the teenagers screamed. "We're going to throw you in first," Ponytail Two said, her voice lisping and raspy. Her breath reeked of rotten fish, musty swamp.

"Blondie next!" Ponytail One said. "She's *such* a bitch."

They pushed me against the edge of the boat. The cold metal dug into my back. My hair hung into the water. I could feel the tugging, the pulling, as claws raked through my hair. Snarling, gurgling, ready to devour me as soon as my body hit the water.

I shut my eyes tight, bracing myself –

Thump.

The hands released.

Blondie stood over me. She had Ponytail One by the neck, holding her halfway over the boat. "That's for calling me a bitch, you slimy monster!" she growled. Tall Guy ran over and grabbed her feet. In one coordinated motion, they threw her overboard.

Splash.

Geeky and Purple Hoodie wrestled with Ponytail Two on the floor of the boat. She writhed and slashed at them, but Purple Hoodie didn't back down. *Smack. Smack.* She landed several punches – before Ponytail Two wriggled out of her grasp.

Crack.

Purple Hoodie's body made a sickening *crack* on the floor of the boat.

Ponytail Two dashed over to the front of the boat. She turned to Eric. The dock light was already in sight, a twinkling star in the blackness.

"No!" I screamed, stumbling up.

I wasn't fast enough.

She grabbed Eric and yanked him from the steering wheel.

The boat swerved.

She toppled him overboard.

Splash.

"Eric! No!" I screamed.

The boat was veering towards a dense thicket of cypress trees. Before I could react, Tall Guy ran into the seat, grabbed the steering wheel, and righted our course. Purple Hoodie, with renewed vigor, tackled Ponytail Two.

Splash.

Purple Hoodie leaned over the boat, panting, a triumphant smile on her face.

"Eric? Eric?" I called. I leaned over the side of the boat, staring at the rippling patch of water where Eric fell in.

His head broke through the surface, spraying dark, swampy water everywhere. "I'm okay!" He began swimming towards the boat, closing the several-foot gap between us. "I'm –"

He plunged under the surface.

"Eric! Eric?" I screamed.

The water was still.

"Turn around!" I yelled at Tall Guy. "We have to save him!"

Tall Guy shook his head, pointing towards the water.

Where Eric had been, several of the creatures were diving under the surface. Their faces came up bloody and grinning.

"Faster!" Blondie screamed. I whipped around – the horde of creatures was still advancing through the murky water, now joined by two very angry comrades.

Beyond the halo of light, the shadows shifted between the cypress trees. *Squelch, splash.* The water frothed and bubbled as more heads broke the surface.

Tall Guy's hands were rigid on the steering wheel; sweat glistened on his skin. "I can't go any faster," he said. "I can't, I can't..."

The lights of the dock were brightly in view, piercing the darkness of the swamp. We were close. The stench of funnel cake and cotton candy filled my nostrils. The distant laughter and cheers of people filled my ears.

"Keep going!"

The motor groaned under us. The dock was just several feet away.

Behind me, hisses and splashes, rasping groans –

Thunk!

We collided with the dock.

"Everyone out!" I yelled. I leapt onto the wood; it creaked beneath me. I wrapped the rope around one of the posts. Tall Guy and Blondie climbed out, followed by Geeky and Purple Hoodie.

Splash, splash. Beyond the light, the shadowed heads plopped back into the water.

And then the water was glassy and still.

***

The four teenagers did okay.

Blondie is in college now, a track and field star. Tall Guy is a basketball player at the same place. They've been dating for a while. Geeky and Purple Hoodie remain good friends, despite living in different cities. I'm still here, in New Orleans, giving boat tours every evening. I just never stay out after dark.

As for the Eric and the girl who was thrown overboard... they were never found.

The police investigated and took statements from all of us, but ultimately, their deaths were ruled accidental drownings. Despite no bodies ever washing to shore. Despite Eric being a champion swimmer in college. Their files sit somewhere in the police office, collecting dust, never to be opened again.

I should step forward and tell them the truth.

But I'm not sure they'd believe me.

Some days, I'm not sure I believe myself. I pace the paths near the water, wondering if the whole thing was some sort of hallucination. Some sort of mass hysteria.

But then I look up at the swamp, and I know it was real. Because – just for a second – I see heads poking out of the murky water.

Watching me with glittering black eyes.

VIRTUAL REALITY VACATION

Feeling Tired? Stressed? Take a Virtual Reality Vacation!

The what's the billboard said on the way from Franklin to Country Springs.

At the moment, Finn was screaming bloody murder in the backseat because he dropped his car. Aaron was listening Jason Mraz's *I'm Yours* and head-bopping to the beat. I was driving, my right foot stiff and my left one numb.

"Let's take a vacation."

"What? We can't afford a vacation."

"What about a virtual one?" I asked, pointing to the billboard.

He scrunched his face at me. "No way. That stuff is dangerous. They say some guy played some game on it, and then he couldn't tell reality from the game, and straight-out murdered some people —"

"Wasn't that Cards Against Humanity?"

"Oh. Well, still. All those *games* are the same."

"No, they're not."

I drove the rest of the way home in silence. When I got home, I handed Finn to Aaron. "He needs a diaper change."

"But —"

I went up to our room, pulled out my laptop, and typed in the website.

Stunning photos of beaches filled the screen. Aquamarine waters. Palms swaying in the breeze. Bold, black text read: **PLAN YOUR VIRTUAL REALITY VACATION FOR ONLY $39!** I scrolled down.

5 reasons to book a VIRTUAL REALITY vacation:

- **It's cheap**
- **No jet lag**
- **No bug bites**
- **No sunburn**
- **No embarrassing bathing suit mishaps!**

Pack for 3 days. But don't worry! Time travels differently in our virtual reality system. You'll feel like you had a full two-week vacation!

I needed this. Just a few days ago, I'd accidentally skipped breakfast – and lunch – because I was so busy with Finn. A week ago, I'd almost shelled out a hundred bucks for book that claimed to put babies to sleep without fail. *Goodnight, Precious.* That's how desperate I was.

I clicked the big red button. BOOK NOW.

"Aaron!" I said, walking into the kitchen, which reeked of baby poop. "I'm going away to my mom's for a few days."

He lit up. "Oh, that's just great!"

"*Without* Finn."

"...What?"

"You two will be okay without me, right?"

"I... I guess."

"Mama mama!" Finn said, smiling at me.

I leaned in and kissed his forehead. I *would* miss his sweet, smiling face.

But I needed this. I couldn't remember the last time I had a day to myself. I'd been stuck for almost two years in this rut of dirty diapers and tantrums. Even just taking a 15-minute shower felt like a luxury.

"When are you leaving?" he asked.

"Tomorrow morning."

"Okay." He reached over the mess of poop and gave me a hug. "I'm sorry if I made you sad. I didn't mean to — in the car —"

I shook my head. "It's okay. I'm not mad, Aaron. I just need to get away."

He nodded.

"I'll miss you," he added, as I climbed the stairs to pack.

"I'll miss you too."

***

The building was not what I expected.

Suite 4A, in a dilapidated office building. The few suites next to it were empty, the wallpaper torn where the business placards once hung. I raised my fist and knocked three times.

"Come in!"

My doubt evaporated as soon as I walked in. The office was modern and professional. It mildly resembled a doctor's office, with a secretary behind sliding glass panels and tiled floor. A sign read *Virtual Reality Vacations by Black Widow, Inc.*

"I'm Danica Kelly," I said.

She clacked at the keys. "You may go into Room 3!" she said in a perky, chipper voice.

I followed the white halls to the room. A leather recliner stood in the middle, next to a small desk, a laptop, and a headset.

A tall, blonde woman came in after me. "Please, have a seat," she said in the most soothing voice I've ever heard. "So, Danica — are you ready for your vacation?"

"Yes," I groaned. "Please. I need this. I have a toddler."

She laughed. "I know how it is. Don't even feel like yourself, right?"

"Exactly."

She laughed. "Well, don't worry. You will be *so* refreshed after it, your family won't even recognize you."

She picked up the headset and lowered it over my face.

"Just relax," she cooed. The image of a sunny beach faded in. Aquamarine water. Palms swaying in the breeze.

"Relax."

***

The vacation was incredible.

I sunbathed on a private island. Built a castle out of pink Bahama sand. Swam with dolphins. Snorkeled in a coral reef. Pet a turtle.

And it all felt so *real*.

The "two weeks" went by all too soon. Before I knew it, I was watching the sun rise over the ocean, waiting for my 11 AM checkout time.

Surprisingly, though, I wasn't sad.

In fact, I was happy.

I can't wait to hug Finn again. And Aaron.

I smiled to myself as I imagined Finn, sitting on the floor, playing with his cars. *Vrrrooooom! Vrrrrrrooooom!* he'd say, pushing them along the carpet. When I walked in, he'd look up and say "Mama! Mama!"

And that was more beautiful than any sunrise — real or not.

Soon enough, the credits rolled up on the screen. **THANK YOU FOR CHOOSING VIRTUAL REALITY VACATION. WE HOPE YOU ENJOYED YOUR STAY!**

Beep, beep.

Click.

The headset loosened. I reached up to pull it off. My arms felt surprisingly stiff and achy, and a sharp pain jabbed me inside my elbow. *I guess I have been just sitting here in this chair for three days.*

The headset came off.

What?

The room looked... different. Dilapidated. Old. The clean white paint was peeling; the floor was cracked.

"Hello?" I called. "I'm done."

No reply.

I started to get up. The sharp pain jabbed in my elbow, again.

I looked down.

My heart stopped.

A needle was taped to the skin. Leading from it was a thin tube, that curled and coiled up to the ceiling. Some sort of fluid passed through it.

"Hey! Is anyone there?" I shouted.

Silence.

I ripped it out with a yelp of pain.

I looked down, again. My pants were gone. I was instead covered with a thin sheet. Two more tubes snaked out from under it.

I ripped those out, too, whimpering in pain.

Then I hobbled up, pulled on my pants, and walked over to the door. I yanked it open. The hallway was in the same state of disrepair. Peeling paint. Cracked floor.

What the hell is going on?!

I ran out into the waiting room.

It was empty.

I ran down the stairs, out into the parking lot. The asphalt cracked and buckled; weeds poked through. My car was gone. In fact, all the cars were gone, save for a red Civic at the end of the lot.

What the hell is happening?

I pulled out my phone. It was dead.

I walked out onto the sidewalk. Cars whizzed past me. I walked until I reached the main road. I held my hand out for a taxi, but none passed.

Finally, a pickup truck rumbled to a stop next to me.

"Hey, lady," the guy said. "Need a ride?"

"Oh, no, I'm just waiting for a taxi —"

"Taxis don't come here no more," he said. "Come on. Hop in. Where ya goin'?"

"Uh… Monmouth Place."

"It's outta my way, but I'll take you there."

I weighed my options. It was cold out. My phone was dead. There were no taxis.

I opened the door and climbed in.

We drove in silence, only broken by loud *smacks* of chewing gum. Finally, we pulled up to the small ranch on the cul-de-sac.

"Thanks for the ride."

"No problem, ma'am."

I stepped out. I grabbed my keys and put them into the lock.

They didn't fit.

I jammed them in again.

Not even close.

"Aaron! Aaron, can you let me in?" I called. "My keys don't fit, and —"

The door creaked open.

A woman I didn't recognize stood there. "Who are you?" she snapped, eyes narrowed.

"Who the hell are *you?!*" I shouted back.

My confusion boiled into anger. *No. Gone for three days, and he invites some woman over? Hell, no.* "Where's Aaron?"

An 11 or 12-year-old boy peered out from behind the woman. "Oh! Are you the new mail lady?"

"Where's Aaron?" I asked again.

Footsteps thudded inside the house. The tall, lanky shape of a man appeared. His eyes were sunken with wrinkles; his hair was peppered with gray.

But it was undeniably Aaron.

As soon as he saw me, he went pale. "Danica. What are you doing here?"

"Where's Finn?" I asked, my voice shaky. "What's going on?"

"I'm Finn," the boy piped up.

"No — what —"

Aaron stepped out onto the porch and closed the door behind him. "You can't just come back here. After so long."

"What are you talking about?"

"The last ten years!" he shouted, his voice halfway between a scream and a sob. "Why did you leave, Dani? Why? We were happy. We were a family."

I stared at him, confused and terrified.

"The first few weeks, Finn cried for you everyday. And, if I'm honest — so did I. But I guess you didn't even care."

"I do care. I didn't —"

"No." His eyes glittered in the light. "Now I finally have a good life. A good family. Don't take that away from me."

"Aaron, I —"

"No. I'm done."

He walked back into the house and slammed the door. Inside, I saw Finn smiling at his new mom, eagerly grabbing a sandwich.

It *was* Finn. The upslanting brown eyes, the olive skin, the pointed nose. Not a baby anymore. Grown up.

I missed everything.

I started away from the house, missing the clumsy toddler hugs Finn used to give me. The cold wind nipped at my face, my hands. The snow crunched under my feet.

I waited until the sun sunk behind the trees. Until Aaron and his new wife were in bed. Then I went in through the back door – he always left it unlocked – and crept up the stairs.

I can't believe he just married some new woman. His wife… and Finn's new mom. I felt the heat rush to my face as I stepped towards the bedroom. *He never cared for me.*

The door creaked open.

I stepped inside.

Finn slept peacefully under the covers. Various awards and diplomas hung on the wall – things I'd never been part of. Things I missed.

I covered his mouth.

Then I pulled him out of bed.

I dragged him down the stairs. He thrashed and wriggled against me. I didn't remove my hand until we were out in the cold night air.

"You're crazy!" he yelled. "Get away from me!"

"I'm your mother," I said, dragging him by the hand. "And you're coming with me."

TUTORING

I met her on the internet.

My daughter needs help with Algebra 2. Please contact me ASAP. – Gina T.

She gave me her address for an appointment. XX Laurel Ct.

Rolling up her long, wooded driveway, I couldn't believe my eyes. Her house was enormous – easily five times the size of mine. Carved columns rose up to the sky. Two stone statues of lions flanked the front door. I grabbed the bronze knocker, carved in the shape of a boar's head, and swung it hard. *Clank, clank, clank.*

For a minute, there was complete silence.

Then I heard the *thumps* of footsteps and the *clink* of the lock. "You must be Annie," said a short, plump woman with bright blue eyes. "I'm Gina."

As I stepped in, a strange feeling settled in my stomach. The house… was weirdly empty. The kitchen didn't have a table. The living room had a single, dusty sofa. The air was damp, cold, musty.

And – all the lights were off. Only natural light, pouring in from curtainless windows, lit the place.

"Just moved in?" I said, despite the lack of boxes.

"Oh – uh – yeah," she said hurriedly. "Yeah, we're just moving in. Come on, Greta's in the study." She led me into a back room. A nervous-looking girl sat at the desk, her hands folded over a blank notebook. She was tall and lanky, with dark eyes and hair, unlike her mother.

Greta didn't say much as we started the session. Since Algebra 2 classes begin with a review of Algebra 1, I wrote out some $y=mx+b$ equations for her. She graphed the lines perfectly. *Struggling?* I thought. *What kind of standards does this mother have?*

I'd tutored kids like that. Where the mother thinks "struggling" is an A-. So I rolled with the punches and gave her some more questions.

As her pencil scratched away, I looked around at the study. Like the rest of the house, it was mostly empty. The bookcase in the corner only held dust. Curiously, on the back of the door, there were long, indented lines that ran almost the entire height of it.

Almost like scratches.

"Where's your textbook?" I asked, when I ran out of questions to give her.

She looked around. "I don't have one," she replied.

"You didn't buy one yet? Or the school didn't give you one yet?"

"School?" she asked, eyes unblinking. "I don't go to school."

278

Oh, a homeschooler. I'd dealt with them too. Generally they were smarter – and weirder – than the public school kids. Which fit Greta perfectly.

I wrote out another equation and handed it to her.

That's when the noise started.

Eeeeeeeeee!

A high-pitched whine, coming from outside the door. "What *is* that?" I said, before I could stop myself.

Greta didn't reply. Her pencil scratched quickly over the paper, working on the problem.

"Greta?"

She ignored me, scribbling furiously over the page. Her hair hung limply over her face, concealing her expression. Fear pounded through my body.

"Greta, what is it?"

She wordlessly slid the piece of paper back to me.

Under the chicken scratch of x's and y's were six letters.

GET OUT

"Greta, what –"

She held a finger to her lips and shook her head. When I didn't move, she leaned over me and furiously wrote another word:

NOW!

Stunned, I grabbed my bag. I walked over to the door, swung it open. Stepped out into the hallway.

That's when I understood.

Gina – if that's even her real name – was in the kitchen. In her hand was a whirring, whining bone saw.

The stove was on; the blue flame shimmered. A greased metal pan sat over it, the oil sizzling and popping.

I ran to the door. My thundering footsteps drew the attention of Gina; she looked up, her eyes wide with fright.

Then she stepped towards me.

I yanked the door open. I ran over the stone walkway, the damp grass, and didn't stop until I was sitting in my locked car.

Then I peeled out of the driveway and never looked back.

***

By the time the police came, the house was empty.

Well, emptier than it had been before. Greta and Gina were gone. The house – XX Laurel Ct. – had been abandoned for months, they told me.

In the basement, the police made a gruesome discovery. Three bodies were found. They were identified as local missing people – a professor, a teacher, a scientist.

All of them were missing their brains.

CHOO-CHOO

We found the train set for $5 at a garage sale.

I couldn't believe my eyes – something like this would sell for $100, or more, at the local toy store. It was a complete set, with railroad ties that fit together like pieces of a jigsaw puzzle, a beautiful red engine with painted gold details, and ten train cars that hooked up to each other. And it had all the extras – little spruce trees made of wood and plastic needles, a few stoplights that flashed for train crossings, and even a little conductor man.

"Get it," Jake replied. "For five bucks, that's a steal."

We happily loaded it into the car. As soon as we got home, we started setting it up. "This is so cool!" Danny said, greedily grabbing the pieces from our hands. In less than ten minutes, he'd snapped the pieces together to form a circular track, and was pushing the trains along while making *choo-choo* sounds.

"Danny, let me put some batteries in for you. Then we'll *really* see it go choo-choo."

He reluctantly handed over the engine car. I turned it over in my hands; smooth, black plastic. No battery compartment.

"I thought it was one of those electric ones," I grumbled to Jake.

"Still worth the five bucks," he replied. "Besides, Danny loves it."

And he did. For hours, I heard him *choo-chooing* in the family room. Before long, the track was snaking into the kitchen, in front of the cat's bed and next to the oven. I internally swore as I tripped over it half a dozen times.

That night, Danny fought bedtime. "I want to play with the train more," he complained, as I pulled on his dog pajamas.

"Tomorrow you can play with it all you want," I replied, pulling the blankets over him. "I promise." Then Jake and I retired to our room. After watching a bit of TV, we were fast asleep.

Rrrrrmmm.

I jolted awake. A low, rumbling noise filled the house, like distant thunder. *That's weird. I didn't think it was supposed to storm.*

Rrrrrrrrrrrrrmmmmm.

But it didn't fade, like thunder would. It was a constant, rumbling noise, accompanied by a low *click-click-click* sound. *An earthquake? A bomb?*

"Jake! Do you hear that?" I whispered.

Silence.

I stretched my hand out to shake him. "Hey, Jake –"

My hands fell on empty covers.

282

"Jake?"

I sprung out of bed. I walked into the bathroom; it was empty. "Jake?" I whispered, walking out into the hall. "Jake, where are you?"

That's when I saw that Danny's bedroom door was hanging open.

And his bed was empty, too.

My heart throbbed painfully in my chest. "Jake? Danny?" I yelled, running down the stairs. The rumbling sound grew louder. "Where are you?"

I flicked the lights on.

Ch-ch-ch-ch-ch.

The room was empty, except for the train. It slowly moved along the tracks, rumbling and clicking as it went.

Why's the train on? I gingerly stepped over it, and peered into the kitchen. Empty. *Maybe Danny had trouble sleeping, and Jake started playing train with him to calm him down.*

But then, where are they now?

Wooooo – ooooo.

The sharp sound of the train's whistle broke me from my thoughts. I looked down at it, as it chugged along.

And then I remembered. *How is it moving? It doesn't have batteries.*

I snatched it off the track. The wheels still spun, almost angrily, as if the train was mad I ripped it off the tracks. I looked it over, again; the smooth plastic bottom, the meticulously-painted exterior.

My eyes fell on the windows.

And then, the two pairs of hands pressed against the glass.

I brought the train closer to my face. There were two figurines inside that I hadn't noticed before. Frozen still, hands pressed against the glass, mouths painted wide open. The larger one wore a white T-shirt; the smaller one wore dark blue pajamas. With little dogs on them.

The train clattered to the floor.

MY NAME WAS ON THE NEWS

I was sitting on the sofa, eating a reheated slice of pizza, when I saw it.

My Facebook profile picture. On the local news. Underneath the text: *PRIME SUSPECT IN JACKSON MURDER.*

I blinked. Rubbed my eyes once, twice.

"The prime suspect is 24-year-old Hamburg resident, Amanda Duffy." *My name. She said my name.* My heart doubled its tempo in my chest. "Kaylee Jackson's family demands justice. We all do."

"Who the hell is Kaylee Jackson?" I shouted at the newscaster.

As if to answer my question, a photo flashed up. A little girl. Curly black hair, tied into tight braids. Denim overalls. A beautiful smile.

I've never seen that girl before.

"Kaylee's mom dropped her off at school on the morning of December 7th. But she never came home.

Around 7 PM, her mother called the police. It wasn't long before..." The newscaster coughed, clearly overcome with emotion. "It wasn't long before they found her body, at the bottom of a ditch along I-95."

My heart pounded in my chest. *December 7th, December 7th...* I eyed the empty whiskey bottle, tucked behind the trash can. *Sure. I drank that morning... Like I have every Friday morning, since the breakup.*

But I've never seen that girl in my life.

The news cut to a video. A tear-stained mother. "We lost everything because of her," the woman said through sobs. "We need... we need to bring Amanda to justice. What she did to my little girl..." She never finished the sentence. She just crumbled into choking sobs.

I stared at the TV. Numb. Paralyzed.

I've never seen that girl in my life.

I eyed the empty bottle of whiskey again. Peeking out from behind the trash can.

Then I stood up. "I didn't *do* anything!" My knee collided with the table; the pizza slid off, hit the linoleum with a wet *slap*. "I've never seen that girl in my life! Don't you understand? I never even met her!"

"As we speak, police are heading to Miss Duffy's door," the newscaster said. "She will be brought to trial — and no doubt punished severely for this heinous crime. Now, on to the weather..."

No. Police? Now?

My heart thudded in my chest.

I ran over to the doors. Instinctively, my fingers turned the locks. I shoved a chair against the door. *Don't*

286

let them in. No — no, you have to let them in. The truth will come out. You're innocent. You are.

You never met her.

I grabbed my cell phone. *Call Mom. She'll know what to do.* But as my fingers slid over the screen, I saw the message:

39 New Messages

Shaking, I began to read.

You are fucking devil spawn. Don't you ever contact me again. Rot in hell.

From my best friend of nearly 20 years, Shawna.

I hope you get the death penalty. I can't believe you killed that poor little angel. Blocking your number now.

From my sister.

I dialed my mom's number. "Mom?" I cried, when she picked up. "Mom! Did you see —"

"I gave you so much," Mom said, nearly unintelligible through sobs. "I raised you... I loved you... I gave up everything for you. Why did you do this, Amanda? Why?"

"I didn't do anything!"

"How can you lie to me? How can you lie, at a time like this?!"

"Mom, I didn't —"

"Tell the truth. I don't — I don't care if you lie to me. But tell the police, tell those poor parents, the truth. That's the least you can do."

Click.

I walked over to the front door, removed the chairs, and unlocked the door. With a deep breath, I yanked the doorknob and swung it open. The icy air stung my face, fluttered through my blouse.

I didn't do anything.

The truth always comes out.

Doesn't it?

I waited there for what seemed like hours. Until my arms were numb with cold, my legs stiff and aching. Until the night grew still as a tomb, and tiny stars winked down from above.

No one ever came.

So I began driving to the police station. *I'll tell them exactly what I know.* I slowed as I approached the stop sign. *That I saw the broadcast, but I didn't —*

I froze.

A woman was crossing the street, holding the hand of a little girl.

A girl with braided pigtails, denim overalls.

What the hell? I shook my head. *No. I didn't just see that.* But as I took a second look, I recognized the mother, too. Short brown hair, wine lipstick, heavily-tweezed eyebrows.

If they're alive...

How am I guilty of murder?

I rolled down the window. "Hey! Are you Kaylee Jackson?" I shouted out the window.

The little girl turned back to me, fearfully. As soon as the mother saw me, she hurried up, practically dragging her along the sidewalk.

"Hey! Come back here!" I yelled. "Aren't you the Jacksons?"

They disappeared into the night.

I sat there at the stop sign, the car rumbling underneath me. *If they're alive... why did they broadcast that story?* A terrible dread filled me. Something was very, very wrong.

So I didn't turn left for the police

I continued straight — to the news station's office.

The building was still lit up, despite the fact that the broadcast had ended more than an hour ago. I pulled into a parking space in the back, shoved my hands into my pockets, and tried the door. It was open.

Creak.

The lobby was empty. A low buzzing sound filled the room. The HNN logo on the wall shined in the light, along with the familiar little icon of a dove.

I turned left and walked down the hallway. As I walked, a low rumbling sound filled my ears.

Voices.

I walked towards them, careful to keep my steps quiet.

"Alright, good job, everyone!" a man was saying loudly, in a chipper tone. "Especially good job to you, Rebecca. Wow."

I flattened myself against the wall. The door at the end of the hall hung open a few inches, spilling out golden light.

"Thank you," a woman's voice said.

"Really, you outdid yourself. With the tears, and the calls for justice. Amazing." The man — or someone —

clapped his hands together. "So, Amanda Duffy is ruined."

I started at my own name.

"Who's next?"

The sound of papers shuffling. "Looks like it's Reginald Smith," a third voice piped up. "What do you want to do with him?"

"Who is he?"

"He's one of the bums. Homeless for a good part of his life, now lives in one of the crappy apartments on Maple Ave. Trying to get his life together, keep his job."

"Ah, I see," the man replied. "How about rape?"

"We could do that."

"Make it a pretty blonde woman. Everyone loves those."

"I'll make some calls, see if we can get one of the college students."

"And you, Rebecca — you write up a script to read on air."

"Of course."

"Okay! Well, that's all for tonight. Good job, everyone!"

Rustling movements. Heavy footsteps.

Coming towards the door.

I ran out of the building as fast as I could. The icy wind slapped against my skin. My heart pounded in my chest. I raced across the parking lot, towards my beat-up sedan.

"Hey! It's her!"

I looked up to see a couple was crossing the parking lot, from the offices on the other side. "It's the woman who murdered that poor little girl!" the woman shrieked.

"Rot in hell!" the man shouted.

Crash.

A glass bottle exploded at my feet, hurled by the man.

I scrambled to the car, yanked the door open, and peeled out of the parking lot. *Clank* — another projectile clanged against the bumper.

I pulled out into the dark street.

Then I turned left for Maple Ave. When I got there, I ran up to the building and buzzed the button next to REGINALD SMITH.

"Hello?"

"Hi, um. My name is Amanda Duffy, and —"

"The *murderer?!*"

Dammit. I shouldn't have led with that. "Listen. You're in danger," I said, ignoring him. "Tomorrow night, the local news is going to accuse you of rape —"

"Sounds like you're threatening me."

"No, I'm not. *They* are. Listen to me — there's something terrible in this town —"

"Yeah. You."

Click.

After a few moments of silence, I started away from the door.

That's when I saw the police officer.

Smack, smack. His footsteps smacked against the cement. The crackles of a radio echoed through the darkness.

291

What if he sees me? Tries to arrest me? I ducked behind a hedge.

He stopped in front of the apartment building. But he didn't ring the bell. He just stood there, outside the door. Watching.

Then he picked up his radio.

Crackle. "John's here. Outside Smith's building now."

"You got eyes on him?"

"No. But he's home. I'll make sure he doesn't leave."

"Good." Pause. "Make sure no one — and I mean *no one* — can give him an alibi. We don't want our viewers losing faith in us, after all."

"Of course."

I snuck behind the bushes, around the back of the building. Then I slipped into the parking lot, ducked in the car, and drove home.

***

The next day, I tried to warn him again.

This time I got lucky. Someone was exiting as I arrived. I barely caught the door in time.

When I got to his apartment, the door was already hanging open.

"Reginald?"

I took a step into the apartment. The smell of whiskey hit me like a truck. An open suitcase lay on the floor, spilling clothing. "Reginald?" I called.

The door swung shut behind me.

"Don't move."

I whipped around. There he stood, between me and the door. Dark curls, touched with gray. Tired blue eyes. A bottle of whiskey in one hand, sloshing its contents onto the floor.

"It's you. Amanda Duffy."

I nodded, backing away.

"You know, there was a police officer outside my apartment all night," he said, pointing a shaking finger at me. "Did you call him?"

"No, I —"

"I was just getting my life together! I got a job. The apartment. My ex-girlfriend is finally letting me visit our son again." He quickly stepped towards me, closing the gap between us. "And now you're calling the police, so they can put me in jail for a gram of weed?"

"No! I was trying to warn you! The officer was one of *them*. With HNN."

"What are you, some kind of tinfoil-hat conspiracy theorist?"

"No! Didn't you see the news? They accused *me* of murder! I'm not a murderer!" I backed away from him. My heel hit the wall. I shrieked in fear and closed my eyes.

"Okay, okay! Sssshhh." He backed away, set the bottle down. "I'm sorry. I didn't mean to scare you. I just... I thought you were trying to get me in trouble. I have a lot of enemies." He stared at me, blue eyes soft. "What are you trying to say, then?"

I took a deep breath. "Okay. Last night, I was in HNN's building." I took a seat on one of the lumpy couches, keeping my distance. "I overhead them —

planning today's story. They said they were going to accuse you of raping some pretty, blonde woman. And the officer outside your apartment was there to make sure you didn't leave... so you wouldn't have an alibi."

His face paled.

Then he spoke in a quiet tone. "I'm not saying I believe you. But, if you're right — we need to stop them. This is my last shot — at everything."

We made it to the HNN building in ten minutes flat. As we pulled into the parking space, my heart plummeted.

A pretty, blonde woman — wearing a hoodie with the words CARLTON UNIVERSITY — was standing on the sidewalk. Talking to a tall, thin man with spiky black hair.

"No, no, no. I bet that's her." My heart dropped. "She's probably going to go on air, read the script. Everyone's going to believe her and —"

I stopped. Rebecca was swinging the front door of the building open. She motioned them inside with a smile.

"Okay. We'll go in behind them. When they get ready to film the broadcast... we'll intervene. And then we'll tell them everything. That we're not going to stand for it." The doors swung shut behind the three of them. "That sounds good. Right?"

But Reginald was already yanking the car door open. Before I could stop him, he was running across the pavement.

"Wait!" I sprinted after him.

The air inside the building was uncomfortably warm. The HNN logo shined in the dim light. Down the dark hallway, a green light glowed: ON AIR.

Rebecca's voice echoed out into the hallway. "Good evening, Hamburg. Tonight, we have tragic news to report. Last night at around 11 PM, Marisa Fox — a sophomore at Carlton — decided to go for a quick jog. But that decision cost her everything."

A high-pitched voice began: "I was... I was so scared. He suddenly jumped out of the bushes and ambushed me. Like he'd planned it all along. I tried to get away but he — " sniffle — "he was too strong."

"Marisa has already spoken with police. She identified her attacker as Reginald —"

Reginald yanked the door open.

"Hey!" he yelled. "Hey, you!"

Rebecca turned, eyebrows slightly raised. Marisa leaned towards Rebecca, fear on her face.

"I didn't do anything! I'm innocent!" He aggressively stepped towards them. "You hear? Innocent!"

Two burly men moved towards him from the perimeter of the soundstage. But the tall, thin man — who was sitting behind the row cameras — shook his head. Rebecca gave a small smile, and continued: "The attacker was —"

Reginald lunged at them.

"No!" I shouted.

But it was too late. Reginald charged the stage and roughly grabbed Marisa. "I didn't *do* anything to you," he shouted. "You know that. You *know*. Tell them."

"Get off of me!" she shrieked, her fake tears turning to real ones. "Please, stop it!"

Rebecca shot a smile to the tall, thin man in the back. Then she immediately twisted her face into a fake look of terror. "Somebody call the police!" she moaned.

"This is my *last chance*. My last chance at a normal life," Reginald growled. "I won't let you ruin it all with some fake story. I won't."

The red lights of the cameras blared through the darkness, like dozens of tiny eyes. The faceless cameramen hunched behind them, chattering excitedly. Swiveling their equipment towards him.

Reginald. No. Please, please stop.

His arm looped around her neck, squeezing. "I'll let you go if you tell them," he said, his voice taking on a hurried, manic tone. "Tell them I didn't do anything to you. Tell them."

"Okay," she coughed. "You didn't — do anything — to me last night."

"Hands in the air!"

The door burst open. Two police officers charged in, guns cocked. "Hands in the air, or we'll shoot!"

Reginald backed away. Put his hands in the air.

He shot a glance at me. *Go,* he mouthed. *Go.*

I took off. I climbed in the car, peeled out of the parking lot. Thankfully, no one followed; they were all too distracted by the commotion.

The next day, the headline on HNN read:

LOCAL NEWS ANCHOR AND COLLEGE STUDENT ATTACKED BY REGINALD SMITH.

***

The next day I made a decision.

I slipped a knife into my pocket. Zipped a hoodie up to my neck. Slipped a flash into my hoodie in case I needed it later.

Then I drove over to the HNN building.

The halls were quiet at this time of night. Fluorescent bulbs flickered overhead, casting the hallways in shifting, dancing shadows. My hands were shaking. And my legs. I took a sip of whiskey from the flask, and felt the pleasant burn creep down my throat.

I can do this. I can do this.

I entered the elevator. Every floor I stopped at seemed empty – except for the top floor. This one was remodeled with sparkling-white walls, birch linoleum, and brass doorknobs. Low murmurs flowed and ebbed through the halls.

I took a shaking step off the elevator.

The first door on my left had a light on. Gripping the knife, I walked towards it.

Creeeeaaaak.

It was filled with clutter. But not news-related clutter. A small bottle read *Dr. Widow's Face-Tastic Exfoliating Mask,* rolled it in my hands. Stacks of pamphlets sat on the table – *book a Virtual Reality Vacation today!* and *take our Love Simulator for a spin.* There was even a random pamphlet for Lasik surgery.

What is all this junk?

Then my gaze caught on a stack of small, white AirPods.

My friend Emily had been *obsessed* with those. She wore them constantly – never took them off, even when she was talking to people. It was really weird, but she somehow seemed to hear even better with them on.

It was only a few days after she started wearing them that she disappeared.

I turned over one of the cases. On the back, rather than showing the classic Apple logo, it read *Black Widow, Inc.*

Why is all this stuff here?

I shook my head and walked out of the room.

As I continued down the hallway, the voices got louder. I peeked into the second room on the right – a man and woman were arguing. I didn't recognize either.

Just find Rebecca.

I crept past the door and continued down the hallway.

At the very end there was a closed door. Holding my breath, I peeked into the small window installed in the door.

A head of dark hair. A red blouse.

Rebecca.

I pulled out the knife and turned the doorknob.

GOODNIGHT, PRECIOUS

My son is 2 years old and does. Not. Sleep.

So when I saw an ad online for **Goodnight Precious: the only book GUARANTEED put your child to sleep,** I clicked. I was skeptical — but there was a video demonstration on the website.

"I'm going to show you how this works. Right now, I've got a child in bed." The goateed man motioned to a 3 or 4-year-old boy lying in bed, wide awake. "I'm going to read the book to him. Watch what happens."

The video cut to him finishing the book. "The sun is set, and you slumber. Goodnight precious, little wonder."

As soon as he closed the book, the boy's eyes fixed straight ahead. Blank. Motionless.

Then they fluttered shut.

"No wakeups in the middle of the night, either. Once he falls asleep with this book… he *stays* asleep," the man said, over the boy's light snores.

I was sold.

I clicked the order link. It was close to a hundred dollars, but I didn't care. In three days, I had the book in my hands. It was a lot thinner than I expected — only a few cardboard pages. The cover was a drawing of a boy sleeping in bed, as an old woman (maybe his grandma?) watched him from a rocking chair in the corner.

I read it to Jackson that very night. "It's time to go to sleep, little dear. When you wake up, I'll still be here," I read softly. The illustration showed an old woman tucking a child into bed. She wasn't smiling.

I glanced at Jackson. Still wriggling and wide awake. But he seemed to be enjoying it, at least.

"Night has fallen, stars are out. Go to sleep now — don't you pout." This image showed the same woman, sitting in a rocking chair next to her sleeping child.

"You'll sleep through sadness, sleep through pain. And when it's done, we'll do it again." *That rhyme's really a stretch...* I glanced at the image. The woman was getting out of her seat, walking towards her son's bed.

"Go to sleep now, little one. Be patient, now — we're almost done." In this drawing, the woman was looking down at her sleeping child from the bedside. She was holding a pillow.

I turned the page, to the last one.

My heart stopped.

The old woman was pressing the pillow over the child's face. Smiling, with one of those cartoonish grins you often see in kids' books.

I read, in a soft, cautious voice: "The sun is set, and you slumber. Goodnight precious, little wonder."

I closed the book and looked over at Jackson.

He was fast asleep.

300

It really works! I moved him to his bed, and enjoyed some well-earned alone time. *Who cares if the book is a little weird... it really works!*

An hour later, I was asleep.

***

I woke up at 8.

Jackson didn't wake me — at all. A welcome change from the usual. I looked over to his still, slumbering body and smiled.

But by 11 AM, he still hadn't woken up.

He never sleeps this late.

Maybe he's sick?

I turned on some light music, talked to him. I patted his back. No response. "Jackson?" I said. I picked him up, put him on my lap.

His head slumped against my chest.

"Jackson? Are you okay?"

Nothing. Just his soft, deep breaths against me.

"Jackson? Jackson, wake up!"

Nothing.

I yelled in his ear. I bounced him up and down. I brought him out in the sun.

Nothing woke him up.

Now, it's almost 3 o'clock. He's been asleep for 19 hours. I'm about to load him into the carseat and drive him to the doctor. I think something is terribly wrong with him.

MY HUSBAND
CHANGED

My husband changed after I married him.

Ben used to be loving, kind, amazing. Every day, he'd tell me I was beautiful. Call himself the luckiest man alive.

But just a few days after the wedding, everything changed.

I'm miserable, he said.

You're ruining my life.

I wish I never married you.

You're an ugly, stupid, thoughtless bitch.

From there, the abuse got worse. I vividly remember the day he called me up while I was at work. As soon as the call connected, he began to shout:

"I'm miserable, Lydia! Don't you get it? I feel trapped. I can't do the things I want. I never have time to myself."

"Mmm-hmm," I replied.

"Are you even *listening*? You know, I don't have endless time to talk to you on the phone. You're wasting my time if you're just sitting there, not even –"

"Mmm-hmm."

"Fuck you. This is *your* fault, Lydia. *You* did this to me."

"Mmm-hmm."

"You stupid *bitch*. You know what? I shouldn't have married you. When I met you at Nightshade, in that skin-tight, tiny dress, I should've just –"

I dropped the phone. It tumbled to the ground. His voice exploded out the earpiece – tinny and incoherent.

But I knew exactly what he was saying.

I left work in tears. I spent the night at my mom's, alternating between crying and eating huge bowls of ice cream. A night turned into several nights, then weeks.

I decided to visit Ben, in broad daylight, after a month had passed.

When I saw him again, I felt a tinge of sadness. He looked so pale and pitiful in his orange shirt, his lip trembling and his eyes wet. He immediately apologized.

"I was just stressed," he said. "I didn't get much sleep that night. I was frustrated. I'm so, so sorry."

I decided to stay with my mom. But I also I decided to say those three, terrible words:

"I forgive you."

That was the wrong decision.

I woke up at 3 AM, in my mom's guest room, to a noise.

Click, click, click

I rolled over and tried to fall back asleep. But the sound continued, pounding in my ears, keeping me from falling back into wonderful sleep. *Click, click, click.*

I slowly sat up in bed.

Click, click, click

It was coming from outside.

I walked over to the window. With a trembling hand, I grabbed the edge of the curtain and peeled it back. The yard outside was filled with moonlight. The grass swayed in the wind.

And on that grass...

Was a running figure.

My heart sunk. I ran over to Mom's bedroom door, pounded on it as hard as I could. "He's out there, Mom! He's out there!"

She hobbled out of bed. "Oh, Lydia, there's no way he could be out there. Are you sure you aren't imagining –"

Thump!

The front door shook under a mighty blow.

"Lydia!" the man's voice yelled on the other side. "I know you're in there!"

I clung to Mom. For a minute, we both stood there, eyes wide, hiding in the shadows of the hallway. Afraid to make even the tiniest sound.

But we didn't have to wait long.

Sirens broke through the darkness – and the thumps ceased.

***

I visited him one last time.

He stared out at me from behind the glass, looking pale in his orange jumpsuit. I picked up the phone and sat down in the chair. I took in a deep breath, hoping it would fill me with confidence.

"Enjoying prison?" I said.

"Didn't enjoy it before. Doubt I'd enjoy it now."

"How exactly did you break out? That's quite a feat, you know."

He ignored my question. "We could've had everything," he muttered, low and clear under his breath. "We could've been happy together. Marital bliss." He sucked in a deep breath through his nose; it almost sounded like a sniffle. "But because of you – I've been rotting away, here in prison, for almost all of our marriage."

"What, you expected me *not* to go to the police when you told me?" I asked. My voice wavered; I stopped, bit back the tears, and continued. "When you were drunk out of your mind that night, you told me what you did to that woman. Every last detail. You deserve this, Ben."

"But –"

I set the phone down. I could hear the tiny sounds coming from it. But I didn't care. I ignored it, not even turning back to look at him one last time.

Ben got what he deserved.

MEMEGWESI

"Grandpa, what's that?"

I pointed at one of the boulders on the riverbank. A hole had been carved in the center, just a few inches above the water's surface. About two feet tall, one foot long.

"It's just a natural formation, Emily."

"It doesn't look natural."

The top was arched into a perfect circle, as if drilled by a machine or painstakingly carved by an artist. The bottom flattened out into a straight line. It looked deep, too; the sides of gray rock faded quickly into complete darkness.

"Maybe it's a rabbit burrow."

"Rabbits can't dig through stone."

Grandpa sighed, pushing his paddle against the water. It made a gentle *splash*. "I don't know what it is. But I think you'll have more fun if you don't think so much."

He was right, of course. This was my once-a-year trip with Grandpa, to get away from the hustle and bustle of city life. I was supposed to relax and have fun. But I usually just ended up with a thousand mosquito bites, ugly sunburn, and another weird story about my great Uncle Carl.

"Just close your eyes. Listen to the birds. Forget about everything," he said with a reassuring smile.

I closed my eyes. I heard the chirps of birds, flitting from tree to tree. The steady splashes of Grandpa's paddle cutting through the water. The *thump-thump-thump* of footsteps across the grass.

Footsteps?

My eyes shot open. But when I whipped around to the shoreline, I only saw a deer, grazing several feet from the riverbank.

"Look at that deer!" Grandpa said, steering the canoe towards the shore. Long grass poked out from the shore, brushed against my arms. "Beautiful, isn't she?"

"She's *okay*."

"What! You don't like her?"

I shrugged. "I see deer all the time upstate."

"Well, *I* want to get a better look at her."

Grandpa quietly paddled along the shore. Roots and rocks jutted from the dirt, nearly brushing the boat. I noticed two more holes – one in the moist dirt of the riverbank, the other carved into the trunk of an oak tree. I didn't point them out to Grandpa.

Before we knew it, fifteen minutes had passed. The forest grew darker, quieter. Gnarled trunks and branches stretched up to sky, blotting out the sunlight. I turned to Grandpa. His brows were furrowed in concern.

The deer was nowhere to be seen.

"Where are we?" I asked.

307

"Don't worry. We'll just go back the way we came."

But as we paddled against the current, none of the surrounding forest looked familiar. Grandpa pulled out his phone and squinted at the screen. "No service," he grunted, tossing it back in his bag.

With every passing second, the forest seemed to get darker. The sunlight dimmed; the shadows stretched across the ground. The chirps of the birds faded into the gurgles of the water.

"We're lost."

His silence confirmed it.

"I knew it. You have no idea where we are."

"We're not lost. We just haven't found our way back yet," he said in his calming, gentle tone.

"That sounds like lost to me."

"Emily," he said, "please, just relax. Enjoy this. Your time away from the city –"

"Heh! You think I *enjoy* getting lost in the middle of nowhere? Getting eaten alive by mosquitos? Hanging out with an old guy who doesn't even know how to use a smartphone?"

"You know, Emily, when I was in middle school like you, we didn't have Internet. We had –"

"Just *stop* it, okay? I don't want to hear your stupid stories! I just want to go home—"

I stopped, hearing the sound of pattering footsteps. Fast, rapid, light.

"What was that?"

"Just the deer, Em."

But he looked concerned. Scared. He paddled us towards the center of the river, watching the forest with wide eyes. I clung to my seat. *What if it's someone watching us?* I glanced into the canoe. We had no weapons – just oars and some half-eaten peanut butter sandwiches.

Thump!

The sound didn't come from the forest, this time. It came from the bottom of the boat. As if we'd just tapped a turtle or scraped a rock.

"Did we hit something?"

More tapping sounds. Soft and hollow, from the bottom of the boat.

Grandpa's eyes widened. "Go. Go!"

I grabbed the two small oars on the bottom of the boat.

I plunged them into the water. The canoe cut through the current, racing across the surface as we both paddled. As the riverbank whooshed past us, I noticed more holes. In the soil, the trees, the rocks. Staring back at us like dozens of eyes.

Rapid taps sounded along the bottom of the boat, matching my pounding heart. I pulled the oars harder, faster. The water churned into white foam underneath me.

Clunk!

My paddle collided with something hard.

I looked down to see something small and gray floating on the surface of the water. About three feet long and spindle-shaped.

Splish-splosh.

Splashes erupted around us. *Fish? Birds?* I thought. But when my eyes met Grandpa's, my heart plummeted.

309

I'd never seen such a look of terror on my stoic grandfather's face.

"It's too late," he muttered to himself. "Too late."

The boat rocked furiously underneath us.

Then it tipped.

I plunged into the cold, dark water. No sight. No sound. Just cold blackness all around. I thrashed and swam blindly, until my head broke the surface. I took in a gasp of breath.

"Grandpa!" I screamed.

The canoe floated on the surface of the river, slowly sinking. Grandpa was gone.

"Grandpa!"

That's when I felt it.

A light touch, brushing across my leg. Under the water. I yanked it back and screamed. The touch multiplied – I felt touches, like tiny fingers, brushing my shoulders. My back. My legs.

Something tugged me under.

Icy water filled my nose. I kicked and thrashed, mouth open in a silent scream. Something was pulling me down, down, down –

Strong hands grabbed my shoulders.

Then I was lying on the shore, flat on my back, gasping for air. Beside me was the canoe, pulled into the wet dirt, and our bag of supplies. Grandpa leaned over me, an expression of horror cut into his face. "Emily. Are you okay?"

"I think so." I pulled myself up. The cold wind blew against my drenched clothes, my wet hair. "What happened?"

"We need to get out of here."

Motion caught my eye. I looked down. A short, flesh-colored creature dipped back into one of those strange holes, cut in the large oak tree. *Some sort of hairless cat? Or weirdly-colored lizard?*

"Grandpa? What's going on?" I asked.

He didn't have a chance to reply.

Thump-thump-thump – the tiny, pattering footsteps again. This time, from the entire forest surrounding us.

Grandpa grabbed my wrist and yanked me forward.

We ran over the grass, over the rocks. The tiny footsteps faded into the wind. The evening calls of birds and low hum of crickets filled the air.

"Grandpa? What's going on?"

"Nothing" was all he muttered back.

After several minutes of running, we stopped in a clearing. Grandpa leaned over a boulder, his breaths coming out in loud wheezes. I tugged at my shirt, still ice-cold against my body. The forest was silent and dark as night.

"Best for us to set up here. If we go any further, we'll just get lost." He pulled at the backpack strapped to his shoulders. "We can go back for the canoe tomorrow."

"You mean... we're going to spend the night out here?"

"I have before." He roughly opened the bag and pulled out a few blankets, a pile of snacks, and a lighter.

311

"Good thing I decided to bring the waterproof backpack, huh? Here, get yourself into some dry clothes." He tossed me his spare shirt.

I stared at him and felt the sting of tears. "Your clothes are wet too, though."

"I'll live." He shouldered off his wet shirt and threw it into the dirt. Then he pulled the lighter out. A flickering, orange flame appeared.

Soon we had a small fire going. The forest flickered with the flames, as if it were moving itself. I spread the blanket across the ground, lay on top of it. The rocks still bit into my back, and the soil still felt cold and wet.

Somehow, despite the discomforts, I fell into a deep sleep.

***

I woke with a start.

For a second, I didn't remember where I was. But then I felt the wet hair against my neck, the rocks cutting into my back.

What woke me up? I wondered. But then I heard it – the chilling note of a flute, piercing the air. Then another note, and another after it. Piecing together to form a haunting, beautiful melody that rode on the wind like a lullaby.

My eyes adjusted slowly to the darkness. An endless sea of black slowly became indigo sky, tangled branches, a scorched campfire. Listening to the melody, I yawned and rolled over.

That's when I saw the feet.

Small and fat, like a child's. Covered in thick, brown hair.

I sat up, my heart pounding in my ears. I opened my mouth, but only a dry squeak came out.

The humanoid figure took a step forward. It was about the height of a toddler, with all the wrong proportions. Long, stick-like legs. A flat, large face. Thin patches of hair that covered its face and body.

And it was missing a nose.

I tried to scream, again. Only a low hiss came out.

It leaned forward. Cold drops of water fell onto my face. It opened its mouth and spoke. "Come with us." Its voice was hushed and high-pitched, like the whine of a dragonfly.

I backed away. The rocks cut into my hands. My feet tangled up in the blanket.

"There is only sadness for you here," it rasped. As it spoke, I noticed several short shadows, standing at the edge of the clearing. Slowly closing in. "Only sadness, boredom, heartache. Come with us." It lay a cold, damp hand on my shoulder that felt like a child's.

"No," I croaked. "Get away from me!"

Those little black eyes turned from sympathy to fury. Tiny eyebrows furled, wrinkling a hairy forehead. The hand tightened its grip.

"You will come with us," it growled in a deep voice.

The rest of them ran forward and closed in. Cold, little hands grabbed my arms. My legs. My shoulders.

And then they pulled.

I slipped out of the blanket and skidded over the damp soil. Rocks scraped against my chest. They chittered excitedly among themselves, in a strange language that I couldn't understand. Warm, rotten breath wafted over my face.

I took in a deep gulp of air. "Grandpa!" I shouted. "Grandpa!"

A rustling sound, from across the campfire.

Then the flicker of an orange flame.

I fell hard into the soil. The creatures scattered, disappearing into the shadows of the forest.

Grandpa stood up. The orange light threw his face into harsh relief. He brandished it like a sword, walking through the clearing. With each *whoosh,* the shadows retreated; I couldn't tell if they were just shadows, or some of *them* scampering back home.

Finally, he stopped in the center of the clearing. "They're all gone, now, Emily."

I ran over to him, buried my face in his shoulder. "Grandpa, I'm so sorry. For what I said to you. For everything. For –"

"Sssshh, sshhh. It's okay."

"What... what were those things?"

"Memegwesi."

"I've never seen anything like them." I grabbed the blanket off the forest floor and wrapped it around my shoulders. "They look so... human. Almost like children."

"They're not human," Grandpa replied, with bite in his voice. "Not human at all." He sighed and bent down to relight the fire. "I thought we were safe. They usually don't stray this far from the water. But I should've known that they'd follow us."

"Why?"

The fire crackled to life. He sat in front of it, hands stretched out towards it. "Do you remember those mushrooms I found in the woods, last year? And you were terrified I'd poisoned myself by eating them?"

I nodded.

"I found them in these woods. What I didn't know… is that they were *planted*. By the Memegwesi. In the weeks after I took them, I found little footprints around the cabin. My stuff started disappearing. Garden tools. Bags of birdseed. Anything they could get their hands on outside my house. But they saw it didn't bother me." He looked up and gave me a small smile. "So I guess they decided to try and steal the thing that means the most to me."

"I'm sorry, Grandpa."

"Don't be sorry! It's not your fault. I'm the one who took their damn mushrooms in the first place." He poked the fire; it sparked and flickered. "Try to get some sleep, okay? I'll keep watch until dawn."

"Okay, Grandpa."

I wrapped the blanket around myself, and after almost an hour, finally drifted into a deep sleep.

***

In the morning, we headed back down to the river. The canoe was as we left it, dragged up onto the shoreline. As we got close, Grandpa's face fell.

"Where are the oars?"

Tiny footprints scattered the sand, around two oar-shaped imprints.

"Dammit," Grandpa muttered. "Okay. We'll have to walk back, along the riverbank. Get back to the car. We'll worry about all this later. Let me just get my bag out."

Grandpa grabbed the side of the canoe and began to lift.

"Grandpa! Stop!" I screamed.

In the sliver of shadow underneath, two dark eyes glinted out. Glinting with fury.

Then the forest thundered with footsteps. Much louder than yesterday. Small brown shapes darted out of holes in the trees, the rocks, the soil. Shadows converged on the horizon, darting between the trees, forming a crowd.

An army.

"Run."

Grandpa yanked me forward.

We ran along the riverbank, my feet slipping over the stones and mud. The entire forest shook underneath us. "We're not going to make it!" I shouted. "We don't even know where we are!"

"We'll make it," he shouted back.

The river roiled and churned. Dark shapes flitted underneath the surface, like enormous fish closing in on their next meal.

We ran as fast as we could. My legs ached; my lungs burned.

And then, suddenly, the forest cleared.

We dove into his truck and locked the doors. I coughed and panted; Grandpa wheezed. He fished the keys out of his pocket and stuck them in the ignition. Then he turned to me.

"Promise me one thing, Emily."

"What?"

"Don't tell your mother about any of this. Deal?"

"Deal," I replied with a smile.

***

A few days later, I left Grandpa's. I promised to visit him again over the holidays – a year was too long to wait. He gave me a tight hug, and Mom and I began the trip back to the city.

Over the coming weeks, I tried to forget about the Memegwesi. But it was difficult. They lived in my nightmares and fears. Sometimes I woke up with the *thump-thump-thump* of their little footsteps still pounding in my ears. Sometimes I swore I could feel their warm breath on my face.

One night in September, I woke from a particularly horrible nightmare. In it, I was back in the forest, sleeping in that dark, cold clearing. The fire had long been reduced to embers, and in the purple shadows, I could just make out the form of a short figure standing over me.

I woke up gasping for air. I jumped out of bed and flicked on the lights, my entire body shaking.

That's when I saw them.

317

On the carpet – right next to my bed – were two wet imprints.

Shaped like little feet.

BABYSITTING

"The diaper's backwards."

"No it's not."

"*Yes*, it is. Just hand me the baby, okay?"

Through an unfortunate series of events, Brit and I were babysitting the neighbor's baby. We're 13. We have no prior babysitting experience.

I reluctantly picked up the baby – who was a *lot* heavier than he looked – and handed him to Brit. "Wait. He feels hot. Is he supposed to be that hot?"

"I don't have a frickin' clue."

I placed my hand on the baby's forehead. He stared at me, blankly. Poor thing didn't even know how clueless we were.

"He's burning up, Brit. We need to take his temperature." I grabbed at the various items Mrs. Dunlap left us – a nose suctiony thing, a nail clipper... ah! The rectal thermometer.

"We have to put it up his butt? Ew." Brit sighed. "He doesn't feel that hot to me, Kasey. Maybe we should just skip it."

I ignored her and slowly slid the probe in. *Beep, beep.* The numbers blared back at me.

104.3

"Brit. He's got a fever, and it's high. 104.3." I pulled out my cellphone. "I think we should call her. This is bad."

"No! She's gonna think we did it!"

"She'd going to think *we* gave him the fever?" I shook my head and groaned. "Do you even pay attention in Biology class, Brit? Colds take a few days to incubate. They don't just instantly happen." My fingers tapped across the phone as I dialed her number.

I wasn't prepared for what I heard.

Beep, beep, beep!

The number you have called has been disconnected.

"Shit. We put the wrong number in." I tried it a few more times. It never went through.

Waaaaaaaahhhh!

Waaaaaaaahhh!

I looked down. Poor baby. His face was flushed and red. Mouth open in a terrified, heart-breaking cry. I grabbed him and pulled him to my chest, rocking him.

"I'm going to call the doctor. Or 911."

"No. You're overreacting," Brit said. "Babies have fevers all the time. He'll be fine."

"I don't think so, Brit. He feels *really* hot."

She grabbed my arm. "Kasey. You're overreacting. Just like at school, when Mr. Thomson said your poem could 'use work.' I'm telling you, there's nothing wrong. Mrs. Dunlap will be home in an hour. We can talk to her then."

"Okay. But I'm going to take his temperature again."
I laid him back down, got the thermometer out.

Beep.

105.7

My heart sank. I didn't know much about fevers, or babies – but that sounded really high. "That's bad, right? The highest fever I ever had was 104," I said to Brit. "I think we should call someone."

"Babies can handle higher fevers than we can. He'll be fine. Stop overreacting." She picked up her phone and started texting again.

I sat down in the rocking chair, baby Logan resting against my chest. As soon as I started rocking, he stopped crying. His eyes closed. The heat of his little body burned through my thin top, and I wondered if Brit was wrong. Wondered if I should call a doctor, even though she said not to.

But I didn't.

We sat like that for a half hour. Brit splayed herself out on the sofa, texting some boys, no doubt. *Mrs. Dunlap will be home soon. She'll know what to do,* I told myself, to the rhythmic beat of the rocking chair. *She'll be home soon.*

But she was late.

At 8:15 PM, Baby Logan hadn't woken up. He lay still and silent in my arms, sleeping. He was so hot, now, it was uncomfortable to hold him against me.

I looked down, wondering if I could shift him without waking him.

No.

He wasn't moving.

321

His little chest didn't rise and fall with breath. His toes didn't wiggle and twitch. I poked him and jiggled him; he remained still. "Brit?" I asked, my voice reaching fever pitch. "Brit! Brit! He isn't moving!"

She jumped off the sofa. "What are you talking about?" She stared down at him. "Oh my God, Kasey."

I couldn't breathe. Tears rolled down my cheeks. A horrible cry burned my throat.

I whipped around to Brit. "You *told* me not to call a doctor! You *told* me he was fine!"

"I thought he was fine!"

"This is your fault –"

My finger brushed against baby Logan's skin.

It easily gave under my fingers.

"What the hell?" Brit said.

With a trembling finger, I poked his bare arm. The hot material caved easily. Like putty. Or wax. In the darkness of the hole that was formed, metal glinted out.

"I don't understand," I said.

Brit grabbed him from my hands. She viciously started poking, peeling, prodding. "Brit, no!" I yelled. *Maybe he's somehow still alive. Maybe he's –*

She ripped off the right half of his face.

Underneath was a metal, glinting skull. Wires snaked in and out of the metal. Some plugged into the naked eyeball, poised in the metal socket; others disappeared back into the flesh, traveling somewhere else through the body. Stamped on the metal were the words *Made by Black Widow, Inc.*

"It's not a baby," she said. "It's a robot."

322

BANDERSNATCH

by Blair Daniels & Craig Groshek

The effects were instant.

Seconds after I swallowed the tablet, I felt lightheaded. Faint. I gripped the side of the armchair; the house swayed underneath me.

"You feelin' it, huh, Kasey?" Sandra said.

I'd never done drugs before. Ever. And this... this was some home-brewed concoction, called "Bandersnatch," by a friend of Sandra's. *What was I thinking? What did I just get myself into?*

I pulled my coat tighter and closed my eyes.

"No, don't close your eyes!" Sandra said. "You're missing the best part! Look — the walls are moving!" She let out a high-pitched, weird laugh.

"No," I replied, shutting my eyes tighter. "I don't want to see."

"But look! There's something moving under the wallpaper!"

"Okay, fine!" My eyes flew open.

The walls were dark green, covered in gold damask. Fancy like the rest of the house. But now... the damask pattern rippled and warped, as if something large were moving underneath it.

My heart began to pound.

Sandra let out a wheezing laugh. "You look so scared, Kasey! Don't worry. It's not real. It's just the chemicals taking effect in your brain."

Smack! The wall convulsed, shaking the large oil painting Mr. and Mrs. Bencht had hung up. It clattered loudly against the wall, threatening to fall.

But there was something wrong with it.

The little painted farmers, who were usually happily scattering wheat seeds, ran through the fields in terror. Behind them, the silhouette of something large and gray bounded towards them.

"Sandra. Look at the painting," I said, my voice shaky.

"What about it?"

"There's something wrong with it."

The little farmers were now at the edge of the painting. They clawed at the frame, mouths open in terror. The shadow loomed closer behind them.

"They're running from something."

"Peasants running from menial labor? Sounds about right."

I snapped towards her. "Are you not seeing this?!"

She shrugged.

Underneath them, the wallpaper churned faster. As if rats, or immense bugs, were skittering underneath. The farmers were thrashing in terror, now, as the shadow bounded forth.

"Make it stop. Make it stop, Sandra!" I shrieked, my voice reaching fever pitch.

She laughed in response. "I can't make it stop. It'll wear off eventually. Come on, just enjoy it. Ha, look! There's a three-legged woman sitting on the couch!" She grinned at the thin air. "Hi! What's your name?"

I didn't see the three-legged woman.

I just saw the walls, rippling and shaking with growing force. The farmers in the painting, crying and thrashing as the large mass on the horizon grew ever closer.

"Stop, stop, stop," I muttered to myself. "Please, stop —"

Smack.

The painting flew forward, as if something had punched it from the back. It narrowly avoided my head before crashing to the floor.

Behind it was a gaping, dark, rectangular hole.

I didn't see beams, or insulation, or drywall. Just darkness. Like the sky on a moonless night. Or the depths of the ocean.

I stood up, took a step towards it.

I ran my hand along the wall, then grabbed the raw edge. Bits of drywall crumbled in my hands. I leaned my head forward, to peer inside —

Crrrrack!

A hand shot out.

I leapt back, screaming. The hand gripped the side of the wall, fingers groping for a better hold. Bits of drywall crumbled to the ground.

"H-hello?" I called. I whipped around to Sandra.

No.

The room was empty.

Not *just* empty. Abandoned. It looked like, in the span of seconds, decades of dust and grime had appeared. The armchairs were covered in white sheets. The wallpaper had faded to a sickly shade of grayish-green.

What happened? Where... where'd she go? I turned back to the hole, my pulse pounding in my ears. The hands had crawled up the side of the wall, now, and a dark shape was taking form in the shadow.

A face emerged.

No, no, no...

It was Sandra's face. Smeared with blood and dust. Contorted into a look of panic. "Please, help me," she whispered. "It's coming for me. Please —"

I jumped back.

"Kasey!" She pulled herself up a bit. Then she slipped, disappearing halfway back down the hole. "Give me your hand!"

Shaking, I took a step forward. Extended my arm.

My fingers brushed against hers.

"Closer," she choked. "You have to get closer."

I took a step.

Slap!

Her hand grabbed mine. *Hard.*

326

I yanked forward. "Hey!" I yelped. "Hey, stop! Sandra!"

"I'm not Sandra."

Before my very eyes, her skin cracked like a mirror. Dozens of black cracks webbed across her face, her arms, her body. The pieces, one-by-one, fell off like eggshell — leaving tufts of gray hair in their wake.

I looked down and screamed.

It was no longer a hand latched onto my wrist.

It was a gray, furry claw.

It yanked me forward. I skidded across the floor, towards the hole. "Stop it!" I screamed, trying to pry it off of me. "Get off! Get off!"

The creature stared at me with milky-white eyes. Its gray fur bristled like a lion's mane; its mouth hung open to reveal rows and rows of sharp teeth.

"Hey! Stop!" someone shouted from behind me — but they sounded so far away. "Kasey!"

Slam! My body hit the wall.

My face leaned into the hole.

And for a second, I saw it all.

Stars, twinkling in the utter blackness. Shimmering and pulsing in colors I couldn't begin to describe. Eras of history, happening all at once. Pyramids built as men landed on the moon. Christ born as fleets of spaceships fought in World War X. Everything melted into each other. Connected. Unified.

But beneath it all — a rippling, gray mass. With the head of a dog, the mane of a lion, the claws of a bear. It had reached up to grab me, but it was present in all that I saw. Hideous and revolting. Grabbing at every moment, every man, every soul. Trying to pull every particle of existence towards it.

"Kasey! Hey, Kasey!" Hands grabbed me roughly by the shoulders. "Kasey!"

I blinked.

I was pressed against the wall. Blurry damask patterns filled my eyes. The back of the painting pressed into my head; my nose smushed against the wall.

"Kasey? Are you okay?

I slid my head out. Sandra stood in front of me. Her brown eyes were wide; her hair stuck to her forehead in wet curls. "Kasey. Talk to me."

I looked down.

My own fingers were dug into my wrist, clawing at the flesh. Deep, red marks bloomed into shining blood.

"I... I don't think so," I said.

***

"Tell me what happened."

"I don't know."

"You don't know?" she scoffed. "Of course you know. You just don't want to tell me."

It was true. Sandra had been a good friend for three years now — yet I couldn't bring myself to tell her what I'd seen. "I can't really describe it," I said, finally.

"Then try."

I ignored. "Why is it so cold in here?" I pulled the coat tighter around me. "Don't your parents believe in heat?"

328

She shrugged. "My mom doesn't like to sweat. She thinks it's gross."

I halfway smiled, for the first time since the high. "Your mom doesn't sound fun."

"No, she isn't. Not at all." She grinned. "I can't complain about her, though. She goes out a lot so I can have my space. Which means —" she did a suggestive eyebrow waggle — "I get to do Bandersnatch with my friends."

"What is Bandersnatch, exactly?"

She shrugged. "I'm not sure. All I know is the name." She pointed to the small, plastic baggie sitting on the table. In Sharpie, someone had written *Bandersnatch – Black Widow* over it. "It's a reference to that guy who played Sherlock, I think."

"No, it's not. It's a creature from *Alice in Wonderland*."

"Oh."

We fell into an awkward silence. Finally, I said: "I should be off. I need to go to get some stuff done before Monday."

She nodded, not meeting my eyes. "Go and do your thing."

I walked out into the cold. The sun was beginning to set, outlining the trees in gold. I pressed the button on my keys — the lone car in the driveway blipped back at me.

For all the riches the Benchts had, they never bought their daughter a car.

I shook my head and started it up. Through the thin veil of trees, their neighbor — Mr. Dickinson — was shoveling snow off his deck. When he saw me, he gave his usual frown. As if to say *what the fuck are you doing here?*

I smiled and waved to him. Then I turned for home.

***

That night, I lay in bed and stared up at the ceiling.

I'm never doing that again. That much I was sure of. I'd never had such a terrifying, weird experience in my life.

I closed my eyes.

But sleep never came. Every time my lids shut, images of that hideous creature filled my mind.

I rolled over and pulled the blanket over my face.

Snap!

I jolted up.

All was silent once more, save for the steady rush of city traffic. "H-hello?"

Silence.

I pulled off the blanket. Softly, slowly, I stepped out of bed. My hand fell on the cold metal of the doorknob.

With a deep breath, I pulled it open.

The main room of the apartment was dark. Too dark to see anything other than blocky silhouettes. Outside the windows, snow fell, obscuring the skyscrapers across the street.

Snap!

I jumped. "Hello?" I said, louder this time. I stepped into the kitchen. My fingers fumbled across the wall. *Where's the light switch? Come on, come on...*

My hand fell on smooth plastic.

Click.

Yellow light filled the apartment.

"No. No, no…"

Gaping black holes. On every wall. Some so large, the apartment should have collapsed. The edges were jagged and dusty, as if someone tore them out with impossible force.

I backed away.

I'm not high anymore. I shouldn't be seeing this.

Snap!

Something shifted behind the wall. Something huge. Each footstep shook the entire apartment, reverberated through the walls. A flash of gray fur, of milky-white eyes.

"Get back!" I screamed.

I swung the door open and ran out into the hallway.

Ding. The elevator doors whooshed open. I ran inside. Pressed "1" repeatedly.

The doors didn't close.

Snap! Snap! The snapping sound started. Soft, then growing louder by the second. "Come on, come on!" I screamed, pressing the *close door* button. *Maybe this isn't real. Maybe I still have a trace of the drug in me. Maybe —*

The hallway walls began to shake. The lights flickered.

"Come on!" I screamed. "Please, go!" I glanced at the stairwell door. It was halfway down the hallway, barely visible in the darkness. *I'd never make it.*

The walls undulated violently, shedding dust and drywall everywhere. *Snap! Snap!*

And then the lights went out.

331

With it, the walls stopped moving. The *snaps*, the *thumps*, faded into total silence.

My heart slowed. I cowered in the far corner of the elevator, praying it had left. Everything was dark — save for the glow of the EXIT sign above me.

"Kasey?"

No.

"Kasey!" Sandra's voice called, from the far end of the hallway. And then I saw it — the silhouette of a woman. Just barely visible in the red glow. "Kasey! Thank God, I found you. Please — help me!"

I jammed the *close door* button.

"Kasey!"

"I know it's not you, Sandra!" I screamed. "Get away from me!"

I blinked.

And then the silhouette was no longer a woman. It was a hulking, terrible shadow, taking up the entire width of the hallway. Bristled fur. Thick legs. Standing, still, at the far end of the hall.

I felt every muscle in my body freeze.

It took a step forward.

Everything shook. The walls, the floor, the elevator. Its silhouette swayed with every lurching step.

"Move, dammit!" I screamed. In a wild impulse, I slapped my hand against the elevator wall.

Ding!

The elevator doors whooshed shut.

I reached into my pocket, pulled out my phone. Dialed Sandra's number. She never picked up the phone, but I prayed she would answer this time.

Riiiiiiing.

Riiii —

Brzt! Brzt! Brzt!

Busy signal. As usual. My heart pounded as I waited for the elevator to descend. 4, 3, 2, 1...

Ding.

I ran out of the elevator. Out the door, into the snow. Then I drove to Sandra's house.

***

"Something's wrong with me." I stared at Sandra, my lip trembling.

"What do you mean?" Her brown eyes filled with concern. "Kasey, are you okay?"

"I think I'm still high. Because I'm still seeing things." I let out a quavering sigh. "Or maybe... maybe it's real. Maybe it followed me back."

"What followed you back?"

"The Bandersnatch."

I expected Sandra to start laughing madly. Or to say *I'm really worried about you, Kasey. We should go to a doctor.*

But instead, she said: "Tell me about it."

"This creature... it comes out of the walls. Like a huge, gray lion. But it's the most hideous thing I've ever seen." I pulled my coat tighter around me, my breath coming out

333

in puffs of mist. "Ugh. It's so cold in here. Can't you turn up the heat?"

"Sorry. I can get you a blanket, or —"

"No. It's okay." I glanced over at Sandra. She stared back at me, watching intensely. "Do you have any food, though? I'm feeling a little weak."

She shrugged. "I don't think so. But you can check."

I walked into the kitchen. It was mostly bare, as usual. No fruit on the counter, no cookies or bread. I sighed and grabbed the refrigerator door.

Yank.

Nothing.

Not a single piece of food. Just dust, dirt, and grime.

And it wasn't even cold.

"Sandra?" I called, pushing the door shut. "I think there's something wrong with your —"

I stopped.

I was standing in an empty kitchen. Perfectly empty — not a single piece of furniture. Layers of dust covered the counter like snow.

It looked abandoned. Like no one had lived here in years.

"Sandra?" I called, walking back into the room.

I froze.

The armchairs were covered with sheets. The damask wallpaper was cracked and faded. Where the painting hung was a jagged hole instead, spilling insulation and dust.

"Sandra?!"

"I'm right here."

I whipped around.

Sandra stood behind me, smiling.

But something was wrong.

Her pale skin rippled and roiled, as something churned underneath. Her eyes flickered from brown to milky-white.

No... this isn't real. It can't be.

Her lips curled into a smile. "Do you understand now?"

"Understand what?"

She gestured to the empty, abandoned house. "The house. The drug. *Me.*"

I shook my head, backing away.

"This mansion has been abandoned for years," she said, taking a step closer. "It's a popular drug drop-off for the dealers in this town." She grinned. *"Especially* for Bandersnatch."

"I don't... I don't understand. What does that have to do with anything?"

"Do I really have to spell it out for you, Kasey?" She sighed. "You've been visiting this house every day — for the past three years. Each time, you steal a pill. Or three. You take them, you get high... and then you see me."

"What are you saying?"

"I'm not a real person. You've only been seeing me every day because, well... you've been high every day."

"No. You're my friend." I suddenly felt dizzy, faint. "I *know* you. I tell you everything. You're one of the closest friends I have."

"Then how did we meet?"

335

"I..." I faltered. I tried to remember the first time I hung out with Sandra. What drew us together.

But it was all blank.

"Who... who are you?"

"I'm Sandra Bencht," she said, her smile widening into a grin. "Or, if you rearrange the letters... Bandersnatch."

I ran out of the room. I grabbed the doorknob, yanked it open. The snow was coming down heavily, now — thick flakes flitting and twirling in the wind.

And then the snow-covered ground rippled.

I ran across the lawn. I threw the keys in the ignition, started it up; then I pulled out of the driveway.

Through the veil of snow, the dark, abandoned mansion looked back at me. In the doorway stood a hulking, gigantic silhouette.

I pulled out of the driveway and didn't look back.

MY SON IS DEAD

I didn't mean to kill him.

We were walking in the backyard, down the rocky hill that leads back towards the house. While holding Alex's hand, I tripped. Brought him right down with me.

I fell on the soft grass.

He fell on the rocks.

His head made a sickening *thwack*. And then he lay there in a still, bloody heap.

I couldn't process it. It was like I just... broke. I stared at his lifeless body for what seemed like hours, although it was probably just a few minutes.

Then I ran back inside, locked the doors, and sobbed hysterically.

I don't know why I didn't call 911.

I don't know why I left his body out there.

But believe me... I wish I'd done those things.

It was about 4 AM when I woke. I'd fallen asleep in the chair by the kitchen, exhausted after so much crying.

Tap-tap-tap-tap

It was coming from the sliding glass door. I slowly stood up, my mind foggy from sleep, and walked over.

I froze.

My little boy was standing there, in the dark. Blood dripped down his face. His knees were scratched and bruised. His hair was matted to his forehead, caked with blood.

But it wasn't my little boy.

When our eyes met, a chill coursed through my body. His eyes were empty, cold, emotionless. Not the warm, smiling brown eyes of my son.

Tap-tap-tap-tap

"Mommy," he called, his voice muffled through the glass. "It's cold out here. Please, let me in."

I stood, paralyzed, watching him with fear.

"Mommy! My head hurts, and it's dark out here, and I'm scared."

Tears fell down my trembling cheeks. *It's not Alex. It can't be. Do not open that door.* But seeing my little baby like that – even if he was some sinister shell of himself – broke my heart in two.

I walked over to the glass.

Crouched to his level.

Placed my hand against the surface.

"I love you, Alex."

His face was red from crying. The blood mingled with his tears on his cheek. "Mommy, open the door!" he screamed.

All I wanted to do was open that door.

Give him a hug.

338

Never let him go.

But I knew it wasn't him. *Do not open that door,* the words repeated in my head. I steeled myself against my emotions, restraining the torrent of tears that threatened to burst with every breath. *It's a spirit, a devil, a trick...*

I forced myself to turn around.

"Mommy! Where are you going?" he screamed through the glass. *Tap-tap-tap-tap* – fast, panicked, frenzied. "Mommy! Don't leave me! I'm scared!"

I didn't reply.

I forced my heavy legs to take a step. Then another, and another, until I was at the bedroom door. I forced myself to close the curtains. Lie down on the mattress. Pull the covers over my head. Ignore the faint crying from the kitchen.

It began to rain.

The water drummed on the roof, splashed down the gutters. Thunder rumbled in the distance. *Alex was always afraid of thunder,* I thought. I couldn't hear his cries over the rain anymore, but didn't stop me from picturing him there.

Standing at the door. Screaming. Crying.

Telling me he's scared.

Begging for me to let him in.

Somehow, I fell asleep. When I woke up, it was well past morning. I was numb, empty. The image of Alex was burned into my eyes. My mind. My heart.

I leapt out of bed and ran over to the kitchen door. A small part of me hoped he would still be there – but he wasn't. Just the green grass, the rocky hill, and the patio.

And something else.

A small set of footprints in the mud, weaving away from the front door.

Spirits don't leave footprints. A wave of nausea rose in my throat as the realization fell on me. Heart pounding, I raised my eye to the hill. Where I had left his broken body.

It was empty.

He must be alive. I'd left my son out there, all alone, wounded and bloody. He wasn't some monster, waiting for me to let him in.

I was the monster.

I ran into the backyard. "Alex! Alex!" I screamed, until my voice was hoarse. "Alex?"

Only silence replied.

PUNISH THE SINNERS

Have you ever heard of an online game called "Punish the Sinners?"

I was scrolling through Reddit late last night when I saw the advertisement. *Still mad at someone who has betrayed you? Get revenge in "Punish the Sinners"!* Below it was an animated video of a person being whipped by a devil. The face of some "real" person was badly photoshopped on the cartoon body.

It looked kind of funny and different, so I clicked. Then I signed up. Within five minutes I was on a startup screen, asking **Who would you like to punish?**

Underneath were suggestions.

They must've somehow linked my account to my Facebook or something, because the three choices below were actually people I knew. A photo of Melissa Hartford, my roommate from freshman year... Gary Burton, my uncle... and Teddy Lachman, my ex.

Teddy.

There were a million reasons I hated him. He blew off dates for piddling nonsense, like playing video games.

While we were dating, I borrowed some textbooks from him... he asked for them back literally minutes before he dumped me, because apparently I'd be petty enough to hold $50 worth of books hostage. And, the stinger – 48 hours after we broke up, he was sleeping with the girl he'd told me was "just a friend."

I clicked on him.

The scene changed. It showed a cartoon man in his underwear; Teddy's Facebook photo was sloppily photoshopped on. Next to him was a devil character. **Choose your punishment**, it said in big, yellow letters.

Below was an icon of a whip, a knife, and a rock. I clicked on the whip.

Click anywhere to begin.

I hovered the undulating whip over his bare, cartoon backside. *Click.* The whip shot out, and the character jumped. A frown and blue teardrops were superimposed on Teddy's face.

Click.

More tears.

Click. Click. Click.

It was oddly satisfying. Even though it was just a game... it was cathartic. I felt a surge of anger leave me each time I cracked the animated whip, each time my finger came down on the touchpad.

Click. Click. Click...

***

I stayed up until 3 AM playing the game. Then I jumped into bed, and slept in my little dorm room until almost noon.

When I woke up, I automatically checked my email and social media. When I got to Facebook, I stopped.

My newsfeed was filled with status updates from classmates.

> Pray for @Teddy Lachman.

> My football teammate and friend @Teddy Lachman was found this morning with life-threatening injuries. Please keep him in your thoughts.

> @Teddy Lachman, I love you. Please pull through so we can have a life together. <3

My heart dropped. *What happened?* My mind went back to last night... the game. *No, there's no way it can be related. No way.* My heart pounded in my chest, and a feeling a little like guilt seeped through my veins. *I didn't cause this. I didn't.*

But when I saw the photos of him in recovery a few days later, I was terrified.

He had lashes across his face and entire body.

As if he'd been whipped.

After a few minutes, I resolved what to do. I'd done this to Teddy... I needed to take action. I pulled out my phone. With a shaking finger, I tapped across the screen.

I took a deep breath...

And entered by username and password for *Punish the Sinners.*

Who would you like to punish?

My eyes fell on Melissa. The "friend" who told me I was too fat for leggings. Who told my new boyfriend my entire sexual history. Who tried to kiss him at a party.

I clicked on her.

A message popped up.

Your trial has ended. Please enter your credit card for your $24.99/month subscription fee.

$24.99?! I closed out of the window.

I walked to the mini fridge. Poured myself a shot of schnapps.

Then I rifled through my desk drawers. Candy, butterknife... no, no. None of these would do. My fingers finally locked on something cold and smoothed.

A canister of mace.

I grabbed it, yanked my keys off the rack, and headed out of the building.

I'd dole out her punishment the old-fashioned way.

MY TODDLER SAYS HI

My toddler is a smart kid, but he learns things in a strange order. Case in point: his first word was "ant" – not "mama" or "dada." He can say short sentences, like "make a mess," but he still doesn't know how to hold a spoon.

So, when he finally started saying "hi" – at age 1 and a half – I was thrilled. "Good job, James," I said, leaning in close and bopping his nose.

He smiled at me.

Then he bent over, looked under the bed, and waved. "Hi."

"No, no. You say 'hi' to people," I said. "See? Hi, James!" I waved my hand at him.

He stared at me and furled his eyebrows.

Then he bent his knees, looked under the bed again. "Hi!" he said, with a little wave. I patted his head and smiled. *Okay. Good enough.*

The next day, though, I became concerned. We were again playing in the master bedroom; he was stacking blocks up on the floor. Suddenly, he stopped, stood up, and ran over to the bed. If you have experience with toddlers, you'll know they get random impulses like that. Where they just drop whatever they're doing and run in a random direction.

He bent his knees and peered under the bed.

But this time, he didn't wave or say "hi."

He said: "I see you!"

That's another short sentence he knows, from when we play hide and seek or peekaboo. "Peekaboo! I see you!" But I've *never* seen him say "I see you" in any other context.

And *definitely* not to anything other than me or my husband.

"James? What do you see?" I asked, hoping he'd respond with something intelligible. I quickly bent down and checked under the bed myself. Nothing was there. Of course.

"Peekaboo! I see you! I see you! I see you!"

"What do you see?"

He whipped around and ran back over to his blocks. "Block! Yellow block. Red block."

Of course he's not going to answer me. I sighed and sat on the floor, watching him with my arms crossed.

***

That night, I couldn't sleep. Dan snored loudly beside me, sprawled over 80% of the bed as usual. I was pushed to the far edge, arms wrapped around a body pillow.

I see you, the voice echoed in my head. *I see you! I see you!* What did he see?

No. I'm being ridiculous. Listen to me! Taking the ramblings of a toddler seriously.

I rolled over, facing Dan. My eyes fluttered closed, and I tried to think about something else. *Costco trip tomorrow... vacation to Florida in a few months...*

I froze.

Something ice cold brushed against my back.

I flipped around. "Who's there?" I said hoarsely into the darkness. Dan didn't even budge. *Snore. Snore.*

Cold. On my feet.

My eyes snapped to the edge of the bed. Just in time to see a something dark, retracting back behind the bed.

"Dan? Dan?" I yelled. I grabbed him by the shoulder and shook him madly. "Wake up!"

His eyes fluttered open for half a second. "What?"

Cold. Again, on my back.

I whipped around.

A stubby, shadowy little hand poked over the edge of the bed. A *child's* hand. It quickly slipped back under the bed.

I leapt out of bed and peered underneath. My heart pounded in my chest, drowned out by Dan's snores.

Nothing was there.

Just a dark, empty floor. Clumps of dust. A few wayward socks.

I climbed back in bed, shuddering. I wrapped my arms around Dan and closed my eyes.

"Blair?" His snores had stopped, and his eyes were open. Staring at me.

"What?"

"Did you just poke me?"

WHITE BLANKET

Ah, the Jersey Shore.

As I opened the car door, the stench of rotting fish and turbid water hit my nostrils. Hungry greenhead flies buzzed around us, and a dark haze had settled overhead. A storm was coming.

We ran to the porch. "Your Grandma just wants us to check for water damage, right?" Dan asked, swatting at his neck. "From the storm last night?"

"Yup. That's what she said in her text." With a jingle, I pulled out the keys. "Should just take a minute. Then we can get back on the road."

I swung the door open.

Inside it smelled like dust and mold. The furniture was covered in white sheets – as Grandma always did when the house was off-season. This house her "vacation home." I put that in quotes because, well… it's more like a vacation *shack*. It's an old salt box with a kitchen the size of my closet, an outside shower, and a rickety dock in the lagoon out back.

I flipped the light switch.

The lights didn't turn on. "Ah, she cut the power, too," I said. Grandma was always very thorough about that. I pulled out a flashlight, and we continued through the rooms.

"I don't see any water damage," Dan said, scanning the seams where the walls met the floor. I crouched down and began opening the cabinets.

Inside was an unopened jar of peanut butter.

Which wouldn't be weird – except, Grandma's allergic to peanut butter. So much so, when we were kids, we had to eat our PB&J sandwiches outside because she wouldn't allow it in her house.

"Dan? Look at this." I picked up the jar and rolled it over in my hands. EXP DATE: 11/2018. Somewhat new. "I bet my asshole cousin Steve left this here."

I put it back and looked up. Through the glass door, the sun set over the lagoon. It reflected off the black water like a candle's flame, flickering with every ripple. It *was* beautiful, even if the lagoon smelled like dead fish all the time.

"Why does she leave the blinds open?"

I looked at Dan. Then back at the door. He was right – Grandma usually closed the blinds. Even when she was staying here.

I walked across the parquet floor, tugged on the string to pull the blinds shut. "She must've forgotten," I said.

But then my eyes fell to the floor.

Grandma always jimmied a stick in the track, to prevent people from opening the door from the outside. It was a nervous tick – a paranoid old-lady habit. But ever since Grandpa died, she was very conscientious about those things.

The stick was gone.

"There's something wrong," I said. "She never closes the door without the stick." I pulled out my phone and dialed her number. The line rung a few times. *If she isn't home… then where is she?*

But then I heard it.

Priiiiing. Prriiiiiiiing.

The noise echoed through the house, tinny and shrill. I pulled the phone away from my ear. "Is that your phone, Dan?"

But I knew it wasn't. His ringtone is some futuristic space theme.

Priiiiing.

I glanced around. There. On the armchair – from under the sheet – came a white glow. I ran over to it, wrenched at the sheet.

Prriiiiing.

Incoming call flashed on the screen. With my name underneath.

"This is her phone," I said, holding it up. "Why is her phone here?"

"Did your Grandma come up here recently?"

"No. She hasn't been here in over a month…" I trailed off, glancing around the house. *But had I actually seen her since then?*

I started up the stairs.

Light rain pattered on the roof. Thunder growled in the distance. "Where are you going?" Dan called. I didn't reply.

The two bedroom doors were closed. With a deep breath, I opened the first one.

It was empty.

Nothing looked out of place. The armchair by the window was draped in a white sheet, like the furniture downstairs. The bed was stripped of its sheets, pillows, and comforter. Just a twin mattress wrapped in plastic.

My heart slowed. I shut the door. Dan had followed me up, now, and was waiting in the hall. "Everything okay?"

"Yeah. I just want to check this room."

I pushed the door open. But it was empty like the others. Sheets drawn over the furniture; clothing, knick-knacks, décor all put away. After a quick look around, we started down the stairs.

I stopped.

All the sheets had been taken off the furniture.

They lay on the ground in crumpled, tangled heaps. The sofa, the rocking chair, the piano – they were all bare.

Except for one.

The sheet across the dining table was still there, draping to the floor. As we stood there, paralyzed… it fluttered with movement.

"Run," Dan whispered.

We swung the door open, ran out of the house. Thundered down the porch steps until we reached the car. "Go!" I screamed. Dan fumbled with the keys.

Finally, the engine roared to life. We reeled out of the driveway, sped down the road. My heart began to slow; calm washed over me. *We're safe.*

"Melissa," Dan said.

I looked up. His eyes were glued to the rearview mirror.

"Did you leave a white blanket in the back seat?"

SWITCHING BODIES WITH MY SISTER[2]

If this was a Disney move, I'd be the "evil" sister.

Can you blame me? My sister, Eva, got quite a different lot in life than I did. Tall, tan, and buxom, with a placid disposition and a beautiful voice. Me? I'm short and pale, with a habit of eating too many Reese's and a voice that sounds like a dying frog.

Sometimes, when I tell her, she'll laugh (that tinkling, feminine, beautiful laugh) and go "Oh, Cora, don't be *jealous!* We should love each other like sisters, not fight over stupid things."

I wonder if she'd still say that, if *she* were the one who got the short end of the stick.

Last night was the breaking point. We went to a party at one of the fraternities. I waved over one of my classmates, Robby, from Physics. As soon as I did, and his eyes fell on Eva, it was all over. No matter how many

---

[2] Originally published in *Shadow on the Stairs*

jokes I made, no matter how many times I touched his shoulder–he barely gave me a second look.

That very night, after Eva went to bed, I snuck out of our apartment. I'd heard rumors that a real-life witch lived in the abandoned house at the end of the street. It was something no grown-ass woman should've believed.

But I was desperate.

When I arrived at the house, my heart sank. The boards were rotten and splintered; the glass was cut into large, pointed shards that rose from the frame like fangs.

I could tell there was the dim, yellow glow of a light on inside. I raised my hand to knock.

Before my fist hit the wood, a voice called from inside: "Come in!"

Creeeeeaaak. I took a step inside, my legs shaking. "Hello?" The light seemed to be coming from a back room; I made my way towards it.

"Welcome."

A woman sat on the floor, in the middle of a pentagram, wearing a hooded robe. She looked only a few years older than me, her blonde hair poking out from under the hood.

"Uh… are you the witch?" I said, rather awkwardly.

She grimaced. "W-I-T-C-H is not a term we use around here. It's *Woman of the Magical Arts.*"

"I'm so sorry! Uh, well –"

"What do you seek?" she interrupted.

"I want to switch bodies with my sister."

"An easy spell. I can do it for you–but the question is, can you pay the price?"

355

"What's the price?"

She paused, staring up at me with her ice-blue eyes. "Your firstborn son."

"I, uh–I don't know –" I stuttered.

She broke into laughter. "I'm just messing with you. The payment is money–a thousand dollars. Cash or credit?"

"Uh, credit," I said, breathing a sigh of relief. I fumbled for my wallet and handed her the card.

She pulled a smartphone with one of those Square card readers from the folds of her robe. Once she swiped it, she patted the floor and said: "Come, sit with me."

I gingerly lowered myself onto the pentagram. "After it's done–will she know we've been switched?"

She shook her head. "No. I'll cast a memory reformation spell, too, which will reform her memories and make her think she was always you."

I smiled. "Good."

She took my hands in hers. "Lady of Darkness, I beseech thee, switch this woman and –"

Creeeeaaak.

One of the floorboards, creaking from a back room. I shot up, staring into the shadows.

Out of the darkness, a silhouette began to take form. A woman–old and withered, with pentagrams and symbols cut up and down her skin in white, shining scars. She stared at me with two deep red eyes, and I felt my blood run cold.

"Do you need help, dear?" she asked.

"No, Grandma, I got it. She just wants a body swap with memory reformation."

The old woman paced forward. She knelt on the ground beside me, and leaned in close, until I could smell the odd citrusy scent of her hair. "Body swap, again? Did it not work the first time?"

I looked at her, eyebrows furled. "What?"

"Well, you were just in here a few weeks ago. We did this exact same spell."

I stared at her, the realization sinking in. "I... was?"

"Oh, yes." A smile crinkled her pale skin, and her eyes twinkled.

"You were in here, looking to switch bodies with your better-looking sister–and to make sure she never remembered any of it."

I'M A DIRTY GIRL

I'm a dirty girl.

Wait, wait. I should rephrase that.

I'm a *messy* girl.

And now you're judging me. Well, don't. You know, there are *much* worse habits out there than being messy. Like drinking soda every day. Or driving recklessly. Or never exercising.

Can't a girl live in her own filth without judgement?

I mean, come on, guys. It's a victimless crime! I don't live with anyone. I own the house. So what if some toenail clippings are on the floor? Or the stack of dishes looks like the Leaning Tower of Pisa? Or clumps of brown hair roll by like tumbleweeds?

That's the way I like it.

Well... that's the way I used to like it, anyway.

Before the Mouse.

I've never actually seen the mouse. But I know it's there. I hear its pattering little footsteps all night as it scurries around the kitchen, eating all the food I dropped during the day. I hear its feet scratching through the wall as it recedes back into the bowels of the house.

I decided to just ignore it.

Until I the night I *saw* it.

I was eating some leftover pizza while watching *America's Funniest Home Videos.* I heard the *scrtch-scrtch-scrtch,* and looked up.

A flash of brown scurried across the floor.

I screamed.

All night, I barely slept. I couldn't stop thinking about its little paws skittering over my body. Creeping up my neck. Brushing against my face. Its fat, wriggling body pressing against my arm. Its worm-like tale dangling into my mouth.

I hadn't gotten a good look at it – it was too fast – but my mind had no trouble filling in the gaps.

As soon as the stores opened, I bought a mousetrap. I wanted a neck-breaking one, but they only had the sticky ones.

When I got home, I stuck two globs of peanut butter in the goo and set it on the kitchen floor.

Then I went to sleep.

***

I woke up to a horrendous *clack-clack-clack* sound.

In my groggy state, I thought someone was breaking in. I leapt out of bed, grabbed my gun, and tiptoed into the kitchen.

"Freeze! I've got a gun!"

Something was moving in the darkness. Thrashing, shifting –

Oh. The mouse.

I lowered the gun and stepped towards it. In the shadows, I could just make out the silhouette, thrashing in jerky, erratic movements. Its legs flailed. Its head whipped back and forth. A low, hissing sound filled the air.

What am I supposed to do now? Throw it outside, trap and all? Smash it and give it a quick death?

That's why I didn't want a sticky trap, dammit.

Clack-clack-clack

A prickly sensation flooded my body as I imagined the mouse, in the darkness, somehow limping over to me. Climbing on me. Running all over me.

I don't want to be in the dark with this thing. My fingers fell on the light switch.

Click.

I froze.

Then I leapt back. "No," I whimpered, clutching my mouth. Nausea bubbled in my throat; my legs felt weak.

It wasn't a mouse at all.

It was a horrific creature made of… *me.*

Tangled clumps of my brown hair formed its body. Crescent-shaped teeth poked out of its open mouth. My toenail clippings. Its paws – if they could be called that – were formed from flakes of my dead skin. Its eyes were dark, sticky lumps of earwax.

Clack!

It wildly thrashed, trying to unstick itself from the trap.

Clack!

One fleshy paw broke free.

That was all it needed. The plastic skittered across the floor as it ran back into the darkness.

I didn't sleep a wink that night.

***

I'm a neatnik now.

I moved into an apartment on the top floor of a skyscraper. Every night I mop the floors, take out the trash. I never leave a single hair – or crumb – on the floor. It's too risky. I can't give that... thing... a chance to re-form.

Please, take it from me.

Always clean up after yourself.

THE WEEPUL

The following was a post that appeared on an online forum in 2018.

Subject: Were you approached by a man dressed like a clown in the '90s?

Hi, Reddit. I'm writing because I had a weird experience I had as a child – and I want to know if any of you experienced the same thing.

A man approached me in a parking lot, dressed as a clown, when I was 5 or 6.

It was somewhere between 1995 to 1997. I don't remember the exact date, as the years have fogged my memory. I think it was probably in the spring or fall, as my mom left me in the car, and I don't remember being too hot or too cold.

That day, my mom had parked at a Kings to get groceries. (Kings is like Whole Foods or Trader Joe's; it's pretty popular here in NJ.) My mom rolled down the windows halfway and left me in the car.

"I'll be right back, Blair, okay?" she said, swiftly walking across the parking lot.

I sat there in the car, bored, playing with the locks and staring at my feet. But it wasn't long before I heard a voice through the open window.

"Hi there!"

I looked up to see a man.

He was standing right outside the car door. His face was painted like a clown's, but it wasn't a very good job. He didn't have a blue afro wig, a brightly-colored outfit, or the white face makeup. He basically just had two large circles painted on his cheeks, and some black makeup around his eyes. He was also pretty short, as I remember his face looking directly through the window.

"Do you like weepuls?" he asked.

Weepuls, if you don't remember, are these little toys that were popular in the eighties and nineties. Each one is a pom-pom, with googly eyes, antennae, and sticky feet attached. I vividly remember he gave me a *weepul*, not some other sort of toy.

"Yeah!" I said, with a grin.

"What's your favorite color?"

"Purple."

He reached into a small bag he'd been carrying and, after rummaging around for a few moments, pulled out a bright purple weepul. He reached his hand through the window – it barely fit – and handed it to me. I grinned, ripped the paper off its feet, and stuck it to the center console of the minivan.

"What are you doing out here alone, sweetheart? Isn't your mommy with you?"

I shook my head. "She's in the store."

He opened his mouth to say something. But just then, I recognized my mom's purple hoodie and bobbing ponytail in the distance, slowly walking down the parking lot. "She's there!" I said, pointing, grinning. I couldn't wait to show her the weepul.

His blue eyes widened, he said he had to go, and he slipped away between the cars in the parking lot. As a kid, I was confused why he so hurriedly ended our conversation.

"Okay, I got everything," my mom said, as she loaded a few bags into the back of the car. "Hope you didn't get too bored."

"I got a weepul!" I said.

My mom was in a hurry. She didn't even glance at the new toy that had inexplicably appeared in our car.

She didn't pay attention when I ripped it off and brought it inside, shedding purple fuzz everywhere. Or when I stuck it in the dollhouse and pretended it was Barbie's new pet. Or when I made a little paper hat for it.

She only paid attention when one of its feet fell off, onto the parquet floor.

And she noticed sloppy handwriting across the gray foot:

To: Blair.

VICTORIA'S ROAD

I live in New Jersey – the state known for its "haunted roads."

Crack open a copy of *Weird NJ* and you'll see what I mean. *Clinton Road* – a body dump site for the Mafia and home of a little ghost boy. *Shades of Death Road* – where a woman buried her husband's head and body on opposite sides of the street.

But have you ever heard of *Victoria's Road*?

It's in Warren County, where the congestion of the Jersey suburbs fades out into mountains and trees. It's easy to miss – just a narrow gap in the thick forest, that you'll drive right by if you aren't careful. But if you find it… you'll see, walking along the side of the road, a woman in a purple dress.

You can ask her one question. Any question.

She will tell you the answer.

I went with my best friend Mira late one summer night. We were parked on the side of the road, overlooking the valley below, to review the "rules." The air was thick with the sound of summer crickets and smell of barbeques from the houses on the mountain. The rest of the forest was black with shadows.

Mira handed me the piece of paper, now damp and crumpled. "It was in my pocket all day. Sorry," she said, through *smacks* of gum. I rolled my eyes and began to read.

"1. You must be the only car on the road. For this reason, go late at night, or early in the morning."

Check. It was 12:45 AM.

"2. Your radio must be tuned to 102.2 the entirety of the drive. Turn off all other devices, including your cell phones."

"I don't think it's even possible to get that station," I said, as I turned off my phone. But when Mira gave the dial a spin, it easily landed on 102.2. Static filled the car.

"3. Don't stop your car for any reason *other* than Victoria. No matter what you see or hear, do not stop."

"Weird," I said to Mira. She shrugged.

"4. DO NOT, under any circumstances, attempt to make a U-Turn or go back the way you came."

"Well, that's easy enough," I said. "You ready, Mira?"

She nodded.

I turned back onto the road and rolled down the window. Yellow fireflies danced between the trees; the sounds of crickets filled the air. The breeze was warm and humid. "Are you sure it's this way?" I asked. The road tilted up, climbing the mountain. In a few minutes, we'd be at the top.

366

"Positive," Mira said. "It's just around the bend, there."

She was right. Within minutes, a tilted signpost came into view. Faded and cracked, wrapped with vines and foliage.

VICTORIA'S ROAD

I turned on the blinker – despite the road being completely empty – and swung left.

The road was dark. The headlights barely punctured the thick shadows; it was as if we were submerged in murky water. Mira, however, didn't seem perturbed. She practically vibrated with excitement. "So, if this thing works – which it probably won't, I know – what are you gonna ask her?"

"Oh, I don't know. Maybe what college will accept me."

That was a lie. I knew *exactly* what I wanted to ask her. *Is Dad ever coming back?* After he met Linda three years ago... it's all been missed calls, one-word texts, empty promises. "So, uh, what do *you* want to ask her?"

"If Sarah McCoffrey likes me. Duh."

"*Her?*"

"What's wrong with her?"

"Isn't she super-Christian? Like Bibles and white dresses and cross necklaces all the time? Are you sure she's even –"

Mira stared at me blankly. "Christians can be gay too, Hannah."

I suddenly felt dumb. "Well, uh, I just assumed –"

My foot hit the brake.

367

Screeeeeech.

We jolted to a halt.

A deer sauntered across the road. It stopped in the center and turned towards us, its eyes glowing in the headlights. "Oh my gosh, that scared the bejeezus out of me," Mira said. My heart pounded in my chest.

But then she grew annoyed. "Wait, wait, we're not supposed to stop! Rule #3. We're going to screw it up!"

"What do you want me to do, plow into the deer? We have to wait for it to cross."

"Fine."

But as we sat there, the deer didn't move. It just stood there, in the headlights, watching us. *Get out of the way. Come on!*

Finally – as if my thoughts willed it – it took a step.

Not towards the woods. A step forward, towards our car. "What's it doing?" Mira asked. It walked closer, its fur scratching against the hood of the car, until it was just a few feet from my window. It stared at me with those black, glinting eyes.

Then it reared its head –

And rammed against the car.

Thump!

"What the hell?!" I screamed.

The car jolted forward; we sped down the dark road. "What a crazy-ass deer. It must be rabid or something." Mira shook her head. "Is the car okay? Did it leave a dent?"

"No idea. If it did, Mom's going to kill me."

We drove for the next few minutes in silence, save for the crackles of static from the radio. The road continued through the forest, growing even darker and narrower. *I don't like this at all. Maybe we should turn around.*

We continued down the dark road. It grew narrower and bumpier; Mira and I jostled in our seats, and a few branches scraped at the windows. "I don't know if this is safe," I said. "Maybe we should turn around –"

"Are you chickening out *already?*"

"I'm not chickening out! What if we hit another deer? Or –"

I stopped.

The static on the radio had fizzled to silence.

But when I looked at the car's glowing console, it no longer said *FM RADIO;* it said *BLUETOOTH AUDIO.* Like it does when my phone is connected.

"Hannah?"

A man's voice came through the speakers, cut with static.

"Hannah, hey, you there?"

I gulped. "…Dad? Is that you?"

"Yeah!" He laughed his cheerful, warm laugh. "Sorry to call you so late. But I happen to be driving through Blairstown right now – had a work thing in Philly. Do you want to meet up?"

"Now?" I said.

"Yeah. Where are you? We can meet at that 24-hour diner –"

"I'm with Mira. We're uh, just on a little adventure."

"Oh, sounds fun!" He laughed again, and my heart soared. "Well, do you want to meet up? I'll be there in about fifteen minutes."

I glanced at Mira.

"Yeah, okay."

Click.

"I'm so sorry, Mira. We'll have to do this some other time." I began turning the wheel, swinging left. The headlights swept through the dark forest, cut with lines of trees. "I haven't seen my dad in six months, and we've been trying to reach each other –"

Mira thrust her hand into my pocket.

"Hey! What are you –"

She pulled out my phone. "You turned your phone *off*, remember? It was in the rules." Her voice began to tremble. "There's no way that could've been your dad, Hannah."

"But I –"

"Do not, at any point, attempt to turn around. Rule #4, remember?"

I stared out the window. At the disjointed shadows; at the road that disappeared into the black.

And then I continued forward.

Tears burned at my eyes. *Hearing his voice again...* I shook my head, forcing the thought out of my head. The static faded back in. The road began to dip down, as if we were finally descending the mountain. Wayward branches scraped at the car. I slowly rolled down the window; but the summer air was silent, devoid of crickets, wind, rustling.

And then Mira screamed.

"Watch out!"

A blur of white darted out of the forest. In front of the car. I hit the brakes.

But it was too late.

Thump.

"What was that?" Mira asked, her voice trembling.

"Another deer, maybe."

But I knew it wasn't.

I was numb, frozen, paralyzed. *What did we just hit?* I didn't want to know. I wanted to turn around, speed as fast as I could down the road. Back to safety. Pretend like whatever we hit – it never happened. We were never here.

"We should go out and check," Mira said. But she didn't move to open the door.

"I'll... I'll get out and check."

I forced myself to open the door and take a shaking step onto the cold asphalt.

The headlights shone into the darkness, motes of dust and debris swirling in the light. The surrounding forest was silent. My heart thrummed in my chest. I stared at the ground as I paced towards the front of the car, waiting for something terrible to come into view.

The space under the wheel was empty. Just smooth, empty asphalt, darker than the surrounding trees.

Nothing here, so far. Maybe I'm okay.

I took another step. More of the road came into view in front of the car.

It was empty.

Still nothing. It must've been my imagination...

I took another step, rounding the corner.

No.

Sticking out from under the car was a bit of white cloth. Wrinkled, crushed, speckled with deep red stains.

I crumpled to my knees.

A lifeless figure was halfway pinned underneath the front tires. Pale, smooth skin of an arm became a crushed, mangled mess as it met the tire. Tangles of auburn hair – whether stained from the blood or natural, I couldn't tell – spread out across the asphalt.

I shot to my feet.

Mira's eyes met mine through the windshield. As soon as are stares locked, she understood. "Oh my God, Hannah –"

I broke into choking sobs. "I didn't mean to. I didn't even see her." I looked down again at my feet, as if I expected her to suddenly disappear. But the white cloth was still there, poking out from under the hood. "I didn't mean to. Oh my God, what are we –"

My sentence ended in a strangled yelp.

Something cold grabbed my ankle.

Hard.

It violently tugged. I fell to the ground. The tar scraped against my chest. The metal bumper hit my head with a sickening *thump*.

It was pulling me under the car.

And then all I saw was darkness. Save for the few inches of light between the dark metal of the car and the pavement. "Help!" I screamed; my voice was muffled, muted, under the car. I thrashed and squirmed, but the grip held tight.

I looked back. All I could see was a mangled mess of white cloth, blood, and red hair. Unnaturally contorted and jumbled, as if she were horribly disfigured before I even hit her.

I screamed as my body scraped against the tar, staring at that little gap of light...

Mira's face appeared. She grabbed my hand and pulled. "Hannah! Hold on!" she yelled.

She yanked and tugged with all her might. The cold hand released; within a few seconds, I was out, panting in the darkness. "Hannah, are you okay?" she kept asking, but all I could hear was a ringing in my ears.

"I'm okay," I groaned, stumbling to my feet. "I mean, I think I am – what *was* that –"

Vrrrrrmmm. The roar of the engine.

We looked up.

The woman was no longer under the car.

And the car was rolling forward.

"Run!"

The car roared towards us, flew down the road.

Slap!

The mirror glanced off my shoulder. It sent me flying into the forest. Branches and trees scraped across my chest. Headlights flashed in my eyes. I stumbled blindly; my toe hooked onto a branch, and I fell forward.

"How do we get out of here?" I screamed breathlessly. "I have no idea," Mira yelled back, several feet from me in the darkness.

The headlights flashed across the tree trunks, shifting the shadows. I stood up, backed away. The sticks crunched under my feet; the wind whistled through the trees. Mira's hands fell on my shoulders. She was shaking with fear.

Snap, snap, snap.

The car careened into the bushes, towards the trees. Half off the road, threatening to follow us into the forest. I squinted at the windshield – through the bright light, I could make out that horrendous, misshapen head, staring back at us.

"Help!" Mira screamed. "Someone, please!"

A voice – over the roar of the engine, the sounds of our ragged breaths – replied: "Yes?"

We both looked up. There, among the shadows of the trees –

Was a woman wearing a purple dress.

We ran towards her, aching and breathless and terrified. She stood against one of the trees, thin and tall and smiling. The dress fell to the ground, seeming to melt into the dirt, leaves, roots.

The woman in the purple dress.

You may ask her one question. One question, only, and she has to answer it. I no longer wanted to ask about my Dad. Or colleges. Or anything else. Everything was gone from my mind, except one singular, ultimate question. I took a deep breath, and shouted:

"How do we get out of here?"

I looked up. She was suddenly standing just a few feet in front of us, towering over Mira and I, her long

374

dark hair fluttering in the wind. "That's always the question, isn't it?" she asked, with a sad smile.

Vrrrrrm. The car roared in the distance, headlights flashing over her face.

She lifted a hand and pointed into the darkness of the woods. "Run that way. Don't stop until you've come to a small stream. Turn right; in ten minutes you'll find yourselves on a residential street."

We didn't need to be told twice.

We ran through the darkness. The roar of the car faded into the distance; the bright white of the headlights faded into shadows. We didn't stop until we got to the stream, breathless and aching; then we turned, like she instructed.

We found ourselves on a quiet, residential street and knocked on the first door we saw.

***

The police never found my car. They just tossed our file in with the rest of the strange occurrences on Victoria's Road. Disappearances, injuries, sudden mental breakdowns... we weren't the only ones dumb enough to drive down the road.

But we were one of the luckiest. Other than a few scrapes and bruises, we were okay.

So, to answer your question: yes. The legend of Victoria's Road is true. Every person who drives down it gets one question answered, absolutely truthfully.

But the question they choose to ask is always the same: "How do I get out of here?"

However... that doesn't mean our other questions went unanswered.

The trauma of the experience forced us to ask the questions ourselves, to the people who *could* answer them. In the wake of such terror, asking out the girl you like – or calling up your estranged dad – just doesn't seem that scary anymore.

We got our answers.

Will you?

ASTRAL PROJECTION

by Blair Daniels & Craig Groshek

When I first saw Arron, he was lying on the floor of the Thompson's bedroom, still as death.

"Hey! Are you okay?"

I prodded him with my toe. Then I crouched down and shook him, like mad, until his eyes fluttered open.

"Don't *do* that!" he yelled in my face. His breaths were panicked and fast, as if he'd just come up from underwater. A rustling noise came from the other side of the room, and I noticed there were several other people sprawled out across the floor.

"Sorry," I said. "I thought you were passed out."

"No. I was sleeping."

"Everyone else is out there drinking and dancing, and you're *sleeping?*"

"Not sleeping," one of the girls piped up. "Astral projecting."

"Seriously?"

I'd heard the stories. I didn't believe them, of course — but I'd heard them. In the past several months, all kinds of wild stories had popped up. Especially on internet forums and amateur websites.

Some of the stories were wonderful. Like the girl suffering from macular degeneration, who said it let her see for the first time in years. Others were terrifying. Like the teenage girl who realized one of her classmates was using it to spy on the girls' locker room. Others were just... confusing. Like the woman who preferred the astral plane to real life. Now her family waits by her bedside, watching her comatose body, waiting for her to come back home.

"Does it work?" I asked.

"Yeah. And it's wonderful," Arron said. His ocean-blue eyes met mine, and he smiled. "You should join us."

"No thanks."

"It's far better than dancing to crappy music and drinking cheap beer."

"I wasn't drinking. I was talking to people."

"Well, this is *much* better than talking to people. You'll soar among the clouds. See the stars up close. Swim in the ocean, without ever coming up for air. It's the best thing in the world."

Arron's voice rippled with excitement as he talked. For a moment, I was tempted to just lie down on the filthy carpet with him, and try it out for myself.

But I couldn't.

"Maybe some other time," I told him.

I left the bedroom. As I walked towards the hall, though, footsteps sounded behind me. I turned to see Arron following.

"What are you doing?"

He shot me another hypnotizing smile. "I changed my mind. There *is* something better than astral projection."

"What?"

"You."

I laughed. "Nice pick-up line, there."

"Come on. You liked it." He shot me a wink. "I'm Arron."

"Billie."

We took a seat in the corner of the room, away from the thrashing mass of teenagers in the center. "Do you go to Glenmont High? I haven't seen you around before," I said, over the music.

"I'm new. My family just moved here from Pennsylvania."

"Oh. Do you like it here?"

"Yeah, I —"

A scream rung out, above the music. Then a girl broke through the crowd — face red, eyes wet with tears.

"He won't wake up," she screamed. "He won't wake up!"

Arron leapt up and ran back to the bedroom. I followed. Several people crowded around a still form on the floor. Arron pushed through them. "Eric, can you hear me?" he shouted, shaking him. "Eric! Hey, come on!"

He didn't respond.

Arron thrust a hand under his back. In one quick, strong motion, he pushed him up. Eric's eyes shot open. He began to cough.

"He's okay. He's okay." Eric began to cough. Arron smacked him on the back. "That's it, Eric. You're okay."

My pounding heart filled with admiration. Arron wasn't just handsome and kind — he was a hero.

***

The next few weeks were a blur. Arron texted me everyday, and we often stayed up until the wee hours chatting. He'd tell me about his experiences traveling, his excitement at us being together. Finneas didn't approve; he and Arron were both seniors. "He's too old for you," Finneas would say. "And he's kind of weird. Hangs around with that astrological, spiritual crowd."

I didn't see him like that. I was falling in love.

We'd been dating for almost a month when Arron brought up astral projection again.

"So, I don't want to pressure you or anything, but... I was wondering if you'd project with me."

I turned to him, frowning. "I don't know, Arron. It seems dangerous. After what happened to Eric —"

"That was his fault. He didn't have a partner. You *always* project with a partner, in case something goes wrong."

"I don't know, Arron. It's not really my thing."

"But you've never tried it!" His blue eyes took on that faraway look — the same look I'd seen when he was driving me home that very first night. "Come on, Billie. It'll be romantic. We'll soar among the clouds, together."

"But just last week, some woman projected for several hours. And some people are saying she isn't the same, like she's possessed or something —"

"That's like, one out of *thousands*. Besides — you've got someone with tons of experience to pull you back if anything goes wrong." He looked into my eyes, again. "Please? It would mean so much to me."

I sighed. "Okay, okay. I'll *try* it."

He grinned. Gently holding my hand, he guided me into the bedroom. "Go ahead and lie down on the bed. On your back."

I quirked an eyebrow at him. "You better not be trying anything."

He laughed and lay down next to me.

"Just a few things to remember, before we start. First — don't lose sight of me, okay? I'll be keeping you safe. Second — if anything looks off, don't approach it. There are... things, in the astral plane, that you don't want to interact with. Third — we can't stay longer than an hour. The longer you stay, the harder it is to come back."

"That's not encouraging."

He turned to me, blue eyes locked on mine. "I will be with you every step of the way, Billie. You're going to be fine. Okay?"

"Okay."

"Now... close your eyes and relax. Fade out all the sounds and sights around you. If you feel a heavy, tingling feeling — as if you're falling asleep — that's when you want to act. Imagine you're being pulled out of your body by a rope, or climbing up a ladder."

"This is so weird."

"Just try it."

I closed my eyes and tried to relax. Within ten minutes, I felt the heavy, tingling feeling that he described. I imagined a sort of endless ladder sticking out of my abdomen — and then me, climbing up it, out of my body.

A *pop* filled my ears.

And then I was staring down at myself.

"Holy crap," I said. But it came out as more of an ethereal echo, vibrating through space itself.

"I can't believe you did it on your first try!"

I turned to see Arron hovering beside me. He looked the same — except his clothes and body were washed in neon, as if he were standing under a blacklight. When he smiled, his teeth glowed brightly.

"Are you ready?"

"I guess."

He took my hand and pulled.

We soared right up through the roof. Higher and higher into the sky, until the town below shrunk to tiny pinpricks of light.

"Watch for your tether."

I looked down to see a white string coming out of my chest. It extended down into the darkness, far below, like some sort of ghostly umbilical cord. "What *is* that?"

"The thing that tethers you to your body."

"But *you* don't have one."

"With enough practice, you don't need one. You just snip it off." He reached for my hand again and tugged. "Come on. Let's go."

I didn't reply.

Something had caught my eye. An orange light, in the distance, shimmering and flickering between the mountains. "What's that?"

"What's what?" Arron asked, scanning the landscape.

"The light." As I spoke, it started to grow. A glint turned into a flame; a flame grew into a river of orange. It bled towards the town at frightening speed. Puffs of black smoke clouded the sky, blocking out the moon.

"Arron! Is that fire?!"

He didn't reply. He just stared at me with those ocean-blue eyes.

The orange reached the first few houses at the edge of town. As soon as it touched them, they burst into flame. Then it spread further into town, pooling in the roads and crevices. As soon as it came into contact with a house, it burst into flame.

Then came the screams.

Horrible, shrill screams of pain. Rising up from the town like a chorus. "Arron!" I yelled over the sound. "Please, do something —"

Then I was falling.

Fast and hard, yanked forward by the cord in my chest. The cold air quickly warmed as I neared the town. The orange light licked my face. I closed my eyes. My scream joined the others.

I hit the ground.

My eyes flew open.

"Arron! We have to get out of here. The fire, the fire —"

"Billie, it's okay."

He wrapped his arms around me. The window outside was dark and cold; not a single flicker of light.

"But the fire —"

"Just your imagination." He pulled away from me, ran his hand through my hair. "Sometimes, if you're not totally relaxed… if you're stressed, or distracted… your own thoughts can pollute the experience. Especially the first few times."

"Why didn't you tell me that?"

"I didn't want to scare you. I thought maybe —"

"Maybe I'd say no?!"

He sighed. "I just wanted to have a fun with you, Billie."

I grabbed my things and stormed out. Then I went to sleep, fuming mad.

***

We spent a few days in silence. No texts, no calls, no emails.

Finally, I broke down and drove to his place. After five minutes of knocking, he opened the door.

"Billie." As soon as he saw me, those ocean-blue eyes lit up as if the sun was hitting the water. "I'm so sorry."

He pulled me into a hug. The two of us stood there on this doorstep, hugging each other like we were afraid the other night slip away at any moment.

"I love you, Billie."

"I love you too, Arron."

For the next few months, our relationship was incredible. We spent our days exploring town, and our nights looking up at the stars in Groveland Park. It was on one of these nights, around 1 AM, that astral projection came up again.

"We should be getting back, shouldn't we?"

"You go on ahead," Arron said, stretching out on the blanket. "I'm going to sleep out here. I want to astral project again. See the stars up close."

"Okay. Goodnight." I started across the grass. The park was so quiet, so empty at this time of night. I thought of my bed, too, empty at home. Without Arron.

I turned around. "Actually, I'll stay here with you."

His eyes lit up. "Really?"

"I want to see the stars with you." I took a deep breath and squeezed his hand. "I'll try it just this one more time. For you."

We lay back in the grass. The sky hung over us, scattered with stars. Arron reached for my hand, and we closed our eyes.

It came quicker this time. The tingling, the heavy feeling... it all came on within minutes. I felt my spirit peeling off my body, lifting out of the ground.

Then I was hanging in the night air, looking down at our bodies below.

"Wow, that was quick," Arron said.

"Practice makes perfect, I guess."

The park shrunk away as the two of us soared up towards the stars. "They're so much more beautiful up here, see?"

But I wasn't looking at the stars.

I was looking down at the forest. Something was wrong. The trees were shaking, swaying, knocking into each other. A few toppled to the ground.

"What's happening down there?"

"I don't know."

The trees roiled and quaked, as if something immense was passing through. "Is something in there?" I asked.

Crack!

An immense shadow stepped out of the forest. Thick and tusked, like an elephant; lithe and graceful, like a jaguar. It crossed over the park in quick, rapid strides. The earth shook underneath its feet.

"Arron! What *is* that?!"

Crrrrraaack!

The field tore open under its feet. Grass gave way to a fissure of rock, dirt, and darkness — just several feet from our comatose bodies. The figure had stopped in the middle of the park, sniffing the air.

"We have to get back! Arron, we have to —"

I stopped.

Arron was hovering a few feet below me. Holding my tether in one hand — and a knife in the other.

"What are you doing?!"

But I was too late. The knife touched the tether. Immediately, a shockwave of pain rippled through my body.

I yanked away from him. But he held fast to it; I snapped back, as if on a leash.

"Arron!"

"I want you to be here, with me, forever." He slashed at the tether again. I screamed in pain. *Crrack! Crrack!* More fissures erupted underneath me. The whole world shook.

Another sharp pain stung my chest.

And then I was floating. Drifting away, as if blown by some invisible current. "Arron — help!" I screamed. The world started to blur and shift.

My tether was gone.

I looked around wildly — at the shaking, splitting ground. At the swaying trees. *Where is imy body? Where is it?*

There. A speck of white among the dark grass.

I forced myself to fall towards it. With every fiber of my being, I concentrated on that speck of white, among the blurry, shaking landscape. The current tugged at me, trying to pull me away. I wouldn't let it.

With a pop, I opened my eyes.

The sky lay above me. The earth no longer shook.

I scrambled up.

A hand grabbed my ankle, hard, and yanked me back.

"Arron! What are you doing? Let me go!"

He didn't reply. He just stared at me, his ocean-blue eyes burning with anger.

I yanked as hard as I could. Then I ran. I sprinted through the park, past the trees, to the car. Arron's footsteps thundered behind me.

I yanked the door open and dove inside. I pressed the locks just as Arron's hand hit the handle.

"Let me in, Billie."

"No," I sobbed. "You were trying to hurt me. Why, Arron? Why?"

"Come on, Billie."

"You're scaring me," I said through the glass. "Please, just go."

"I just wanted us to be together."

"Why did I see those horrible things, then? The monster? The cracks in the earth? The fire?"

"It's the future, Billie." He sighed, as if what he was saying truly pained him. "Humanity has sinned against the earth far too much, for far too long. We break through the gates, cleanse the Earth, and start it anew."

"We? Who's *we?*"

"Us on the astral plane."

"You aren't making any sense."

"Didn't you ever wonder why I don't have a tether?"

The pieces slowly fit together in my mind. "No. You're possessing Arron?" I filled with anger. "Get out of his body! He's mine! You can't take him away from me!" I pounded the glass and screamed.

"No. I *am* Arron. But this body... it belongs to some guy in Nevada named Derek."

My heart plummeted. "What?"

"Don't worry. You, Billie, don't have to suffer like the rest. You're one of the good ones. We'll stay in the astral plane, while the rest of the world burns."

"I just want to go home."

His expression turned angry again. "Home? What's there for you, at home? Your brother? Your parents?"

I nodded.

388

"Then I'll bring them with us."

"What? No, Arron —"

He took off across the park. He lay down in the center of the lawn, on the rumpled blanket, where we had held hands just an hour before.

I leapt out of the car and ran. I didn't stop until I was standing in front of my house, weak and breathless.

I ran in the door and ran up the stairs. "Mom? Dad? Finneas?" I shouted.

I ran into the master bedroom first.

Mom and Dad lay on the bed, silent and still. "Mom?" I yelled. I grabbed her shoulders and shook her. "Mom, please. Wake up."

Nothing.

"Dad?"

I ran out of the room. "Finneas! Finneas!" I shouted as I ran down the hall.

Finneas lay in bed. His body jerked and twitched wildly.

"Finneas!" I grabbed him by the shoulders and shook him. "Finneas, please! Wake up!"

He fell still.

Then he rubbed his eyes. "Billie?"

"Oh, thank God. Finneas, we need to get help. Mom and Dad won't wake up. We need to get out of here, before —"

I stopped.

His eyes had fluttered open.

They were a bright, ocean blue.

"Hello again, Billie."

MADELINE[3]

I was sitting at the nurse's station, reading trashy tabloids and drinking coffee when Olga — the other nurse on duty — poked my arm.

"The little girl escaped," she said, with a giggle.

"What?"

She pointed to the security camera feed.

Little Madeline was standing in the hallway, her image grainy and pixelated.

We'd admitted Madeline at 8:23 PM. A little girl, no more than six. Her face covered in blood. She'd taken a nasty fall down the stairs. Dr. Thompson was worried she might develop a subdural hematoma, so we were keeping her for overnight.

"Ugh, no. She shouldn't be up." I paused, leaning towards the monitor. "And where'd she get those clothes?"

---

[3] First appeared under the name "Nurse Jolene," another pen name of Blair Daniels.

She wasn't wearing the hospital gown we'd put her to bed in. No — she was wearing a black dress, white stockings, and shiny black shoes. As if she were all dressed up for church. Or a funeral.

And she kept whipping her head back and forth. As if expecting someone to come down the hallway.

"Well? Are you going to go get her or not?" Olga said, looking up from her phone.

"Yeah, yeah, I'll get her." I pushed the chair out, leapt up, and speed-walked down the hallway. "Madeline?" I called, as I rounded the corner. "Madel —"

My breath caught in my throat.

There was no one there.

I walked up to her room. "Madeline?" I called, poking my head in.

She was sleeping peacefully in bed.

In her hospital gown. With her IV still attached.

Weird. I walked back to the nurse's station. I couldn't help feeling a bit unsettled. I know kids sometimes do freaky shit, but there's no way a 6-year-old could reattach an IV.

I plopped back down at the nurse's station.

Olga raised her eyebrows at me. "You found her?"

"Yeah. She's sleeping in her room." I leaned towards her and lowered my voice. "This is going to sound really weird, but I don't think... I don't think she ever got out of bed."

"Oooh, spooky," she said, with a grin. "Maybe she's possessed by that slime thing you wouldn't shut up about last week." Back to texting.

391

I narrowed my eyes at her. "That's not something to joke about."

"Oh, really? What are you going to do, murder me?" She held up her hands in front of her. "I'm so scared!"

I rolled my eyes and turned back to reading about the half-mermaid that apparently washed up on the shores of Lake Erie. *Psh, I can't believe people actually believe this stuff,* I thought.

It was 3:40 AM when it happened again.

I happened to look up at the hallway, and the security monitor caught my eye. Madeline was standing just outside her door. In her dress and stockings.

Except she looked scared, this time.

"Look. It's Madeline again," I said, poking Olga.

As I said it, one of the lights flickered out at the far end of the hallway. The video feed grew darker.

Olga looked up from her texting (who was she even texting after 3 AM?!) and followed my gaze. "Oh, it's the little demon girl again! Ha, ha!"

I narrowed my eyes at her. "If you think all of this is *so* funny, *you* go check on her."

Her eyes widened a bit. "Uh, okay." She slowly got up, taking as long as humanly possible. Then she disappeared down the hallway.

I turned back to the video feed.

Another light had gone out at the end of the hall. The video was darker and grainier now. But I could still make out Madeline's little form standing in front of the room — barely more than a silhouette.

Click!

Another light went out.

Then another. And another. The hallway was quickly engulfed in darkness, until the only light on was the one above Madeline's door.

"Well, crap," I muttered to myself. "We're going to need an electrician."

I drank the last dregs of my iced coffee. When I put the cup down, I saw it.

My blood ran cold.

It was a shadow. A grainy, pixelated silhouette, roiling and shifting in the darkness. At first I thought it was Olga, coming from the other end of the hall.

It wasn't.

It was too tall, stretching from the ceiling to the floor. Too thin (no offense, Olga.) I leaned into the monitor. *What the hell?*

The shadow got darker. Larger. It slowly bled out of the darkness and into the light of the hall.

Right next to Madeline.

It was so dark and subtle, I thought it might be just some trick of the camera. Some error of the low light.

But Madeline saw it too.

Because she was backing away. Stretching her arms over the open hospital room door. Shaking her head violently.

The shadow advanced.

Beep! Beep! Beep!

My eyes snapped away from the security system to the nurse's console.

No.

Madeline's vitals were plummeting. Her heart rate, blood pressure...

I shot up and sprinted down the hallway.

Olga had just gotten there, her hand on the doorknob. Half the hallway was dark, just like in the feed. But no tall shadow like I'd seen, no Madeline standing in the hallway.

"Call Dr. Thompson!" I screamed. "She's in trouble!"

I flew past her, into the room.

Madeline lay still and motionless on the bed.

Her heart had stopped.

I ran over. Started CPR. *Come on, come on,* I screamed, internally. *Please don't take her from us. Please* —

Blip. Blip. Blip.

Her heartbeat returned just as Dr. Thompson rushed in.

I fell against the wall and began to sob.

***

We kept Madeline in the hospital for a few more days, but I don't think we needed to. She seemed to recover quickly. As I checked her vitals to release her, I'd nearly forgotten all about the shadow.

"How are you feeling?" I asked her, as I took her blood pressure.

"Great," Madeline said. She turned to her parents. "She saved me!"

"Aww, it was nothing."

She glanced at me. "Not *you,*" she said, condescendingly. "Maggie."

Maggie? I furrowed my eyebrows at her. *Ungrateful little kid.* "Who's Maggie?"

Madeline's mother uneasily stared at the floor. Her father wrapped an arm around her, and coughed strangely.

Okay, then.

"You're all set," I said, ripping off the blood pressure cuff.

"Yay!" she squealed. She grabbed her mom's hand, and the two of them walked into the hallway. But the father stayed behind.

"Thank you so much for everything," he said, with a smile. "As I understand it... you saved Madeline's life."

"No, that was *Maggie,*" I said, rolling my eyes.

He coughed again, strangely.

The curiosity bit into me. Completely overstepping my bounds as a nurse, I asked: "Who's Maggie? Her imaginary friend?"

He sighed heavily. "Uh... sort of. When my wife was pregnant with Madeline... she was actually pregnant with twins."

My heart stopped.

"Identical twins. But one of them passed away in the womb," he continued. "We told Madeline, since we don't believe in keeping secrets. But it appears we made a mistake. Little Madeline has an overactive imagination. Always talks about 'Maggie,' as if she's actually still with us."

He coughed again, strangely, and I realized it was to stop an impending sob. He reached out to shake my hand. "Thank you so much again."

He turned and followed his family down the hallway.

But all I could think about was the little girl.

Who looked exactly like Madeline, standing outside her door.

Protecting her.

BLACK WIDOW, INC.

Amanda Duffy killed Rebecca.

I was quite impressed. She just charged right up to her and stabbed her in the stomach. That took guts... no pun intended.

We did a good job. When we set out on this project – using the evening news to falsely accuse people of crimes – we used a computer program to select "high-risk" individuals. People who were likely to become criminals eventually.

It did a fantastic job picking Amanda.

You're probably wondering who I am. I'm the president of Black Widow, Inc., and I'm writing this because... well, I'm proud of all we accomplished. Now that we're closing it down, I want *some* record of all the havoc we caused. All the chaos. All the fear.

Fear.

It's a funny thing, isn't it? Some people – like you – seek it out voluntarily. Others avoid it at every point they can.

Still others feed on it.

When we started the company, that was the million-dollar question. How do we create fear? And after much research (that involved hundreds of fun tests), the answer was: change your perception of reality.

We first accomplished that by creating simulators – like *The Love Simulator* and *Virtual Reality Vacations* – and reality-modifying drugs, like Bandersnatch. But then, we moved on to bigger – better – things. Like AirPods that tell you other peoples' thoughts – changing your perception of others. Or face masks that change your appearance, your perception of yourself. Or Lasik operations that change your entire reality.

But as I said, we're closing it all down. As I write this, the technology, the drugs, the media takeover – all of it is being destroyed.

Because we found a better way.

A better way to change your perception of reality. A better way to create fear. A way to invade the mind – without the target even realizing it.

All it takes are some words on a page.

FIVE BONUS STORIES

Keep reading for five bonus stories from other books by Blair Daniels.

THE RAIN ISN'T WATER

I first noticed it when I was waiting for the bus.

It was raining. Harder than it had all month, all year. Everyone was crammed into the glass hutch, looking miserable, apparently without umbrellas. I stared at the scene, trying to decide which was worse: getting wet, or rubbing butts with strangers?

It was an easy decision.

I stood in the muddy grass. The rain pattered on my skin, soaking my shirt. Rivulets ran down my forehead, dripping into my eyes; I reached to wipe them away.

I froze.

The rainwater felt… *different.* It was mildly slippery– like a cross between water and oil. I wet my fingers and rolled them against each other, eyebrows knotted.

I thought it was my imagination at first. One look at the road told me it wasn't. Cars were going much slower than usual on this road–maybe twenty miles an hour. And the ones that went faster seemed to career towards the gutter, as if skidding.

I pulled out my phone began to type: "rain in Bloomfield." That's when I heard the scream.

I looked up. Across the sloshing mess of the street, two women were yelling and pointing at a man that had just exited the Starbucks.

"You're bleeding!"

"Are you all right?"

At first, I thought he was wearing some sort of white shirt with red polka-dots. But as the rain beat down on him, the shirt grew redder. "Call an ambulance!" one of them said. I squinted at the scene, confused.

"I'm fine, really, I don't know what's going on," the man said. "Please, don't call anyone."

That's when I figured it out. The red dots were where raindrops had fallen. Red lines ran down his face and arms, dripping onto the sidewalk, tinting the puddles pink.

"I'm fine, really."

Three days later, I saw his face on the news.

John Allard, 45, was arrested for murdering his wife in their home on Tuesday night. The trial will be held...

"That's the guy," I said, pointing wildly to the TV. "The one I told you about—out in the rain."

Molly barely looked up. "Oh, that's nice," she said, as she rummaged through the kitchen cabinets.

Over the next few weeks, more people were caught in the rain. When the rain touched some of them, it ran blood-red, staining their clothes just like their hearts. Within a few days, they always turned to some act of violence—whether it be murder, assault, or rape. The town of Bloomfield was in a state of chaos, a state of confusion. No one knew what was going on, or what to do about it.

Last night, we had another storm. Rain pounded across the back door; lightning flashed across the purple sky. I stood out on the deck, under the awning of the house, just watching.

"Molly, come out here. It's beautiful!"

"The soup's getting cold, Rick," her voice called from the kitchen.

Lines of lightning flashed, cracking and webbing across the purple clouds. *Nature's fireworks show,* Molly always said. "You love thunderstorms," I called back. The rain picked up tempo, cutting into the awning. "Come out here and see it!"

She came to the door. "No. Come in and eat dinner with me," she said through the screen.

"Just for a moment. It's sort of romantic, come on."

She sighed. "Okay, fine."

Molly stepped cautiously out onto the deck. I threw my arm around her, and we stood there for a few moments, watching the lightning flash.

A gust of wind blew through, sending a spray of raindrops into my face. "Sorry about that," I said, turning towards her. "Maybe I shouldn't have forced you out here, after all –"

I froze.

Beads of blood stuck to her cheek.

"Uh, Molly?"

"What?"

She turned towards me. As she did, her arm poked out slightly from the awning. The rain glanced off it, turning to a deep crimson.

I backed away.

"Rick, wait," she said, her eyes widening with recognition. With soft *smacks,* more drops hit her face; they dripped down her cheeks in dark lines.

I ran into the house. *Click*–I closed the door and turned the lock.

"Rick, please, open the door," she said, as her shirt turned red and bloody.

I turned away, and picked up the phone.

***

The police found a bottle of ethylene glycol in the kitchen cupboard, half of it missing.

I like to think the rain caused her to do it. That all of us are innocent in Bloomfield, and we're being manipulated by some unknown chemical dropping from the skies, choosing people to turn into monsters.

But I found the receipt for the poison.

It was dated six months ago.

It continues to rain here in Bloomfield. Every time I see the gray storm clouds overhead, my stomach ties up in knots, wondering what evil will be revealed.

But they've gotten smarter. When I drive down Main Street in the rain, only a few stragglers remain. The rest stay inside.

And the ones that do walk out–

Well, they never forget to use their umbrellas.

THE HITMAN WITH A HEART

Michael Zinsky wasn't my usual type of client.

He wasn't a spurned lover, looking for revenge, or a murderer, looking to snuff out the witnesses to his crime, or a husband, hungry for his wife's insurance policy.

He was just an ordinary guy, looking out for his sister.

"I wouldn't normally resort to… such drastic measures. But Harold has become so awful. Treats her like garbage. Doesn't give a rat's ass about her, or anything, except for that stupid band he sings in with his work buddies." He blew his nose loudly. "You understand that–right, Switchblade?"

I winced. "Uh, that's just my alias, Michael. You shouldn't… like… actually call me that in casual conversation."

"Then what should I call you?"

I blinked. Clearly, he had never done *anything* like this before. "Uh, do you have the cash?"

His eyes darted around the diner. He pulled out a wad of hundred-dollar bills from his pocket.

"You can't just–they'll see it!" I hastily threw him one of the napkins. "Wrap it up in that. And do it *discreetly.*"

He wasn't discreet–but, thankfully, the diner was nearly empty at this hour. "It's *twice* your usual rate," he whispered, very loudly. "I wanted to give you a big tip, so you'll do a good job."

A tip? You're not ordering an ice cream cone, Michael. You're ordering a hit. But I took the cash, smiled, and buried it deep in my pocket.

"And I don't want you to kill him."

What?

"Michael, you know I'm a hitman, right?"

"Yes. But Nancy needs his income–she's been a housewife for the past twenty years. No work experience, no education past high school. There's no way she could support herself on her own."

"*You* could support her, with the cash you just gave me."

He shook his head. "I've tried. She won't let me. Cares too much."

I sighed. "Well, okay. Suppose I did take you up on this... job. What do you even want me to do to him, if not kill him?"

"I don't know! Scare him. Threaten him. Just make him stop being so terrible to her."

"But it's risky business. I mean, he'll know what I look like, and –"

"You'll go on Sunday morning. He'll be napping alone in the house–won't even see you come in." Michael looked down at the table, and then added: "It's the only time he's ever alone in the house. The only time... he *lets* her leave."

My belligerence evaporated and I felt a pang of sympathy. "It's that bad?"

He nodded.

"Okay. I'm in."

***

The house was a tiny little thing, shoved into the gap between a massive brownstone and a dilapidated food mart. It would be a challenge to do this without any witnesses.

Good. I like a challenge.

I snuck through the backyard, creatively using the various bushes and fencing to hide from onlookers. I stepped into the open window, like Michael told me to.

The knife was heavy in my hands.

I turned left at the kitchen and crept into the living room. In the center stood a microphone, a music stand, and some sheet music–presumably for Harold and his band. Nancy's needlepoint supplies were pushed into the corner, taking up as little space as they possibly could.

I walked into the next room.

There, in the armchair, sat Harold.

Fast asleep.

I retrieved the chloroform from my pocket. With the grace of a dancer, I lay it against his nose.

Then I set to work.

***

I visited Nancy myself a few weeks later.

I like to do that sometimes: pose as a friendly neighbor, see how their lives have changed in the wake of my work. Yes, I know it increases my chances of getting caught, but as I said, I like a challenge.

When she flung open the door, her eyes were bright, and she wore a smile. "Hi! I'm Smith Baker," I said. "Just moved here–a few houses away from you, behind the food mart."

"Oh, how nice! Please come in."

She led me into the living room and I smiled. The music stand and other equipment were thrown haphazardly in the corner. Nancy's needlepoint was sprawled across the sofa, taking up as much space as it possibly could.

"Smith, this is my husband, Harold."

He just stared at me. Still, silent, pale.

And then he started shaking wildly, clawing at the raw, red mark across his throat.

"Oh–sorry–I should explain." She sat down, with a small smile. "He's not trying to be rude. It's just that… well, he had an accident a few weeks ago. Now he can't speak, I'm afraid."

She patted his arm, comfortingly, as he clung to her. "Or sing, unfortunately."

Hmm.

An 'accident.'

That mysteriously cut his vocal cords–

And left the rest of him untouched.

I could see Harold's hands shaking, his lip trembling. I wonder if he was thinking about the first thing I said to him when the chloroform wore off.

If you don't treat Nancy right–I'll slit your throat again.
And next time you'll lose more than just your voice.

I smiled at Harold. "Would you like a cookie?" I asked, holding out the tray. "I baked them myself."

HOW WILL YOU DIE?

Have you ever heard of an app called *How Will You Die?*

You tap a button, and it tells you (supposedly) how you will die–and when.

My friends all thought it was hilarious. "I'm going to die at 72–run over by a taco truck," Morgan said through fits of laughter.

Amber added with a grin: "95, choking on a piece of chicken. Not a great way to go, but hey–95, I'm not complaining!"

"What does it say for you, Alexis?"

"I didn't download it."

"Why not?"

"I don't know."

In truth, it was because I was a little scared.

But of course, nobody respected that. Amber leapt over and snatched the phone from my hands. "Stop it!" I said, but she held it out of my reach, tapping madly.

"There."

She handed the phone back. The screen was now black, with white letters:

HOW WILL YOU DIE?

TAP TO FIND OUT!

"Do it."

Now that it was right there, just a tap away...

I felt the irresistible pull of curiosity. With a shaking finger, I tapped the screen.

Ping.

"Cause of death: virus," I read.

"Age of death: 24."

Morgan's smile fell from his face. Amber looked at me with wide eyes.

Because we all knew–

My 25th birthday was in five days.

***

I couldn't sleep that night.

A virus? I thought. *I had all my vaccines... didn't I?* I rolled over, pulling the covers over my head. *Maybe it's the flu. Wait, is the flu a virus? Or bacteria?* I turned the pillow over. *Why am I even thinking about all this? It's just some stupid app...*

At four AM, I finally gave up on sleep. I leaned over and clicked the lamp on; yellow light filled the tiny apartment. Outside, the din of sirens, cars, and city noise came through. *Nice to know at least* some *other people are awake,* I thought.

I went over to my computer. I'm getting worried over nothing. I'm sure people have already proven it to be a hoax. *"How will you die app,"* I typed into the search bar.

The first hit was an article entitled: DEATH APP ACCURATELY PREDICTS FREAK ACCIDENTS ALL OVER THE COUNTRY.

My heart began to race.

Leslie Baker, 36–app said 'chocolate'; died in a collision with a Hershey's truck.

Tommy Carmen, 54–app said 'Marilyn Monroe'; died when a reproduction of the Andy Warhol painting fell on his head.

Jenny Lee–

Snap. I closed the laptop and pushed away from the desk.

Then I picked up my phone from the nightstand.

And opened the app.

A few links now appeared underneath my cause of death.

The first one was *COUNTDOWN.* I tapped it.

3 days. 12 hours. 22 minutes. 10 seconds.

I suddenly felt hot. My vision swam; the phone nearly slipped out of my hands. *It's just a stupid app,* I repeated to myself. *Nothing to worry about.*

The next one was *AUTHOR.* When I tapped it, it said *"App created by Atwell Industries."*

The final link was *FIND FRIENDS.*

When I tapped it, a map showed up. A little white pin icon was at the apartment building on 3rd St., showing my location.

FILTER BY:

TIME OF DEATH

METHOD OF DEATH

I clicked the first one. The map showed a few other dots around me. *David [1 month]. Cassidy [2 weeks].*

It was showing the people destined to die soon.

Like me.

I clicked the second option. No dots appeared.

But viruses are contagious, I thought. How could I be the only one?

I zoomed out.

Way out.

Several dots appeared. *Cameron [virus]*, all the way on the other end of the city. *Lydia [virus]*, in a townhouse on Eagle Ave. *Tyler [virus]*, in a bar on 15th.

I tapped on one of them. To my surprise, it opened a texting screen.

My hands were still shaking. My shirt was damp, from the layer of sweat that had formed between me and the chair. I took a deep breath and typed out a quick message.

Hey, I saw you have the virus too. I'm kind of freaked out. Want to talk about it? 5pm tomorrow, video call?

I figured meeting in person, when we're all going to catch a contagious virus, was a terrible idea.

Ping.

Yes. Definitely.

I tapped on the next dot.

***

Cameron set up the 4-way video call the next day.

"Hey! Alexis! Nice to 'meet' you," he said, making air quotes. He was a mammoth of a man, dwarfing the recliner he sat in. And handsome… from what I could see of his pixelated face, anyway.

Lydia showed up next. Skinny, blonde, with a fat gray cat skulking behind her.

Tyler entered last, about 15 minutes late. "Yo guys," he said, through *smacks* of gum.

An awkward silence. We all stared at each other through the screen.

"Here's what I was thinking," I started, fiddling with the fat stack of notes on my desk. "If we're the only four people in the whole city of C__ to get it… that means we all have something in common. Like maybe we go to the same restaurant? Or –"

"I never eat out," Lydia said. "I have two kids under the age of two. It's a nightmare."

"Well, what about the gym?" Cameron said. "I go to the gym on 8th every day."

I glanced at his pixelated biceps.

Tyler shook his head. "No man. I've got exercise-induced asthma."

"What about groceries? I get mine at the Super Mart on Willow St. –"

But the other three shook their heads.

"Do we even, like, all die at the same time?" Tyler asked, spitting the gum offscreen and unwrapping a new piece. "What does everyone's countdown say? Mine is 6 days."

"7 days," Lydia said. The cat mewed plaintively behind her.

"4 days," Cameron said.

I stared at the screen. It began to blur and smudge, as tears filled my eyes. "Alexis?" Cameron said, but his voice sounded so far away.

2 days, 22 hours, 13 minutes, 5 seconds...

I was first.

"Sorry," I said, wiping my eyes. "Uh, 2 days."

An uncomfortable pause.

Then Lydia began to shout. "You probably already have it!" she said, her shrill voice warbling through the speakers. "In fact–*you're* probably the one who gives it to *us!*"

"Hey, calm down," Cameron said. "We're all in this together. And –"

"Alexis, you need to lock yourself in the apartment," Tyler said. "Do not go *anywhere*. Do not have contact with anyone. Do not –"

Click. Click.

Lydia and Tyler's images disappeared as Cameron bumped them off the call. "Assholes," he muttered.

I reached for a tissue. *Honk.* "Thank you."

He leaned in close to the screen. "Listen, they're right–you probably already have the virus. But whoever you caught it from already touched a million things in this city. It's too late; our odds of survival are, essentially, zero." He broke into a smile. "So don't spend your last days locked in a tiny apartment. Go out, have a good time. Okay?"

I nodded. *Honk.*

"Alright. Unfortunately, I've got to go. Late for my appointment with Dr. Rosenfield." He smiled. "Take care of yourself, okay?"

Click.

I shut the laptop.

But then a thought occurred to me. I pulled out my phone. Tapped through my settings, found *How Will You Die?*, and pressed UNINSTALL.

For a several minutes, all was silent.

Then–

Ping.

A text.

Morgan: Why are you sending me these? You ok?

Huh? I scrolled up through the conversation.

10 selfies.

Selfies I don't remember taking. Or sending. I was smiling widely in each one,–but there was something cold about my eyes. As if the smile was forced, or fake.

I tapped on the first one.

Wait…

I zoomed in on the background. A small, hilly street, with a familiar oak tree leaning slightly askew. A wide, buckled driveway, leading up to a little blue house…

My parents' house.

Ping.

New voicemail.

I dialed in and listened.

"Hey, Cookie! I didn't know you were going to visit! Dad said he just saw you–in that ring camera he has by the door. Don't worry, you're not waking us up! Come on in–door's unlocked!"

Click.

I looked down at the phone. The countdown popped up on the screen.

1 day, 21 hours, 24 minutes, 53 seconds.

It had taken away a day.

Riiiing.

Morgan. "Hey, Alexis! Just callin' you back, since you texted –"

"I didn't text you. Listen, Morgan, something terrible is happening." My voice warbled with impending tears. "I tried to uninstall the app, and now–it's threatening my parents "

"Wait, slow down. What now?"

"The 'How Will You Die' app!" I shouted through sobs. "It's going to do something horrible to them –"

"Hey, hey, it'll be okay, Alexis, uh –"

"It's *there!* At my parents' house!"

"Why don't you meet up with us for lunch tomorrow? We'll help you figure it out," he said, his voice a forced calm.

Ping. A text.

Mom: Hey, so, the power just went out. Maybe it's best if you visit a different time–we might not have heat all night. Need a ride back to the city?

"Alexis?"

"We'll pick you up tomorrow, okay?"

I nodded, swallowing my sobs. "Okay."

***

But I wish I hadn't gone.

Because, as it turned out, "lunch" was an intervention. An ambush. A lie. After finishing our salads, Morgan and Amber swept me downtown, up two flights of stairs, and into a cold doctor's office.

"We're just worried about you," Amber said, patting my arm.

That's funny–because I wouldn't even be in this situation if it weren't for her.

The waiting room was terrible. It felt like the color had been sucked out of the room. The walls were gray. The people were pale and ashen, wearing gray clothes, black jackets. If I hadn't been 'depressed' before, I was certainly now.

"Alexis Johnson?" the nurse called.

We walked down the hallway into the doctor's office. Once seated, the barrage of questions began–questions that my 'friends' were all too happy to answer for me.

"She freaked out yesterday," Morgan said. "Saying this app on her phone is going to get her parents."

Amber added: "She's really jumpy, too. Jumps every time her phone makes a noise."

"How do *you* feel?" the nurse asked, turning to me.

What do you think?! I was wasting precious time in this ugly doctor's office. I had been tricked by my best friends. But I forced a smile, and said: "I guess I've been feeling okay."

416

The nurse left, and we waited for the doctor to come in. Morgan tapped his shoes furiously against the floor. Amber stared on her phone, never looking up.

Finally, the door creaked open.

"Hi, Alexis," the doctor said, extending her hand. "I'm Doctor Rosenfield."

I felt the strength drain from my arms. My vision swam and rippled. I wavered, nearly fainting right there on the couch.

This is the common thread.

This is where I catch the virus.

Dr. Rosenfield pressed a cold stethoscope to my chest. "Now take a few deep breaths in…"

It's over. The voice pounded in my head, deafening everything else. *It's over, it's over, it's over…*

"Your vitals look good," she said. She sat down in the desk chair, looking over a file. "Now, tell me why you're here today."

Maybe it was the finality of it all—the fact that I *knew* it was over. Or maybe it was just how nervous I was. But as soon as I opened my mouth, it all spilled out. I told her about the app, the virus, the sleepless nights. Everything.

When I had finished, she gave me a warm, comforting smile. "It sounds like you have a bit of anxiety, Alexis. Nothing to worry about—very common for your age. I'll prescribe you something to help, okay?"

I nodded and put my sweater back on.

"I'll send your prescription over to the pharmacy on 12th. Sound good?"

"Yeah. Thanks."

The entire way back, I didn't speak a word to my so-called friends.

***

When I got back to the apartment, I video-called Cameron.

"I figured out the common thread. It's Dr. Rosenfield."

His face fell. "Oh, no."

"I can't believe I didn't think of it yesterday. Doctors have so much contact with illness. She's probably infecting everybody she sees." I scoffed, and looked down at the floor. "And we're just the ones lucky enough to die from it."

He nodded.

"There's so much I wanted to do." The tears crept back into my eyes; I looked away. *Should I say it? At this point, I have nothing to lose, right?* "I wanted to get to know you. I thought... we *had* something. And I know that sounds stupid, since I've only talked to you like once, but you seem–well, amazing."

He was silent.

"Do you think we have a chance? To stop this?"

His eyes grew dark.

And then he slowly shook his head.

"No."

The frames jumped. His face became pixelated, distorted, as if there was a bad connection.

"Cameron?"

Through the blocky pieces of pixels, a wide smile formed on his face.

No–

"There is no way to stop us," it said in a chorus of voices coming from every device in the room.

Snap.

I closed the laptop, threw my head into the pillow, and began to sob.

***

"The funny thing is, I still don't feel sick."

I sat on a park bench, overlooking the river. Cameron sat on the next one over, several feet away. The yellow rays of the sinking sun glinted off the river, cut by the wakes of a few ducks.

"How are you holding up? Mentally, I mean."

"I'm okay, actually." Then I laughed. "But that might be more due to the pills I just took than my state of mind."

He smiled. "Hey, whatever it takes."

No, I didn't tell Cameron about the video call last night–or my budding feelings. I decided to keep it simple; just enjoy my final moments in the company of someone who understood. I had already done everything I needed to–called my parents (they are fine, by the way, despite the scare), prayed a whole lot, read a book, and ate the best cheeseburger I ever had.

Now it was just time to wait.

"Did you finish *How I Met Your Mother* last night?" Cameron asked, turning towards me.

I laughed. "No. Still on Season 8."

"So you didn't meet the mother!"

I smiled at him. "And I guess I never will."

And that's when I felt it.

The sudden pang of dizziness. The hitch in my breathing. The world spinning around me, growing darker with every second.

"Alexis!"

But he sounded so, so far away.

***

"Alexis?"

I opened my eyes.

White walls. Tubing, wires, equipment. Murmured voices, clacking shoes, faint beeps.

I was in the hospital.

I turned. There sat Cameron, leaning over the bed.

"What happened?" I groaned.

"Something wonderful," he said, breaking into a smile. "As we were there on the riverside... I got the craziest idea. To switch the SIM cards in our phones. Had about a ninety-percent chance of killing both of us, and a ten-percent chance of confusing the system and resetting everything."

"But the virus –"

"You were dying from the pills, Alexis. Not a virus." The smile faded from his face. "You took more than double the amount you should have."

He stood up. "Were you trying to kill yourself? To defy the prediction?" His voice cracked, and his eyes locked with mine. "Because–I risked everything to save you. And –"

"What? No! I took three pills. Exactly what Dr. Rosenfield prescribed."

"Then she made a mistake. Or –" Cameron lowered his voice. "Wait. Do you think she *purposely* gave you the wrong prescription?"

"Why would she do that?"

"Maybe she's working with them."

Cameron shot up and darted into the hallway. Ten minutes later, he was back with a wide-eyed Dr. Rosenfield trailing behind him.

"Why did you do it?" Cameron asked. He loomed over her, taller by more than a foot; she took a step back.

"What are you talking about?"

"Yesterday you prescribed Alexis some anti-anxiety meds. It was the wrong dosage. And it almost killed her." He took a deliberate step forward. "Are you working with them? You are, aren't you?"

"With whom?"

"Look, we're not trying to accuse you of anything," I said, shooting a glare at Cameron. "But–why did you give me the wrong dosage?"

"Uh, let me pull up your file," she said quietly, taking a seat at the computer. Her hands flew over the keyboard. After a few minutes, she turned back to us.

She swallowed, her face pale.

"It looks like your file... accidentally got swapped with Cameron's. I gave you the dosage–not for a 110-pound woman, but for a 250-pound man." She said it with a mix of guilt and terror in her eyes, as though she were confessing to a murder.

Well, I guess she kind of was.

"How?" Cameron asked. "How did the files get switched?"

"A lot of our patients' files got corrupted and mixed up," she said, laying her glasses on the table with a muffled *clink*. "Because yesterday–our computers got a virus."

And before I could respond, motion caught my eye–

A dark shadow, flitting across the computer screen.

LET ME IN

I woke up to my daughter crying at 4 AM.

That's a horror story in itself, right?

Unfortunately, it gets worse.

Let me start from the beginning. My husband, Michael, and I live in the rural town of H____, Michigan. We have a 5-week-old daughter named Riley. She's doing well, but wakes up several times a night. Every. Single. Night.

Thankfully, on weekend nights Michael takes baby duty. He's amazing—he gives her a bath, reads her a story, rocks her, and puts her to sleep. And he sleeps right in the nursery with her. The only thing he's bad at? Singing lullabies—he's completely tone-deaf. (I usually shut the door when he gets to that part.)

So, last night when I heard the baby crying at the ungodly hour of 4 AM, I assumed Michael was on it. I rolled over, and tried to fall back asleep.

But she continued wailing.

Waaaaah. Waaaaah.

I pulled the covers over my head.

Waaaaaaaaaaaaaah.

I turned up my white noise to full blast.

Waaa—aaaaaa—aaaaahhhh!

I jolted up. Dammit, Michael, are you even trying to calm her down?! I heaved myself out of bed, threw on my robe, and opened the door.

Waaaaah. Waaaaah.

I froze in the doorway.

The cries weren't coming from her room.

They were coming from downstairs.

I peered down: dim, golden light shone across the floor, coming from the living room. "Michael?" I called.

No response, other than a blood-curdling *waaaaaaaaaaaaah.*

"Is everything okay?" I shouted, louder this time. The shadows shifted across the floor, but no answer. I took a step down—footsteps, coming from her room.

I froze.

The doorknob turned—

Michael walked out of the bedroom, rubbing his eyes, his mouth wide with a yawn.

"You left Riley downstairs alone?! What's wrong with you?!" I began running down the stairs, my robe flying behind me—

He grabbed my arm.

"That isn't Riley."

"What are you talking about?!"

"Sssssshhh." He pushed his door open. I turned, and my heart began to pound. In the dim light I could see a little pink bundle, rising and falling with each breath.

I held my breath. Slowly, I backed up the stairs, careful to not make even the quietest creak.

He pulled me into the bedroom. *Click*—he shut the door. *Click*—he locked it, dragging a chair in front.

"Maybe it's just the baby next door," I said, trying to calm myself.

"The Johnsons live a quarter mile away."

I looked at him, my eyes wild. "Maybe it's—"

"It was coming from downstairs, Catie. You and I both heard it." He began pushing the dresser. It didn't budge. "There's someone down there."

"But—"

"Ssshhh!" Michael held a finger to his lips.

The wailing continued.

"Hear that?" he whispered.

"Yes, I hear the screaming baby."

"No. There's a pattern. Two short cries, then a long cry, then a raspy cry."

"So?"

He turned to me, his eyes wide. "It's a recording."

I felt the breath catch in my throat.

"Someone's down there, playing a recording of a baby crying?" I said, incredulously. "Why?"

"Isn't it obvious?" With a grunt, he pushed the dresser; it wobbled, and shifted maybe half an inch across the carpet. "To lure us out there."

Waaaaaah.

I jumped. But it was only Riley crying, woken by our loud whispers. Michael swooped her up, singing a terribly off-key rendition of Brahm's lullaby in her ear.

"We need to call 911," I said, feeling my pocket. "My phone. Where's my phone?! I must have left it in the other bedroom—"

In the soft moonlight, Michael was pale as a ghost. "And mine's out of battery..."

"Maybe we can get out the window," I said. Shaking, I wrenched it open. The cool breeze blew in, and the forest was black as ever. Our only neighbors—the Johnsons—were too far away, and the drop... just looking down made my stomach turn. The lawn bench looked like it belonged to dolls; the barren garden beds were like tiles on a checkerboard. "What do we do?"

"I'll get your phone."

"What? You just said yourself—someone is out there!"

"Your door is five feet across the hallway. I'll make it across before they can get upstairs."

"Michael—no—"

"The dresser's too heavy to move across the door. The chair isn't good enough. Sooner or later, they're going to come upstairs, kick down the door, and who knows what. I'm going." He handed Riley to me. "Wish me luck."

Before I could stop him, he opened the door.

And as soon as he did—

The cries stopped.

I froze, clinging to the crib. They know you're out there! I screamed, internally. I rushed to the door, gripping the knob, ready for Michael to rush back inside —

Thump.

A footstep, at the base of the stairs.

Then slow, heavy footsteps, growing louder and faster—the unmistakable sound of someone running up the stairs—

Thump! A crash, a yelp of pain—

Michael dashed back in. I slammed the door shut.

The door rattled.

Thump. Thump.

The hinges groaned.

"Let me in!"

My eyes widened.

It was Michael's voice.

"Hey! Leave us alone!" Michael shouted, holding me close.

"Catie! It's me!" *Thump, thump.* "Let me in!"

I looked at Michael. "That sicko must've recorded my voice," he whispered, handing me the phone.

"Whoever that is – it's not me!" The voice cracked with desperation.

"Get out of our house!"

"Catie—please—it's me!"

Michael grabbed the dresser. Groaning, he dragged it across the door. The pounding grew louder, faster; the cries grew frenzied and shrill, becoming a blood-curdling scream—then silence.

***

By the time the police arrived, he seemed to be gone.

"We'll dust for fingerprints and run it through our database," one of the officers told us, "but most people are smart enough to wear gloves these days." They gave us paperwork, phone numbers, and left.

After checking the locks for the hundredth time, we sat down on the bed. Riley, severely overtired like both of us, began to wail.

"Can you put her to sleep? I'm exhausted," I said, rubbing my eyes.

"Of course." He lay Riley across his chest, rocking her slowly. I stumbled across the hallway to my bedroom. The sun was just rising over the pine trees; bright golden rays shone through the window, lighting up the room. Sighing in relief, I collapsed onto the bed, and closed my eyes.

Across the hall, I could hear Michael's soft voice singing: "Lullaby, and good night... go to sleep now, little Riley..."

Perfectly on key.

OVER THE WALL

"Never go over the wall." My grandpa sat in the rocking chair, massaging his bad ankle through mud-stained jeans. "This isn't the safest area of Florida. Especially at night."

"Okay."

"Also, be careful with that. You could take your eye out."

See, that's why my nine-year-old self didn't take him seriously. He was always warning me about various "dangerous" things. *Don't swim in the deep end of the pool; you could drown. Don't run so fast; you could trip and break your neck.*

So when – one night – I heard a voice on the other side of the wall, I wasn't scared.

I had been playing alone in the backyard, sitting in the grass between the orange trees, when I heard it. A woman's voice, low and soft, echoing over the concrete wall at the end of the backyard.

"Hello?"

Being the curious kid I was, I immediately ran over to it. I wouldn't climb over – even though I didn't believe Grandpa, I didn't want to make him mad – but there was no harm in taking a peek, right?

I stepped up on the old stone fountain, reached for the top of the wall, and hoisted myself up. And then I peered down.

Underneath the intertwining oak branches and Spanish moss was only darkness. I squinted, trying to make sense of the shadows flitting across the dirt floor. Maybe I had imagined it –

"Hello?"

The voice rang out in the darkness, up through the trees.

"Hello!" I called back.

I heard a rustling sound, and the soft thump of footsteps. "Who's there?"

"Jess," I called down.

"I'm Elizabeth." The shadows shifted, but I still couldn't quite make out the figure below. "And I need your help, Jess."

"Sure! I can help!"

"I'm thirsty," she said. The wind picked up, and the branches swayed, scattering the shadows below. "So very thirsty."

"I'll get you some water!" I said, without second thought.

"Oh, that would be so wonderful, Jess."

I jumped down, scampered inside, and fished a bottle of water from the fridge. Grandpa didn't even notice; he was watching some boring World War II movie on TV, rubbing his bad ankle all the while.

I stepped back up onto the fountain. "I got you some water," I called. "Do you want me to throw it down?"

"Oh, well... it might hit me. Maybe you can come down and give it to me?"

I paused. The warm Florida air blew over my face, and there was a strange smell: sour, like when Dad's meat freezer in the basement broke a few years ago. "I can't. I'm not supposed to go over the wall."

I was met with awkward silence.

"Hello?"

"Please, I'm so thirsty," the voice said, again.

I looked at the rough concrete. Maybe I could pull myself up a bit, reach down, and hand her the bottle of water? I swung a leg up over the wall, and with a grunt, pulled myself into a sitting position.

Slowly, I leaned down, and reached my hand through the canopy of branches.

But nothing took the bottle of water.

"Hello?"

Silence. Not even a footstep, or a rustle, from the underbrush below.

"Hel—"

Something yanked my ankle.

Hard.

I jerked forward. The water fell to the ground with a sickening *splat*. My hands flew out, gripping the edge of the wall –

Ch-ch-ch-ch.

A chittering sound, almost insect-like, emanated from the underbrush. Large, dark figures emerged from the shadows, swarming towards me in jerky motions. I screamed, holding on to the wall for dear life, but my fingers were slipping –

"Jess!"

Two rough, strong hands grabbed my shoulders. In one motion, they yanked me back over the wall.

"What did I tell you?" Grandpa shouted. "Never go over the wall!"

"But there was a woman," I said, through sobs, "and she said –"

"No buts!" He dragged me back inside, and sat me down on the couch. "No matter what you heard – what you *think* you heard…" He propped my leg up on the ottoman. An angry red mark had appeared – four long fingers and a thumb.

Fingers so long, they wrapped around the entire circumference of my ankle, and then some.

"Grandpa, what were those things?"

He didn't reply.

Instead, he slowly rolled up his pant leg.

There was a white, shining scar –

Of long fingers wrapped around his ankle.

More terrifying tales in Don't Scream 2!

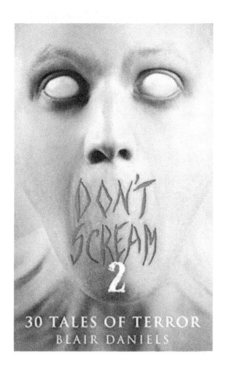

Made in the USA
Coppell, TX
27 September 2021